THE WARD OF EXILES

THE BOOK OF OSIRYS
PART ONE

CORBIN KIME

FLOOR GOBLIN PRESS

This book is dedicated to my Father, Edward.
It took great loss to inspire great achievement.
You will be missed always.

CONTENTS

Map   IX

Prologue   1

Chapter One   7

Chapter Two   21

Chapter Three   27

Chapter Four   57

Chapter Five   79

Chapter Six   87

Chapter Seven   105

Chapter Eight   129

Chapter Nine   157

Chapter Ten   175

Chapter Eleven   185

Chapter Twelve   193

Chapter Thirteen   205

Chapter Fourteen   225

Chapter Fifteen   261

Chapter Sixteen   285

Chapter Seventeen   297

Chapter Eighteen   321

Chapter Nineteen   349

Chapter Twenty   385

Chapter Twenty-One   405

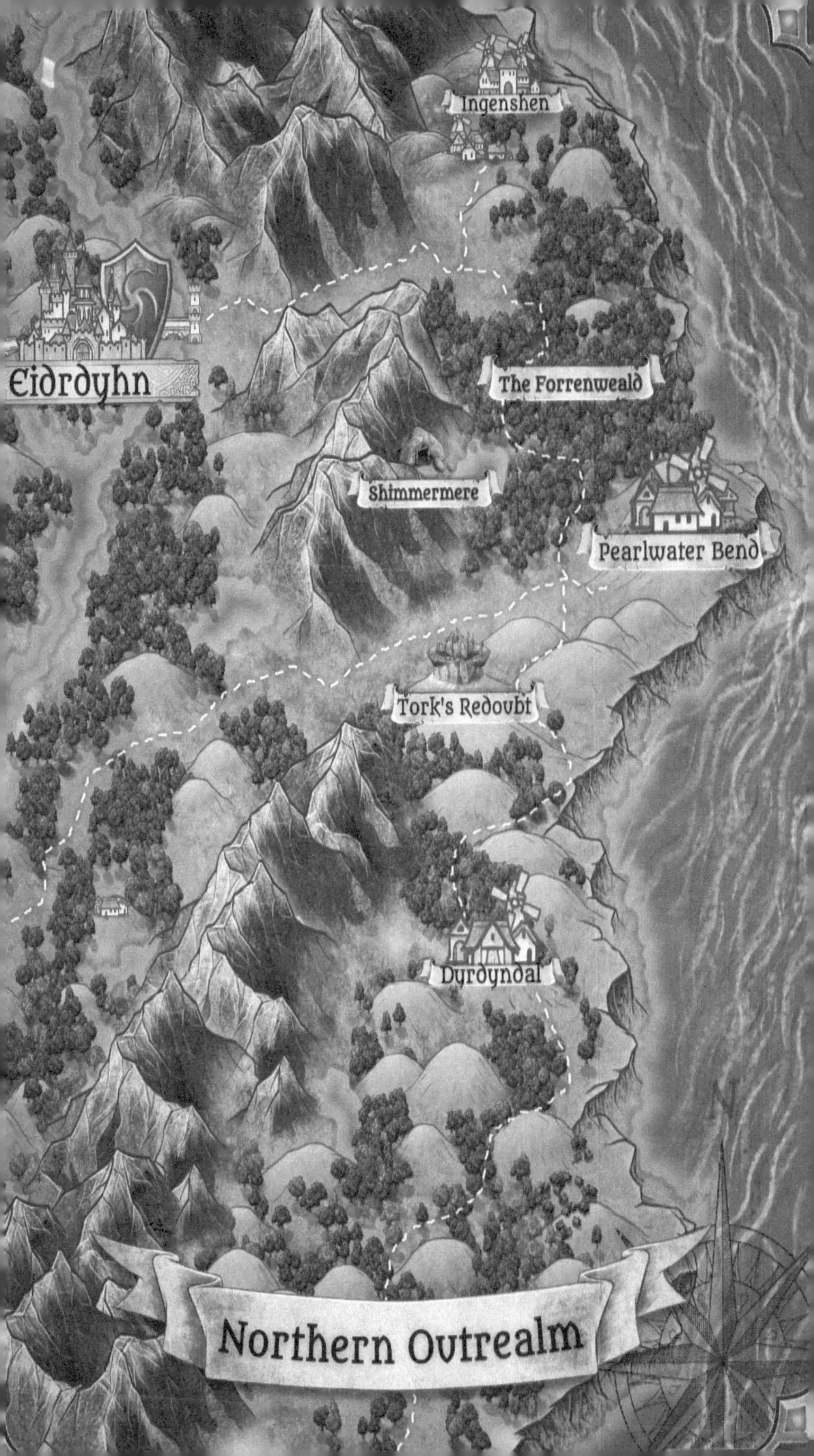

Ingenshen
Eidrdyhn
The Forrenweald
Shimmermere
Pearlwater Bend
Tork's Redoubt
Dyrdyndal
Northern Outrealm

PROLOGUE

THE CHRISTMAS TREE LEANED ominously against the corner wall, half toppled and distressed from the fight. Half a dozen ornaments of various importance lay shattered on the floor, a few lucky managed to avoid obliteration, by some miracle. Osirys avoided touching her face. She could feel the heat of the swelling, and the metallic smell of dried blood when she involuntarily sniffed. She didn't know why she didn't feel like crying - her body was reacting like she was, but she just had nothing left. There was still fear, lingering in the shadows of the room. She dreaded every moment, listening so hard for the sound of heavy footsteps coming up the stairs. The mild ringing in her ears was the only thing she could focus on. The lights of the Christmas tree were blurry, just fuzzy orbs with lines of bright light slowly pulsating with her thundering heartbeat. She kept her eyes mostly closed. Well, she kept the left one mostly closed. The right one was as open as it was likely going to get for a few days.

She was on the couch where she landed shortly after her boyfriend fled the apartment in his rage. She had kept on her feet until he was gone. Adrenaline, fear, and a vestige of self preservation had kept her upright. Moments in silence after the car peeled out of the driveway melted away the candlewax that held her together. She collapsed on the couch, across from the TV that bore a spider's web of purplish-black veins and a kaleidoscope of polygonal colors. Ruined. Osirys watched the flickering of the failing LCD crystals, and found a measure of camaraderie in the floundering television. It could not have reflected her better if it were a silver mirror.

It must have been over an hour in silence by now. He wasn't coming back tonight. Osirys shifted her eyes to the table by the door. She wanted to see if his key to the apartment was still there, but couldn't focus on it well enough. It would be good to lock up anyway. She turned her head slightly, and pain surged across her nerve endings. Her nose was definitely broken. She should go to the hospital. She could probably drive. She tried to get her arms below her to push off the couch. She didn't know if she had it in her. She didn't know if she had anything left at all. One more minute. Was that a car slowing down? She breathed out heavily, giving in to look at the TV once again. Then her hand brushed her abdomen.

Shit. How could she only be thinking about this now? A whole new feeling of dread rose up within her and washed over her, breaking down her apathy and tears erupted from her eyes. She *had* to go to the hospital. Tonight was supposed to be so happy. She was going to tell him the news. The good news. She hadn't told anyone else yet. Not even her sister. She wanted to tell him first. She never got to tell him. It had been bad before, but never this bad. She struggled to remember what set him off. He said something about her acting strange, demanding to know where she was earlier that day. He stopped home unexpectedly from the garage for lunch but she wasn't there. She had spent the afternoon planning how to tell him. She was totally caught off guard. She didn't want to tell him like that, with him already getting worked up. She wanted it to be happy, so she stammered. That was enough. She was in the middle of working through how to respond when the shock of his hand hit her in the face. She tumbled backward into the Christmas tree. She scrambled, but he was coming for her. She threw something. It must have missed and hit the TV. She kicked at him several times but he was just too strong. She had nowhere to go, and all she could do was try and cover her head and face. She deflected one or two hits, but most connected. She was screaming and crying. She finally managed to wrestle free and get up. She grabbed the fireplace poker and held it in front of her, trembling. At first she didn't know if he was going to come at her again, but it was done. He turned and charged for the door, slamming it behind him.

Osirys looked down at the poker that rested by her feet, where she dropped it. She had to get to the hospital. She had to try. She pushed through the pain and cleared her mind. This was more than just about her now. She had someone else she needed to be strong for. Someone who had to live with her choices. Her weakness. Her inability to turn him in, to leave him, to call for help. She had the phone number for the hotline memorized, but she never called. She had used up nearly every excuse to her friends and family for the bruises, the ones she couldn't hide. Her sister once asked her directly if he had hurt her, and she lied. She didn't know why. She couldn't fathom the words that came out of her mouth when she said no. Every fiber of her being wanted to break down in Lily's arms and ask her if she could stay for a while, but she didn't. She couldn't.

Osirys staggered to the bathroom to assess the damage. She couldn't just leave. Someone might see her and call the police. She flicked on the light, and the tears erupted anew. Her nose was… a disaster. Her dark hair hung about her face, strands clumped together, wet with blood from her nose. Her typically angular features were swollen, and round. She looked at her reflection, struggling to recognize the battered face that gawked back at her. Even her eyes, normally amber-colored, were dark and muted. She felt the room spin a bit, seeing herself like this weakened her knees. She held onto the counter with white knuckles and looked away to keep from passing out. She turned the water on. It splashed into the basin, clean and clear. She couldn't hide this. She couldn't lie or make up some story about her clumsiness. She would have to tell the doctor or nurse at the hospital what happened. Then there would be police. Then there would be family. They would find out she was expecting and that her boyfriend was a sadistic asshole in one ruinous moment. Worse, she still didn't have the strength to end it with him. She knew if he came back, she would apologize. She would take the blame for this, and everything else. She was pathetic. She looked at her shattered face and saw the ruined TV in the mirror.

She was weak. She wasn't meant for motherhood. God. How could she bring a baby into the world to be subjected to his wrath? It was irresponsible. An image flashed in her mind of him raising his fist against a child - their child - and what little she had left dissolved. She couldn't do it. Any of it. She squeezed her eyes closed. She grabbed the Ibuprofen, and hovered over the box of Ambien. Maybe one wouldn't hurt. She could try again in the morning. Maybe.

She staggered back to the couch. She still clutched the bottle of sleeping pills in her hand. She wasn't sure why she still had them. Had she taken one yet? More than one? Maybe she should put the bottle down. She wasn't sure any more. She didn't know what she was thinking. Was she really considering it?

"Just close your eyes. We will figure it out in the morning." She whispered to herself. And she did. The empty bottle of sleeping pills clattered from her grasp onto the floor.

Chapter One

O SIRYS FELT HERSELF SURROUNDED by an inky blackness that ate at her, devouring her reservations, one by one. She only vaguely struggled against it, there wasn't much she actually wanted to protect anyway. She strayed through a life that felt filled with regret, filled with shame. She felt as if she should be scolded like a petulant child. She felt the guilt of actions she committed. Mostly, she felt disappointment in herself, and a rage at her incompetence that led her farther from anything that she knew, and deeper into a viscous emptiness, an internal entropy where she clung to disorder as her only defense. Perhaps she couldn't have helped the way things turned out. Perhaps it was some divine purpose or lack thereof, perhaps it was a plan that was laid before her with the purpose to fail. She felt a warm, orange coal of despite and hatred smoldering inside the pit of her heart, fueled by a rejection of the notion that any other than chaos had decided the series of events that led her to where she was now.

Osirys wasn't aware of any measure of her surroundings, it was immaterial, conjured by the darkness within her. It was opaque, smoky, and acrid. The darkness built and swirled into plumes of shadowy smoke that curled about her and licked at her extremities, testing them, tasting her temperature, her fury. She felt the presence of an intelligence in the looming darkness surrounding her, a malice - or was that just her imagination? She felt a hot wind blow through her, lighting her nerves as it passed. She felt the shadow within her. It felt like violation, it felt like everything that she had been feeling, but pressurized, concentrated, and *violent*. It wanted her. It lusted to take what little dignity remained for her, it craved those last few drops of her humanity, to suckle upon her depravity. She felt it digging into her from all sides, drinking her. She felt bereft, powerless, and it felt good. *Oh, did it feel good.* There was a comfort in purposelessness; a measure of safety in subservience. It was sensual, it was narcotic. She was raw, base, and foul. Osirys inhaled the inky blackness, filling herself with it, giving in to the malicious desire lurking about in the unseen shadow. It did not rush to its prize, it lingered, almost in frustrating lethargy, it approached. Osirys could feel it near now, it was definitely not her imagination.

Searing heat tasted her flesh as three pairs of bottomless pits for eyes formed in the swirling shadow before her. They were set vertically, one pair slightly more angular and narrow. They were beautiful and terrifying eyes, the kind that paralyzed with fear and yet were so intoxicating to the sight. They were ink black in a sea of dark smoke.

They were matte and did not glisten. They inhaled light, devouring it and giving no twinkle of reflection. They felt familiar, somehow. She had seen them - or felt them - throughout her life, even in childhood. They were meaningless until now; A pattern in snow that she stopped to consider, grain in a wooden table that she would idly trace with her finger waiting for a coffee - What measure of infinity lay beneath the threshold of the black orbs before her? What depths of depravity lay beneath and within? She wanted it as badly as it wanted her. She opened herself, inviting it to enter, to dominate her.

She felt a rumbling from all about her, more empathetic than verbal.

"Has it been so long already?
It had been far too long for her.

"It is a worthy vessel. At long last."
She would be worthy.

"I will see the light swept from your world, and you will be my tool, luminous one."
Her world deserved no light. This darkness was fitting, it was her pain, her shame. Osirys accepted the shadow, yearning to be filled by it.

"He is sired by Shadow, and he shall be Destruction, The Unmaker."
The darkness about Osirys pressed upon her, it felt coiled like a spring, energy building about and around her. Limitless, raw power. She wanted it to release upon her, within her, through her. It was the chaos she needed,

she craved. The inky, viscid blackness reared and formed a lethal point, aimed at her core. It was moments away. She lamented the length of each second in anticipation. It was an agony she yearned to indulge, a finality she sought with all her being.

She hardly noticed a thin, silvery cord wrap about her waist.

The darkness lunged forward. It pierced her in the belly, directly into her womb. Osirys felt her soul leap to embrace it, but her form was yanked back and away, into the swirling, dry heat of the shadow. She ached for what the shadow offered, but somewhere deep in her mind, she felt gratitude for her unseen savior. The six eyes of entropy fell away from her rapidly. She felt its words, barely a whisper in her mind,

"I have chosen my instrument carefully. Always remember, the brighter you shine, deeper are the shadows cast. We will meet again at the Gateway."

She closed her eyes, consumed by her newest regret and shame.

W HEN OSIRYS OPENED HER eyes again, it was still night. She was standing in a field of snow, up past her bare ankles. She shifted slightly, expecting to shiver from cold, but there was no cold. The snow was fluffy cotton-like flakes that swirled and danced about her. She looked up to see the clearest night sky – ablaze with a multitude of thousands of stars, twinkling in hues of blue, red, orange, and pink. The sky was unfamiliar. It was alien, twinkling as if it had always been there, and yet she'd never seen it before. There was no Big Dipper, no Cassiopeia, no Orion's Belt. Constellations of unknown name and unknown mythology filled the heavens. It unsettled Osirys. Even though this unfamiliar celestial dome was just a different seed of random light noise, somehow it impressed upon Osirys that she was very far from anything she knew. Osirys took a step, and began moving towards what looked to be a small clearing. It was not far from where she was, but she moved slowly, cautiously. Was this a dream? The obsidian eyes of the malignant darkness felt like an eternity in the past, so much so that Osirys wasn't sure it ever happened. She wasn't sure what was real, and what wasn't. In her confusion, she looked at the limbs of the trees, which tinkled with crystals hanging from the branches. Every sound seemed to have a musical tone, as if in direct contradiction to the random chaos of eternal shadow.

Osirys paused as she entered the clearing. Several feminine figures emerged from the dark spaces between the crystalline forest trunks, and began to walk towards her cautiously, but with no hint of malice. Each was dressed in a flowing, supple cloak or robe, embroidered with runic symbols in a language she had never seen, and thickly decorated with ornate metallic discs and embellished with reflective, thick silver lace around the shoulders. Upon their foreheads they wore ornate crowns, upon which small gemstones glowed a warm, starry yellow. Their eyes and cheeks were slightly angled, and their noses slender. Their skin was almost stonelike, smooth and matte, but rough and ancient looking. They were large of stature, and each seemed to tower over her, immense in some way that Osirys could not quite measure. They wore jewelry of crystal, clear prisms that seemed to capture the light of the stars and hold it, burning with color inside the stones. Osirys had never met these women, but something inside her told her she knew much about each one of them. One began to whistle as she approached, it reminded Osirys of water bubbling in a swollen stream, then the crags of a windy cliff and soaring clouds, and the haunting peace of a deep forest. Osirys met Nature's eyes, and knew her. Another figure hummed, warm vibrations of two connected points and the harmony of movement between. Osirys closed her eyes and felt for her tune, resonating in her heart with affection for friends and family. She felt the warmth, but also the chill cold of fear; of isolated desperation. She recoiled, and Love's tune dissipated into the night air. Love's gaze lingered upon her for a moment, hesitant. *Yes, that was it.* She put a hand on her abdomen. Love, fear, shame. All combined within her.

Yet a third, much older woman moved more slowly, more purposefully behind the group. She made no sound, but her silence echoed the embodiment of memory. The eyes of the woman narrowed slightly, studying Osirys. Her eyes scanned from her belly, slowly upward, to her face. Osirys was only briefly able to meet her gaze, before looking down at her feet. There were others, as well. All told there were seven, not including the elder that remained behind. Most she knew instinctively, few she did not. She pulled down inside herself, as the women closed in upon her, forming a semi-circle about her where she stood.

They began to speak. Their words were piercing, poignant, and full of musicality. They spoke in riddle, following each other's statements as one:

> *"We did not forsee her.*
> *She was beckoned by Shadow.*
> *What is her purpose?*
> *Pandemonium seeks the Silver Enclave.*
> *She will either set Pandemonium free-*
> *Or destroy It completely.*
> *Hers is the power of the Virdi.*
> *And its chaos.*
> *And its violence.*
> *And its vitality.*
> *What is her fate?*

It is unwritten-
As are all travelers from her world.
She carries great pain.
And great promise.
What of our Progeny?
They must choose for themselves now.
They are guides no longer.
She will be their undoing.
That is not certain.
She will be protected-
By those whose lands refuse them protection.
She shall be the Ward of Exiles.
She carries great darkness within her.
She will grant Pandemonium access to the Great Gateway.
The keepers must be warned.
Must we intervene?"

Finally, the elder stepped forward, her bare feet carefully placed with each stride. She approached Osirys, and towered over her. It seemed that she was being examined to the core of her being, but not judged. A warm yellow glow began to pour forth from her, as if she were made of starlight. Behind her, the celestial heavens seemed to bend and whirl. The gems in her headpiece sparkled and leapt aflame, dancing about her. Her thick white hair cascaded along her shoulders, and for moments, they stood, regarding one another. She spoke, looking at Osirys but addressing the others behind her.

"We must trust the River.

It shall weigh her worth.
If she truly serves Pandemonium-
The River will not protect her.
Her memories cloud her potential.
Her past dims her light.
I will keep her burdens.
They are many.
Hide them, so she may become unfettered.
She will not remember His venomous whispers."

Her luminosity intensified, and a warmth spread through Osirys. Osirys shuddered, what was going to happen to her? For reasons she couldn't explain, she remained unafraid. The Aethereal beings before her were gentle of manner. She understood innately that they were immensely powerful, though they betrayed none of that strength in their appearance or demeanor. The eldest Muse addressed Osirys directly, and though it seemed to Osirys like she was speaking plainly, her voice carried weight, rhythm, and tune as though she were singing:

"Hello stranger, I am the one called Mnemosyne,
The daughter of the lovely Goddess Gallumine,
My father was a mortal of her undying affection,
To honor him I am the one called Recollection"
"Be still and heed my daughters, called the Muses,
They speak the truth of feelings that each chooses,
None here mean you harm, and you are in no danger,
Though we have many questions you cannot answer, dearest
stranger"

Mnemosyne's light wrapped around her, the gemlight that danced about Mother Memory's head bobbed like fireflies and encircled Osirys. She felt the bones of her face groan and knit, as if they were compelled to return to their former shape. Her pain subsided in what could have been moments or weeks. Her mind quieted, and she felt fear and doubt slip away, little by little. Shame that continued to plague her became muted, dull, and far away. She stared at Mnemosyne, who stood before her, palms up, eyes closed, light surrounding them both in that surreal place. She felt moments of sadness, regret, and anger snuff out like candles being pinched, plunging her past into dim, dusky darkness. She tried to bring faces of her life before into focus, but it was like her recollection of her life was scrambled, and hollow. She felt like she knew pain, but she couldn't remember the source. She remembered the grip of fear, but couldn't place what she was afraid of. She remembered shame and doubt, directed toward herself, but she couldn't recall what she had done to be ashamed of.

The Muses and Mnemosyne turned as one and began walking out of the clearing, down a path into the crystalline forest. Osirys turned with them and followed, not knowing exactly why – passing ethereal beauty as she descended toward the shores of an unimaginably large glassy lake. The terrain was hilly, even mountainous, with wide clearings that bathed in starlight. Looking up, Osirys felt small amongst the comparatively large Muses that guided her, and even more minuscule as she watched the matte of twinkling stars, in the uncountable millions, flickering coldly from their immeasurable distance.

As they walked, Osirys stopped in her tracks, amazed. In a clearing glade, she saw what seemed to be a fox - sitting with its large bushy tail wrapped around it, but it was transparent, and blue-hued. The Muse Nature paused along with her. They both stood and watched the spirit beast for a moment. It eventually looked in their direction. It saw Osirys, and its large ears rotated to regard her curiously.

"You are more strange to them
Than they are to you,"
Nature rested a hand on Osirys' shoulder to signal her to continue the walk. Osirys looked up at Nature, her angular, gemlike eyes twinkling like the stars above her.

"What is it?" Osirys asked, slowly beginning to walk again, but eyes still fixed on the ethereal creature in the glade.

"It is an Ideal" Nature responded musically.

"It exists here so that more like it may exist elsewhen"
Osirys didn't understand, but Nature seemed satisfied with her explanation, so they continued walking in silence until they had caught up with the other Muses. The path was easy to follow, and downhill. Osirys did not become exhausted from the trek, though she didn't quite know how long they walked. It could have been minutes, or it could have been days. Time felt thin and imperceptible

here. It was as if one moment could not be measured, even the time between the beats of her heart felt like it was difficult to quantify.

At long last, they came to the shore of the lake. It was like a mirror, the stars and nebulae that painted the sky met the water and melded, as if there were no border between them. The body of the lake may as well have been as deep and vacuous as the cosmos. The water was nearly motionless, the waterline slowly and gently pulsed, making no sound. While there was snow covering the ground, Osirys expected ice along the water's edge, but peculiarly there was none. The water ended, and the snow began. The Muses continued walking, entering the shallows of the lake, clothing and all. They waded up to their knees, beckoning Osirys to follow. Osirys hugged her thin bathrobe about her. She prepared herself for the icy, frigid lake water. Mnemosyne stood just beyond the waterline, with her hand extended. Osirys took it, and stepped into the water, expecting a shock of cold, but there was none.

She stood before Mnemosyne, the water of the lake lapping at her ankles. Mnemosyne removed a length of silver chain from her cloak, along with one of the disc-like clasps, and carefully wrapped it around Osirys' waist and tied it, cinching it snugly, but not uncomfortably so.

Osirys played with it, sliding the end between her fingers.

"*A gift, and a message to the keepers of the Great Gateway,*" Mnemosyne said, her voice barely a whisper but perfectly clear in the complete silence of the quiet shore. Osirys nodded, though she did not understand.

Mnemosyne and her daughters led Osirys into the water, gently lowering her onto her back, where she floated easily, making no ripples on the surface. As Osirys slipped down into the water, Mnemosyne cradled the back of her head with one hand and rested the other lightly on her belly. Mnemosyne smiled, ever so subtly. She did not speak, but she didn't have to. Mnemosyne was, after all, a mother herself. What did that shadow monster - Pandemonium - do to her unborn child? Perhaps Mnemosyne's light had cleansed it like she had healed her physical hurts? Memory's face fell to sadness and their eyes met squarely. Mnemosyne leaned forward and kissed Osirys on the forehead.

In an instant, her thoughts of her pregnancy dwindled and disappeared. For a split second she panicked. She knew she had forgotten something paramount, something unforgettable, yet it was gone all the same. Why was Mnemosyne resting her hand on her stomach, and why did she look like she was crying?

Osirys felt connected to all things. Those feelings surrounded her, left no room for anything else. The holes in her were filled with the song of the world around her, the rhythm of the moon and tides, and the rising notes of all things that grow; the plants, the creatures, even the mountains as they slowly reached for the clouds and beyond. The Muses sung softly, their voices propagating off of the water and echoing through the open, clean air, until Mnemosyne gently pushed Osirys away from the shore. She felt herself picking up speed, what began as static on the fringe of her mind soon became more and more prominent and turned to the deafening roar of water. She lifted her head and saw that she was heading straight for an immense waterfall, miles above the land below. She focused on the rhythm of the land and world about her, and laid her head back down as she was pulled over the edge of what seemed to be reality and fell, swallowed by the immense Virdi River.

Chapter Two

S HE FELT HERSELF BEING dragged. Not violently, but urgently. She tried to breathe in but couldn't. Her diaphragm wasn't working. It was as if Osirys had the wind knocked out of her immediately upon awakening. She tried to force a cough, it was weak.

"Hold on, girl. I hear you. Keep trying."

She didn't recognize the voice. It was female. It was rough. It was strong. It commanded a measure of authority; not from fear, but rather from weathered confidence. It wasn't old, but it wasn't young. It was experienced, but not exhausted. It reminded her of someone she must have known, but couldn't picture. Osirys coughed again. She felt cold. Very, very cold.

"I don't know how you got into that river, but it's a miracle that you came out. The Virdi isn't a swimming hole. I don't know how you didn't get crushed by tumbling boulders. Come on. Keep trying. I need more out of you. Water out. Air in. Come on."

Osirys sputtered and shook, her chest was on fire and she was teetering on unconsciousness. She thrashed, curling up on her side and forcing water out of her lungs. She gasped a tiny bit of air. She was trying. The voice told her to breathe. She gurgled. A little more air. She tightened her body and coughed as hard as she could. A hard hand connected with her back. Water spilled out of her mouth and nose. She gasped and air filled her lungs.

"That's the way. That's it. Push through the pain. You aren't done yet. One more."

She coughed again. It was easier. It hurt. She had sand in her mouth. She took one deep breath, then another. She heaved the air. It was painful. It was life like she'd never felt before. Osirys cracked open her eyes. Light blazed through tree branches. A dark silhouette of a woman leaned over her. No features yet. Too much light. There was another sound. It was like a train. A roaring and grinding of weight, highlighted by the crack of stone on stone. It was water. A river? No. Not like any river she had known. It was as if a building was collapsing mere feet from her. She felt the ground trembling under the tumult.

"Good enough."

Osirys felt herself lifted from the ground. She turned her head and looked at the voice. She didn't know what she was expecting. The woman was stern-faced, with several scars scattered between her features, but they seemed to enhance a kind of raw beauty. Her chest was covered in polished metal, with a thick leather jerkin beneath. It was covered in dents and thick scratches. Osirys stared in amazement. This woman was her size, maybe a bit larger, but carrying her with ease, as if she were a child. They climbed the embankment and the woman set Osirys down, propped up against a large rock. She had gotten control of her breathing now. She was soaked. Her hair was a tangled knot full of pebbles, sand, and mud. She closed her mouth and felt the crunch of sand in her teeth. She could only imagine what she looked like, covered in filth and wearing a thin linen bathrobe. Oh, how embarrassing. Around her waist, however, was still the silver corded belt, cinched tightly, that the Muses had given her. So that wasn't a dream either?

"Thanks."

Osirys wanted to say more but it was painful. Her ribs screamed when she tried to speak.

"You owe me one. What are you about, girl? How did you wind up in the river? Did you jump in, thinking you'd be better off dead?" The woman chuckled.

Osirys felt shame, but couldn't remember why. She looked down, unsure how to respond.

"Really? You thought 'this is how I'm gonna go!' and just cast yourself into the river? You're braver than me, girl. I've faced down three to one odds at the hands of mirelings before, but even I'm not that crazy."

The woman shrugged, "Ah, well. Let's have a look at you. For a swim in the Virdi, you don't seem that worse for the wear." She scanned and examined Osirys, obviously looking for injuries. After a few minutes, the woman sat back, raising her eyebrows.

"How do you get out of that without a scratch on you? How is it possible?"

What in the world was this woman talking about? Osirys looked at her, puzzled. The woman stood up, shaking her head. She walked a dozen paces to a nearby rock, picked up a backpack, and strapped a scabbard onto her back containing a five foot long blade. The pommel was weathered, the leather wrappings on the hilt were dark from sweat and blood, and the crossguard was notched with dozens of deep gouges. The woman slowly walked back towards Osirys, digging in her leather satchel bag, producing a wrapped package containing jerky. She took a piece for herself, and tossed a piece to Osirys.

Osirys looked around. She didn't need to pinch herself, the pain of breathing let her know she wasn't dreaming. There were leaves on the trees. It was a warm spring day. Something wasn't right. She couldn't remember why, but she was expecting it to be winter. She grabbed a fistful of warm, green grass and tore it and the dirt beneath, squeezing it in her hands in total confusion.

"Where- where am I right now?" Osirys asked. Her voice rattled, shaking. She felt herself trembling.

"About an hour North of Pearlwater Bend, little miss."

As if she had any clue where that was. It wasn't any place she had heard of before. She stared at the woman, blinking.

"Pearlwater Bend? You must have gotten your little nogg scrambled right when you went for a swim. Come on, let's get you to town and get someone to take a look at you, maybe a warm meal and a bit of rest will help you put yourself back together." The woman pulled her hand from a heavy leather glove, and extended it down to help Osirys to her feet.

"My name is Naivarra. What's yours?"

Naivarra. That was a strong name. This woman was everything Osirys was not. Whatever life she lived, Naivarra oozed strength and purpose. Osirys looked down at her tattered robe and sprawled form. She was a waif, a spindly wretch in comparison. She held up her hand, and Naivarra grasped it. It was a strong grip, one that was familiar with pulling someone to their feet after being knocked down. Osirys felt courage swell within her as she was hoisted to her feet. Naivarra met her eyes, they were gray-blue, and kind. For a moment, she imagined herself in Naivarra's image. Maybe she could learn? Osirys bore her own weight again and immediately stars wheeled in her vision. Her knees buckled, and everything went black.

"Didn't think it was that tough of a question-" Naivarra trailed as Osirys' limp body crumpled back to the ground. The Virdi River crashed nearby, the violence of countless tons of water smashing through the landscape echoing across the plains.

CHAPTER THREE

O SIRYS CAME TO ABRUPTLY, and her disorientation deepened. Naivarra had pulled her to her feet, and was whispering something. She blinked to adjust to the light of the bright day, and heard the clacking of hooves and the grinding of wooden wheels on stone nearby.

"Do you need aid?" A deep gravel-toned voice called.

"Aye, mayhaps," Naivarra replied.

Osirys turned and looked at the silhouette, perched on top of a weathered and highly reinforced cart, drawn by two enormous, and equally weathered horses. The cart was the leader of a small caravan. Several carts rolled to a stop behind the leader. Each cart had several menacing men sitting astride their fronts, and their backs were covered in a thick canvas top, so that she could not see what they carried.

The shadowed figure continued speaking, "There are Musefolk around these parts. Can never be too careful, you know."

Naivarra glanced at the caravan of carts and narrowed her eyes, before taking a step in front of Osirys.

"The Vamanari have always been allies of the Empirate," Naivarra countered, cautiously.

"And what of yourself?" The cart driver asked. "Do you consider yourself an ally of the Empirate as well, this far on the North Road with no house sigil?"

"I think it wise that you move along and mind your own," Naivarra growled.

The cart driver chuckled, stepping down from the seat. His head was bald and tattooed, blue and black patterns inked precisely into his scalp. He wore thick dark colored robes that hid his hands.

"One might get the wrong idea, you know. You wouldn't be the first fugitives of the Empirate we've apprehended on this long, desolate road."

He gestured over his shoulder at the line of caravan wagons.

The robed caravan driver glanced at Osirys and his eyes lingered on her silver corded belt, given to her by the Muses. He quickly turned and signaled to the caravan wagons behind him. Osirys noticed weapons. Clubs, swords, and the like. What was happening here?

"Girl," Naivarra whispered under her breath, "Stay behind me. Don't let them get behind you, you hear? If you need to run, you run."

"Who are these people?" Osirys whispered into Naivarra's ear, before the caravan driver could return his attention.

"Slavers, by the look of things." Naivarra responded.

Osirys gulped and began to tremble with fear, but nodded. If Naivarra could stand alone and hold her nerve against a dozen armed men, she could agree to run. Naivarra stood like a pillar of stone between the caravaneers and Osirys. She didn't yet reach for her weapon, rather, she was cool and poised, almost conversational. But beneath her demeanor, Osirys saw her feet shift to a more balanced stance, and her eyes focused intently, never dropping her attention from the approaching crew.

"There are many that credit me with the gift of foresight, you know," the tattooed caravan driver said, staring at Naivarra ominously, "and if I had to take a guess at your future, I'd say you had a choice to make."

"What choice would that be, then?" Naivarra responded casually, her hand resting on her hip.

"You seem like you've done an admirable job helping your friend out this far. What say you hand her over to us and we'll bring her safely to town where she can get some proper help from the clerics?"

Naivarra looked around at the empty road behind and before them. The Virdi river groaned and rumbled distantly to the East, and mountains rose like shadows of the heavens to the West.

"She's my cousin, family best look after family, you know." Naivarra lied, crossing her arms and narrowing her eyes at the bald man. "What's my other choice, fortune teller?"

Several of the other caravaneers had reached them, and they stood, threateningly, nearby.

The bald man groaned, "I'd say you're a little out of your depth there, miss. I have no doubt that you can wield that blade of yours well enough, but let's be smart. There's no need for us to come down hard on one as young and full of promise as yourself. You give us the girl, and we won't take you, too."

"I've never been one for gambling." Naivarra responded, sarcasm dripping from her words. "But these aren't the worst odds I've beaten."

A chorus of threatening chuckles passed over the thuggish crew, and some drew their blades as they approached.

"Aye, maybe," said the robed man, "but you're no good to us as the bloody mess we'd need to make of you if we all had a good rout right here. I have a better idea!"

He bellowed some words that Osirys couldn't make out, sweeping his hands over his head in a flourish and then violently down. Naivarra's face flushed ghostly white nearly instantaneously. She wavered for a moment, fumbling, and then toppled, unconscious.

It was over in mere moments. Osirys instinctively turned and began to run, full tilt and barefoot away from the captors. She felt the thud of Naivarra's body as it connected with the ground. She didn't look back. What had he done to her? Naivarra was so strong, what chance did she have against these horrible men? She stifled a scream and just focused on breathing and running. She had no idea where she was going. She had no place to hide. She had no one to call to. Her heart pounded in her temples as she fled. She heard pursuit. Not footsteps. Hooves. She looked back and couldn't help but cry out. A devilish looking thinner man with leather straps across his chest was bearing down upon her. He wielded a club, and was grinning savagely as he raised it to bring it to bear upon her. She cried out and dropped to the ground to avoid the strike. He laughed and dropped from the horse, landing in a roll and coming to his feet and rushing her. She scrambled and grabbed a fistful of grit, throwing it at his face to blind him. He seemed unphased, shielding his eyes with his sleeve. She turned to run. Pain surged through her, the sharp gravel had shredded the soles of her feet as she ran.

She didn't get far. A thick hand wrapped around her hair and yanked her back and down. She landed heavily, the wind knocked from her instantly. She sputtered and gasped, trying to draw breath. The man loomed above her, raising the club over her head, smiling.

"Now don't get carried away, son." The bald man said casually, "A corpse isn't worth a pint, even if it's pretty." He moved up and put his hand on the man about to kill her in broad daylight. "Besides, this one might be particularly special. My master will want to see her personally. Go ahead and put her with the others. You did well."

He seemed placated. He stepped back and lowered the club, still grinning savagely. It was sickening. Osirys began to cry against her will. He moved toward her and she flinched and tried to scramble, but it was no use. He grabbed her by the hair again and hauled her to her feet, half dragging her, half leading her to one of the carts in the rear of the caravan. She struggled, and a heavy fist connected with her temple, sending stars across her vision. She felt herself lifted and dragged into the back of the cart, where she landed heavily on her backside, whimpering. It was too dark to see and her head was still spinning. She felt cold iron across her wrists and ankles, and the heaviness of a thick chain affixed to the sturdy cart. She curled up on her side and squeezed her eyes shut.

A trickle of blood dripped from the side of her head across her face. It was warm. It was familiar. She hated that she knew the difference between blood, sweat, and tears on her face intuitively. She hated that she wasn't appalled by her treatment. It felt, almost, normal? She was terrified, but resigned. She shuddered and wrapped her arms around her, keeping her eyes closed. She felt like she was in a bad dream that she couldn't wake from. She tried desperately to remember anything from before that day. She remembered groggy glimpses of living darkness, and after that the lake with strange crystalline trees and the peculiar women with angular eyes and prismatic features, but it was foggy, incoherent. She felt as if those were dreams, conjured memories that never actually happened, but the silver belt around her middle suggested otherwise. She heard the shouts of commands from outside, and the cart began to move, rumbling over the dirt road, rocking back and forth. She kept her eyes closed, waiting to wake up. The rhythmic sound of crunching stone on wood took on a sound almost like a record that had spun out of its last track, and was now amplifying the emptiness on the vinyl. She kept her eyes shut.

It could have been several hours or ten minutes- Osirys couldn't really grasp the passage of time, but she began to make out other sounds over the crunching of the wheels on the road and clop of hooves. She heard the vague rumbling bustle of civilization. She heard the far-off sound of a hammer striking metal, and the clamor of a marketplace in the distance. She heard the groan of wind driven mills turning heavy millstones and the grinding of grain into flour for bread, the timber groaning under movement and constant stress. At first the sounds progressively got louder, and Osirys' began to hope that someone would find her, she could cry out for help, maybe someone would hear her – but then the caravan turned, and the sounds of salvation began to recede into the distance one more.

Of course her captors wouldn't be stupid enough to ride into town without means to keep her quiet. Goodness knows, if she couldn't make enough ruckus, Naivarra certainly would. Osirys wondered for a moment about Naivarra's fate. Was she alive? Osirys thought so. If she was alive, perhaps they could communicate, and form a plan for escape. Osirys cracked open her eyes, and saw a row of feet nearby where she lay. She jerked upright and looked about her. She wasn't alone in the back of this wagon. There was a dozen others, of small stature, the size of children, she would estimate, but they were of all apparent ages. They had angular features, big eyes, and slim noses. Most strikingly, they had a stone-like complexion that reminded her of the Muses. Their skin color was gray-hued, though some were more umber, while others were nearly marble-white. Some had elaborate hairstyles, some had long beards, some were robust and muscled, and others were covered in wrinkles, but not one an inch over three feet tall. Osirys gasped. Several of them reacted to her sudden movement, looking up from their binds. Seeing her shock, one of the small women spoke to Osirys in a soft, barely audible voice:

"It never gets familiar, waking up and seeing these bindings. I keep thinking I'll wake up back in bed in our village, but so far the luck of our people has failed me. It pains me to see a beauty such as yourself in this mess with us. Just awful. These ruffians are an unscrupulous lot."

Osirys inched closer to the seemingly older woman, leaning down and in towards her, whispering. "Who are you? What happened to us?"

The woman sagged even deeper into herself for a moment, before replying.

"We were the Vamanari of a small village far to the North called Ingenshen. We thought we were remote enough. We had heard of the Vamanari of other villages being captured, but they were farther South, easier to transport. We had been receiving refugees for several weeks. It must have been that these slavers tracked a group of families North to us after their village was raided. Our Queen Lavis dispatched aid in the form of warriors to help protect us, but the slavers arrived first. We didn't stand a chance. Those who fought were killed, those who surrendered were thrown in chains, piled in wagons, and whisked away South. What unfortunate circumstance brought you to us, lass? We didn't know they were stealing anyone they came across, the mongrels. I'm afraid we're bound to be sold into slavery. Not a life I imagined for my children…" She trailed off.

Osirys processed the words of the small, wrinkled, stoic woman. Several of the individuals blinked while staring at her, their large reflective eyes perfectly attuned to the dusky shadow of the cart. She closed her eyes and slumped against the back of the cart, and began to laugh. Softly, at first. She couldn't help it. Overwhelmed, she began to crumble, laughing as tears streaked down her face. The Vamanari were all staring at her, mouths agape.

"Shh, hush, hush!" the older Vaman woman pleaded with her. "Stop! Please!"

Osirys couldn't stop. She didn't even try. Whatever this fantasy was that her mind had conjured, she was ready for it to end. Her laughter built and grew, until she was holding her stomach. She heard shouts from outside the cart and the vehicle lurched to a halt. Several of the Vamanari in her cart cried out and buried their heads in their tattered clothing. Hurried footsteps ran to the back of the cart and the back flap of the canvas was ripped open, light suddenly flooding the space. Osirys looked at the lanky brute who had first captured her with defiance. She began to shout and thrash at her binds as he climbed into the back of the wagon and approached. He raised his club, just as the older Vaman woman clapped her hands over Osirys mouth.

"You monster, leave her alone." She growled. The other Musefolk gasped. Fear gripped their faces. Tears from some of the younger ones began streaming from their eyes. Osirys stopped laughing for a moment, confused.

The lanky ruffian grinned menacingly, and grabbed the old Vaman. With a flick, he unlocked her chains and hauled her up off the floor of the cart. Osirys couldn't see her face as she was tossed over his shoulder. A younger Vaman cried out as she passed, "No, Granna!"

"Hush, my son. I knew what I was doing. Better me than her."

And she was gone. The Vamanari in the cart turned and looked at Osirys, mouths open, eyes wet, but no words. Moments later the man returned, and headed towards Osirys.

"You thought you weren't gonna get any because the little hag stood up for you, eh?" He chuckled insanely. "After this you'll never open your mouth to laugh again."

She offered no resistance as he roughly dragged her out of the cart. Osirys shielded her eyes as they adjusted to the brightness of the daylight once again. She looked at her surroundings, hoping for anything that suggested she recognized where she was. The plains rose up to the North, an immense knob on the landscape that was flat at the top, like a spired plateau. The peculiar geology was itself not terribly huge, maybe five hundred yards in length, and three quarters as wide, vaguely shaped like an anvil. It stood tall, however, with a path winding up a grassy slope to its summit. The face that was closest to the caravan was rocky and sheer, and imposing. Atop the formation, she saw what appeared to be stone ruins, the crumbling remains of something that could have been a castle or fort. It was captivating, and she held her gaze upon it as she was being unceremoniously led several paces away from the caravan.

Osirys looked back to the situation at hand, sobered from her laughing outburst by the sunlight and the group of slavers that had assembled. The bald, robed man that had spoken earlier approached like a darkened sky about to storm. He was humming as he moved, his voice was dark and full of gritty undertones, as if the sound were coming from under the heel of his heavy boot that crunched along the rocky dirt road. As he approached, he softly began singing.

> *"I hear the Muses in the rain,*
> *What else might explain,*
> *Sacrifices of the slain-*
> *Their wisdom is the cause of all our shame,*
> *Sets our heart and soul aflame,*

> *And at our feet, the blame-*
> *I hear their voices in the wind,*
> *Our spirits flayed and skinned,*
> *For redemption of the sinned-*
> *The purest arcane echoes hold us thrall*
> *Make us feel so small*
> *Makes us want to feel at all-"*

The Vaman woman stood as tall and as straight as her aged and curved spine would allow.

"And you-" He spun, putting his pointer finger directly on Osirys' forehead, smiling viciously. His pitch was cryptic, and threatening, he held onto the sounds of his words just longer than normal, giving his speech an element of unhinged madness.

"Everyone seems to want to protect you. We're going to find out why." He scanned her for clues, his eyes once again lingering on the silver linked belt.

"Perhaps the wind is speaking after all," He mumbled, running his thick digit from her forehead, down the bridge of her nose, and wrapping under her chin, grabbing her lower lip and pulling it down slightly with his thumb. She felt as though he was exerting a pressure upon her, something unseen, something just under the surface of his demeanor. Her skin prickled as he scanned her face, a hint of malicious glee tugging at the sides of his mouth.

"Just as Master Sheol foretold," He purred. "How exciting! He will be very happy to know you've arrived."

Osirys stood, shaking. His touch was corrupt, and every instinct told her to flee, but firm hands on her shoulders and the cold point of steel in the middle of her spine kept her where she stood. She glanced back at the caravan. She could see the canvas pulled up on the sides of several of the carts, and the reflection of dozens of sets of Vaman eyes peering from the shadows. She looked down at the old stone-skinned woman, stout even through her old age, who had thrown herself into harm's way for her sake, and frowned. She stared straight forward at the side of the plateau spire.

The bald man continued, addressing the old Muse-folk. "You know where we are, don't you?" He gestured behind him, waving his hand at the rocky slope. "You know how many gallons of blood this hill has seen over the years, don't you? The ground drinks it, they say. You know how many thousands of lives were ended on these fields, don't you? All of them were fighting for something, but you? You're going to end here, for nothing."

He turned and thrust his finger once again towards Osirys, "You best watch closely. This old creet isn't worth the coin to drag her filth from the North to where you're headed, but you! You'll be worth our time, unless you make any more trouble like you just did. One more peep out of your pretty little face and you'll be right here beside your "Hero", where the crows can pick out your pretty little eyes."

Osirys wasn't looking at him, she was focused on the little woman who stood fearlessly before her, staunch and resolute as the stones in front of them. The man grabbed Osirys face and forced her to look at him. He held her gaze and his face pressed in close to hers. She could smell his breath and sweat, sickening and bitter. She looked into his eyes for a moment. She wasn't sure what she was supposed to see. She figured if she looked into the eyes of someone as mindlessly evil as a man such as this, she would see some sign betrayed in them. But they were just brown, with gold flecks. He was just a bad man. No more, no less. She knew she had stared this kind of man in the eyes before, and felt afraid. The slaver released her face, and she turned to look at the Vaman woman again. Osirys wanted to apologize for something. Somewhere inside of her, Osirys wished the woman would look at her. She probably would have apologized anyway, but the woman didn't even so much as flinch as the tattooed monster spun on his heel, and in one fluid motion brought a spiked truncheon down upon her skull, caving it in and splattering gore all about the ground beneath. The sound, though sickening, wasn't loud.

O SIRYS INSTINCTIVELY CRIED OUT. She stared agape as the body of the old Vaman crumpled to the ground and lay motionless, soaking the dirt with blood. This was no dream, this was a nightmare. Osirys shrieked, involuntarily pressing back into the blade against her spine. She felt its tip bite into her skin, and she felt the hands on her shoulders clamp her in place. She heard the big slaver speaking to her but it was muffled, as if she was underwater. All she could hear was the static of adrenaline demanding she flee for her life, but she couldn't. He was moving toward her, pointing one finger of his large, deadly hand towards her and a cool, murderous look in his eyes. She was terrified. She looked back at the caravan. Dozens of Musefolk peered from the shadows under the canvas, the only hint of their presence the glim twinkling of their reflective eyes. Where was Naivarra? Was she still alive? Osirys looked back at the slaver. He was two paces away.

"Help! Help me!" Osirys screeched, attempting to thrash her way to freedom. Her voice bounced off of the rocks of the outcropping and echoed across the plains, blending with the wind.

"There's no one helping you, little girl." The man said, venom dripping from his words. "So if you know what's good for you, and you don't want to end up like your friend here, you best learn to keep that big mouth of yours shut."

Osirys was staring at him, but something caught her eye past him, on the cliff. It looked like one of the boulders moved. She fixated her eyes past him, no longer concerned with his threats. Two, then six, then a dozen tiny figures leaped from the top of the plateau, landing and sliding down the shear face of the crag in a full run. They were closing fast. They were Vamanari, clad in leather with purple cloth wraps, hoods, and face coverings, wielding impressively long spears for their size, several hoisting javelins as they sprinted towards the caravan. Suddenly everything was in motion. A warning horn sounded from one of the caravan drivers nearby. Osirys was thrown to the ground, landing mere inches from the body of the Vaman woman killed mere moments ago. She heard blades being drawn from their scabbards.

"Stay near the caravan! Use the carts as cover!" The bald man shouted. Osirys heard the cry of one of the horses. She looked to see the beast that pulled the middle cart of the caravan rearing up, the shaft of a javelin protruding from its hind quarter. It cried in pain, and toppled over, wrenching the wheels of the cart off of the road, sending it crashing onto its side, breaking in several pieces, spilling supplies from a compartment underneath the body of the cart. Osirys caught the glint of metal – it was weapons. It must have been where the slavers had stored the arms of the Vaman village when it was raided. Osirys saw her opportunity. She began to crawl on all fours toward the capsized wagon. She heard the cries of Vamanari inside.

Several came scrambling out of the cart, freed from their bonds.

Osirys heard the sounds of battle rise around her. Shouts mingled with the clash of steel on steel. She looked back to catch a glimpse. A Vaman flourished its spear and swiped it low, catching a slaver's leg as he lunged. The Vaman twisted the spear, raising it and changing the much larger opponent's momentum, causing him to stumble. The Vaman lowered its shoulder and threw itself against the side of the man's knee that had caught his weight to keep him from falling over. She heard the pop of the joint and the man's leg bent unnaturally. He howled in pain as he fell. Like a wind, the Vaman had moved past him and thrust the spear up and behind, its lethal point catching him in the lower back as he fell. It was so precise. Surgical, even. The small warriors were so adept at fighting larger enemies. They worked as a team, flowing like the breeze across the plains, using weight and momentum as weapons against their foes.

Their initial onslaught was effective, taking down several of the caravaneers before they could react. But the more experienced fighters were not to be taken so easily. They were more cautious, recognizing the experienced fighting style of the Vamanari. They had fought Vamanari before. They kept themselves balanced, and stood close together, not leaving openings for the Musefolk to weave into their dance. Three of the slavers had moved together near the toppled cart, facing off against two Vaman warriors, between Osirys and the scattered weapons on the ground. They kept their stances low, and defended each other from the prodding test strikes of the Vaman warriors in purple. A younger Vaman crawled from the wrecked cart behind them. He pulled himself free, and moved up behind the slavers, picking up a small dagger-like blade from the ground as he moved. He stalked cautiously, and then sprung, launching himself at the larger man and burying the weapon deep into his side. The man cried out in pain, and his partner spun, and brought his broad falchion of a blade down upon the small attacker. The Vaman ducked away, avoiding a direct chopping blow, but the blade caught the outside of his shoulder, digging deep into his sinew. The Vaman grunted and dropped, clutching his shoulder and scrambling away, deep crimson soaking through his rent shirt, and a determined look of defiance on his face. The slaver turned to finish off the young attacker, but the warriors in purple did not hesitate to capitalize on the opening he created. With two of the three men wounded or distracted, the pair leapt into motion, one ducking and dashing to the right of the slaver, the other demanding his attention with a thrust to his left, forcing him to parry, leaving his right side exposed. The flanking Vaman turned and thrust upward, sending the tip of the spear in under his ribcage, seeking his heart with a precise, controlled thrust.

Osirys watched the man fall, and felt the glimmer of hope as the warriors in purple seemed to be gaining advantage. She scrambled across the ground and slid beneath the overturned cart, grabbing a small blade. Her hopes were shattered when the large man waded into view, swinging the heavy truncheon in a low sweep, catching both the Vaman warriors with the blow and sending them head over heels, sprawling out in the road. Their spears clattered away, one of the Vamanari did not stir. The other clutched their arm and side, bones clearly shattered from the blow. He turned, and Osirys ducked in under the cart, hiding from sight. She wanted to help, but there was no way she could stand against these men. She held the little blade in both hands, she hoped he didn't see her. She inched away and slipped in under the canvas. She couldn't see the fighting any more, she could only hear it. It was nothing like she'd ever heard before. All she wanted to do was hide, but she knew she had to do something. The Vamanari weren't winning decisively. They were fearsome, but they were so small. The large men clad in armor that were still standing were experienced fighters, and after the initial attack their numbers did not dwindle. The Vamanari were counting on an overwhelming assault, their tactics were not designed for a prolonged battle. They were too few and too spread out. As the slavers organized a defense, the tide of battle began to turn.

The Vamanari were separated from each other and forced to defend themselves without partners, the slavers spread out but kept themselves in pairs, and moved in circles, flanking and striking between the Vamanari to separate them, and then circling between them so that their comrades could assist. The Vamanari were being forced back and away from the caravan carts. One of their number was singled and flanked by two slavers, using their spear to deflect strikes, but the strength of the blows was exhausting for the small warrior, the slavers used their size and just alternated hammering strikes. Osirys peeked out of the canvas to see the Vaman backing away from the assault, being herded away from their allies as the slavers pounded against their defense. The purple cloth fell away from the Vaman's face and Osirys saw feminine features. One of the slavers pushed forward, sending a knee into her chest as she deflected a blow from his partner, throwing her onto her back. She raised the shaft of her spear to attempt to block the overhead chop of his club, but the shaft splintered and broke, and the club crashed down onto her chest with a sickening crack. The Vaman's arms fell to her sides, motionless, and the slavers turned, and ran back toward the fighting.

Osirys watched in horror at the motionless warrior in purple, smote upon the road. She turned and looked about her in the overturned carriage. It was otherworldly. Several Vamanari dangled by their bindings, unconscious. At least one was crushed under the gunnel of the cart. Her eyes widened though, when she saw Naivarra, upside down and suspended by chains, hanging from the far wall of the wagon. Osirys pushed herself towards Naivarra, whose unconscious form dangled limply. Osirys pushed herself up under Naivarra to take her weight, and she whispered,

"Naivarra! Naivarra! Wake up! Please!" Osirys slapped her face lightly to try and rouse her. Her time was running out. She heard the battle turning sour outside, there wasn't much time left until the Vaman attackers were routed. She raised her voice, risking it all: "Naivarra! Now! Help!"

Naivarra's eyes fluttered open, and there was only a moment of confusion in her face as she focused on Osirys. "You can explain what happened later."

Osirys smiled briefly in relief and nodded, taking her blade and jamming it into the wood below the plate that held Naivarra's chains. She pushed into the lever, trying to pry it free.

"Come on girl, lean into it!" Naivarra urged. Osirys pushed, gritting her teeth and setting her legs against the wooden gunnel behind her. She felt the blade bend, but the nails were beginning to pull from their sunken positions.

"Good, good, keep going, almost there!" Osirys strained, adrenaline pushing her muscles beyond what she had ever used them for before in her life, but it wasn't enough. She struggled and lunged against the plate, but it wasn't moving any further. Naivarra saw that Osirys had reached her limit, and sucked in a sharp breath of air, grabbing the chain with her other hand, and yanked. The wood groaned and pulled, shafts of light began to streak through near the plate's housing. Together they pushed and pulled, and with a crack the chain housing wrenched from the plank. Naivarra slid down and landed with a thump on the ground. She groaned, and rolled over, and pushed herself out and toward the battle.

Osirys couldn't fathom running toward the fight. Every instinct in her body now told her to run, to flee away, but Naivarra didn't hesitate. She forced herself to move, to follow. In a moment she launched herself from the cart. Naivarra was there, and extended her hand once more to Osirys as she emerged from the wreck. In her other hand, was her blade, recovered from the spilled supplies.

"I'm Osirys", Osirys managed to sputter, "You asked my name before, and I never got to answer. My name is Osirys."

Naivarra grinned, "See? It wasn't that hard of a question."

Naivarra turned and charged toward the battle. The Vamanari were nearly broken, splintered from each other and on full defense. Naivarra howled as she descended upon the nearest slavers. Her blade flashed over her head and she brought it to bear, with a fury Osirys had never seen before. It was gruesome. Naivarra slammed into one slaver and cut down another, twisting her weapon like it were an extension of her body. Though it must have weighed a considerable amount, Naivarra wielded it as if it were an orchestra conductor's wand. A burly man with a longsword stepped in front of her and caught her blade with a wooden shield. She growled and spun, pushing him back and away. He clapped his blade against his shield and laughed. Naivarra advanced on him like a dark omen. She raised her weapon to strike, and then feinted, he raised his shield expecting the blow but it never came, instead she ducked to the side, dropping the tip of her blade to the ground, then bringing it in an upward arc up the middle of his body, splitting him open from groin to chest. His look of surprise only lasted a moment as the crossguard of her sword connected with his face, sending him backwards, his innards spilling as he fell.

Osirys realized she was still holding the blade she used to free Naivarra, and she began to run to help. She wasn't sure what had possessed her, but she knew she couldn't stand by uselessly. Rather than fight, she jumped up on the next nearest wagon, and plunged her dagger into the canvas, cutting it smoothly. She made a large enough gash to climb through and she pushed into the darkness, spilling light into the wagon as she entered. The Vamanari inside gasped at her, ragged as she was, covered in blood, and wielding a bent dagger. She knelt and slashed at their ropes struggling with her bent blade to rend their bindings. She sawed at them until her arms screamed but she refused to give up. She freed one, then another, then another. As they were freed they scrambled from the wagon. Soon there was a Vaman by her side, of sandstone complexion. He regarded her as she looked at him in the shadow. He held two daggers, reclaimed from outside. He held one toward her, pommel extended, for her to take. She looked at her bent and blunted blade, nearly useless in its current form, and she tossed it, grabbing the new one and together they freed the remainder of the Vamanari in the cart. Her mind was focused, every Vaman she freed was an ally. An ally for Naivarra, another wrench in the slavers plans. She knew she didn't stand a chance in combat, but this just might be enough. She emerged from the caravan to see the Vamanari she freed rushing from the overturned cart with weapons in hand, a small army of tiny reinforcements.

Naivarra looked back and saw Osirys, dagger in hand, standing by the large slit in the wagon she had just freed. Naivarra's eyes had the gleam of victory in them, and in moments, it was all over. The slavers could not stay coordinated, and they broke, running from the battle, the robed leader grabbing a horse and leaping astride. After the horse made several long strides, he pulled it around and it reared back on two legs as he swept his gaze across the wreckage of the caravan. His eyes came to rest on Osirys, and she shuddered at his stare. He held her gaze, even from the considerable distance. He bared his teeth and wheeled his steed, galloping away at great speed. Several of the Vaman warriors in purple hurled javelins in pursuit, but they they didn't move to chase - instead they immediately started to assess their wounded. All told, there were two dozen or more bodies on the road, a mix of slaver men and Vamanari. Osirys felt the weight of the battle drop upon her like lead, and she leaned against the wagon, heaving. Her stomach revolted at the sight before her.

A dozen yards away, one of the Vamanari in purple approached Naivarra, and bowed their head in thanks. Naivarra knelt and said a couple words that Osirys couldn't make out, but she gestured toward Osirys. The Musefolk turned and looked and began walking towards Osirys. They didn't get halfway when another of the warriors called out: "Pae- Pae come quick!" The Vaman turned and saw the lifeless form of the purple warrior that had been singled out and crushed by the slavers that Osirys had witnessed.

The warrior cried out and ran, her feminine voice catching Osirys off guard, dropping her spear and falling to her knees by the body. The Vaman howled, clutching at the vestment of the fallen. She saw the Musefolk pull an ornate dagger from the belt of her dead comrade, and clutch it to her chest. She couldn't watch any more. She turned away.

Osirys tested her knees and began to walk towards Naivarra. The remainder of the enslaved Vamanari had been freed, and they began to congregate off the road, looking towards the warriors in purple that had gathered over their fallen. Whispers ran through their number, Osirys caught fragments of their words, she heard one young Vaman whisper 'Is it really the Vipers come to rescue us?' It seemed that no other of their number had been slain, but several bore fresh wounds, many that would undoubtedly be lifelong reminders of the day. Naivarra approached the purple warriors, Osirys sheepishly in tow.

One of the purple warriors turned to regard Naivarra, nodding in appreciation for her assistance, and removing their face covering. They too were female. Her face was the color of a dry shale. She addressed Naivarra:

"You have our thanks, warrior. Had you not arrived to turn the battle, we would have surely been routed and many more of our number slain. Our leader, Pasea, would see to our gratitude, but alas, it is her sister Pemme that has fallen today. I am Mirabyll, second in command to Pasea. We are our Queen's royal guard, known abroad as the Violet Vipers. We tracked the slaver scum from Ingenshen, we arrived too late to stop the attack. Queen Lavis sends her regards to all allies of the Vamanari in these dark times. I will pass word of your heroism. Your kindness and bravery will be rewarded, I'm sure."

Osirys' heart sank. Sister? She could not keep her thoughts from drifting. Did she too have a sister? Her emotions suggested she did, but she had no recollection in name or face. She despaired at her inability to remember as she felt tears begin to fall.

"Aye, but don't thank me alone." Naivarra replied, "Had this girl not freed me and many of your kin, we would still be dangling in chains where we hung."

Osirys stood nearby, clutching her thin robe between her fingers. She was fixed on the fallen Vaman warrior Pemme and her sister, Pasea.

Mirabyll nodded and stepped closer to Osirys. Osirys looked down at her. Mirabyll was perhaps three foot four, a half of a head taller than the other nearby Musefolk. She lowered her hood to reveal a thick braid of auburn hair, restrained with several gemmed pins. She had large, yellow eyes that reflected the sunlight. Her body was lean and muscular, not disproportional. Her stone-like poise was imposing, but not unfriendly. Naivarra seemed unphased by the existence of Vamanari, as if she were accustomed to seeing them, but Osirys was still awestruck. Mirabyll regarded her, hands on hips, with those deep yellow eyes. Osirys felt slightly uncomfortable, she felt as if she was being examined, like a scientific specimen.

"Hm."

Mirabyll nodded at Osirys, but didn't say any more. Her piercing stare lingered on her for several more moments before she turned back to her comrades as they lifted the body of Pemme and began walking toward the plateau. Mirabyll addressed the group of Vamanari that had gathered. "You are all safe, for the time being. You are free to go where you wish, though I suspect the slavers will return for their horses and belongings before day's end. There is a safe house for our kind in Pearlwater Bend, if you have no where else to go, I suggest you start at the Lost Lantern Inn. Be safe, and trust no-one. These are dangerous times for us. We will return there shortly as well, after we have finished up here."

Mirabyll turned to Naivarra and Osirys, and nodded. "Same for you two." The majority of the Violet Vipers carried their fallen warrior up the path toward the summit, while two others built a small pyre for the dead near the caravan, unhitched the horses, and scrounged some supplies.

Osirys watched the Vamanari disperse, and followed the Vipers up the path with her eyes. "What is that place?" She asked Naivarra, who stood, arms crossed, looking down at the poor Vaman woman who was the first to die that day.

"Hm?" Naivarra looked up, her thoughts interrupted by Osirys' question.

Osirys pointed at the crumbling structure on top of the anvil shaped plateau. "That place, what is it, or I guess, what was it?"

Naivarra cocked her head. "You worry me, girl. Everyone for leagues knows what that place is. Even these Vamanari from Ingenshen, two weeks ride by horse away from here to the North know what that place is. It's Tork's Redoubt. Do you really not know where you are?"

Osirys shook her head, shuddering, suddenly feeling cold, even in the bright sunlight. "I- I'm not from here. I don't think I belong here. I'm not even sure if any of this is real."

Naivarra gave her a puzzled look. "Well, you're a mystery then. But if you've never seen the ruins of Tork's Redoubt, we should go and have a look. No sense wasting such a nice day on death and violence without a good view afterwards." She began to walk after the Vipers, who were climbing the path to the summit. "Come on, girl, before those slavers come back for you. If they catch you again, I'm staying out of it."

Osirys looked around her, it was surreal. Dead bodies of people were piled on a fire, and the wreckages of horse drawn carriages lingered on the road, like an apocalyptic scene. She just watched people die in front of her, and now she was going to go take a pleasure hike to a vista with a woman dressed in battle regalia, a five foot long sword, and a handful of mythical stone-skinned Musefolk. The two Vipers that remained paid her no heed as they lifted the body of the old Vaman woman whose name she never learned and began to carry her towards Tork's Redoubt, to rejoin the rest of their kin and bury their fallen. The Vipers had put torches to the wagons and they were now aflame, any supplies left would not be usable for the slavers should they return. Osirys was soon standing alone, and shuddered at the thought of the slavers returning. She took one last look at the caravan, smoke billowing into the clear sky, and turned to begin walking to catch up with Naivarra, suddenly keenly aware of the myriad of hurts that she had acquired in such a short time.

Chapter Four

T HE SUMMIT WAS HIGHER than it appeared from the lower vantage point of the ruined caravan. Osirys was exhausted, her legs burned as she ascended the verdant road that ran the length of the anvil-shaped plateau, steadily sloping upwards towards the ruins above. The grass was lush, almost cushion-like. On one side, the rocky earth rose precipitously, bending upward. The rocks were sturdy and old, rounded by aeons of weather and wear. Where vegetation could take purchase, it did. Small scrub trees and shrubs wedged their stubborn roots into the cracks of the rocks, syphoning what little sustenance they could out of the stone. The formation itself felt strange to Osirys, as if it was pushed up from deep beneath the surface of the world, evenly and shapely. The path before her steadily climbed on. It wasn't steep, but it was wide. It was more of a road than a path, really. Two of the caravan carts and their horses could ride side-by-side comfortably, maybe even three. Along the sides of the path, Osirys saw stones occasionally break through the thick grass, some indication of intentionality in their regularity along the way.

Naivarra was a dozen or so paces ahead of Osirys, and showed no hint of fatigue. Naivarra paused and looked back over her shoulder, waiting for Osirys to catch up. Osirys stumbled to a halt to catch her breath. Naivarra produced a waterskin and held it for Osirys to take, her muscled arm outstretched and a smile on her face.

Osirys grabbed hold of it and awkwardly held it to her lips, unsure of how to get the water out of the container. After a few moments of fumbling, Naivarra rolled her eyes and chuckled, taking the skin back, and biting the stopper to pull it free. Osirys could feel her cheeks get warm with embarrassment. She had never felt so strange and helpless before. Naivarra shook her head and smiled in amusement, handing the skin back to Osirys, who promptly took to the waterskin. She didn't realize how thirsty she was until the cool water touched her lips. She slugged on the waterskin for several moments, before sighing heavily.

"What did you say this place was?" She asked, wiping a few drops from her chin.

Naivarra looked around and squatted, plucking a few pebbles from the ground and tossing them over the edge of the road, sending them bouncing down the sheer face of the slope to the plain below.

"Tork's Redoubt. It's an old fortress. A big battle was fought here, once. Long, long ago. Well, more than one, but it's known for the one in particular. This was the spot where the clans of old united against the most powerful Auric in history, and turned the tide in his conquest across the land, or something. I was never one for history, never paid attention, really."

Osirys held the waterskin out for Naivarra, who stood and accepted it, taking a small drink and then putting the stopper back in firmly, tucking it back into her satchel.

"Come on, let's keep going. Those Vamanari have already reached the top, they'll be done with their memorial by the time we catch up."

Osirys looked out over the plain as Naivarra began trudging along up the path again. From her vantage, she could see steep jagged mountains in the distance to the West, running north and south, and beyond a wall of cloud, seemingly held back by the peaks. The clouds bled through the valleys of the mountains, and were torn South by a crosswind, pulling them in streaks along the horizon. The sun was past the mid day height, and was slowly starting to sink towards later afternoon. Osirys felt much better after the drink of water. She took a deep breath and continued up the path towards the plateau above.

She was breathing heavily again, sweat beading on her forehead when she finally crested the plateau. She was nearly at the point of the anvil, facing Westward towards the mountains. The afternoon had progressed, and Osirys felt hunger for the first time in what could have been weeks. The summit of Tork's Redoubt was breathtaking. Ancient buildings, many crumbled and in ruins stretched along the flanks of the plateau. The lush grass swayed in the steady breeze that blew across from the East. Several aged watch posts still stood, ancient and stoic. Osirys looked out over the plains and marveled at the strange land. She saw the hazy smoke of a town in the distance to the East, and beyond that, a wall of mist that stretched from North to South as far as she could see, the water droplets shining prismatic colors as they rose into the sky.

She saw Naivarra and the Vamanari not far away, near a decayed but still standing chapel in the center of the plateau. She tightened her thin robe that had begun to flutter in the wind and wrapped it about her, and walked towards the gathering.

Osirys saw fresh turned mounds of dirt, presumably where the Musefolk had laid their comrades to rest. The lot was somber now, but the leader, Pasea, stood from where she was resting and moved toward Osirys purposefully as she approached. The other Vamanari had taken notice of her as well. Mirabyll looked over her shoulder, squinting at Osirys. A firm but inquisitive look on her face.

Pasea stopped in front of Osirys, hands on her hips. Her spear rested against a stone pillar of the chapel where she had left it. Her violet cloak was folded nearby, and her armor sat discarded, leather straps in a heap on the weathered stone. She wore a tunic, squared at the seams but perfectly cut for her size. The tunic buttoned halfway down so that it was still a pullover, but the top two buttons were undone, leaving a deep cut of her chest visible, which glistened with drying sweat. She was visibly feminine, and yet bore herself with a masculine authority, her stance square and forward. Her skin, like the other Musefolk, resembled worn stone, though hers was somewhat lighter. The beads of sweat gave her the appearance of schist, glistening with quartz embedded within. One of the other Vamanari was making herself busy de-tangling the mess, and Osirys assumed she had been the one to fold the cloak as well. None of the others spoke, but they kept their eyes turned towards Pasea and Osirys.

"Do you know of this place?" Pasea asked bluntly.

Osirys shook her head. "I was told that it was an old fortress, long ago."

"That's correct." Pasea responded, frowning. She lowered her gaze, studying Osirys from top to bottom, her eyes lingering on the silver belt that was wrapped about her middle, stepping forward and taking Osirys by the hand.

"Come, I will show you."

Pasea led Osirys into the chapel. Despite the age of the building, it was in remarkably good shape in comparison to the other structures on the plateau. She gasped as her eyes adjusted to the dim lighting. Stained glass miraculously survived the ages, letting in streaks of light to illuminate the stone and plaster walls within. Upon the surfaces of nearly all the walls, weathered and faded paints still displayed an amazing scene. At the back of the chapel, a weathered stone dais presided over the assembly. To her left was depicted Tork's Redoubt, but not the decayed version that she had walked through. It was a bulwark, tall walls and parapets topped the plateau like a crown. Behind the fortress, the sun was depicted, spilling light over the walls and onto the battlefield below. A vast army was shown assembled on the plains, many colorful banners were illuminated by the streaks of sun, made even more surreal by the actual sunlight shining through the stained glass, showering the painted battlefield in hues of greens, yellows, and reds.

Behind the dais, a highly decorated looking man was depicted, with shining regalia. He stood in front of a stark white banner with a worn symbol emblazoned in the center. In one hand, a scepter, in the other, a sword outstretched, gleaming in the fading light. His expression was too faded from age to make out features, but even without the detail, Osirys could imagine a look of desperate determination on his visage, looking out at the approaching opponent. Behind him stood a figure, but Osirys couldn't make out any details of the face, in fact there was no face present. The plaster had decayed and crumbled somewhat. Barely readable above the figure, there was an inscription:

Osirys fumbled with the lettering for a few moments. It was alien to her, script that she had never before seen. She moved on to examine the rest of the mural.

"It is the old tongue," Pasea commented. "And these are written in Illumari, the language of the Muses," She said, running her fingers along an inscription on the Dais. She read them aloud:

"Gaei Lumi Immateri - Praetu Adver Tenae ad Inifini"

"It means 'Halo of mother's light - protect against darkness for Eternity." Pasea stood for several moments, studying the words.

The opposite Western wall was clad in shadow, the late afternoon sun did not come through the stained glass on the Eastern Wall of the united army, but the rays of the Western light filtered through the windows on the darkened side of the mural. Pasea had released her hand and let Osirys move about the chapel to examine the images therein. Osirys moved closer to the darker wall. She saw an opposing army, wreathed in shadow. Gaunt faces and skeletal forms clawed their way towards the united armies bathed in light. In the rear of the army depicted on the Western wall, upon a throne of dark stone, sat a terrifying figure, tall, lank, and with glowing pits for eyes, wearing a crown of black metal. He wore ornate blackened armors, and about him was wrapped a dark cloak, spilling down his form. From around and behind his throne poured what seemed an endless tide of warriors. Living, feral looking men, charging together with the skeletal and partially fleshy remains of the un-living. Osirys ran her fingers along the plaster.

"How did this happen? The dead coming back to life, I mean?" Osirys asked.

"A forbidden form of Auric magic, one that didn't exist before Or'qan the Immortal rose to power, and the like of which has never been seen again since his downfall." Pasea replied.

"Or'qan, the Immortal," Osirys whispered, her fingers tracing his dark throne.

"A sad story, one that begins long before the moments pictured here, with the fall of the Old Empire of Eophaetha, beyond the Virdi River. For ages long lost to knowing, Eophaetha was vast and prosperous, or so the history says. The enchantment of the Virdi River was stronger then, and there was no way to cross to these shores. This land was a wilderness, and Eophaetha was the pinnacle of society, thick with magicks, and the birthplace of Auguries. Legend has it that other magic existed then as well, many point to the existence of us Vamanari as evidence of such magic…"

Pasea trailed off. Osirys studied the mural, touching the weathered stone as if it were some kind of braille writing that she could decipher with her fingertips. Osirys looked back to Pasea, who shook herself from her internal thoughts and continued.

"Anyway, the Empire fell, all at once. It's referred to now as the '*Incursion*'. As is the way of power, it sours and infects the world it's born into. Over the many years, the power, wealth and prosperity of Eophaetha attracted the attention of a fiend from the shadowed otherworld, who saw the Old Empire as a means to expand its shadowy demesne. It sought to link the two planes, our material world and the twisted interpretation of our reality that is Pandemonium. It sowed the seeds of Eophaetha's downfall, and over time its servants spread through the Empire, to every corner. Using the theurgy of the old world, the planes were linked, and Pandemonium assaulted the entirety of the Old Empire at once. There was no way to fight, and Eophaetha went from prosperous to naught but ruin from one day to the next. Legend has it that was the moment when the first Harbinger arrived. With the help of the most powerful Aurics in the Old Empire, they fled Eophaetha and dared the raging and impenetrable Virdi River, preferring death at the hands of the torrent to the horrors of Pandemonium. With the help of the Harbinger, they forged the first crossing to these shores."

Osirys considered Pasea's words, puzzled. These things were strange to her, and none of it made sense. "If this shadow world was linked as you say, why did Pandemonium not reach these shores as well? Why weren't they followed across the River?"

Pasea sighed, and the corners of her mouth tightened in apologetic frustration. "The theurgy of the Virdi River prevented the forces of Pandemonium from following. You see, the Virdi River is not just water and stone, raging as it may be. It is also a conduit, a font of magic that sustains and gives life to our world."

Osirys had no concept of what Pasea spoke of. It was as if she were speaking a different language entirely. She stared at the small Musefolk, blinking in the deepening dusk of the chamber.

"Suffice to say, crossing the Virdi was something that was impossible before the appearance of the first Harbinger, and by the power of the River, the legions of Chaos were held on the shores of Eophaetha, unable to cross to these lands, and so we were allowed to endure, and rebuild. The old magicks of Eophaetha were lost, and the grand power and riches of the Old Empire were abandoned and left to legend."

"So what do these images have to do with any of that?" Osirys asked, still confused.

"Those secrets were what Or'qan sought, and what brought him to these lands. Before the Dread Wraith had united the lands against him, the nearby town that you saw to the East, now called Pearlwater Bend, was a much larger and more prominent settlement. It was known as *"Haltaborgi"* in the old tongue - Pronounced 'Haltberg' in common dialect. During the war, Or'qan fought for control of Haltberg for unrestricted access to the ruins of Eophaetha, and the dark secrets of the old world. Haltberg was the site of the only known safe passage across the Virdi River then. It was the Battle of Tork, on the plain surrounding this old, crumbled stronghold, that began the turn of the tide. Haltberg's armies were outnumbered and would have been defeated had Villem Uteriel not arrived with a coalition of warriors from the Southern lands to cut off the wraith's Armies. Though Haltberg was ultimately razed to the ground in the fighting, It was the first time Or'qan had been defeated on the battlefield, and it was proven that through unity, he could be overthrown. After the formation of the Empirate, Haltberg never recovered, but the new town of Pearlwater Bend sprouted from the ashes and dust many years later."

Pasea moved and stood near the depiction of Villem Uteriel, studying the images therein. Osirys joined her.

"That was also the day that my kind gained our freedom, if you could call it that. Look closely at the figure behind Uteriel."

Osirys did as she was instructed. The smaller figure was flanked by what appeared to be warriors of smaller stature, wielding spears similar to that which Pasea and her companions bore. The figure itself, though largely featureless, wore a very distinct, silver belt.

"That was the last time a Harbinger was borne to us from the Muses."

Osirys rolled Pasea's words around in her head. She thought back to the fuzziness that preceded her arrival on the shores of the raging Virdi River not long ago. She had thought those images and feelings were the remnants of a dream. Looking at the stone-skinned Vamanari before her, she saw obvious resemblance to the mythical beings on the snowy plateau.

She struggled to think back farther than the shores of the Aetheral Lake, farther than the colorless Shadow World, and the malignant eyes therein. Before that... Was there a before that? She felt like there must have been, but whatever it was, it was beyond her reach. It was just vague emotions; sadness, regret, fear, pain. No images, no faces.

She must have been lost in thought for some time. Pasea stood nearby, studying her carefully. After a few more moments, she continued:

"Legend has it our kind, the Vamanari, were created by the Muses to protect the Harbingers. We accompanied the first Harbinger across the Virdi River the day the Old Empire fell, and several times thereafter we were stewards and protectors to the strange visitors. The Battle of Tork was a day to celebrate for most, but not for our people. We failed that day. The last Harbinger to visit these lands sacrificed themselves to Chaos to give Villem Uteriel the opportunity to win the battle. We fought bravely, but ultimately we could not prevent our ward from being consumed. Before they fell, the Harbinger absolved us of our failure. Our forebears, however, felt that we were no longer worthy as protectors of the Muses and their unknowable kind, or the Harbingers that appeared from time to time at their behest in moments of dire need. So, in a way, by failing their kind, we bought our freedom from protecting theirs with our lives. Since that day, no more Harbingers have appeared in these lands. Until now, I suspect."

Osirys blinked at Pasea, and turned from the wall where they stood. Several others of the Vamanari had gathered by the entrance of the chapel to listen to Pasea speak, and they held her gaze when she looked at them. Osirys paused and looked down at her feet. Pasea moved past her and out of the open doorway without another word. The other Vamanari lingered in the entryway for a small while, before leaving one by one, wordlessly. Osirys stood in the center of the chapel, studying the ancient mural, looking for answers to questions she didn't know the words to ask. For reasons she couldn't explain, she felt tears on her cheeks. She felt like she had wronged these strange Vamanari just with her presence. From somewhere deep inside, she felt an old pain from a life she couldn't remember bubble upwards from within, an unworthiness, that just her existence caused anguish.

Osirys shuddered, overcome with emotions she didn't understand. She didn't hear Naivarra approach, but she felt a firm hand on the back of her shoulder. She jumped, startled.

"Come, girl. This place has seen much death."

Osirys looked at the tall, broad shouldered fighter. She had tied her hair back with a band of what appeared to be thick linen or canvas.

"Why do I get the feeling that they don't like me?"

Naivarra shrugged. "Musefolk are a strange people."

"Did I do something wrong?" Osirys asked.

"Not that I can tell. I don't know much about all that history stuff, but I do remember my Nan telling me stories when I was young. From the little I understand, Harbingers represent a different kind of slavery to them – a reminder that they were created for a specific, inescapable purpose."

Osirys shivered in the dwindling daylight.

Naivarra kicked at a small stone, sending it skidding away on the smooth stone floor, "Or something like that."

They left the chapel, stepping onto the plateau, through the remnants of what had once been a regal courtyard.

The sun had dropped below the peaks of the Western mountains, igniting their slopes in gold and silver, and the smoldering wall of clouds loomed like a dark omen. Osirys looked to the East, where the shadow of dusk crept across the land. The Vamanari had laid bedrolls and had set a campfire. Several of the younger warriors sat in the decayed lookout towers, eyes towards the ruined caravan far below on the road.

"We should be safe here," It was Mirabyll, who was resting against the exterior stone wall of the chapel.

"Those slavers would be daft to attempt to ambush us up in these ruins. They know it too. They returned some time ago, and it looks like they've moved off with what they could salvage from the wreckages. We didn't leave them much, that's for sure."

Osirys nodded. They fell into silence. Osirys felt like Mirabyll wanted to ask something, but she just gazed up at her, large reflective eyes flashing in the dying light.

"Do you hate me too?" Osirys asked, a tone of acid in her voice.

Mirabyll narrowed her eyes briefly, and considered her words before responding.

"Don't let Pae get to you. She did just bury her sister, after all."

Osirys dropped her gaze, ashamed.

"I know, I'm sorry."

Mirabyll softened. "I must admit, our kind has never been one to favor the idea of coincidence. Pasea is conflicted. It is her duty to land and kin to hunt the slavers who have been stealing our people from our homes and bring an end to our persecution, but.."

She trailed off. "If a Harbinger is in our midst, she is compelled toward a much older, much more sacred duty. One that she is much compelled to honor, even though we have claimed to be free of the responsibility for generations. It is a source of great conflict. No matter what path she chooses from here, it will mean she is turning her back on the lives of those she feels responsible for."

That made sense to Osirys. She felt like she was familiar with situations that had no right answer. She looked over at Pasea, who had sat down next to the fire, which was spitting glowing embers into the air above the ruins.

Osirys' shoulders quaked and her teeth clicked in the cold, the temperature had dropped significantly as the sun slid behind the mountains. The cool breeze that blew across the plateau did not relent, and her thin robe provided no protection whatsoever against the elements. She instinctively hugged it about her anyway, as if the act would somehow help it retain more of her warmth, but the wind pierced the fabric and stripped her of that heat. She looked on at the fire from a distance, the warm glow tempting her. She took a step towards it, but stopped herself. She couldn't face Pasea right now. She turned and walked a short distance into the ruins, until she found a husk of a building that was intact enough to shelter her from at least the wind. She pulled her legs up under her and sat against the cold rock. It sent shivers through her body, but it was solid, and it stood impervious to her presence, as it had for ages.

She was cold, but she was beyond exhausted. As the last light of day faded from the sky, Osirys looked up at the strange night that felt so unfamiliar. Thousands of stars twinkled indifferently above her. She felt suddenly very much alone, but the feeling wasn't enough to keep her awake. Shivering and distraught as she was, she found herself slipping into an uncomfortable sleep filled with strange dreams.

WHEN SHE AWOKE, SHE felt weight upon her. She stretched her fingers to feel a thick fur blanket laid on and about her. It was warm. She heard quiet motion nearby, and she opened her eyes, feeling disoriented. Across from her in the small decayed stone building Naivarra was standing facing away from her, back exposed as she pulled her tunic over her head. Osirys saw a deep crisscross of scars on her shoulders. A clean bandage dotted in crimson circled her middle. It wasn't neatly done, but it was functional. Osirys felt her mouth hanging open. Naivarra's skin was a patchwork of old wounds, rough and bubbled in places, blotched with pink discoloration of hurts that never had enough time to heal before more took their place upon her body. Despite the old wounds, Naivarra's back rippled with toned muscle as she pulled the tunic down over her head. Her shoulders tapered to a disciplined and solid core. Her waist wasn't visible under the bandages, but Osirys could make out dimples in her lower back, just above her trousers.

Osirys shifted, the ground beneath her was hard, and uncomfortable. Her body ached too, and she let out a soft groan. Naivarra tensed and yanked her tunic down, covering her back, quickly glancing over her shoulder. Their eyes met. For the first time, Osirys saw a measure of weakness in Naivarra. She looked ashamed, bashful. It only lasted a moment before being replaced by her typical cavalier visage.

"How do you feel now that you've had a few hours rest?" Naivarra asked, picking up the padded leather that laid folded on top of her breastplate, by her weathered rucksack. The tinkle of the buckles against the metal of the armor pierced the quiet of Tork's Redoubt, the silence of the place was almost disconcerting.

"Sore." Osirys voice croaked from beneath the furs.

"From your thrashing and moaning through the night, I gathered that you were not accustomed to a bed of stone."

They lingered, looking at each other for several moments. Naivarra inspected some new stitch-work she had performed on the back of the leather jerkin, mending a slash that corresponded with the bandages in the middle of her back. "It seems I am not the only one who covers their scars." She pulled the jerkin about her and fluidly cinched the buckles.

"Are you hurt?" Osirys asked, feeling slightly uncomfortable.

Naivarra shrugged and pulled at the fit of her leathers. "It's not bad. One of those thugs managed to get a hit off when I had my back turned. The coward's dead now."

Osirys decided to change the subject, Naivarra clearly was not willing to engage further into her inquiry. "Did you give me this last night? Did you have another for yourself?" Osirys patted the thick fur.

Naivarra chuckled. "I don't typically pack for company, little miss. Usually, if I have another to bed down with, we're sharing the blanket."

Osirys blushed and was surprised to hear herself giggle. Naivarra grinned devilishly and looked down to latch her belt. "Don't worry about me. I was just fine. I'm accustomed to getting rest out of doors. I probably wouldn't have used the fur last night anyway. Would have sweat myself to death."

"Thank you." Osirys said.

"I assure you - my motivation was selfish, until I threw that thing on top of you, there was no way I was going to get any shuteye with all the racket you were making. Afterwards you calmed down enough for me to get an hour or two." Naivarra glanced over at Osirys while digging through her pack.

Osirys wasn't sure, but the look on Naivarra's face suggested slight exaggeration. Naivarra did look tired, but Osirys was pretty sure it was an attempt at humor.

"Well, you could have slept in another pile of rocks," Osirys mumbled in response.

Naivarra dismissed her with a wave and threw a pair of trousers and a thin linen tunic at the only part of Osirys that was visible above the furs.

"Get yourself moving, the Vamanari are already packed up and ready to go. You can wear those until we get to town, then we can find you something of your own." Naivarra picked up her breastplate and her pack and walked out of the collapsed building, leaving Osirys to herself and her thoughts.

Osirys heaved in some of the crisp morning air, and threw off the furs. Her body ached from the hard ground, and she stretched several times to try and work out the kinks that had developed in her arms, legs and back. Her thin robe was tangled and twisted about her, covered in dirt, grime, and spatters of dried blood. The events of the day before swirled up to meet her, and she squashed a surge of nausea as she recalled the old Vaman woman who had stood up for her in the caravan, and paid for it with her life. She pulled the robe off of her and threw it aside, disgusted. She stood naked as a newborn, shivering in the morning air. The wispy remnants of dreams of darkness, crystalline forests, and threatening prophecies slipped away with the rising sun. She hastily pulled on the trousers, hopping on one leg as she attempted to navigate her leg through the thick fabric. The pants were slightly too large, and fell off of her hips unless she held them in place. She looked around, and saw the silver cord, tangled with her bathrobe. She picked it up, leaving the robe, and studied it. The cord was made of tiny overlapping silver ringlets, reticulated in such a way that they would bend in multiple directions. It gleamed in the morning light. It bore none of the dirt and grime of the rest of her garment. She looped it through the trousers and buckled the clasp. That would do the job. She pulled the linen jerkin over her head and shoulders. it billowed in the sleeves and was largely a shapeless piece of attire. Her thin frame swam in the garment, but it wasn't uncomfortable. She felt strange in the outfit, like it was archaic and peculiar, but she couldn't point to any reason why. Truth be told, she kind of liked it. The top hid her meager curves; curves she for some reason felt keenly aware of. It kept her body as a mystery, something that she didn't want advertised - particularly following the previous day - and the predatory men that captured her with the intention to sell her into slavery, or worse. She tried to run her fingers through her hair, which was matted and full of knots, as well as sand, grit, and tiny sticks. Hopeless. She pulled it behind her and did her best to get it out of her face. She folded the fur bedding. She picked up her tattered thin robe. She began to fold it, but her fingers ran over several bloody patches that had dried overnight. She looked at it with disdain, and cast it back down to the ground. She turned and left the ruin, carrying only the folded pile of furs.

The sun was up, but it was still early. Osirys gaped. Atop the plateau, she could see the sparkling of the mist arising from the Virdi River miles in the distance. The sun burned through the water droplets, millions of tiny prisms separating the light into colors. The Eastern sky was ablaze with a gorgeous rainbow that flickered and danced with the billowing, rising mist. She stood in the morning light, in awe at the spectacle of nature. She felt the warmth of the sun on her skin, and she smiled. Beauty surrounded her in this place. The colors of the morning sun painted the landscape in saturated hues; the plains surrounding Tork's Redoubt rippled in gleaming gold as a soft breeze rode its way across the landscape. Soft clouds drifted Southward from the mountains to the west. The embankment of distant, dark thunderheads walled behind the peaks was gone from the night before.

CHAPTER FIVE

T HE VAMANARI WERE DRESSED in their battle regalia, purple cloaks draped over their shoulders. Pasea watched Osirys approach quietly. Mirabyll moved to her side and nudged her shoulder. Pasea visibly softened, and turned to acknowledge Osirys.

"Good morning, Harbinger. I must apologize for my… Temper, yesterday. Only long after you had retired, I realized I didn't even introduce our company to you." Pasea was matter of fact, but sincere. She gestured with her spear at the rest of the Musefolk, who straightened themselves to attention.

"From left to right - There's Syndal, Fernip, Olaavi, Flembe, Wavu, and Vim. Mirabyll, my second in command, you met yesterday. They are all trained in the Vamanari spear and hand to hand combat, and are proficient with blades. For the time being, we are at your service." She bowed deeply, sweeping her spear to the side, and crossing one foot back and behind the other, in an elegant, balanced motion. The other Vamanari bowed as well, some reluctantly.

They remained bowed for several seconds. Osirys shifted her weight, unsure if they were waiting for some kind of response from her.

"Uh, thanks." She stammered. She wasn't any good at formality like this.

Mirabyll nodded perceptibly at Pasea, and the Vipers returned to formation as one.

Pasea forced a smile in Osirys' direction, and began walking down the path they had ascended the day before, followed closely by two of the younger Vamanari, Flembe and Olaavi.

Mirabyll stood next to Osirys as the Musefolk began to file down the wide path. "We are headed to Pearlwater Bend. We need to resupply and prepare for the journey North."

"We should be following those slavers," commented Wavu over her shoulder, her spear rattling against her mail.

Mirabyll frowned as Wavu hoisted her pack and turned away, quickening her pace to catch up with Pasea and the two other Vamanari.

Naivarra had finished securing the furs to her rucksack with sturdy straps, and tossed a hunk of stale bread to Mirabyll and Osirys. "Let's get to town."

The two nodded and began plodding down the green pathway, descending from the plateau much the way they had come, in relative silence. The path was still clad in the shadow of the morning, and the grass was wet with dew, and was slippery. Several times, Osirys found herself starting to slide, and had to proceed much more slowly and carefully than her companions. Before long, she could tell that the Vamanari were holding back their pace to accommodate her. She fought the embarrassment back. After all, she didn't even have any shoes. Still, she felt like a child, unwelcome and foreign. She couldn't relate to these warriors, and even if she could, she would have kept her mouth shut, well aware that she was the source of the chagrin that still lingered in the air.

Even still, the descent was more swift than the climb, and before an hour had passed, they found themselves at the base of the plateau, near to the remains of the caravan, which had more or less stopped smoldering. Osirys was winded from concentrating on her balance, and her feet were red and sore. The road was even less welcoming. The cuts from the day previous on the soles of her feet were wet from the grass and open, sending stinging reminders every step of the way. She clenched her jaw and plodded onward, determined not to slow or limp. It was a long morning. She felt blisters well up and pop on the ball of her foot, the skin peeling away and the sand and dirt caking the wounds and grinding into her flesh. She cried, but made no sound as she followed Naivarra, who trudged along ahead of her without difficulty. There was a part of her that took penance from the pain. She felt her suffering was justified as she thought back on the lives that were lost on her account less than a day ago. She turned back and looked at the spots of dark blood on the sand of the road, and it reminded her of the old Vaman woman, laying on the ground, bludgeoned. Her pain was fitting.

She started to walk normally, forgoing the beleaguered steps she was taking to try and avoid the pain. She wanted to feel it, she wanted to be aware of each cut. She didn't last long that way. Within a hundred yards, she stumbled and fell to her knees, sobbing. The caravan of Vamanari and Naivarra halted and turned to look at her. She felt weak. She hated their attention. She wished they didn't pay her any mind and just kept walking. She squeezed the tears from her eyes and shoved herself back to her feet, and took several more steps before dropping to the ground again. Her feet screamed in agony. She shivered from the pain, and realized she was sweating.

Naivarra turned and glared at Pasea. Pasea sighed, walking back to help Osirys to her feet again. She gasped when she saw Osirys' feet, shredded and flayed as they were. Osirys saw the shame in Pasea's eyes as she dropped to her knee to assess the damage.

"Girl, why didn't you say something?" Pasea scolded, before sighing heavily. "I… I should have been more observant, I'm sorry."

Osirys winced as Pasea pulled some cloth from her pack, and began to clear some of the sand and grit from her wounds.

"This is bad. It looks like there is already some infection setting in. When did you get these injuries?"

"Yesterday, when we were captured," Osirys replied.

Pasea clicked her tongue, frowning. "And you climbed that plateau path all the same." Pasea shook her head. "Syndal, here!" Pasea called out. "Bring the field kit. See what you can do for our outlander. She has gone and let bravado get the best of her."

Pasea put her hands on her hips and looked at Osirys. Though Pasea was standing and Osirys was sitting, their heads were about the same height. There was a softness in Pasea's visage that Osirys had never seen before. Pasea didn't seem annoyed or upset with Osirys like she expected. In fact, her compassion felt strangely genuine to Osirys.

The smallest of the Vipers arrived moments later with a kit of medical instruments and small satchel of tinctures.

Syndal hunched over Osirys and tended to her feet, washing them with some cool water and applying some ointments. "This is water from an underground spring that is fed by the Virdi River. It is pure and will help purge the infection, and your wounds will heal faster. It is called Viqua, it is rare, and can save lives if used correctly. Viqua itself is remarkable, but with a little skill, its powers can be amplified."

Syndal crossed her legs and sat in front of Osirys, concentrating. She began whispering with her eyes closed. Her complexion was the hue of a soft pink granite, with dark specks. At first there were words that Osirys couldn't understand. and then her words began to change. They took on the tone of a bubbling brook, as if the words themselves were water washing over smooth stones. Then Syndal opened her eyes, and spoke:

"*Ba-ahal.*"

Osirys felt the command more than heard it. The Viqua that beaded on her skin rippled in response to the words. She watched in amazement as she felt the pain suddenly dull in her feet, and saw thin filaments of skin begin to knit along the edges of the wounds.

Syndal breathed out, and her shoulders slumped slightly. Pasea put her hand on Syndal's shoulder and squeezed. Syndal nodded, and steadied her breathing. "I am but a novice, and have not the skill needed to fully mend your hurts. I hope at least your suffering is lessened." She stood slowly. Osirys noticed her balance was slightly unsteady, and Pasea's hand helped her keep her footing. She winced and nodded to Pasea and began walking slowly towards the other Vamanari.

"That was amazing!" Exclaimed Osirys.

Pasea smiled.

"How did she do that?" Osirys wiggled her toes slightly. Her feet felt stretched thin, but the pain was nearly gone.

"Syndal is an Auric. She performed a minor incantation of restoration. She commanded the Viqua to restore your body." Pasea paused. "She also commanded the pain to be shared. While the incantation holds, she will feel some of the pain, so that you do not."

Osirys' smile evaporated and her head spun to look for Syndal, who had returned to the group, and was replacing the field kit and satchel of tinctures in her belongings.

"Wh-why would she do that?" Osirys stammered.

Pasea looked up and away from Osirys, back towards Tork's Redoubt and the final resting place of her sister.

"Because she is kind."

Chapter Six

The town of Pearlwater Bend sat atop a craggy bluff, rising out of the plains and defiantly jutting Eastward. Trees sprouted in clusters on knobby knolls, lending the rocky spit a lumpy, weathered aesthetic. The road led the group through the outskirts of town. They passed aged, weathered farmsteads that intermingled with old stone walls that ran in straight lines, and stayed low to the ground. Interspersed through the lumpy fields, Osirys could occasionally see the remnants of rocky foundations poking their way out of the ground, as if they had been slowly sinking into the soft earth over generations. Moss and thin grasses climbed their fractured sides, like tiny arms pulling the stones deeper into the ground.

Mirabyll walked next to Osirys, matching her pace and looking about with a measured and satisfied curiosity. She nodded towards a tilted and tumbled rock structure.

"The remnants of Haltberg," She said softly. "It used to be a city. Where we walk now used to be a great market."

Osirys looked about. As the road gently wound up towards the hamlet on the cliffs, farm animals grazed on the sparse grasses that clung in between the rocky clusters. Sheep slowly chewed on cud and absentmindedly watched Osirys, Naivarra and the Vipers pass, with very little curiosity. Neither Osirys' appearance nor her ginger gait caused them pause or alarm. She spotted several lambs, standing on spindly legs and wobbling about. She smiled. 'Now, that's something I have a lot in common with', she mused internally.

"Why didn't they rebuild it all?" Osirys asked.

Mirabyll walked in silence for several moments, considering her reply

"Only a handful of families survived. Even fewer stayed after the massacre. Neither the people, nor the land ever fully recovered."

The road meandered East. To the South, the farmlands had given way to a lowland field that sloped down and away from the crags. The grass was sparse, but low wildflowers bloomed in abundance. Dotted along the ground in regular intervals, small stones poked out of the loamy soil, barely inches above the blooms. Osirys paused, looking out and down over the expansive plain. From the altitude of the road, Osirys could see that it extended for miles. Osirys was afraid to ask, and glanced at Mirabyll, who had paused with her.

"Graves." Mirabyll responded. "For those who had remains to bury."

Osirys hand instinctively covered her mouth. There must have been a million or more stones. They were not ornate or rounded headstones with engravings and kind words carved into their surface. Rather, they were irregular chunks of stone plugged into the ground. Some wide and rounded, some jagged and thin. Different types of stone followed the terrain; a strip of schist markers stretched along a low ridge, a patch of thin slate slabs darkened a low valley, a hill sprouted uncountable chunks of lumpy granite. The stones were just that - stones - of approximately appropriate size exhumed from the ground and used as they were found.

Osirys stood agape for several moments. Mirabyll stood beside her, head only coming up to Osirys' hip, looking across the plain. A light breeze blew from the East, ruffling the violet cloak of the Vamanari warrior, causing it to snap lightly in the wind. The sound broke Osirys from her thoughts.

"So many…" she said softly, under her breath.

Mirabyll turned and made to continue walking, but hesitated, waiting for Osirys to follow in step. "Come, Osirys, the others are waiting for us ahead."

She moved more slowly, aware of every step. She picked her way around sharp looking stones and walked on the grass when she was able, and kept checking on Syndal. A few times she had inadvertently stepped on something that would have caused her pain, and in the awkward moments that followed when she expected a sharp twinge to run up into her leg that never came, she would look at Syndal and wince. Not once did Syndal ever turn about or indicate she suffered in any way. Osirys cursed her clumsiness each time. The road remained relatively smooth, though the solid packed earth was unforgiving and she had to move even more slowly to avoid the many stones that threatened the wounded soles of her feet like caltrops.

As they ascended, Osirys began to notice something was peculiar. Every now and again she felt the ground beneath her feet shudder, as if it were a battered shack in a storm driven gale. She thought it a trick of her mind, maybe an extension of her fatigue at first, but as they trudged on, the palpable fear of the earth beneath her feet became too obvious to ignore.

"What is happening, is it an earthquake?" Osirys asked, pausing and leaning on a tall tumbled boulder and turning to Naivarra.

"No, girl. That's the Virdi. We are getting close."

The river? How could a river cause the land to buck and shudder so - it was as if the earth was fighting a losing battle from being torn from the bedrock beneath their feet and being ripped away, as the wind might rip the roots of a tree from the ground in a cyclone. Soon enough she began to hear it as well. Initially just the reverberating far-off crack of stone that followed the tremors in the ground beneath her wounded feet. Then came the deep rumbling, rhythmic and persistent roar; the reverberation of the primal rage of the river. It was dull but mighty, Osirys had never felt such raw power - it was as if the full fury of a natural disaster raged just beyond her sight.

Despite the ambient violence that surrounded her, Osirys couldn't make out anything but a peaceful town up ahead. Amidst the clustered boulders atop the bluff, squat, rigid looking buildings huddled together. They were mostly single story, and kept low profile. The foundations were tall and very highly reinforced. The town was built to withstand the extremity of its clime, and the weathered, rounded edges of the stones advertised their success.

They passed low farm houses and stables, the faces of animals and their caretakers peered out from their dwellings at their passing. Osirys caught their gaze, which lingered upon them.

Mirabyll nudged her, "These are suspicious folk. They live simple lives and thrive on the tales that arrive with the travelers from Eophaetha. They are not accustomed to our kind. Don't mistake their suspicion for unkindness, however. They are a hardy people, one sympathetic to a life with purpose."

Osirys mused on Mirabyll's words. 'A life with purpose'. They rang through her and rattled her uncomfortably. She knew what Mirabyll meant, but it felt to her as a point of contrast between her and her traveling companions. She felt about as far from purpose as she could get.

Her musings were interrupted by Naivarra, "Girl, with me. I want to show you something." She had paused by a wide path that split off from the main road into town. She nodded at the Musefolk who had paused. "Go on ahead and get supplies. We'll meet you later at the "Lost Lantern".

Pasea leaned on her spear for a few moments, considering. "Very well." She turned to Syndal and nodded. "Go get some rest, Syn. You would have done Pemme proud this day."

Syndal bowed deeply. Her face was pale and lips were slightly blue-tinged. She closed her eyes and breathed out slowly. Within moments, Osirys felt the heat of pain in the bottoms of her feet keenly again. She winced, and Naivarra frowned. "I suppose we should probably stop by the healer first, and maybe find you some boots."

Osirys nodded, but wasn't looking at Naivarra. She was fixed on Syndal, who leaned heavily on Wavu. The Vamanari warriors moved together as a group toward the market and were soon lost in the comings and goings of the townsfolk. The canvas of the market tents were muted, their colors drained from many long years of sun and elements. The thick ropes that tethered the marketplace to the rocky earth were frayed, but resilient. The town felt old, the roads were deeply grooved where thousands of footfalls had gradually worn away the smoothness of the packed earth and stone. Still, there was a softness about every edge, every line, and every corner. Age and wear had rounded nearly every surface of Pearlwater Bend, giving each structure an oblong, but cozy feel.

"How old is this place?" Osirys asked Naivarra.

Naivarra kept her hands on her hips and looked about, gauging the state of the buildings that surrounded them.

"I never paid attention to history." She replied matter-of-factly. "These buildings survived the battle of Tork and the fall of Haltberg, though. This part of town was all that was left, or so they say."

"Those fields earlier," Osirys began. "The gravestones-"

Naivarra nodded. "Don't trouble yourself over the long dead," she said, squinting at Osirys with a cocked head. She scuffed pebbles on the road with her boot. "Your pain can't change what happened to them."

Osirys felt a strong arm around her back and under her arms, supporting her. She and Naivarra picked their way towards a small steepled building with stained glass windows, reminiscent in style to the small dilapidated buildings atop Tork's Redoubt. An aromatic smoke billowed from a chimney in the back of the building. Naivarra paused by the door, and sighed heavily before pushing it open, "Let's make it quick." She said matter-of-factly. "I've never enjoyed the company of the Clerics."

THE HEAVY DOOR SWUNG open easily and they stepped inside. Osirys was expecting heavily incensed air, but instead it smelled *delicious*. The smell of freshly baked bread and roasted nuts filled her head, nearly making her swoon. The floor was made of small stones that were worn smooth with age and use. They created a pattern of two interlocked circles that overlapped in the center of the medium sized room. There were two sets of heavy benches arranged into facing rows. In between the benches there were a dozen or so heavy stone basins on short pedestals, filled with water. The ambience was quiet, save for the dim crackling of two braziers that glowed in the back of the room. There was a dais with a larger basin nestled in the rear as well, flanked by two small doorways leading further back into the building. All told, the room could hold twenty or thirty individuals comfortably, or fifty if need be. Naivarra cleared her throat loudly while scanning uncomfortably.

The door to the right of the dais opened and an older, slender looking fellow entered the main chamber. His robes were dark and flat of color, with oversized buttons running down the center and thick braided fabric flowed from the shoulders of the garb. The sleeves were wide but ended just past his elbows. The robe was cinched with a very thick belt of supple leather, notched along the bottom end with many various attachments, presumably religious in nature. A pair of small glass orbs dangled on his left hip, while a brass clasp held a tasseled metal container that reminded Osirys of a thurible, but much smaller. He was bald, and his skin was dark, much darker than hers, but had a very red hue to it. She wasn't sure if it he was tattooed or if it was his natural skin tone.

He paused by the dais before stepping down and moving hurriedly over to Osirys after she took a labored step.

"Are you hurt, young *Pathyk*?" He asked. His voice was heavily accented. As he moved over toward her he met her eyes. They were kind, but sharp. He was a discerning man, and Osirys did admit his presence was somewhat intimidating.

"*Pathyk*?" Osirys asked, glancing at Naivarra, who shrugged.

"It is a word - for pilgrim," The cleric clarified. "You are not from here, this is true, yes?"

Osirys checked her response, unsure of how these folk might react to her revealing how much of a stranger she actually was. "That's right, I think."

"Then you are *Pathyk*, and welcome here. You did not answer, but it seems plain that you arc hurt. Please, let me look."

Osirys sat on the heavy bench and groaned. Naivarra moved and sat across the chamber uncomfortably. The Cleric knelt in front of her, and gently lifted her leg to examine her wounds. He frowned, and his brows furrowed deeply.

"You have come very far, *Pathyk*. Very far, and without shoes. I have the skill to heal this. Please, come."

He stood and offered his hand to Osirys, who looked at Naivarra. Naivarra raised an eyebrow and waved her on. "I'll be here, girl."

He led her through the door from which he emerged earlier and into another small room with several beds. Two of them were occupied. On one bed a child slept, bundled in blankets. Osirys found herself staring at the child, as if transfixed. She felt something sink like a stone in the pit of her stomach. She shook it off. In the other bed there was a thick man of short stature and large, full beard. His features were squared, and he had very prominent ears, whose lobes were three inches long at least.

She sat on the edge of a bed and the cleric moved to the back of the room, where a series of cabinets lined the wall. He pulled a decently large basin from one of the low shelves, and placed it under a cistern, opening a valve, letting water run into it. While it filled, he moved swiftly through a couple other cabinets, running his fingers along rows of things in jars, pulling a couple small bags and a vial or two from them, and emptying their contents into the filling basin. Within a few minutes, he returned, the basin half full and steaming, the aromas of several different leaves and salts filling the air. He put it in front of her and gestured for her to put her feet in the water. She complied. The water was hot, and after the initial sting on her wounds, she felt herself sigh. It did feel good.

The cleric knelt and hummed in a deep tone. His voice resonated and took on a harmonic, as if there were two or more of him humming at the same time. The water began to simmer. Osirys looked on in awe. He raised his head and said "*Jakh Mbarana*". The water jumped into a full boil, but it was not any hotter in temperature. Osirys felt health run through her veins. It was so hot it was almost painful, but she wasn't in any discomfort. She couldn't describe the feeling, but it was as if any infection was instantly seared away from her flesh. She flopped back onto the cot and closed her eyes, and focused on the feeling that filled and surrounded her. She didn't notice that the cleric had moved to check on his other wards.

She opened her eyes to a round, friendly face peering down at her. It was a woman's face. She had soft features and thick eyebrows, and several inch long earlobes attached to prominent ears. Her hair was neat and braided and long, and she smiled down affably at Osirys. She raised a small tray, upon which several golden brown biscuits steamed.

"Oh haloo there, wouldja care fer a bit-a-biscuit?"

Osirys sat up abruptly. She did very much want a biscuit.

"Go-on-'en, help-erself."

Osirys took one. It was warm and flaky. She devoured it. Sitting up, she realized she was at eye height with the round woman, who was beaming at her.

"I made a-plenty. Go-on-'en."

She took another. She didn't inhale the second one. She ate it more slowly, enjoying it.

"Thanks."

The little woman bowed, nearly spilling the tray of biscuits.

"Oop! Almost lost them there butter-tops! Think nothin' of it, miss. My name's Troodie. Troodie Van Hootan." She giggled and re-stacked the biscuits on the tray.

"Osirys", she replied, mouth full of biscuit.

"Looks like yer feet got all sorts of torn up there. Did you lose yer boots runnin' from the unliving too?"

Osirys blinked, shaking her head slowly at the absurd inquiry, suddenly wondering about the sanity of the small woman.

Troodie shrugged, popping a biscuit into her mouth and looking over her shoulder at the older fellow resting in the cot nearby.

"Excuse me, did you say, the unliving?" Osirys swallowed.

"Oh, yes. Me and the Leventus were charged with their dismissal. We're warriors, ya'see. Them unliving been spookin' the locals. We were on our way to visit the Old Empire, and don'tcha know, we heard tell of some rumor of no-good happening. Well, the Leventus assumed it was just some local boys and girls playing tricks on the folk of the town, them bein' so superstitious and all. Anyhoo, him bein' the hero he is, up and volunteered us to go do some investigatin'. Wouldn'tcha know, turns out there actually is some no-good evil at work - We were on the path to Shimmermere nearby, and a living corpse shambled out into the path in front of the Leventus, spooked his steed something good! It threw him, knocked him silly I think. I dismissed that there undead with a good swat of my trusty axe, and brought the Leventus back here. He's been out since. Figured I'd make myself useful and make a couple of these here biscuits while I wait for him to get himself back and sorted."

Warriors? This small woman certainly did not resemble any definition of the word warrior that Osirys had ever encountered. Whereas Naivarra looked and breathed the part, this soft pumpkin of a woman with a tray of biscuits seemed entirely unlikely.

Osirys nodded slowly. "Well, good luck with that."

Troodie replied, bubbling, "Oh why thank you dearie! I'm sure our next try will go better!" She turned and scooted towards the door, leaving the tray of biscuits within reach of Osirys.

"Appa Morvrel, I made some biscuits!" She called to the cleric before leaving. He turned from his study of the older man that Troodie referred to as the Leventus, and nodded in her direction.

The bubbling of the water in the basin had calmed and stopped. Osirys studied the water. It was so difficult for her to believe that the clear, unassuming liquid had the power to undo hurts that should have taken weeks to heal. She searched for something that gave its power away; something she could understand. She was pulled from her concentration by the sound of Morvrel entering the room carrying a heavy satchel. He placed it on the floor in front of her.

He knelt and began pulling pairs of boots out of the bag, looking for a pair that would be close to her size.

"Where did these come from?" Osirys asked, puzzled.

Morvrel looked down and paused, unsure of how to answer. "Many cross the river. The Old Empire is dangerous. There are always more that leave these shores than return. Sometimes, belongings are all that come back."

They fell silent as Morvrel pulled a pair of sturdy leather boots from the satchel. They looked to be nearly new.

"Such shame. I remember this boy. He came to receive a blessing before leaving for Eophaetha. He was reverent. I had hoped the Divines would preserve him, alas. Many find their faith insufficient in the great shadow of that land. Perhaps his boots will guide you on a lighter path."

Osirys studied the boots. The uppers were long, and the pull straps were stamped with a sigil of a bird with a wide wingspan, inlaid with gold.

"If it's so dangerous, why do so many travel to the Old Empire?" Osirys asked.

Morvrel considered his words before replying. "The Old Empire fell at the height of its wealth and power very suddenly. The unclaimed riches of the old world still remain, buried in the ruins, and guarded by the shades of the shadow realm."

Osirys began to understand before he completed his thought.

"The allure of the treasures of the Old Empire is strong for many. Others seek to test themselves against the wilds. Some fight for glory, some fight against the shadow, hoping to drive it from the world to reclaim the land for the light."

"Have you ever been? Seen the Old Empire, I mean?" Osirys asked, pulling on the boots to test their fit.

Morvrel stood and winced at the question. "I did, when I was young. I wanted to fight the Shadow. Avenge the many dead in darkness. My order sent thirty. Four returned. I fight the Shadow from here now, with blessings and healing the hurts that can be mended."

Osirys looked away.

"*Pathyk*, if your pilgrimage takes you from these shores, remember to keep the light of the Divines with you. There are few who believe in its power these days. It may save you."

Osirys nodded. "Thank you, Morvrel. I did not deserve your kindness."

He smiled for the first time.

"Deserve is a funny word. Your gratitude is honest. You are welcome in these walls, *Pathyk*." He took her hand and patted it, meeting her eyes. "I am glad for you."

Naivarra was waiting for Osirys with one biscuit in each hand.

"Better?" She asked.

"Much." Osirys replied.

"Good, let's go." Naivarra wasted no time getting out the door. Osirys glanced back hoping to bid Troodie and Morvrel farewell. Not seeing either, she sighed and followed Naivarra through the door. They talked as they walked through the town of Pearlwater Bend. The town center was crowded with a flavorful variety of folk of many shapes and sizes. Naivarra gestured toward a small, squat building with a multicolored banner hanging above the door. It had few windows, and it was one of the few buildings in town that looked like it could have been relatively new construction. The stones weren't as weathered evenly, though they were rounded in their own way, it seemed far more likely that the stones were taken from the ruins of an ancient foundation and re-arranged, leaving it awkwardly old and new at the same time.

"Pearlwater Bend is the only settlement along the Virdi that is technically part of the Empirate." Naivarra explained. "The Empirate was built on the foundations of the coalition that started with Villem Uteriel, after the defeat of the Dread Lich, Or'qan. The influence of the Empirate is very weak outside of the core cities, but they have made a point to maintain control, even if just in name, of this town. This is the most reliable crossing to Eophaetha, and so the Empirate maintains a presence here."

They had left the market square behind them, and were walking along a gently sloping path Eastward out of town. The buildings had become sparse, and eventually stopped completely. Osirys began to see large boulders instead, resting on the ground, some buried halfway, some fresh atop the soil, as if they had just been placed there. Osirys was puzzled, and stared at one boulder as they passed that seemed to have turned fresh earth nearby, as if it had just rolled to a stop. The ambient sound of the river was getting more intense.

Osirys asked, "Why are there so few ways to cross the river? Is it really that difficult to cross?"

Naivarra smirked. "You really aren't from here, are you?" She remarked with some sarcasm. "Come, see for yourself."

CHAPTER SEVEN

*L*ILY SAT ACROSS FROM *her. The waitress of the Whistle Stop had taken their breakfast order. Osirys winced as she leaned into her hand, the heel of her palm pressed against her cheekbone, which smarted. She had applied some coverup concealer to hide the impending bruise that would assuredly follow, but she still felt the heat of slight swelling. Lily looked at her. She had seen that look before when they were growing up. Her older sister always knew when she was hiding something.*

"What excuse do you have for me this time?" Lily asked sarcastically.

"What do you mean?" Osirys asked, rolling her eyes.

"Your face, Siry. Your face looks like a balloon."

"No it does not." Osirys insisted, looking away and out the window.

Lily pouted, skeptically. "We're seriously not gonna talk about this?"

Osirys just shook her head. "Can we just enjoy breakfast? You know how much I love this place."

Lily, crossed her arms, sitting back into her chair. They sat in silence. Lily tapped her foot. Osirys knew she wanted to say more, but the conversations never ended with anything but a fight. She never told her sister the truth, and her sister knew it.

"I got put on a special project at work this week," Osirys offered, trying to change the subject.

"Oh yeah?" Lily responded, feigning interest.

"Yeah, my boss actually said that my talents were being wasted up at that front desk."

"Does that mean they're actually going to promote you this time?" Lily asked.

"Probably not."

"Well did you ask? Siry you've been there for three years without so much as a raise. You do the job of three people and they know it."

"Of course not, that's just not me." Osirys said, dismissively. Her job was the only thing in her life she felt like she was good at. She didn't want to jeopardize it by pretending they needed her for anything more than she was.

"You need to." Lily said. She was chewing on her lip. Osirys knew it was coming. There was no way Lily was going to let it drop.

"This is the third time in as many months I've met you for our Saturday morning breakfast and you're all beat up."

"I don't know what you're talking about Lil," Osirys said, sighing heavily.

"Three weeks ago you came in here with a split lip, it looked like you had a round in a boxing ring before coming to have pancakes with me, for Chrissakes."

Lily had her hands on the edge of her table. Her eyes were serious. "You said you ran into a door."

Osirys nodded. "Yeah. Jumped right out at me."

"Sure it did." Lily wrung her hands. "Fine. Then what gave you an egg on the side of your face this time?"

"I told you I don't want to talk about it." Osirys said, slightly louder than she meant to. Conversations around their table quieted, she noticed several other patrons of the small diner looking their way. The waitress had noticed too, and looked like she was going to head over with their coffees to diffuse the situation.

Lily looked like she was going to begin digging at the topic more, but the waitress arrived just in time with their cups.

"Everything okay?" She asked. She was round and rosy-cheeked. Her name was Stella, and she knew them both by name. They had been coming to the restaurant for a couple years nearly every Saturday for breakfast, and Stella was there to take their usual orders every time.

"Yeah, Stel, my sister's just being a pain in the ass again." Lily said. Osirys saw her considering saying more, but instead she just smiled at the affable waitress.

"Well keep it civil, I'll tell Randy to hurry with your orders so you can calm those hunger attitudes, alright?" She winked at the girls and started to make her way back toward the kitchen.

"Thanks, Stel," Osirys said as she left. She unfolded her napkin and dabbed a drop of coffee that had dripped onto the table.

Lily seemed like she had no intention of letting things go or keeping things civil. She looked like a tigress that had cornered its prey.

"Lil, please. Can we talk about this another time? Somewhere else, maybe?"

Lily huffed.

"I'm just worried about you, Osirys." It was rare that Lily used her full name. It felt almost like her mother, when she would use her first and last name together. It hit Osirys a bit differently. She let her guard down just a bit.

"I know, Lil. Don't worry. It's nothing I can't handle."

Lily opened her mouth with a comeback, then snapped it shut, and said nothing.

"Just promise me that you'll let me in when you're ready, ok? I'm here for you."

"I know," Osirys said. She saw their food emerge from the large swinging silvered door. Stella stopped briefly to hand a check to an older man at the breakfast counter, then began heading their way. Her stack of pancakes steamed as they made their way across the diner, the smell of warmed butter and fresh fruit jam filled the air.

Lily looked over her shoulder, she only had a few more moments until breakfast was upon them.

"You don't have to say a thing. If you need to stay for a little while with me and Tom, you just show up. You don't even have to call or ask. I won't tell Mom or Dad, even." Lily was making hard eye contact. "I'll keep a bed made up for you, okay?"

Osirys nodded.

"Okay?" Lily repeated, demanding a response from her little sister.

"Yeah, I got it."

"And here we are," Stella announced, setting Osirys' plate down. "Your usual, a half-stack with mixed berries and butter,"

Osirys smiled, sending a twinge of pain through her face. Stella blinked, seeing her puffy cheek. She glanced at Lily quickly, likely making the same assumptions, but she wiped her suspicions from her mind, and put Lily's plate down.

"And a Belgian waffle with chocolate crème and two fresh strawberries for you, my dear." Stella stood for an uncomfortable moment more. Osirys smiled again at her and nodded before the waitress moved off to her next table without another word.

They crested the rise and Osirys found herself on a broad cliff, looking out over the full fury of the Virdi River. She was stunned. If it was a river, she would have never known. It was so wide that she could not even see the other shore. She had never seen such force before in her life. The river spit mist hundreds of feet into the air, blowing a wet wind across the cliffs. Below in the furor, she saw the shadows of massive boulders, larger than the buildings of the town hurled through the current.

She watched as a massive boulder was pulled from the depths of the torrent and launched into the cliffside below. She felt the land beneath her shudder with the force of the impact and out of reflexes she braced herself, preparing for the cliff to give way before her, but the land held fast. The boulder cracked and split into several pieces that were instantly ripped back into the current and swallowed by the Virdi once more. Every now and then, a rolling boulder would lock into place temporarily, rerouting the course of the river, sending a gout of water launching into the sky, sending spray hundreds of feet from the riverbed.

The roar was deafening. Without the land to temper the din of the river, Osirys couldn't even hear herself think. The repeated cracking concussions of stone on stone was hypnotic and maddening at once. Osirys stood agape at the spectacle of nature. How was it even possible to cross the Virdi? She suddenly understood the extremity of need that must have caused the first voyagers to risk the wrath of the Virdi to escape the collapse of the Old Empire. She felt tears streaming down her cheeks. She felt so small, so insignificant before the river. She took a step forward, remembering the words of Mnemosyne and the Muses -

She felt the words within her, rhythmic and consistent. The phrase built within her into a chant. She closed her eyes:

"We must trust the River,
It will weigh her worth."
Somehow, she swore that the chaos of the river began to fall into the cant of her words, as if the concussive sounds of the boulders smashing into each other fit perfectly into her cadence. She began to be able to feel when the next crushing reverberation would rumble through the rocks beneath her, anticipating it, even. She felt the River coursing beneath her as if it were an extension of her being. Just as she reached out from within her, she heard Naivarra call out her name-

"Osirys!"

She felt a strong grip on her arm that wrenched and pulled her backwards. She opened her eyes as a large stone passed mere inches from where she just stood, sailing across the outcropping and falling a hundred feet or more to the riverbed below. Osirys landed on her backside, breathing heavily. Naivarra sat nearby, glass-eyed.

"How- how did you do that?" Naivarra asked.

"Do what?" Osirys replied, confused.

Naivarra blinked several times. "Never mind, I thought I saw something. It must have just been the River playing tricks on me."

Osirys stared at Naivarra, puzzled.

"Legends speak of manifestations of the Muses, immense elemental beings known as the *Furies* - though they exist mostly in cautionary tales for children now. I could have sworn I saw one just now. The *Fury of Mnemosyne,* the mother of all aspects, as the children's tale would tell it. It was *watching you.*"

Naivarra shook her head. "You're not the only one who has a scrambled nog, I guess."

Osirys turned and looked back at the river. The rhythm of the words were gone, and the Virdi returned to unbridled chaos. Osirys scanned the river, squinting. No trace of anything like what Naivarra described was in sight. They climbed to their feet, and started walking down the path towards town to meet back with the Vipers.

Naivarra and Osirys entered the Lost Lantern tavern just as the sun began to dip from the sky into evening. Closing the heavy wooden door, Osirys looked for the Vamanari. She didn't have to look very hard. The small Vipers were all at one large table, and there was a significant berth of space between them and any of the other patrons. There were a diverse group lining the barstools. Some sported armors and weapons, others wore wool tunics and were covered in dirty stains. Osirys figured that this is where travelers that were bound for the Old Empire had their last friendly drink, and where those that returned washed away the horrors of their experience. Many of the locals hung about the tables of the well-clad adventurers, hanging on their words like children hearing a bed-time story. Shouts and cheers followed words of triumph, and then the din would melt away to suspenseful silence as a tale became tense.

Naivarra and Osirys picked their way through the crowd to the Vipers' table, taking seats on the long benches.

The Musefolk were clustered around a map of the area, and had clearly spent some time restocking their supplies. A number of rucksacks hung on chair frames were filled to bursting.

Pasea looked up at Naivarra, and acknowledged Osirys with a curt nod. "The slavers move south. Several of their number were in town yesterday to resupply, and were seen leaving on the Southern road 'ere the sun rose this morning. We received word that there are a number of Vamanari families in the hills Southwest of here, in a village called Dyrdyndal. More than a few of the folk we rescued from the caravan were bound that way. If the slavers are aware, which is a safe assumption, they will no doubt be in significant danger."

Wavu slammed her fist on the table. "Why then are we here at this table in this tavern? We know their destination, we know that our people are in danger. We must protect them! We swore an oath, Pae. An *Oath,* to our *people.* We can't abandon them."

Pasea's head hung close to her chest. Mirabyll put her hand on Wavu's shoulder, attempting to calm her, but Wavu brushed it off.

"You cannot be serious." She hissed.

Flembe leaned forward, nodding. "We can save them. We *must* save them. We swore to the Queen. We paid homage to our old purpose. The girl is safe in this town, and protected. Whatever purpose she may have here does not concern us any more. You must see this."

Pasea raised her hand. "I hear you. My heart yearns to finish what we started on the slopes of Tork's Redoubt; My spear seeks vengeance for my sister. Do not presume I make this decision lightly. You all know my loyalty to Queen Lavis."

Pasea's words held a restrained venom. Osirys could feel the divide in her heart and mind.

"It is that loyalty that demands we return to Eidrdyhn at once. The appearance of a *Harbinger* in these lands after so many years cannot be ignored. If it is the Queen's will for us to return to hunt the slavers as I hope it will be, then so it shall be."

Syndal leaned in, speaking almost too softly for Osirys to hear. "Pae, are you *sure* Osirys is a Harbinger, as you say it? What proof do we have? How would we even know? What if she's not what you say she is? What if we turn our backs on our people for nothing?"

The table fell silent. The Vamanari turned and looked at Osirys, who shrunk into her seat at their scrutiny.

Naivarra suddenly had a large flagon in her hand, and was sipping at it eagerly.

"Well? Are you?" Wavu asked impatiently.

Osirys didn't know how to respond. "I- I don't know."

Wavu clapped her hands. "She doesn't know. How can you know and she doesn't know, Pae?"

Pasea gritted her teeth and pulled a dagger from her belt, slamming it deep into the solid wooden table, snarling. The tavern fell silent, and all eyes turned to the large table of small Musefolk.

"I have spoken." Pasea turned and stormed off, leaving the dagger buried several inches into the table, still wobbling. The hilt of the dagger was polished white stone, with a blue gem inset into a pommel which curved out, nearly mirroring the curled, carved crossguard. On each side of the cannelure spine of the dirk, narrow cutouts in the metal left hollow channels that ran nearly the entire length of the blade, terminating in ornate filigree near where the metal met the stone hilt and tapering at the point which was buried in the wood of the table. Ornate runes ran the length of the edges of the weapon, etched into the metal, which started as a dull, almost golden yellow luster near the hilt that blended to a nearly white silver at the tip. Osirys recognized it as the dagger that Pasea took from the body of her sister.

The tavern returned to its usual frivolity within moments, but Osirys noticed a thin man, sitting at a small table in the corner of the room had held his eyes on them, more specifically the dagger, firmly planted in the wood.

Mirabyll sighed. "Those that we freed will warn the families, I'm sure of it. They will be long gone before the slavers arrive. We are a cunning people, and not helpless. We did swear an oath to our Queen, Wavu, but it went somewhat different from what you seem to remember. You swore to follow Pasea's lead in the fight against those that sought our suffering, as I recall."

Mirabyll's eyes were kind, but fixed on Wavu. She continued, "And in Pasea's absence, I am her voice. You would do well to contain your passion. It comes from a good place, but I must remind you to know your boundaries, young warrior, unless you want to endure a *trial of contempt.*"

Wavu faltered, and lowered her gaze. Mirabyll straightened her posture. "That's what I thought. Go make ready the room. We will rest here tonight and set out at first light for Eidrdyhn."

The Vamanari cleared out. Mirabyll remained, head bowed somewhat. Naivarra gave Osirys a side-eyed look and raised her eyebrows, tilting her large flagon back and slugging down her drink eagerly.

Mirabyll shook her head and hopped down from the bench, and followed in the direction that Pasea headed. Osirys stared at the dagger, still wobbling slightly in the middle of the now empty table. She noticed the strange fellow still idly watching. She reached across and took hold of the hilt, pulling it from the table. She struggled more than she thought she was going to have to in order to get it free. She examined the detail in the metalwork. She studied the runes etched into the cross guard; she ran her fingers along the etched metal, feeling their shapes. The blue gem twinkled in the flickering firelight from the hearth. Naivarra wiped a bit of foam from her lip with the sleeve of her tunic.

"That's a pretty little knife," Naivarra remarked. "It's an Auric's blade, if I'm not mistaken."

Osirys barely glanced up from the dagger, "What do these runes mean?"

Naivarra shrugged, taking another big gulp from her flagon. "I'm not the one to ask. I have never seen eye-to-eye with Aurics."

Osirys looked up, "You mean you don't trust them?"

Naivarra crossed her arms across her chest. "I have my reasons."

"Why?" Osirys inquired.

Naivarra frowned and didn't respond, downing the rest of her drink instead.

"I'm going to get another. You want one?"

Osirys shook her head.

"Fine." Naivarra said, sliding from the bench and walking to the bartop counter, flagging down the innkeeper with a practiced hand.

Osirys returned to studying the Auric blade, trying to unlock its secrets with intense examination. Some time later, she looked up and saw Pasea sitting next to her, watching her intensely. Neither Mirabyll nor Naivarra had returned to the table.

"That was my sister's blade." Pasea said, climbing up and sitting on the edge of the table, sliding a little bit closer to Osirys.

Osirys immediately put it down and apologized. "I'm sorry, I shouldn't have touched it."

Pasea cocked her head slightly. "It's not a problem."

Osirys looked at Pasea. Pasea didn't move the dagger from where Osirys had placed it on the table, but traced its silhouette with her finger, and began slowly spinning it, causing the blue gem to flare with reflected light as it bounced off of its many facets.

"Was she a- an Auric?" Osirys asked.

Pasea nodded. Osirys saw a hint of a smile on her face. "She was - A powerful one, too."

"Tell me about her," Osirys continued.

Pasea looked Osirys in the eyes. Her matte complexion seemed darker, somehow more soft in the light of the tavern. She straightened her posture, and as she dropped her gaze, she smiled wistfully.

"Pemme was… everything I couldn't be. When we were young, she was identified early as an Auric, where the best I could do with the water was drink it." She laughed lightly, her eyes welling up slightly.

"I trained hard. I wanted to earn my place. Pemme was actually the youngest Vaman ever inducted into the

Queensguard, such were her talents. She was Abjurer to our Queen Lavis while I was still learning my stances. Despite her duties to our Queen, her Grace would always allow my sister to come down to the training grounds to watch my sparring matches.

I remember the day of my Proving- I had entered to be tested two years early, admittedly in hubris. My Havatis of course, she advised against it. She knew I wasn't ready. I wasn't even the best in my rank, let alone competent enough to face a seasoned Viper in battle. I insisted, however. I needed to prove that I was as gifted as my sister in something. I had some minor wounds from my training leading up to my Proving, and Pemme asked to see me before the rite, so that she might heal those hurts before I faced my trial.

She performed an incantation I had never heard her use before, but I was too excited to take much notice. Regardless, my hurts were mended and I entered the arena to face my Proving trial against the most senior of the Vipers at the time. I was no match for her, naturally. I fought bravely, and every time I was struck, I regained my feet and continued to fight. I thought the fact that the blows didn't hurt as much was just the thrill of battle in my veins. I remember thinking '*I was born for this*', as the sting of her spear and blade was muted and almost non-existent. After many minutes of punishment, I remember pressing a reckless attack, one that I thought would surely end the fight one way or another. Somehow it connected with my opponent. Looking back, it was obvious to me that she allowed it, the alternative would have surely slain me.

The result was that I stood victorious, but at that moment, when the focus of the fight drained from me and I became aware of myself again, I saw what caused my opponent to hesitate. My body was veritably flayed. I bled from more than a dozen grievous wounds that should have ended my will to fight many times over. My opponent was skilled enough to avoid striking lethal blows, but at some point there's only so much a body can handle before it fails. Still, I didn't feel any of the pain that should have ended me."

Pasea trailed off for a few moments before continuing.

"I'll never forget looking at the arena stands for her in my moment of triumph, and seeing her pale and quivering, curled and clutching her body, writhing in torment. You are familiar with the magic. Pem had known I was in over my head. She must have. She couldn't bear to watch me suffer, so she took the pain for herself. I remember her visiting me in the ward, healing my wounds while also bearing my agony. I saw it in her face for months."

Osirys stammered, trying to find a response. "I–I'm sorry."

"I never thanked her or apologized." Pasea stated, flatly, almost aggressively. "More accurately, I never forgave her."

The dagger spun slowly to a stop. Pasea blinked away some tears and climbed down from the table without another word, and began walking towards the chambers of the inn.

Osirys sat alone at the wide table, grieving for Pemme and Pasea. She couldn't help but feel responsible in some capacity for Pemme's death. The tavern had cleared out somewhat, only a few grizzled adventurers and smattering of locals remained. She looked for the strange fellow at the corner table, but it was empty. She looked around, suddenly she felt very vulnerable. She felt bewildered, overwhelmed, and plagued by a lack of purpose. She considered for a moment leaving the tavern, just walking out and not coming back- but she had no idea where she was or where she could possibly go. Worse, she doubted she'd get very far before she got herself into trouble again, or got someone else hurt or killed. She tried again to search inside for anything before the past few days, looking for some vague sense of direction, to answer why she was there and what she was supposed to be doing. She knew there must have been something, the shadows of her past lingered just beyond the edge of her mind. She could feel the reverberating emotions of her life, but it was as if she was trying to use ripples on water to guess the geometry of an object that fell into a pond.

She gave up, frustrated. She grabbed a cold roll from one of the plates left on the table, tucked the dagger between her belt and her tunic, and headed toward the chambers. She was caught off guard when a hand caught her by the arm as she moved past the hearth. She spun to see the peculiar thin man holding her. She yanked her arm free and made ready to run.

"I'm sorry, please, don't go. I didn't mean to frighten you." He said.

Osirys paused, and regarded him suspiciously.

"It's just, you remind me of someone. Someone very dear to me that I lost. I was just wondering if your voice was such similar."

Osirys felt her flight instinct rise up within her. Something didn't feel right about this man, but for some reason she believed that what he said wasn't deception. He wore a sadness about him that was pervasive- it saturated his guise, he wore it on his shoulders, and his eyes were dark and sorrowful. She glanced about her. There were still a handful of patrons including some well armed adventurers at the bar, their presence calmed her somewhat.

She swallowed, and replied: "I'm sorry for your loss, though I really must be going." She turned away from him to continue to the chambers.

"Wait," he called. "You probably think I'm crazy. Look. Here." He pulled a small locket from within his tunic hanging from a chain that he wore about his neck. "Look."

She turned back and glanced at the locket. Inside there was a picture of a young girl. The metal of the locket was inscribed in delicate writing. It said: "For Byzzim, my love". She did admit they had very similar features. She felt a pang of sympathy for the man.

"That was my Hyara." He said, choking up somewhat. "We were to be married."

"What happened to her?" Osirys asked.

He took a sharp breath in. "An illness took her. She was so strong and healthy, then… She fell ill, and over the course of the summer she got weaker and weaker. She never recovered."

"Was there nothing the Aurics could do?" Osirys asked.

"The Aurics!" He spat. "Useless, the lot of them. They didn't have the *knowledge*, they said." He wrung his hands together, and an ember of anger burned in his eyes that unsettled Osirys.

She recoiled instinctively. He regained his somber composure. "Thank you," he said, closing the locket and tucking it away back under his tunic.

She nodded, and turned to leave once more.

"Uh- miss?" He asked, his voice small and meek.

"Yes?" She responded. She didn't know why she kept indulging the poor man. Clearly her being there was torturing him.

"Ah, never mind. It's probably too much to ask."

Osirys folded her arms across her chest, losing her patience. She raised an eyebrow at him. "Go on, then-"

He stood suddenly and caught her in a hug. She stood, paralyzed, unsure of what to do. She felt some wet tears on her cheek. Several moments went by, and she began to panic internally. She looked for Naivarra. She was nowhere to be found, but all hope was not lost. She saw one of the adventurers at the bar had taken notice and had stepped down from his seat and was approaching, hand on his sword.

Finally, he released her. She took several steps backwards and fought the urge to yell. Byzzim saw the adventurer who had paused his advance but still had his hand on his weapon. He met Osirys' eyes, and dropped his gaze instantly to the floor. "I'm sorry, thank you." He said, sweeping his cloak up from his seat and moving for the door of the tavern. He paused as he passed the adventurer, who kept his hand firmly on his blade. The tavern had dropped into silence at the commotion.

Byzzim spun on his heel and muttered something under his breath before hastily exiting the building. The adventurer watched him go and the door close completely before relaxing. He then turned to Osirys.

"Young miss, are you alright?"

She nodded. The man was tall and strong, his features were well defined. He wore a linen tunic that buttoned three quarters the way up, but the buttons were offset to one side. The longer side of the tunic front was folded back slightly, such that she could see the top of his chest and part of his left shoulder. His breeches were a thick dark fabric, with buttons that ran down the outsides of the legs. His hair was medium length and light colored. He was very attractive, and Osirys felt herself suddenly in a new situation feeling very awkward and uncomfortable.

"Yes, thank you, I'm fine." She managed to get out.

He smiled, and took his hand from the hilt of his blade. Osirys felt her face flush.

"Good, I was afraid I was going to have to step in there for a moment."

Osirys brushed some of her hair out of her face, pulling it behind her ear and forcing a smile. "That's very kind of you."

He gestured to the bar, "I pray you don't intend on walking alone so soon - I could walk you to wherever it is you call home, if you prefer?"

She winced. It was always the same song and dance from men. "Oh, thank you, I'm staying here at the inn, actually, so that won't be necessary."

He smiled, "Ah, even better, care to join me for a drink then?"

Something inside of her was panicking. Part of her wanted to accept. She saw her reflection in the tavern window for the first time in Naivarra's clothing. She was surprised, she actually looked... pretty? She took a step towards him, but something inside wouldn't let her proceed. She felt afraid, vulnerable, anxious. She just wanted to get out of there. She didn't want to be focused on. She stood there awkwardly until she heard footsteps on the stairs coming down from the tavern chambers and watched Naivarra walk in. Naivarra raised an eyebrow and paused, leaning on a nearby support beam, seemingly amused.

"I would love to, I really would, but my companions are waiting for me." Osirys stammered, "I really must be going. I'm– I'm sorry."

She moved past him hurriedly, darting for the stairs that led to the chambers above the tavern. She bolted past Naivarra and climbed to the landing, pausing and running her fingers through her hair. Damn it! She considered going back down. There was no reason why she had to act like that. She slapped her thigh lightly, in frustration. She froze. Looking down, her stomach flipped and her heart beat into her throat. The dagger was gone from her belt. It must have been that Byzzim character! She took a couple hurried steps down the first couple stairs, then stopped. He was long gone now. She gripped her temples with both hands. "Damn it!" She hissed, squeezing her eyes closed.

She opened them to see Naivarra jeering at her from the bottom of the stairs. Osirys turned and fled to the room, the sound of Naivarra's chuckling chasing her at her heels.

She entered to find the Musefolk kneeling together in silence. None of them so much as looked up when Osirys entered. She saw Naivarra's rucksack and belongings by a bunk close to the door. She froze, afraid she had interrupted something. She stared at Pasea, terrified that she would notice she didn't have her sister's blade. When the Vamanari didn't react to her presence, she slinked to the back of the room, and found a bed that was separated from the others with no personal affects. She sat down on it gingerly. Even so, the frame groaned loudly as it accepted her weight. She saw Syndal shift uncomfortably at the break in the silence. She laid back and stared at the dark ceiling, ashamed and embarassed.

Chapter Eight

Osirys pulled on her new boots as the sun rose and the first rays of sunlight filtered through the small window of the Lost Lantern. She tried not to think of Pemme's lost Auric blade or the events of the night previous. Instead, she thought about the circumstance that brought the boots to her, and tried to be thankful that she had them at all, so that she didn't have to make the trek North with the Vamanari shoeless as she was previously. Though her feet were healed by Auric sorcery, they still felt tender to the touch. She hoped she didn't have to rely on any more of the magic to continue her journey.

"How far is where we're going?" Osirys asked Mirabyll, who stood nearby, looking out of the upstairs window over the town.

"Eidrdyhn?" Mirabyll asked, turning.

"Yeah, I suppose."

"Two weeks by horseback, three by foot." Mirabyll answered.

It was a long way. Osirys had never walked anywhere near that distance before in her life.

"What's it like?"

"The city, or the road?" Mirabyll stepped away from the window, coming to sit by Osirys.

"I was talking about the trip, but I suppose I'd like to hear about the city too." Osirys responded. She looked out the window over the low homes of Pearlwater Bend. Several plumes of gray smoke drifted up and away from rooftops. Osirys unclasped the pane of glass on the hinge, and cracked it open slightly.

The smell of baked goods and primitive industry filled the air. It was comforting, even wholesome. She turned and gave Mirabyll her full attention.

"Just North of here lies the Forrenweald, it's an old, old forest. It runs the length of the road North along the Virdi. Much of our journey will take place amongst those trees before we turn west towards Syrpent's Gap."

"Syrpent's Gap?" Osirys asked.

"Aye, it's a pass through the mountains. The land built a curtain of stone on either side of the River, or the River pushed the land as it carved its way through, none rightly know."

Osirys remembered the tall mountains in the distance from atop Tork's Redoubt.

"There are few places that the range eases. Syrpent's Gap is one of them. Long ago, far before our people crossed the River from Eophaetha, it is rumored to have been the roost of a mighty dragon. The road is difficult there, but it is undoubtedly one of the most beautiful places I've ever seen."

Osirys blinked. "Dragon?"

Mirabyll smiled. "Worry not, Harbinger. Such legendary beasts are just that now - Legendary. Intimidating as the few histories claim them to be, they are no more. Some say they were created by the Muses, just like the Vamanari."

"What happened to them?" Osirys asked.

"What's left is rumor and folktale," Mirabyll sighed. "But, the stories say that the dragons of old were the pioneers of magic. They were wise, and friendly."

Osirys found herself hanging on Mirabyll's words, entranced. "Until?" She urged.

Mirabyll chuckled. "Until," she said, patting Osirys' thigh. "The dragons discovered a magic that they would not share with the people of Eophaetha. They claimed the knowledge was too dangerous."

Mirabyll's eyes shone in the morning light. Her rough, stonelike complexion caught the sun in such a way that it almost scintillated.

"There was a war thereafter, naturally. Some of the dragons believed it was not their place to decide which knowledge was safe and which knowledge should be forbidden. Others believed it was their duty to use their given gift of wisdom to guide the peoples of the world on a path that would not tempt them to ruin."

"Who won?" Osirys asked.

"There are rarely winners in war," Mirabyll replied. "That war least of all. Those dragons that held fast to their belief in purpose were driven from the lands, exiled to a realm that none alive know the location of. The others were fabled to have been cursed by their creators, losing their wisdom, and becoming feral, wild beasts, the knowledge and magic over which they fought lost to both sides, forever."

Osirys had to admit she was fascinated by auric magic, even just the concept of it all. It felt like parts of her childhood awakened whenever she thought about dragons, or magic of the river, and she was filled with wonder. At the same time, she also thought she began to understand Naivarra's feelings towards it as well. She didn't want to rely on it. It felt fake, like an unfair augmentation that she didn't deserve, at the cost of someone else. She fumbled with her feelings on the subject as the rest of the group put themselves together.

There was also the matter of Pemme's dagger that the strange man had stolen from her the night before. Osirys grimaced. She bit her lower lip. She had to tell Pasea. Maybe there was some way they could track him down and recover it? She took a breath and approached Pasea, just as the door opened. Vim, the youngest of the Vamanari, had disappeared shortly after waking, and now returned in a flourish, knocking through the door with a loud 'Whoop!', hefting a heavy bag of breakfast pastries. They smelled like they were baked fresh that morning.

"Where did you find these?" Flembe, one of the more seasoned Vipers asked.

The Vamanari swarmed Vim and the sack of goods. Osirys stood nearby, deflated.

"A Duarf was on her way out of town and had just finished setting up a stand with a sign that said 'Free!'. She seemed rather pleased to see her goods go. Duarfs are peculiar folk indeed."

Osirys looked at Naivarra. It must have been that strange short woman from the chapel the day before. Naivarra just shrugged and popped a pastry into one cheek while simultaneously grabbing another in her other hand.

"What did she look like?" Osirys asked.

Vim regarded her, puzzled. "Well, I'm no expert on Duarfs, but she was rather round, homely looking. It was peculiar though, now that you mention it. She had donned armor and there was a sizable twin-bladed axe holstered on her back. Seems odd an adventurer would just leave dozens of fresh pastry in the town square, doesn't it?"

Pasea looked at Osirys inquisitively. Osirys shrank away, purposefully not making eye contact. "Was there anyone with her?"

Vim thought for a moment. "No, just her. What is on your mind, Harbinger?"

"Oh, nothing. It's just there was someone like you just described at the chapel when I visited yesterday. She was there with someone that she referred to as her 'Leventus', who had gotten injured. She seemed crazy, claiming they had fought the dead."

The Vamanari gaped at Osirys. Pasea stepped toward and grabbed Osirys by the arm. "What did you say?"

Osirys backed away a step. "Her Leventus? Is that a bad thing?"

"No, no, the last part. Leventus is Duarfish for Holy Knight. Did you say, fighting the dead?"

Osirys nodded her head slowly. The Vamanari's faces fell into one of abject dread as they exchanged worried looks.

Mirabyll's voice was barely louder than a whisper: "The Risen have not been seen on this side of the Virdi River since the time of Or'qan the Immortal. The knowledge has been locked in the Avhakamora in Geagana for centuries, and any practice of that kind of Aurancy is met with lethal punishment throughout the Empirate. It would take a powerful, dangerous Auric to accomplish such a thing. Are you *sure* that's what she said?" Mirabyll had walked across the room and stood directly in front of Osirys, her large, dark eyes like pits as they stared at Osirys in disbelief.

Osirys nodded, slowly.

Pasea looked up at the ceiling and sighed. "We must get to Eidrdyhn with all haste. This news must reach the Queen's ears. She will know what to do. First a Harbinger falls into our midst, and two days later tales of the dead walking once more on this side of the Virdi? This cannot be coincidence."

The other Vamanari nodded in agreement, turning on their heels and wasting no time in leaving the Lost Lantern for the road North out of Pearlwater Bend.

THE MORNING WAS COOL, a wet wind blew from the North, and thick clouds piled in from the Northwest, colliding with the rising air from the Virdi River. They swirled ominously overhead; Osirys heard the dim rumblings of thunder through the ever-present roar of the Virdi River nearby.

She fidgeted uncomfortably. Pasea didn't seem to notice Pemme's dagger had gone missing yet. She thought about trying to broach the subject with her again, but didn't get very far. Naivarra had appeared, walking alongside her.

"You're joining us on the trip North?" Osirys asked, casually.

Naivarra looked at her with a sidelong glance, perhaps feigning offense. "And miss an opportunity to save you again? I think not. Besides, if the unliving are truly roaming the land this side of the River, I'd see it with my own eyes, and meet it with my blade. There are few warriors that can claim to cross with the Risen and can later speak of the events. There is a saying that if a warrior openly speaks of an encounter with the Risen, he is a liar. Those who survive are typically too horrified to ever speak of it."

Osirys glanced at Naivarra, skeptically. "And that makes you *want* to fight them?"

Naivarra shrugged. "I want to see for myself is all."

"Sure." Osirys replied.

"Besides, the Vipers promised a reward from their queen for my *heroic actions*." Naivarra flexed and blustered with her words. "How could I refuse?"

Osirys giggled. She noticed that Naivarra was wearing her armor and battle clothes. Her sword looked freshly oiled and she was wearing some new leather gloves.

"Where did you get those?" Osirys asked, pulling at the cuffs.

"Oh- Mirabyll gave them to me as a gift for helping back there at the caravan. How do I look in them? Do you like them?" She held her gloved hands out in front of her, wiggling her fingers.

Osirys was taken aback. She paused for a moment mid-stride before continuing. It was a rare moment where Naivarra exposed any semblance of feminine side. Osirys found herself smiling.

"I think they look great. I wish I had a pair."

She watched a thin smile pass over Naivarra's face. It was only there a moment before it vanished.

"You just got nice new boots. Don't be greedy." Naivarra admonished.

Osirys smiled, and chuckled quietly.

"I think we're in for a Riverstorm today." Naivarra said, changing the subject abruptly.

"What's a Riverstorm?" Osirys asked.

"Nasty lightning and wind, mostly."

Osirys nodded slowly. "I sort-of figured that. I meant, what makes them different than normal storms?"

"Nastier lightning and wind, mostly."

Osirys shook her head in frustration.

"They're called Riverstorms because they only happen near the River." One of the Musefolk called back, the Onyx-skinned Viper Osirys recognized as Vim.

"Thanks." Osirys called back.

"Totally unhelpful." She muttered under her breath.

Osirys turned the conversation back toward the topic of the undead. "What's so bad about, what did you call them? The Risen?"

Naivarra took several steps without replying. She seemed stuck in thought.

She finally responded, "Supposedly, that kind of magic gives the flesh of the dead an extra… Ferocity. I'm not exactly the right one to ask about how it all works, but Aurancy uses the power and magic of the River to *command* things to do what they otherwise wouldn't be able to. The Risen are more than just animated bodies, they carry the *violence* of the River within them. Those who encounter the Risen in Eophaetha, if they survive, usually struggle to find words to describe them. But, like I said, I've never seen one, and the tales that come back from the Old Empire are difficult to believe."

Osirys shivered in the cold, wet wind. She recalled the unbridled fury of the Virdi from atop the cliffs the day previous.

"Do you believe that one?" Osirys asked quietly.

Naivarra shrugged, and they plodded on in silence.

The Riverstorm wasted no time in setting upon the travelers. They were only a few hours out from Pearlwater

Bend when it began, early into the afternoon. Osirys watched the swirling clouds condense and descend, as if pushed down toward the land by some great force. It was as if the sky were pressing down upon her; and then the wind began. It was cyclonic and bestial, thrashing in gusts. The Musefolk wrapped their violet cloaks about them and continued, pressing on into the storm. Naivarra made no attempt to dissuade the storm from exacting its wrath upon her. She remained alert, rain and wind whipping her hair into a knotted mess; water streamed from her armor and skin. Osirys followed closely behind. The Riverstorm was vicious. The wind did not consistently blow from one direction, so she struggled against the changing gusts. The rain hit her from every direction, mercilessly. Even though the sun was high in the sky, the gloom of the storm would have had Osirys believe that it was dusk. The thick, dark clouds that blew down and about them deepened the shadows as they struggled on into a forest that rose in front of them like an ill omen.

Osirys paused at the scrub tree line, the boughs and trunks dancing to the chaotic cadence of the storm. The limbs of the trees waved a warning to her, and she shuddered. The clouds of the Riverstorm blew into the forest, before the direction of the wind would change and they would come surging out again, giving the illusion that the forest was breathing - inhaling and exhaling the madness of the tempest. The Vamanari had darted into the shadow of the trees, Naivarra not far behind. Osirys wiped strands of her hair from her face and steeled herself. As she took her first step into the wood, she felt the sizzle of electricity and felt the concussion of lightning as it blasted the ground on the plains several dozen paces behind her, where they had just passed. The light of the strike lit the umbral forest, the skeletal limbs of the trees momentarily lined in white-blue against the dusk.

Osirys stumbled and caught herself on a gnarled sapling that twisted its way in between larger, more hardy trunks. She regained her footing and pressed on into the woods. Naivarra had paused for her several paces ahead.

"Come girl!" She called against the gale. "There is an ill about this storm. I don't wish to linger here. The Vamanari make haste, we must do our best to follow."

"This place is dreadful," Osirys called back as she drew closer to Naivarra.

"Welcome to the Forrenweald," Naivarra muttered sarcastically.

They caught up with the Violet Vipers, following the winding and narrow road through the Weald.

Suddenly, the forest opened up to the West, revealing a large lake. The wind blew the surface into an uneasy chop. Looking out over it, Osirys could watch the rain fall and cascade in sheets that would catch crosswinds and contort, sometimes even coalescing into small cyclones. She could make out a large, dark cliff face on the far side of the lake.

A brilliant flash of lightning ignited the lakescape, briefly unveiling a breathtaking, tall, thin waterfall that cascaded from the top of the cliff into the lake below. As the lightning struck, Naivarra froze. The thunder rolled through and between the trees, and Naivarra took a couple steps and vaulted onto a rock by the lakeside, taking hold of a limb above her head she\ stopped, staring out over the water, motionless, as if waiting for something.

Osirys moved to her, trying to see what she was staring at. She wiped water from her eyes and face, squinting in the dim light. She followed Naivarra's line. She realized she was holding her breath.

"What are you-" Osirys began.

Naivarra silenced her with a gesture, pointing at a dark spot at the bottom of the cliffs.

Again the lightning flashed. In the briefest of illumination, Osirys saw the opening to some kind of cave or tunnel on the far side of the lake.

Naivarra relaxed slightly, and jumped down from the rock. "I thought I saw something." She said.

"Is that-" Osirys began again.

"Shimmermere? Yes." Naivarra answered. "It used to be a source of great wealth for the region."

"It was a mine, then?" Osirys said, following Naivarra as they hurried to catch up to the Vamanari once more.

"Yes, in ages past. It is no longer used for such things."

They fell into step behind the Vipers. Suddenly, Pasea halted, whipping her head to the side, and throwing one of her hands up, palm outward. The rest of the Violet Vipers froze mid step. Naivarra halted as well, so abruptly that Osirys nearly ran into her.

"Something approaches." Naivarra whispered over her shoulder.

Pasea dropped her hand out to the side, and as a well oiled machine, the Vipers disappeared from the road, deftly ducking into the brush. Naivarra reached up and behind her, un-clipping the strap that held her sword fast to its scabbard, and drew the blade, her eyes fixed on the road ahead of them.

Osirys took several steps backwards, staring ahead into the mist. Whatever it was that the Vipers and Naivarra were detecting, Osirys was blind and deaf to it. The mist swirled between the tree trunks, and the wind whistled and howled through the limbs and branches. Even though it was the middle of the day, the deep dusk of the weald combined with the thick storm blotted any hint of the sun.

Lightning ripped through the gloaming woods - Osirys stared ahead in disbelief; several dozen paces ahead on the road there was a form, illuminated in the flash. The flickering lightning exposed the frame and visage of a corpse, half rotted and decayed, crouched in a feral position. In that briefest of moments, Osirys saw its face - the sockets of the eyes were filled with a viscid liquid-like blackness that streaked down its hollowed cheeks, like ink mixed with too much water. The corrupted liquid seemed to drip from its twisted maw as well, running like thick molasses or rotten mucus. She didn't know why, but she was especially unnerved by the lack of reflectiveness of the fiend. It was opaque, matte, as if it drank the light.

It completely vanished into the gloom when the flash of light from the storm dissipated, but it was more than enough for Naivarra, who lunged into a run, her blade drawn and angled defensively ahead of her. A shrill caterwaul filled the forest air, setting Osirys' teeth on edge and raising the hair on her neck and limbs. The wail was nearly unbearable. She clutched at her ears. In the noise there was chaos that reminded her of the Virdi river - a violent cant that ground against her nerves and pressed deep into her mind, maddening and unforgiving. It assaulted her senses, sending her sprawling into the dirt, scrambling for any means of escape. She stared into the darkness, terrified. Another flash of light revealed Naivarra embattled with the Risen dead in freeze-frame animation - her blade raised to fall upon the horror before her, which was coiled like an unnatural spring. In a series of frozen moments, Osirys saw Naivarra's blade descend and the Risen erupt forward, lunging directly into Naivarra's middle, it's clawed digits gaining purchase on her armor. The power of the Risen was incredible. Even though Naivarra's stance was balanced, the force of the impact lifted her from the ground and sent her sprawling backwards into the mud, the ravenous dead atop her in a fury of gnashing teeth and claws. She swung the pommel of her sword across the top of her, connecting with the Risen and sending it skittering to the side, momentarily freeing her. She scrambled, trying to regain her footing, but the Risen was preternaturally fast, righting itself and springing back towards its prey.

As it lunged, it raised a clawed fist to bring to bear upon the disadvantaged fighter. Naivarra swiped her sword across her to attempt to parry its strike, and connected, only to find that the strength of the monster was so great that her blade was blasted from her grip, clattering into the muck several feet away. Osirys heard Naivarra growl as she rolled to her feet, spinning to face her attacker, sending a cascade of muddy water spinning out and away from her and watched her pull a curved dagger from its scabbard on her belt. She held it in a reverse grip, her other hand held in front of her like an open claw. She kept her body low, her center of gravity by her hips and legs wide. The Risen slowly crept to the side, drooling black ooze hungrily.

Another lightning strike ignited the forest in white light. Osirys cried out - From the limbs of a wide tree above Naivarra, another Risen corpse dangled eagerly in ambush. She watched helplessly as its shadowed form dropped from the height like a sinister missile to land atop Naivarra. She gasped, however, when a streaking javelin hissed through the air and caught the creature square in its center of mass, sending it toppling to the ground nearby instead. Naivarra leapt to the side, taken by surprise by the wretched mass landing in a screeching heap mere feet away. The other Risen responded with a fury that Osirys had never seen before. It threw itself with vehemence at Naivarra, who struggled to keep her balance in the wind, rain, and disorienting lightning. She batted at its strikes, giving ground and stumbling, but keeping it from overwhelming her, if only just barely.

The Vipers leapt from the shadows of the trees, spears raised overhead. They pounced the fallen Risen, thrusting again and again. It shrieked and thrashed about, seemingly impervious to the spears piercing it time and time again. It grabbed the shaft of a spear that punctured its gut, swinging it - and the Viper on the other end of it - violently to the side, crashing into another cloaked Vamanari warrior, sending them both tumbling. It moved to press its advantage to leap upon them, but the other spears of the Vipers held it at bay. It struggled, tearing its flesh and sinew on their weapons to get to the small warrior, who scrambled in the mud away from it, kicking away its grasping claws, and grabbing a cobblestone from the mud and smashing it into the side of the skull of the corpse, with a sickening crack.

Naivarra had backed herself to the trunk of a twisted tree, and ducked a vicious strike that ripped bark and wooded meat from the trunk as if it were the flesh of a beast. She grabbed its arm and twisted, throwing her weight down and to the side, using its momentum to throw it over her body to slam into the tree trunk. She spun on her knee and drove her dagger deep through its neck, burying the blade into the wood, pinning the

Risen to the tree. The crossguard of her dagger crushed its throat and allowed no amount of struggle. The Risen's eyes poured their thick ebony fluid and its mouth snapped and hissed at her as she scrambled away from it on all fours, searching the mud for her sword. The Risen dangled awkwardly from the trunk, its head halfway to upside down and the body twisted around the dagger trying to find purchase on any surface. It grabbed at the blade, trying to rip it free.

Osirys pointed frantically, at the spot where she saw Naivarra's sword come to rest, and yelled; "Naivarra, there!" Naivarra followed her line, and dove upon her weapon as the Risen hauled against the dagger. Naivarra rolled and swung the blade, causing a sharp wake of mud to rise in its path as it cut through the water towards the neck of the Risen, hacking straight through its bone and sinew, the blade coming to rest deep in the wood of the tree. It was as if the energy that animated the Risen evaporated instantly, the body crumpled into a disgusting mess and ceased moving; inanimate, like it had never been given vitality in the first place.

The Vipers had pinned the other Risen from half a dozen spears through its body deep into the muddy earth, but it was still thrashing.

"The head!" Shouted Naivarra. "Sever the head!"

In the blink of an eye, Osirys saw the glint of a short blade flash in the glim light and the thrashing ceased instantly.

The rain pounded around them, the sound of battle and the unearthly wails of the Risen suddenly seemed like a different reality. Osirys sat in the mud where she landed at the start of the frenetic row, panting. Naivarra wiped the wet hair from her face, and stood a few feet away from the Risen that she had brought low, hands on her hips. She shook her head and stepped forward, bracing her leg on the tree and pulled on the dagger that still pinned the body of the undead in a distorted upright position. Osirys realized she had begun to hold her breath, half expecting the body to re-animate as it was freed. As the dagger came loose, however, the torso obeyed gravity and landed with a wet plop in the mud.

"Looks like the rumors are more than rumors." Pasea said. She stood nearby keeping a lookout for more attackers.

The Vipers looked at each other. It was if they were conversing with each other without using words or body language. Osirys wondered at their ability to communicate non-verbally. It was not at all uncommon for the Musefolk to stand about and look at each other for a minute or so, then act as one without so much as a word being uttered.

Mirabyll nodded, and the warriors brandished their weapons and as one began moving down the road cautiously.

"How do they do that?" Osirys mumbled.

"I've been wondering that myself," Naivarra replied, wiping the blade of her sword with a cloth and shouldering it, walking after the Vamanari.

"Somehow, though, I know that they intend on investigating Shimmermere, to find the source of this corruption. Don't ask me how." She turned and shrugged at Osirys, who frowned.

"Great. At least we'll be out of this storm for a bit." Osirys said dryly.

Naivarra smirked, "Ever the optimist."

They followed the Vamanari closely, until they found the overgrown path that led away from the road towards the grotto. The Vipers paused, surveying the sounds of the land and looking out into the gloom, their glassy eyes shining.

One of the more quiet Musefolk, Fernip, moved about the path, examining the stems of plants and ground. "Someone has been through here recently, other than the Risen, I mean."

She took several steps down the path, looking at what must have been tracks in the mud. "Several someone's, actually. One much earlier, potentially last night, one this morning, perhaps only an hour or so ahead of us."

"There is something foul afoot here, I can feel it on the wind." Syndal replied. She was grasping a pendant that swung from a chain about her neck.

Naivarra sighed, chuckling. "You didn't need Auric's sense to figure that one out, Syn. We just left two headless Risen on the road fifty paces behind us."

Syndal frowned, and didn't reply.

"Let's go." Pasea said, moving down the overgrown path with a Javelin in one hand and her blade in the other. Osirys didn't know what to do. Every instinct in her told her to turn the other way and flee the area. This was no place for her. She would only be a hindrance, and a liability. She didn't move from her spot, rain pouring down on her.

But what if there were more of those *things* hanging about in the trees? She shuddered and reflexively glanced around, scanning for the malicious black inky pits of eyes that were burned into her memory in horror. Naivarra paused, glancing back at her.

"Coming?" She asked. "I thought you wanted to get out of the rain."

Osirys wasn't sure how to respond. She felt helpless. "When those... Risen, attacked..." She trailed off.

"Yes?" Naivarra said, impatiently.

"I couldn't do anything. I froze. I just don't want to get anyone hurt. I don't know how to fight."

"You have that Auric's dagger," Naivarra replied. "Maybe try to do something with that." She turned and continued walking down the path after the Vamanari, still talking.

"I won't let them get you, and I don't think the Vipers mean to let them eat you, either."

Osirys grimaced at the mention of Pemme's blade.

"About that," Osirys began.

"Hm?" Naivarra said "About what?"

Before Osirys could reply, Fernip called out, ahead of them. Naivarra turned back.

"You can ask your question later." Naivarra said, firmly. She turned and started jogging down the path, disappearing into the mist. Osirys stopped, and slapped her thigh in frustration, and forced her legs to move, jogging after her.

She caught up to the others. Several of the Vipers were in combat pose, defensively. The others were standing about, looking at something in the brush.

The rise of the cliffs was not far away, Osirys could see them looming ahead, even through the rain and mist. The forest was less dense here by the lake, scrub bushes and small trees clustered in stands around large boulders.

Osirys halted near the group, peering to see what they were looking at. The ground was trampled, and several thin trees lay severed from their trunks. Something definitely had happened here, and recently, too.

Her hair stood on end as she heard the sounds of small rocks clacking as they fell from somewhere nearby.

Pasea's hand shot up, and the Vamanari dropped into a practiced defensive stance, encircling Osirys. Pasea motioned in the direction of the sound, and began to move slowly in that direction, javelin and blade at the ready.

They rounded a large copse of thin trees that lined a massive glacial boulder, and then Pasea halted, dropping her stance and planting the heel of her javelin in the wet grass. Osirys moved up beside her.

On a small boulder nearby sat a scraggly and wet Duarf, wrapped around the middle with a bloody cloth, munching on what appeared to be a muffin. She waved affably at Osirys and the Vipers as they stepped from the brush, and called out to them, mouth full.

"Oh halloo there!" She said. Osirys instantly recognized her as the same Duarf from the day before at the chapel in

Pearlwater Bend. A large battle axe sat across her lap and a pair of headless Risen slumped on the ground nearby.

"I wasn't sure if I was gonna haf'ta put my muffin down to deal with more-a-these here nasties!" She said, smiling from atop her rock. "Good thing I brought extras!" She grabbed her rucksack and began digging through it, pulling a bulging cloth sack from within.

"Troodie?" Osirys asked, wide eyed. The plump Duarf took a big bite of muffin and hopped down from the boulder, wincing and favoring her uninjured side.

"Hiya! I didn't expect to see friendly faces here, that's fer'sure."

Syndal was already rummaging through her belongings, pulling tinctures and ointments from her medical kit.

"Why are you here alone? Where's the Leventus?" Osirys asked.

"Ah," Troodie began. "He ah, he joined his fathers last night." Her smile faded. "I came out here continuin' his good work in his absence. Can't have these here nasties roamin' about so close to town, and seein' as how he'd have done it, I figured it's up to me to do it in his stead. I vowed I'd continue his work by his bedside before he faded, and I was just now tryin' to figure out exactly how I was gonna keep my promise when you all arrived." She opened the cloth sack revealing a dozen or so muffins.

Pasea stepped up, taking a muffin and bowing in thanks. "I'm sorry to hear about your Leventus." She said. "We have seen too much death ourselves recently. These are dark times."

"Yer tellin' me!" Troodie puffed.

Syndal approached Troodie with her field kit. "I can tend your wounds," She began.

"Oh, dearie, you don't hafta do that. It's just a little scrape there on my side, I'll be right as rain after I have a little breakfast." She attempted a smile, but a sheet of wind-driven rain blew off of the lake over the group. "Maybe 'right as rain' ain't exactly the right phrase for the moment."

Syndal looked at the blood-soaked bandage, and back at Troodie, frowning.

"Oh, fine. I was never a good liar. One of the buggers got me pretty good."

Syndal went to work. The Musefolk sheltered their muffins from the soaking rain and wind. Osirys looked to the cliffs, and saw the dark crevasse that was the opening to the abandoned mine. She shivered.

Troodie looked at the Vamanari, Osirys, and Naivarra. "So, what brought you all out this way?"

Pasea sat down on a rock next to Troodie and Syndal. "We set out to travel to Eidrdyhn, to counsel with the Queen of our people, when we encountered the unliving on the road."

"Oh, I missed a couple?" Troodie interjected, "Sorry aboot that."

Pasea squeezed her thighs as she sat, nodding towards Osirys. "We believe our companion, whom I believe you've met, is a Harbinger, such as the kind from the reign of Or'qan."

Troodie winced as Syndal worked, looking with interest at Osirys.

Osirys tried to stand up straight, but felt awkward and slumped. She hated this kind of attention. It was like she was being analyzed for some kind of worthiness that she didn't have. She was just a girl, lost and scared in an unfamiliar land with no memory of how she arrived. Everything about this place was alien to her, strange peoples with peculiar appearances and mannerisms that she didn't have any knowledge of, and everyone regarded her as some kind of legendary hero. She didn't feel heroic, she felt displaced and ashamed.

"I sorta thought the Harbingers were more… I don't know… Somethin'." Troodie said. "No offense there, o'course. It's just that Leventus always described the last Harbinger as the bravest of heroes that stood against the might of the Tide of Darkness."

Osirys stood, resembling a drowned rat, her tunic clinging to her sapling-thick arms and hanging about her, dripping. "Well, I'm not that." She said flatly.

Syndal stepped away from Troodie, finished with her work, and nodded. Troodie shrugged. "No cake came straight out of a mixing bowl!" She said casually, sliding off the rock, landing heavily on the ground near Osirys.

"At least that's what Matron Van Hootan would tell me when I was young."

Troodie looked up at Osirys, placing a heavy gauntleted hand on her forearm and smiled. "I'm sure your ingredients will come together too."

Somehow, Troodie's strange words and demeanor were comforting, even if she found it hard to believe them. Even in the height of the tempest, Osirys shrugged off some of the doubt that hung about her like the dark clouds above and around them.

Troodie bowed deeply to Syndal, who had put her supplies back in her satchel. Syndal nodded. "Now," Troodie said, turning to the rest of the Vamanari and Naivarra. "What say we find out what's makin' all this fuss?" She hoisted her axe, gripping it in a sure fist.

They moved as a group toward the dim opening of Shimmermere at the base of the cliffs nearby.

Chapter Nine

OSIRYS SHIVERED AS SHE stepped under the dilapidated beams of the grotto. The aged wood bore the weight of the entryway, but not without betraying the strain of untold years at the task.

"How old is this mine?" Osirys asked.

Naivarra shrugged. "Don't know."

Troodie ran her fingers along the stone as she stepped into the dark tunnel.

"Don't worry," she said, her friendly voice echoing off the narrow stone passage. "This stone is stubborn. It will stand for many thousands of years yet."

It didn't make Osirys feel any better. An un-natural cold hung in the air; a heaviness that she wasn't able to place. She couldn't discern whether it was the tons of stone above and around her, or the damp rock, slick with water and green with lichen and moss, but she was itching all over. Her heart was pounding in her chest. She hoped against hope that the worst of the abominable undead were behind them, but she felt more than knew that the source of the evil lurked somewhere within the darkness before them. The shadows of the abandoned mine loomed long. Naivarra produced a brand from her rucksack, wrapped in oiled cloth to keep out the rain. She knelt by the entrance with a flint firestick. She pulled a knife from her belt and dragged it expertly across the firestick, sending a wide shower of sparks onto the soaked brand. The light of the sparks lit the entryway of the mine, and thousands of points of light reflected around the group, sending the shadows spinning for a moment, revealing dark crevasses in the rock walls, perfect hiding spots for the shambling Risen.

Osirys knelt down by Naivarra. "When you're done, could I borrow that dagger, in case one of those Risen things…" She trailed off.

Naivarra sent another shower of sparks onto the torch. She didn't look up. "What of the Auric blade that Pasea left to you?"

Osirys looked down and away, and lowered her voice to a whisper. "I lost it."

Naivarra stopped mid-stroke on the firestick. "Lost it, girl?"

"Er, I think someone stole it. There was a man, named Byzzim, I think, from last night at the Lost Lantern. I think he took it off of me. I didn't notice until he was gone. I tried to say something before, but I couldn't. I don't know why."

Naivarra resumed striking the firestick, two or three heavy strokes in rapid succession, sending wide showers of sparks bouncing onto the brand and the rock it sat on. One tiny coal stuck and the dull orange hung on the torch, a thin wisp of smoke rising from the cloth. Naivarra cupped her hand around it and blew on the ember, feeding it with her wind. It shined in response, spreading and glowing brighter. Naivarra stood, whipping the brand down and around in a vertical circle in a practiced motion. Her circle completed overhead and the torch leapt aflame, sending bright light dancing down the stone tunnel where the Vamanari and the Duarf had continued walking, unhindered by the darkness.

Naivarra paused, and looked at Osirys for a moment before flipping her dagger and catching it by the blade. Naivarra stood, stern faced, waiting for Osirys to take it. Osirys grasped it by the handle gently, and Naivarra lingered for a moment, then let go. She turned and began walking after the Musefolk and Troodie. Osirys followed close behind, gripping the dagger in both hands.

The passageway widened and the low ceiling of the tunnel vaulted above Osirys and Naivarra as they picked their way through the tunnel. It turned slightly once or twice, keeping the others out of sight.

"How can they see in here without one of those?" Osirys asked.

"They are children of stone," Naivarra said matter-of-factly. "Both Vamanari and Duarf-kind are accustomed to a life underground, and their sight is more keen to the deep places of the world."

They stepped around a partial collapse of the tunnel, and saw the others gathered around an abyssal chasm in the stone, leading down, in what appeared to be a wide chamber. Old, weathered beams braced the walls and ceiling, and ropes wound about heavy looking gear mechanisms above the pit. Ropes hung taut, delving into the darkness below. Naivarra and Osirys paused, and then joined their companions. Pasea wore a strange smile as they approached.

"Harbinger, come here, look." Pasea instructed. Osirys quickly tucked the dagger in her trousers. Naivarra shook her head, nearly imperceptibly.

"Shimmermere," Pasea began as Osirys approached. The leader of the Vipers neared the edge of the precipice. Osirys didn't dare get that close, her stomach swam even as she approached several paces from the rim. "Once one of the most fruitful mines of the early Empirate."

She gestured at the heavy gear above the center of the vertical shaft. "Mylt was so plentiful here that they forged their mechanisms out of it. Look."

Naivarra handed Osirys the brand. She inched a bit closer to the edge and looked at the mechanism. The metal reflected a dull sheen, gray with blue hued undertone. The light of the brand reflected off the surface, which was clean of any corrosion or wear, in sharp contrast to all the other materials in the old mine.

"Is it rare or something? Mylt?" Osirys asked.

"It is only found in the most specific of places. Syndal, if you would?"

Syndal breathed a command, barely louder than a whisper. "*Ka'amat,*"

The mechanics above the pit glistened with a pale luminance, and began to move.

"Behold," Pasea said, quietly. "Mylt is the metal of magic, some call it Magisteel."

The wheels and gears bit into each other and hauled on the ropes. The ropes vibrated from the tension, and the closed air of the shaft groaned ominously, as if the earth itself was growling.

The Vamanari took a collective step backwards, and brandished their poles in low, ready position. Osirys heard the click of Naivarra releasing the buckle on the scabbard of her sword, and the ring of the blade leaving the sheath. Troodie stood squarely with her axe in one hand at her side, perilously close to the open abyss, gazing down.

"Why did they stop mining here?" Osirys asked.

"Depends who you ask," Mirabyll said. "The folklore is that the miners left and refused to work because they thought Shimmermere was haunted. They claimed that shadows would move by themselves in the depths."

"And what do you think it was?" Osirys asked, following Mirabyll's skepticism.

"I think it was most likely that after hundreds of years of plumbing the root of this mountain, it became harder and harder to find what they were looking for, and it cost more and more to protect what they did find on the long road back to Aefemar and the core cities."

Osirys breathed out, somewhat relieved.

"Or it could have been that the place is truly haunted. After seeing the Risen here today, who knows." Mirabyll followed.

"Great." Osirys said, glaring at Mirabyll, who winked at her mischievously.

"What'cha think might come up?" Troodie asked. None of the others responded. Troodie frowned at the lack of reply. "Whatever it is, it might be friendly-"

"I doubt it will be friendly," Naivarra growled.

Troodie shrugged, and hefted her axe, backing away a step from the ledge. Long minutes passed, the gears wound on and the ropes coiled on huge flat spools that turned slowly, inset into the vaulted ceiling of the chamber. The sound of the ropes began to change pitch, rising to a hum as they shortened. Osirys held her breath as the gears began to slow.

A rigid wooden platform inched into view. The gears stopped moving, and fell opaque and dull.

Troodie dropped her axe to her side. "See, told you it might be friendly! It's a way down!"

Naivarra rolled her eyes and cautiously stepped onto the platform, sword still in hand. She tested the sturdiness with her weight. She held onto the rope and gave a test jump. Troodie looked at her with a cocked head, stepping onto the platform without any hesitation. The rest of the

Musefolk, and finally Osirys joined them. Pasea nodded to Syndal, who closed her eyes, focusing.

Before she could speak, Osirys asked, "Can I try?"

The Musefolk collectively stared at Osirys. Naivarra raised her eyebrows. Troodie beamed.

"I mean, I'm supposed to be some kind of, something. If I'm what you all say I am then there must be something to it. Maybe I can do this."

The Vamanari looked at each other, communicating silently. Mirabyll stepped forward, seemingly prematurely. The rest of the Vipers jerked their heads towards her as she acted.

"Go ahead, Harbinger."

Pasea drew her mouth to a thin line, and several of other warriors huffed.

Osirys moved to the center of the platform and closed her eyes. The group gave her space and everyone fell silent.

"Now what?" Osirys asked.

Syndal glared at Mirabyll, hesitating before moving to the center of the platform, standing in front of Osirys. She took Osirys by the hands, looking up to meet her eyes.

"Are you sure you want to try and open this door?" Syndal asked.

Osirys nodded.

"Then we shall try." Syndal said. "Focus your mind on that which you wish to command, but not the individual or particular thing. You must first find the *ideal* of what it is that you seek. The *ideal* is… like a signature. It carries a pattern, a rhythm. That rhythm fits into the world around us in complex melodies and harmonies. Find the *ideal* of the gears, then speak the command word I used earlier, 'Ka'amat'. It is an ancient tongue, born in the Old Empire of Eophaetha. Any language will technically work, but scholars wise in histories claim Eophaethan is descended from Illumari, the language of the Muses, and as such the words carry a rhythm that help the mind keep focus."

"What does 'Ka'amat' mean?" Osirys asked.

Syndal paused. "It can be used as 'function' or 'physics' in the common tongue."

Osirys nodded, and closed her eyes. She remembered the translucent fox from deep within the Aethereal plateau, from her brief time with the Muses. *'The Ideal'*, she thought. That's what Nature was referring to. She remembered Nature's words:

"It exists here so that more like it may exist elsewhen"

How could she expect to know what the *Ideal* of this mechanism could possibly be? She tried to force her doubts from her mind. She had to try, even if she didn't have the answers. Osirys could feel the eyes of her companions upon her as she stood in the tunnels of the ancient mine, making it all the more difficult for her to focus.

She thought back to the feeling within her when she stood atop the cliffs exposed to the raw power of the Virdi River. She tried to recall the rhythm of the current, the deep rumbling of the boulders as they crashed and tumbled in the raging current. She didn't know where to look to find the *ideal* of the gearworks above them, but she had a feeling that her experience outside of Pearlwater Bend the day before was a good place to start. She pushed the images of the Risen and their black, inky eyes from her mind, and focused on the feeling of standing above the Virdi.

She felt nothing. Her experience above Pearlwater Bend may as well have been a fancied dream. After several moments of internal struggle and no progress, her shoulders slumped.

S HE OPENED HER EYES and lowered them. Syndal frowned, thoughtfully. "The door remains closed to you, though you know where it is."

Syndal closed her eyes.

"Attend, Harbinger." She said. She flipped Osirys' hands over and held them, palms up. She began to lightly tap and drag her finger along the center of her hands. Osirys tried to find a pattern in Syndal's touch, unsuccessfully. It felt random and chaotic. After several moments, Syndal spoke.

"Ka'amat."

The gearworks sprung to life once again, shining faintly in the dim light above, and began to spin the opposite direction.

Syndal looked up at Osirys. "Did you understand?"

Osirys shook her head.

Syndal dropped Osirys' hands. "This was no surprise, Harbinger. It was a crude and challenging first attempt."

She turned away, but paused, and spoke over her shoulder, "Most Aurics study for years before they attempt their first incant, and rarely do they succeed even then." Her tone was blunt, but not insincere.

Osirys tried to find any amount of solace in Syndal's words, but something within her recoiled at her failure. Even though she knew Syndal had no reason to exaggerate the difficulty of the task she attempted, she felt small and pathetic once again anyway. She wanted to believe that she was more than she was, like Pasea and the others believed, but inside she knew they were wrong about her. She was mundane, ordinary, and broken.

She made a mental note to ask more on the subject later, but the platform had begun to descend; slowly at first, then picking up speed. It barely cleared the walls of the shaft, the cut of the stone was precise and carefully wrought.

It may have just been in her mind, but as the platform descended into the depths, Osirys felt the weight of the mountain enclose and surround her. The air was cool and damp, but remained consistent as they descended. She shivered and clutched the hilt of Naivarra's dagger, still tucked in her linked silver belt. Even in the chill, Osirys noticed that she had begun to sweat, and her nerves were alight with the precursor of a panic that she felt all too familiar with, but couldn't place why. Anxiety bubbled in her stomach like sour milk, and she glanced around nervously. Syndal met her eyes. They were wet and reflective, and Osirys got the feeling that Syndal too, felt something was amiss. Syndal pulled her small blade from its sheath, and glanced around nervously.

"Something is amiss. I fear dark Aurancy is at work-" Syndal whispered, barely audibly. The Vamanari shifted uncomfortably, drawing weapons. Naivarra sucked in air. The area was far too small for her to swing her massive sword effectively. She drew it anyway, holding it high, above the heads of the smaller Vipers, who took low battle postures, wielding their short blades.

Moments went by as the platform descended further into the depths of Shimmermere, until suddenly the shaft fell away to an immense underground cavern. Osirys gasped, the platform was descending, suspended above a massive underground lake. They were far above the surface of the water, and Osirys stomach flipped from the height. She instinctively grabbed one of the ropes, clutching it in a white knuckled fist. She felt a wave of nausea wash over her, and she bit the inside of her cheek, fighting the urge to retch over the side of the platform.

Osirys glanced to see Syndal on one knee, pale and shaking.

"What is this?" Osirys asked. It was as if the air were a poisonous fume, but there was no foul smell. The others aside from Syndal seemed unaffected.

"The water, it is corrupted." Syndal choked, looking up at Osirys. "Mylt is made by ore that has been infused for aeons in the magic of the waters of the Virdi. The River's power is strong here, but something…" She trailed off.

"Oh, oh no." Syndal pointed over Osirys' shoulder. "Weapons!"

Osirys whipped her head up to see the distended forms of several of the Risen, their clawed digits holding them tight to the roof of the cavern. They moved in swift, jerking motions as they grabbed for the ropes of the elevator, sending vibrations down the length of cordage. There were four of them, inverted, clawing their way rapidly down the platform's suspension as Osirys, Naivarra, Troodie, and the Vamanari dangled still well over a hundred feet above the subterranean lake. The first of the Risen closed in, preternaturally fast, leaping from on high. It's clawed limbs were extended and its inky, streaked face was held in a perpetual, soundless scream. It fell like a silent fusillade. Naivarra ducked under it, thrusting her sword straight up towards it to catch it on the point of her weapon.

It impacted directly on the blade, the sharp metal impaling it right through its middle, sliding down the length of the sword, and landing atop Naivarra in a frenzy. Naivarra dropped to one knee and deflected the impact, sending a shudder through the timbers. She pushed back and up to attempt to send the Risen tumbling off the edge, but the platform moved under her feet instead, sending her and the Risen sprawling together onto their backs in the center of the platform, which had begun to sway.

The other Risen lunged downward. The Musefolk kept their low center of gravity as balanced as possible. Two javelins launched into the air, catching one of the Risen in the chest, the impact tearing it from the rope and sending it wheeling into the open subterranean cavern, flailing noiselessly out of sight as it dropped. Three of the unliving remained. One of the Risen leapt, landing amongst the Vamanari. The other swung its bottom half down in a kick aimed at Troodie, who caught the legs of the abomination under her arms, spinning and yanking it free from its mooring on the ropes, howling. She rotated and hurled it, sending it pinwheel spinning toward the edge of the platform. It didn't quite clear the edge, but skidded, clawed hands digging into the wood in vain for purchase. It slid over the side, disappearing from sight.

Naivarra punched and wrestled with the Risen atop her, its gnashing jaws inches from the flesh of her neck. One of Naivarra's forearms was all that separated the lethal, jagged maw of the Risen from her exposed flesh. Naivarra's arm was corded and she strained against the monster, but it had supernatural strength, and she was losing. With her other arm, she punched at its temple repeatedly, to no effect. It pressed closer. Naivarra stopped punching and grabbed at its face, trying to pry it away. Osirys watched in abject horror, helplessly. There was only a mere dozen feet between Osirys and Naivarra, but the other of the Risen and all the fighting Vamanari were between them.

"Naivarra!" Osirys called out, desperately.

Troodie spun, seeing Naivarra's failing strength against her unliving foe. Breaking into a full run, Troodie dashed across the platform, through the Violet Vipers and past the thrashing Risen between them. She moved like a rolling boulder, pushing her stout form surprisingly fast. With a hearty bellow she launched a heavy punt kick toward the side of the creature, but the platform twisted and lurched from the force of all the fighting, throwing her from her balance, and sending her crashing into the Risen atop Naivarra, its teeth just a knife's breadth from her throat. The force of Troodie's impact ripped the Risen from atop Naivarra, but they both tumbled for the edge of the platform.

"Oooo!" Troodie called out as she rolled off the edge, Naivarra's gloved hand around her wrist. Naivarra's face was covered in blood and her lower lip was torn open, but her eyes burned with ferocity and adrenaline. She hooked her leg around the mooring of the rope on the platform, and the two warriors dangled, the Risen tumbling into the darkness below.

"Gotcha!" Naivarra gasped.

Osirys looked for a path to help pull them up, but froze. The Risen that Troodie had first tossed was clawing its way back onto the platform, its inky eyes fixed upon her. She held the dagger in front of her with both hands, shaking. It lurched, staggering toward her as the platform twisted and swung beneath its feet. Osyris could barely stand. She watched it approach, raising a clawed hand. It swung at her and she stumbled to the side to avoid the blow. She backed away, swiping the dagger in front of her in crisscross patterns, hoping to deter its advance, to no avail. It dropped low, coiling for a lunge. It sprang at her, it was *fast*. She dodged one blow, but the other clawed hand was already moving. She desperately tried to block the strike with the dagger, but the strength of the creature was unnatural, blasting her in the side and sending her sprawling.

The dagger was thrown from her grip, and spun away from her, toward the center of the platform. She screamed in pain, her ribs were aflame and the air that rushed from her lungs wouldn't return, her diaphragm was stunned and paralyzed from the strike. She choked and sputtered as the Risen coiled to pounce on her. She couldn't stop it. She kicked impotently and struggled to scream for help.

At the sound of Osirys' scream, Pasea turned to see Naivarra's dagger, not Pemme's Auric Blade spin to a stop at her feet. Osirys met Pasea's gaze, and shame washed over her. Even as the Risen coiled to pounce upon her and rend her flesh, she saw confusion and sadness in Pasea's eyes. Osirys squeezed her eyes shut, waiting for the razor sharp jaws of the Risen to clamp into her neck, tearing into her. When it didn't come, she opened them again, to see Pasea, Naivarra's dagger in hand, sliding between her and the Risen, plunging the tip of the blade deep into the maw of the undead. It shuddered and retched, swatting Pasea away, violently. The leader of the Vipers bounced away, unconscious, toward the edge of the elevator. The Risen staggered backwards against one of the ropes tethering the platform to the shaft above and grabbed at the dagger lodged in its mouth. Mirabyll yelled commands to the rest of the Vamanari and spun away from the fight. She launched herself over Osirys in a graceful acrobatic spin and brought her blade across her body in a powerful slicing motion, connecting with the neck and severing the head of the Risen. Her knee connected with its chest as she finished the strike, sending it backwards over the edge of the platform.

The momentum of her blade, however, carried through the undead, and bit into the rope, sending several of its fibers springing away. The platform shuddered. Mirabyll landed on her other knee, looking at the damage to the rope. It was fraying quickly.

"Hold on to something!" She yelled, rolling to the side and burying her blade through Pasea's cloak and tunic into the platform as the rope let go with a snap. Osirys felt a small but strong arm around her middle as she slid towards the abyss, the corner of the platform suddenly dropping away, launching the other combatants from their positions, flailing. The remaining Risen was hurled like a stone from a catapult, and the Musefolk were tossed about as the platform shuddered and spun, sliding towards Osirys, Mirabyll, and the darkness beyond. The torch, which Naivarra had thrown in the center of the platform at the start of the melee, tumbled down and over the side, suddenly casting the entire area in darkness as it fell to the lake below.

It was as if Osirys senses were being blended. She couldn't see, and the sounds of screaming and groaning echoed around her off the walls and ceiling of the cavern around. She heard the splash of something hit the water far, *far,* below. She was disoriented, and fear gripped her as she heard the sharp sound of another of the ropes snapping, and another. She felt herself become weightless, and suddenly heard nothing but the sound of wind rushing by her ears as she fell. It seemed like an eternity, she couldn't tell which way was up. She heard Mirabyll's voice in her ear:

"Hold your breath!"

She sucked in as much air as she could and squeezed her eyes shut. The water may have as well been concrete. The impact on the surface of the water blasted the air from her chest and she lost consciousness.

Chapter Ten

OSIRYS GROANED AND ROLLED over, pressing herself up and away from the cold rock with her hands. She opened her eyes; they saw nothing but pitch blackness. She heard the soft purring of water moving nearby, and felt the chill of her wet clothing and hair about her. She was *cold.* She had never felt so cold in her life. Her limbs felt numb and ached, as if she were climbing from a bath of ice. Her body convulsed and shook, trying desperately to keep her core warm. She struggled and sat up, leaning against hard stone behind her, breathing heavily. Moments passed, and as her memory caught up with her, she began to panic. She remembered plunging into the darkness of Shimmermere, among her companions, and the terrifying Risen. She sucked in breath and held it, straining her hearing for what her eyes could not see.

She remembered Pasea's unconscious body pinned to the platform by Mirabyll as the ropes failed. Images of Troodie clinging to Naivarra and the savage Risen; their sable pits for eyes filled the emptiness of what her vision couldn't reveal in the absolute darkness that surrounded her. Osirys shook and gasped, pulling her legs close about her, and burying her face in her knees, squeezing her eyes shut, as if it would make any difference. Were they alive? Any of them? She thought of all the Violet Vipers, Troodie, and Naivarra - Unconscious and drowning, their bodies being found and chewed on by the voracious undead.

"Hello?" She squeaked out into the abyss of the deep.

Her voice reverberated off the cavern walls and melded with the quiet lapping of the water nearby, but she heard no reply. Oh, what would she possibly do if she were truly alone in that forsaken pit, with no supplies, no way out, and no means of defending herself against the evils she knew were lurking, unbreathing, and unseen in the dark? Calling out was as much a risk as seeking her companions.

"Naivarra? Pasea?" She mewled.

Osirys listened and winced as she heard her voice bounce off the cavern walls, echoing for what seemed like eternity. No reply. If her companions were alive and conscious, they were not close enough to hear her. She remained curled for several minutes, paralyzed with fear. The dark of Shimmermere was menacing, and the corruption of the water was thick and fetid, her whole body felt *wrong*. Something inside Osirys felt comfortable here, however. It was as if the solitude and hopelessness were second nature to her, the ever-present threat of something unseen and unheard felt normal. She hated it, and rebelled against it, giving her strength. She had to do something, had to try. If she didn't, the comfort of nihilism would take hold of her and she would perish where she sat.

She lifted her head from her knees, and reached out, feeling about her in the darkness. She found only stone - sharp, hard, and resolute. She crawled on all fours until she reached the water, it was mere feet away. From the sound of her voice, she knew she was no longer in the immense cavern. If she had floated away from where she had landed in the lake, then it should stand to reason that if there was a current in the water, if she followed it upstream, she could return from whence she came. If her companions survived, and hadn't floated further down the passage than she, that's where they would be, and perhaps she could find and recover some supplies that were lost along the way in the tumult.

Osirys stayed on all fours, picking her way along the edge of the underground river. Progress was agonizingly slow, but she clenched her jaw, and put one searching hand in front of her after another, constantly checking to make sure she still headed upstream.

She jerked her hand back when she blindly put her hand down and felt something clammy and soft. She stifled a small yelp, and she trembled. She built up her courage and reached out again. Her fingers probed the surface of the object, it was slimy. She whimpered when she discovered fleshy nostrils. She reached for the rest of the body. Finding none where it should be, she recoiled in terror, sobbing. She quavered and steeled her nerves, reaching out once more. She searched its features, shivering. Her fingers found something that was protruding from the mouth of the head. Hard, smooth metal. She fumbled with it and closed her hand around the hilt of a blade. Naivarra's dagger. The one Pasea had buried deep in the gaping maw of the Risen just before the elevator fell. It was something. She battled internally, simultaneously terrified and inspired. She braced the disembodied head of the Risen with a foot and pulled on the blade, which was firmly lodged in the cranium. She strained against it, and it began to budge. She cursed and yanked the dagger free, with a sucking *pop*. She scrambled away from the water, hyperventilating, clutching the dagger in her hands and getting as far away from the skull of the Risen as she could.

Finding it was a terrifying reminder that the events that brought her to her current predicament had actually happened. Somehow, it made her more afraid and the feeling of hopelessness surged within her. She studied the feel of the handle of the dagger and thought back to her feeble attempt to defend herself against the Risen that attacked her on the platform. She didn't stand a chance against it then, when she could see. How could she possibly hope to defend herself against such an unnatural foe, blinded and lost as she was?

Her fear manifested with tears, and she cried softly against the cave wall. It was the first time she'd been actually alone since waking on the shore of the Virdi River and being discovered by Naivarra. She felt so overwhelmed, and what began as soft tears soon intensified as Osirys' emotions came pouring out in the isolation of the dark tunnels.

Osirys wept for many minutes, it may have been hours. Time had very little meaning in the depths of Shimmermere. Eventually, she had cried all the tears she could muster, and her eyes stung. She had no choice but to press on, hopeless as it may seem. She found her way back to the shore of the subterranean river and began picking her way upstream once again. Time passed, and as it did, Osirys began to wonder if her sight was playing tricks upon her. Every so often, she felt like she could see her surroundings, dimly, for the briefest of moments. She paused, shaking her head. There was no light here.

She followed the river around a bend, and it became unmistakable. At irregular intervals, the tunnel would become ever so briefly illuminated by some unseen light source. Osirys took in what little light she could when it became available, assessing her surroundings. The ceiling was low and covered with stalactites, some of them inches from her height. The riverbed was tumbled, cubic rocks, with very few Stalagmites. Few as they were, several formed thin columns that connected the riverbed to the roof of the tunnel. The water was dark and opaque-looking. Deep shadows were cast by prominent geology, and Osirys was suddenly aware of thousands of hiding places for the fearsome unliving. She gave pause.

"You couldn't see them before either," Osirys whispered to herself, in a half-hearted attempt to create some artificial confidence.

She waited for the next pulse of light. After several moments it came. She pressed forward, crouching. She began to move a little faster. Osirys consciously recognized how valuable her sense of sight was to her as she moved along the side of the underground river. It bent back, and as she rounded the corner, she caught a glimpse of what was creating the light. In the ceiling, a vein of ore wound between the stalactites, intermittently glowing, pulsing with a muted light before fading to opaque inertness. She gazed upward, mouth agape. Light rippled through the rock like wind through a field of grain.

"Mylt..." She muttered under her breath.

It was unmistakable, but where the color of the gearworks far above was a pale gray with hints of blue, here it was more dull, with a rusty hue supporting a nearly colorless gray overtone. It seemed dusty, almost aberrant to her. All the same, it was breathtaking. She felt the swell of light move through the stone as if it were an extension of her feelings, and its rhythm and cadence became clear to her. She felt as if she were back on the precipice near Pearlwater Bend, before the full fury of the Virdi River. She stood, and closed her eyes, feeling the magic of the Mylt ore, raw and unfettered.

Filled with hope, she pressed forward, following the vein of Mylt as she navigated through the deep. She tracked the ore, neck craned upward, until it split away from the water. It wound along and down into the wall of the tunnel, broadening into a prominent web of pulsing light. A chiseled opening in the stone led away from the river, into the wrought rock. A path was hewn. Ancient wooden beams marked it as a long abandoned mineshaft. Osirys paused at the opening of the mine tunnel, uncertain. The water surely led back to the cavern, but the light of the Mylt beyond the tunnel faded, promising to plunge her back into interminable black. She feared it, and lingered just outside the wrought tunnel, leaning on the aged wood beam that stood fast against the weight of innumerable tons of rock pressing down upon them. As the silence deepened, she became aware of a deep, soft vocal thrum from somewhere deeper along the tunnel. Someone was… singing?

She couldn't make out words or tune, the echoing reverberation of the tunnel melded the sounds and tones together. The eeriness of the dirge wafted ever so faintly through the stone, and with the sound, the Mylt shone with its dull rusty tone, as if the tune itself carried the light with it.

Drawn by the light of the mystical ore and the haunting sound, Osirys found herself taking steps into the tunnel, slowly at first. As she moved, the brightness of the Mylt intensified and the singing became more pronounced.

She focused on it, and winced. The rhythm was errant, twisted, and callous. She hesitated, but something about the voice was familiar, as if she had heard it before. She recognized the voice, but couldn't remember from where. It was deep, soft, and sincere, but the song was laced with pain, its rhythm tore at her nerves. The Mylt was compelled to respond to the song, but now she felt it; the unrefined magisteel anguished with each note, a palpable woe streaked along the walls and ceiling of the tunnel.

Osirys trembled with fear, but was ensorcelled by the melody, compelled onward. She began to hear words stand out among the reverberatory noise that bounced off the walls:

> *"When they met she was but a child,*
> *A lovely rose of just fifteen,*
> *Her body blooming wild,*
> *Though she already knew she was soon to die -"*
> *"She grew weaker day by day,*
> *As the harvest wind blew by,*
> *On a gray day she spoke softly,*
> *"It is my time to die."*
> *"What was our summer like for you?"*
> *She asked him as she cried,*
> *"What's a life of winters without you?"*
> *He solemnly replied.*
> *She said–*
> *"While there is no road that you may follow,*
> *I will always be with you–*
> *Though I won't be here tomorrow,*
> *I'll be near to see you through,*

And I'll love you through death."
But the sadness cut too deep,
The precipice too steep,
And his soul would never mend -
The pain of her loss,
was more than he could comprehend -
He said,
"I will yet remain by you,
As an emblem of my sorrow –
All I will know, or ever knew,
Is I loved you then,
And I love you in death."

Osirys heartbeat thundered in her chest as she moved slowly down the tunnel corridor, dagger clutched in one hand, held in front of her as the other ran across the rough stone walls. She began to see light ahead; the flickering of ochre flames and the pungent acrid smell of smoke. She approached a sharp turn in the tunnel and slowed, tiptoeing as quietly as she was able. She heard the voice clearly, it was very close now. As she moved, she felt the weight of a presence about her. The hairs on the back of her neck stood on end, and she found herself shivering. Though she was terrified, Osirys inched toward the corner of the rock. She sucked in breath and held it, placing her fingers on the cold stone, and peeked around the corner.

Chapter Eleven

OSIRYS CLAMPED HER HAND over her mouth to keep herself from gasping. Beyond the crook, the tunnel opened up into a larger chamber. The walls were a bister color and stained with dark streaks. The mylt ran like arteries through the rock, down the walls and into the floor of the chamber. It pulsed and rippled, arguing with the flicker of flames from two large braziers in the far corners of the room. In the center there was a large dais, upon which lay a shrouded figure, draped in stained canvas. Above the canvas floated a nearly transparent, wispy form that pulsed and oscillated with the cadence of the song. In front of the dais, facing away from her, a silhouetted male figure - slender to the point of gauntness.

She was transfixed, however, on the figure that loomed behind the dais. It wore a gray shroud with hood that hung about it. It's face was covered by a fearsome angular white mask, that was recessed deep within the shadowed hood. The eye slits of the mask glowed a purple energy, twirling in wisps. It didn't seem to have a nose, and the mouth was small, and emotionless. The sleeves of the shroud were long and tattered, but Osirys could not see any arms within. Rather, the frayed ends of the arms fluttered as if in a slight breeze. It moved, raising an arm in a slow, sweeping motion over the body atop the dais. The form of the creature seemed discorporate; the same amethyst colored energy that flickered from the eye slits of the mask licked the ends of the rent arms of the shroud.

It moved around the dais, and Osirys saw that it floated, the bottom of the gray shroud dangled above transparent nothing as it rounded the side of the slab. Sound emanated from it, and with it the mylt roiled with puce light. The sound resembled a sizzling hum, a low, bassy electric noise that modulated incomprehensibly from seemingly nowhere and everywhere at once. It hovered alongside the male figure, looking down. Then it slowly turned its head, and gazed towards the darkness of the tunnel, where Osirys lurked. It swept an arm up towards the corridor, now holding a cruel looking sickle that seemed to float, bound by crackling energy.

The wisp above the body atop the slab pulsed in alarm - the singing stopped abruptly and the silhouetted man whipped around. Osirys froze. The man's face was famil-iar, she recognized it as the man from the Lost Lantern in Pearlwater Bend. She fished her mind for his name, the name that was engraved on the locket he showed her. She wanted to turn and run back the way she came, into the safety of the darkness, but her legs refused to move. It was as if she was losing the ability to control her muscles. She felt compelled to move into the light. She gritted her teeth, but her legs moved anyway, carrying her forward, into the open.

The shrouded figure regarded her, lowering its sickle. She had no way of knowing, but it seemed to regard her with some sort of familiarity. It beckoned her forward, and she obeyed. The wispy orb pulsed excitedly.

"*Byzzim*," it whispered, hauntingly. "*You were right, my love. She is… So much like I was.*"

Osirys glanced down and saw Pemme's Auric blade on the slab dais. She still held Naivarra's weapon, and she held it in front of her, gripping it in both hands.

Byzzim smiled wickedly as he saw her eyeing the Auric dagger. "Ah, you've sought me out, come to claim your blade?"

Osirys didn't make a sound or move a muscle.

"Come now, I should be thanking you." He picked up Pemme's dagger, examining it closely. "This blade was all I needed."

Byzzim gestured at the wraithlike shrouded figure, crackling with energy. "My friend here taught me words. Words that haven't been spoken in aeons. Though I knew the words, I could not achieve the spell, but with your tool…" He trailed off.

"The Risen, they are your doing?" Osirys spat, venom lacing her words.

"Risen?" He chuckled. "A consequence of the failed attempts of the incantation to bring my Hyara back to me. I *told* you, I only knew the words." His eyes darted back and forth wildly. "You think I desired those *things?* Abominations, failures."

He spun on his heel, "No, this, *this,* is so much more. She was taken from me. I swore I would find a way. The Aurics said it couldn't be done. Look how wrong they were! They didn't know where to look. Didn't know *who to ask.*"

The shrouded wraith remained motionless, staring at Osirys. It was so *wrong* to her senses. Her insides squirmed with repulsion at the *un-naturalness* of its form, and the spirit of Hyara that bobbed above the palled figure on the dais.

"I was prepared to love the corporeal form that Hyara had left behind, as… unseemly as others might find it. But now! *Now*," Byzzim panted, "You, will make a much more *seemly* vessel. My mentor has told me the words." He slithered towards Osirys, eyes glistening.

"Come, Hyara is anxious." He was almost giddy, wringing his hands and breathing in ragged, short bursts.

Osirys resisted the call for her legs to move again. The compulsion washed over her like waves crashing on a rocky shore, dragging her - pulling on her like an undertow current.

She locked her knees, but her legs quivered and shook like leaves in a gale. She watched in abject disbelief as she began taking steps forward despite every attempt to remain where she was. She felt violated, intruded upon, in ways she never imagined possible. Her eyes welled up as she struggled internally. It was as if the very baseline of her individuality, her ability to choose how to respond with her own form had been revoked. She felt completely defiled, reduced, as if she were nothing more than the Mylt gears that wound the shaft of the lift that brought her to this dreadful place. She felt as if she were an outsider to her own body; her limbs suddenly weren't hers to control. Was this an Auric incantation? The robed and masked monster floated nearby, glowing ominously, exerting its will upon her. The expressionless mask followed her movements closely.

Byzzim swept up to the altar with a flourish, grabbing hold of the shoulders of the body on the slab and sliding it aside. It rattled like crumpled dry paper on stone. Osirys approached it slowly, deliberately, while straining against the motor compulsions driving her to act. Her willpower felt tiny in comparison to the force of presence that drove her from within, she was quite literally a puppet – an animated plaything for the otherworldly wraith.

She sat on the edge of the stone. She could feel its cold, rough surface. She felt the compulsion to lie back. She threw everything she had to resist. Her body remained upright. She squeezed her abdomen and clenched her jaw. She felt blood rushing to her head as she clenched every muscle in her body to rigidity. Slowly, she began to give way. Like a sandcastle in the tide, her parapets melted and the sharp edges of her defense eroded away and she felt one leg swing up onto the stone, then the other. She wrapped her arms through her legs in fetal position and dug her fingers into her flesh like she was hanging from a cliff.

She cried out in agony as she was compelled to let go.

"Now, don't be so dramatic. This will all be over soon." Byzzim cooed from nearby.

Osirys looked up, tears streaming from her face. The wispy orb of Hyara's spirit bobbed just above her, eagerly. She looked deep into the pale light for a trace of humanity, some kinship of womanhood that would put an end to her torment. She only saw and felt a hunger to live, to have what was taken. There was no help to be had there.

"Please!" Osirys called out anyway, in a desperate plea as her arms released from her legs and she began to recline. "No!"

"There, there. See? It's not so hard to just relax now, is it?" Byzzim loomed over her, Auric blade in his hands, point down, leveled at her breast.

"*Hurry, my love-*" Hyara's disembodied voice hissed softly.

The dagger descended, slowly. Byzzim's eyes were shut, and he was muttering. The wraith stood at the foot of the altar, sickles crossed across its chest and hooded head bowed. The veins of Mylt in the wall leapt to light, erupting in sickly luminance, seeming to crawl within the stone like worms in soil. The tip of the Auric blade touched Osirys' skin, biting into her. She howled. It gleamed, the runes along the blade matched the hue of the Mylt in the cavern walls and ceiling, and the gems hummed with energy.

Osirys saw a dark bead of blood where the tip of the dagger dug into her flesh, a fingertip's depth into her chest. She tried to kick, flail, or throw herself from the dais, but her domination was complete. Her scream trailed into a whimper. She had known helplessness like this before. She had known fear and dread, and hopelessness of not being able to stop it. It was like a familiar, dark door had opened for her in her mind to retreat to. She had nothing left to fight with. It was all she had. Osirys watched numbly as the orb of Hyara's spirit lit upon the hilt of Pemme's Auric Blade, and tendrils of her essence began funneling into the brightly glowing gems along the pommel, flowing down the length of the blade directly into the core of her being. She exhaled, the last remnant of her defiance slipping through her lips.

"**Y**OU'RE USELESS, YOU KNOW *that right?*"

The tinny voice that came out of the phone speaker was exasperated, and annoyed.

"Like, you wouldn't make it if you didn't have me to get you out of this shit. You know that right? Without me you'd be homeless, or dead."

Osirys didn't respond. She did know that, but she didn't want to believe it. She wanted to believe that she could survive without him. Every time she got the courage to try, though, she wound up exactly where she was now, listening to the same speech.

"You there, Siry?"

"Yeah, yeah I'm here."

"I said you'd be de-"

"I heard you, sorry."

There was a few moments of silence. She knew the words were coming, they did every time, but she hoped they wouldn't.

"Maybe this time you'll learn your lesson."

She let her head fall back against the headrest of her car. The cloth of the ceiling interior hung loose in places. The sagging trim reminded her that she too was undone in spots, barely holding on but visibly worn down. She pulled the visor down and flipped open the mirror. Her lower lip was still puffy and swollen from his last 'lesson'. She touched it softly.

"Yeah," She said. "Maybe."

"Are you being sarcastic? I can just hang up and turn around and you can sleep in your car if you're going to be ungrateful about it."

She hesitated. She could call Lily. Maybe her or Tom could help.

"Let me call you back, my sister's calling," She said.

"Don't you hang up, she can wait."

She didn't know why she did what he said. It was like his voice overruled her, every time. He'd be there before her sister or her brother-in-law would be able to get there anyway. If she told him not to come, he'd be just as likely to show up anyway and then she'd be in a world of hurt when they got home. She better just apologize and play it safe.

"I'm sorry. Thank you, babe. I'm just stressed out. I didn't mean to sound ungrateful."

"Well don't take it out on me," His voice shot back. Maybe she had already gone too far. She felt her face flush. It could be literally anything that set him off these days.

When they met, she found his confidence so alluring. She thought it must have been love. She still thought that way at times. He had a way of holding himself that left no room for debate. It was captivating, in a way. She marveled at his ability to see her mind. After a year or so, though, things *started evolving. Thinking back on it, there was one argument that changed everything. Up until that point, he had kept boundaries. Whether it was intentional or not, she didn't know. Regardless, one night he had told her she needed him to survive. She remembered telling him to never speak like that to her again. It was the first time she had ever really raised her voice at him. She remembered him rising out of the armchair in the living room. She had challenged him, and she remembered feeling like she had crossed a boundary that there was no returning from.*

He stepped forward, towering over her in body and force of personality, taking her face in one of his hands, so that her cheeks were squeezed. She never thought in a million years she would be someone who would allow a man to lay his hands on her in anger, but in the moment, she froze in fear.

"I will speak to you how you deserve to be spoken to." He had said to her. "You don't tell me how to speak. Do you understand?"

She didn't say anything. After that, things were different. It was useless to go through all the details again, like she had so many times before, looking for all the signs she must have missed along the way. She returned her mind to the present, and the silence that hung between the phone speaker and her ear. The parking lot of the plaza where she worked had all but emptied. Her car sat, lifeless, with Osirys inside, feeling similar. She couldn't remember the last time she actually laughed.

"Alright I see you." She heard in her ear before the phone clicked, signaling the end of the phone call.

She turned to see the headlights of his car pull into the lot. He pulled up next to her. Despite everything, she somehow felt safer now that he was there. She shook her head, confused and angry at herself. He got out of his car, and walked around to the front of hers. She rolled her window down.

"Go ahead, try and start it."

She turned the key. They both listened to the faint whirr and clicking of the engine as it didn't turn over.

"It's just your battery. I'll give you a jump."

Of course. She looked at the dial on the dashboard. She had left her lights on that morning when she got to work. She sighed. He had pulled his car around so that it was facing hers, and had retrieved jumper cables from his trunk.

"I'll have to get it tested. We can't really afford a new battery right now Siry."

"I don't think that it's a bad battery. I just noticed, I think I left my lights on this morning."

He stared at her through her windshield.

"Well, that's precisely what I'd expect from you. God, Siry. Sometimes, I don't know how you've managed to get this far."

It was an honest mistake. She wanted so badly to yell at him. She had worked a double shift, taking her coworker's opening shift and working her closing shift as well, trying to bring in a little extra for no other reason than to feel less useless. She was exhausted from the night before which ended in a fight, yet again, leaving her scared and unable to sleep. She knew she had to keep her mouth shut. He did drive a half hour out of his way to help her, after all.

"Are you going to pop the hood or are you just going to sit there?" He asked, irritated.

She was getting flustered. She fumbled with the levers by her knees and opened the trunk and unlatched the hood of the car at the same time. He rolled his eyes at her, opening the hood and disappearing from her sight. She gripped the steering wheel in frustration. She couldn't even place where her frustration should be, and decided it was mostly at herself. She listened to the metallic clicks of the jumper cables being attached. His face appeared from the near side of the hood.

"Give it a shot now," He called.

She turned the key. A wave of relief swept through Osirys as the engine turned and leapt to life.

He nodded, and went about gathering the jumper cables, dropping the hoods of the vehicles back into place. He came back and walked around her car, closing the trunk before leaning into her window.

"Take the long way home so the battery has a chance to charge a bit, okay?" He said.

Osirys nodded.

"Next time, remember to turn off your lights?"

"Sorry," Osirys said, looking him in the eyes, trying to judge his demeanor.

"It's okay, Siry. We had a rough night last night. The least I could do was be your knight in shining armor tonight."

"Yeah." She said, looking away. She hated that he was still charming.

"I'll see you at home?" He asked.

"Yeah, alright." Osirys responded, forcing a smile. "Thank you."

He kissed the pads of his pointer and middle fingers and then pressed them to her cheek, near her slightly swollen lip.

"I would say any time, but let's not make this a habit."

He stepped away and started walking towards his car. She was lost to internal conflict. She clicked the shifter in the console down, frustrated with her own emotions. She let off the brake and looked behind her, but the car didn't go backwards. She realized far too late that she had placed the car in drive, and gasped as her car jerked forward, right into the hood and nose of his vehicle. She felt and heard the crunching of plastic and metal. She slammed on her brake and spun back around, looking forward. He stood looking at her with one hand in the air and one over his mouth, disbelief and anger in his eyes.

It was going to be another long night.

Like a streak of lightning, Osirys saw the wraithlike masked horror leap from its position at her feet and sweep behind Byzzim, bringing its sickles to bear, crackling with energy. Osirys heard the sound of steel on steel, and the noise of something clattering to the stone floor.

She whipped her head to the side, blinking through the tears, disoriented. She heard footsteps and a familiar battle cry:

"*Naivarra,*" She whispered. It was a strange sound that came from her, it was ghostly, imperfect, hollow. Suddenly it was a whirlwind around her. She drifted, swimming in a fugue state of consciousness. She heard voices echoing from nearby but yet they seemed so far away. She watched a shadow pass ever so swiftly over her and then her vision snapped back to perfect clarity as Byzzim's body was tossed away from her, the tip of the Auric dagger ripped from its seat in her chest, sent flying. It was like suddenly awakening from a dream. Troodie lurched to a stop where Byzzim once stood, shoulder down from a full tackle lunge that sent the deranged man sprawling to the hard stone. Troodie glanced at Osirys who still lay abject on the slab, and gave her a reassuring wink, placing a thick, gauntleted hand on her shoulder ever so briefly, before turning her attention back to the man on the ground before her.

"Whatcha think you were gonna do here eh? Whatever it was I don't think it's such a good idea, mister!" Troodie stomped ahead, eyes narrowed and face set in a stern disposition.

Osirys took in her surroundings. The light of the Mylt flickered and sputtered, but the braziers continued illuminating the room, causing her surroundings to be shrouded in spectral flashes. Naivarra and the Vipers had rushed into the chamber and were facing off against the fearsome wraith that spun and darted, wicked sickles flashing with supernatural speed. It lunged and caught one of the Vipers, Olaavi, with the leading edge of one of its cruel weapons, ripping into her side and hooking under her ribs. Viciously it spun and tossed her, screaming, to collide forcefully with the wall of the chamber. Pasea watched as Olaavi impacted and squirmed on the cold stone. She howled, thrown into a frenzy, and leapt forward, weapons flashing in a whirlwind of offensive strikes. Syndal rushed over, sliding and dropping to a knee next to her fallen companion.

"Syn," Olaavi groaned, wincing.

"Peace, Vi. This isn't even the worst you've had." Syndal said quickly.

"It feels pretty close to the worst I've had." She grumbled.

Pasea's fury set the wraith back on a defensive heel. It moved fluidly into a guarded technique, using its long hooked sickles to parry against the flurry of attacks from the small Vamanari. Despite being wildly outnumbered, its stance was flawless. It moved without the encumbrance of gravity, able to switch directions as if it were not bound by momentum. Frustratingly, it seemed to be able to predict where attacks would come from and react, like it knew what its opponents would do before they did. Despite this, it was still losing ground before Pasea's onslaught, supported by Naivarra and the other Vipers.

Osirys rolled off of the slab, finding herself suddenly in control of her body once more. She crashed to the hewn rock floor. Though she could move, it was as if every part of her felt unwieldy, almost alien. She looked about her, and saw the Auric dagger. She scrambled on all fours and grabbed ahold of its hilt, bringing it close to her and backing herself toward the wall. The fighting continued and she watched with horror as the spectral form of Hyara swirled overhead, shrieking. The poltergeist seemed torn, half in this world, half in another, belonging in neither. Her features were distorted, pulled in unnatural directions and twisted almost beyond recognition. Byzzim Roth sat, propped on one elbow, looking up in disbelief.

"NO!" He howled. "The ritual must not be interrupted! Not now! Not after all I've sacrificed!"

Byzzim's eyes didn't leave the phantasmal form of his lost lover as it pulsed and flickered with the Mylt in the walls of the chamber. It sputtered, shooting gouts of light and casting long shadows against the corners of the room. An unearthly wail erupted from the center mass of the ghost, forcing its way through from the netherworld beyond.

"Byzzim, my love! Please!" It called, crackling and echoing across reality. "I can't hold on any longer! I- I- can't…" The voice felt farther and farther away. Byzzim's mouth was agape in abject helplessness, his eyes widened in soundless rage.

"Hyara!" He gasped. "Don't go where I cannot follow-"

The cloaked monster gestured at Byzzim, who was pressed against the walls of the chamber to avoid the barrage of lethal weaponry that spun around and about the cavern hall. It commanded his gaze, and while his eyes burned like coals in deep pits within his skull, he obeyed its call, ducking and dashing between the spears of the Vamanari to the back corner of the room.

The wraith spun away from the onslaught of the Vipers, and as it whirled about, crackling energy hummed what could have been words as it traced an arcane pattern in the air. Then, with its hooked sickles, it cut into the fabric of the space in the room, pulling it aside like a curtain. Osirys couldn't make sense of it. She could only see a glimpse, but it was like she was looking through a glass door at a world that resembled her own but was drained of color.

The emotionless masked wraith thrummed with power, and Byzzim darted, breaking into a run for the arched entryway. Mirabyll ducked low and gave chase, on the heels of Byzzim as he leaped into the rift between realms, instantly vanishing before Osirys' very eyes. The Vaman warrior skidded just shy of the rift, her weapon locking with the vicious sickle of the wraith, its dark cloak billowing as it twisted into the rift and snapping from sight.

As the man and monster vanished, the energy of the specter of Hyara collapsed in on itself and imploded, generating a shockwave through the room, sending all sprawling violently to the hard stone. Troodie and Naivarra landed in a pile near the entrance of the chamber, the rest of the Musefolk tumbled from their feet, head over heels, the clang of weapons against stone as they were thrown from practiced hands. Osirys was already pressed against the far wall of the chamber, and covered her face with her arms as the wave of force reverberated against the rocks. She peeked out to see Mirabyll thrown backwards from the blast, disappearing across the rift in an instant, as the curtain between realities slipped back into place. As they vanished, the light of the Mylt in the walls sputtered out completely, leaving only the light of the braziers flickering in the corners of the room. The only betrayal of the event was a sizzling line on the floor of the chamber. It was barely perceptible, like lines of heat rising from a fire. Osirys and her allies sat, stunned, suddenly alone in the subterranean chamber, overtaken with silence.

Chapter Thirteen

The silence was broken with the sound of Vim scrambling over to the bubbling line of the floor of the chamber.

"If we hurry, we may still be able to follow!" She called eagerly, weapon leveled at the location where the fearsome wraith, the corrupted Auric, and Mirabyll had disappeared. Flembe was already in motion, her weapon back in hand and grim determination in her eyes. She spared merely a momentary glance at their leader before grabbing the other young Viper by the hand and rushing across the threshold, pushing open space aside like a curtain of beads and vanishing instantly.

Pasea lingered on the ground, staring at the popping, sputtering rift. She slowly regained her feet, and walked over to Osirys. Pasea dropped her eyes to her late sister's Auric dagger. Her face held sadness and uncertainty, her lips were tight, the edges of her mouth pursed in anger.

"When were you going to tell me you had lost Pemme's blade?"

"I'm sorry," Osirys began. "I tried to tell you, I swear. He stole it from me that night in Pearlwater Bend at the inn, that man - I didn't know how to tell you then, I was afraid of how you would respond."

Pasea boiled internally, snatching the dagger from Osirys, who flinched instinctively. "You thought this was just some *trinket*, to be discarded? What was I *thinking*, entrusting you with it? I-" Pasea shut her mouth and closed her eyes, trying and failing to force down her emotions.

"My Vipers have bled for you. My sister died-" Pasea's voice quavered.

"We have turned our backs on our persecuted kin and the orders of our Queen," She trailed off. "I thought I had impressed upon you the significance of Pemme's Auric blade-" Pasea had tears forming in the corners of her eyes. "It's all I have left of her now."

Pasea blinked and forced her composure. "Now you see what can happen if it falls into the wrong hands." She finished, quietly. She looked over at the crumpled form of Olaavi, being diligently tended to by Syndal.

"I trust you'll take better care of it now." She dropped the dagger in Osirys' lap, turning from her. Even though sitting upright Osirys was at eye level with the small warrior, Osirys felt minuscule as shame washed over her.

Naivarra stood, sheathing her sword. "If I may-" She began, but was cut off by a fiery stare from the small warrior.

"I'm sure your words are wisdom, Naivarra," Pasea spoke through gritted teeth, "But I have no ear for them right now. It is not the time." Naivarra shrugged.

Troodie sat with her hands in her lap, bemused. "Did I miss somethin'?" She asked innocently.

"Another time, then." Naivarra said, turning from the Vamanari and moving to inspect the rift that still sizzled on the ground nearby.

Pasea had turned her focus to Olaavi and Syndal, seemingly not hearing the question. She assessed the damage to the small warrior by the veiled wraith. The wound was severe. The wicked point of the sickle had pierced Olaavi through her leathers in the upper abdomen on her right side, the curvature of the blade dug under her rib-cage, rending her flesh, causing heavy bleeding, and puncturing a lung. Syndal wore a grim look of determination on her face, sweat beaded up on her forehead. Her field kit was fully deployed, tinctures and salves strewn about the cavern floor in organized chaos. She worked feverishly, using a blend of traditional medical physic that Osirys could understand, enhanced by Auric incantations. Syndal was muttering words in a strange tongue under her breath as her hands moved back and forth, applying medicine and working to slow the thick, dark blood as it gushed from Olaavi, who slumped, pale and covered in sweat against the cavern wall, with gritted teeth. Her eyes were glassy and tremors rolled through her body. Her face was stained with blood and moisture, trickles of bright crimson leaked from the corners of her mouth as she fought off coughing fits. Syndal had cut her clothing and unclasped her armor to access her rent side, her violet cloak stained dark under her where the sanguine fluid pooled.

Pasea stood behind Syndal, careful to not intrude or hinder her in any way, watching her work, hands curled into fists, white knuckled. She kept a kind expression on her face as she looked on over Olaavi, but she clearly felt a great deal of responsibility for the younger Musefolk's injury.

"Pae," Olaavi said softly, a fresh drop of blood running down to her chin as she spoke, "I'm sorry,"

"Peace, Vi," Syndal insisted. She wiped her face with her sleeve, drawing a smear of her companion's blood across her cheek.

Pasea nodded and knelt, taking Olaavi's hand in hers, but didn't speak.

Osirys sat, staring. The Auric dagger still lay in her lap where Pasea had dropped it. There was so much blood. She felt nausea bubble up from deep inside her. She knew that if Syndal did not control the bleeding, and soon, there would be no more battles for the small Vaman warrior. She still reeled from what was only minutes in the past when she felt her soul essence pulled from her corporeal form into the blade that lay innocuously across her folded legs. Something about that experience still smoldered in her chest, as if she could physically feel parts of her that before that moment were indistinguishable. She looked down, at the dagger and the center of her chest and her own crimson wound, like a bulls-eye in her core where Byzzim Roth pressed the tip of the Auric blade into the epicenter of her being, piercing her flesh and soul alike. She wrapped her fingers around the hilt of the dagger. She studied its delicate, runed blade. As she grasped the white polished stone hilt, she swore she saw the runes flash a dim silvery light, similar to the now muted veins of Mylt that ran through the cavern walls and ceiling, but it could have been a glint from the fiery braziers that crackled in the corners of the chamber. Still, there was something different about the Auric blade for her now. She couldn't explain it if she tried, but it felt like as her soul passed through the blade conduit, she felt a flicker of consciousness within it, an attunement that was completely strange yet held a measure of familiarity. It reminded her of Pasea in severity and determination, but more empathetic, and entirely selfless.

Whatever it was, Osirys felt a faint affinity for the blade now, as she turned it over in her hands, and ran her fingers up the hollow channels along the cannelure ridge.

She looked at the trembling Viper bleeding out across the room, and climbed to her feet. She had no idea what she was doing, but she felt like she was being guided. The Auric blade was warm in her hands, and as she held it, she felt a prescience from within the blade, encouraging her to act. It felt like a memory, a bound remnant from a life that wasn't hers. She studied the blade, suddenly terrified.

Osirys slowly made her way towards Syndal and Pasea, who remained with their backs turned to her, and Olaavi, who, by this point, was wholly unaware of her surroundings. The rest of the Vamanari eyed her movements. Troodie raised an eyebrow inquisitively, but didn't speak.

Syndal was covered in Olaavi's blood, and her breath was ragged. She had clearly cast an augury to take as much of Olaavi's pain as she could handle. She was slowly shaking her head. Her vials of Viqua were spent, emptied to the last drop. She frantically rummaged through her belongings, hoping beyond hope that she would find some panacea, but it was in vain. Pasea's eyes were fixed on Olaavi, tears streaked from her face, but she held a warrior's expression. She had seen this many times before. She knew what was going to happen next. Syndal had given it her all, but she was still an inexperienced Auric, and the bleeding was too catastrophic. She had done everything she could and still refused to give up, but it was all but too late. The stout Viper warrior's body refused to give in easily, Olaavi's body still shuddered and heaved for shallow breaths, and her eyes still flashed with flickering consciousness, though the blood in her mouth had begun to foam. Thick, viscous bubbles rimmed her lips, and she coughed and gurgled weakly.

Osirys knelt down beside Olaavi.

"Flame and Shadow!" Syndal gasped, exhausted. "Not now, Harbinger!"

"Osirys," Pasea said softly. "Do not make this harder than it is."

Osirys looked at Pasea, repeatedly opening and closing her mouth. She didn't know what to say, or how to say it, but she knew there was no option to stop. Both Vamanari looked at her with stunned disbelief.

"Osirys, please," Pasea begged. "Move back."

"No." Osirys replied. She held the Auric dagger in front of her, lowering the tip until it rested on the exposed chest of Olaavi. She held her breath, feeling her pulse in her temples racing.

"Harbinger!" Pasea commanded.

A hand landed on Pasea's shoulder. It was Fernip. "Pae-" she pointed over her shoulder. The veins of Mylt in the walls and ceiling had begun to flicker to life once again.

Osirys felt her surroundings, as if she were back in Pearlwater Bend, standing before the Virdi River. She felt the raw, unrefined Mylt surrounding her, pulsing with the current of the Virdi River as it blasted along its course. She felt the anger and hope of the Musefolk, Pasea's rage and tempered resolve, Syndal's exhaustion, Olaavi's pain - and quiet resignation. Osirys gasped and nearly lost her focus. The empathetic experience was overwhelming. She felt the warrior's solemn acceptance of her own end, pushed to the limits of her mortality. Osirys pushed past the feelings and further into Olaavi, feeling her weakening pulse and shallow breathing through the Auric dagger held in her hands. She felt the rhythm of her vitality, the tempo of

Olaavi's synapses firing, the beat of her raw form. She felt the wound in her side like the crashing of a discordant symphony - a cacophony of wrongs that shredded the harmony of her biology, and she reached for it.

She breathed out: "*Zakhaham*".

The word tumbled from her mouth from an origin unknown to her. As soon as it passed her lips, electricity erupted from without and within her. The veins of Mylt in the room glowed with pale light, pouring into Osirys and flowing through the Auric blade, which gleamed with a radiant, white-yellow light. The runes along the blade burned brightly, and the hollow channels of the blade radiated a warmth that rivaled that of the braziers. Osirys directed the energy through her to the multitude of dissonant damage in Olaavi's form. She directed the conflicting rhythms to change, eliminated the grating contradictory elements in the arrangement of her being. She quieted the overpowering, harsh noise of the damage to her flesh, and squelched the aberrant crescendo that rent her inside and out.

It was over in moments. As soon as she had accomplished the inexplicable feat, she toppled backward, utterly drained and spent. It felt as if the pains and uncertainties of everyone in the room rushed in to fill her, beyond overflowing. She was all at once a vessel for their myriad of insecurities, fears, and hurts. She felt her stomach rise within her, and she rolled away, retching onto the cold rock. She heard the Auric dagger clatter to the stone nearby, but not a sound was uttered by any of her companions who gazed on, utterly stunned in disbelief.

O SIRYS FORCED HERSELF UP to her knees, and squeezed tears from her eyes, to look at Olaavi - fear rising in her that she was too late.

The Vamanari warrior slumped against the wall, her chest rose and fell in shallow pace. Her eyes were closed, but a hint of color swept across her cheeks and face. Osirys lowered her eyes to Olaavi's rent side, which still bore a deep wound. The bleeding had all but stopped, the gaping hurt itself was burnt and cauterized, a thin wisp of ozone tinged smoke still curled up and away from her flesh.

Osirys heaved a sigh and swooned, collapsing back to the stone chamber floor, overcome with a tiredness she had never experienced before.

Troodie clapped her gloved hands, standing up and brushing dust from her leathers. "Well wouldn't ya' look at that. If ever ya had any questions about this one here bein' something right special, I think you could just go ahead and put those right to bed, don'tcha think?" She huffed and looked at the small violet cloaked warriors that still stared, wide-eyed in disbelief. She clomped over and stood above Osirys, looking down and smiling.

"I knew you were somethin' special all along!"

Osirys cracked a grin through clenched teeth. "That makes one of us."

Syndal appeared next to Troodie. The two locked eyes for a moment, Troodie's round face and kind eyes were in contrast to the stern Vamanari, whose eyes twinkled with reflected firelight from the braziers. Syndal held Troodie's gaze for several seconds, then turned and looked down at Osirys, who still lay on her back, arms wrapped about her own middle in an effort to suppress any more violent nausea.

"Harbinger- Osirys," Syndal began. Though her face was austere, there was a measure of deference in how she corrected herself, choosing to use Osirys' name instead of the title that she had been given that caught Osirys off guard. "I was wrong to judge you so hastily. What you just performed, and without Viqua - there is no explanation other than that you had been hiding skill far in excess of any Auric I have ever encountered." She extended her hand to help Osirys get back to her feet.

Osirys had no idea what she had or hadn't done. She remembered feeling the guiding hand of something - or someone - 'as she performed the incantation. She couldn't explain how she knew, but in the moment when energy coursed through her and into Olaavi, she felt a measure of kinship to Pasea. She nodded at Syndal and took her hand. Though the Vamanari stood as tall as her hip, she was *strong*. It was seemingly effortless for Syndal to pull her to her feet, even with as little leverage as she had. Osirys turned to Pasea, who kneeled, legs splayed to the sides, holding Olaavi's hand. Her cheeks were wet and glistened in the dancing light.

"Pasea," Osirys said softly, moving over and kneeling down so that their eyes were level.

Pasea turned and smiled through some visible shame, but didn't say anything.

Osirys offered the Auric blade in her hands, palms up. They both stared at it as it flashed with reflected light, no longer glowing of its own accord.

"It wasn't me that did that just now. Well, it was, I suppose, but it wasn't just me. I had guidance. I think it was your sister, Pemme. I felt her in me, and I knew I had to listen to her. She, well, basically did everything. I just thought you should know. I think some part of Pemme is very much still here, in this. You should keep it."

Pasea looked like she was about to fall apart completely. She shook with grief and emotion, but she laughed though her tears. "Of course!" She choked. "How could I possibly believe that death would keep my sister from protecting us, even now?" She rested her hands on the Auric blade, "Pem, you beautiful fool. Leave it to you to rub my nose in my pride, as usual."

Pasea took Osirys' fingers and closed them around the blade, gently pushing it back towards Osyris' chest. "I think we finally understand each other." She said, her voice barely a whisper, looking Osirys in the eyes. "Besides, you obviously will make much better use of this blade than I ever could." She turned back to Olaavi and wiped a few strands of wet hair off her face.

"Thank you," She said, still looking away.

Osirys smiled, but she had no words to say. She stood slowly, still disoriented from the ordeal. Naivarra eyed her with curiosity.

"I don't want to cut this sentimental moment short, but I do not know what kind of augury that was, and don't like it," Naivarra said, sword in hand as she carefully skirted the place where Byzzim and the wraith vanished. "Almost as much as I don't like whatever it was that made it. What was that thing, anyway?"

Pasea chewed on her cheek, crossing her arms. "Fernip, you are well educated on our mythos, please tell me it wasn't what I think it was."

Fernip removed her pack, and started looking through her belongings. She produced a weathered leather bound text. She flipped through the pages with precision, stopping on a page covered in writing and some sparse drawings. "A servant of Pandemonium, beings known as the Pharandi. Servant-kin and lieutenants of shadow, they haven't been seen since the day the Old Empire fell, and never on this side of the Virdi River, unless I'm seriously mistaken."

"By the Furies," Troodie said under her breath. "Pharandi? Here? I thought they were just legend?"

Pasea shook her head. "I'm afraid not. If our kind were created by the Muses as protectors of the Harbingers that would appear in our lands, the Pharandi were created by the dark lords of Pandemonium in response. They were said to be cunning, savage, and without pity or remorse."

"We must make haste to tell the Queen what we have seen here. Not three days from the appearance of the first Harbinger in ages, and we find the foul Risen wandering our shores and lingering in the depths of Shimmermere. What's more, the Pharandi?" She shook her head. "I can only hope her wisdom provides us a path."

Almost as one, the Vamanari turned their heads and considered the sputtering remnant of the rift, and then to Olaavi, who rested peacefully, propped against the stone wall.

Fernip pursed her lips to the side, in reserved contemplation. "If the record is to be relied upon, that breach was a pathway to Pandemonium, a tear in the fabric between our two sister planes. They have not been seen since long ago, when Pandemonium invaded the Old Empire of Eophaetha in the event known as the *Incursion*. The histories say that Eophaetha fell at the height of its power, but few discuss the details." She slowly stood and moved closer to the breach, the only contrast to her voice was its dim sizzling.

"Long ago, the Eophaethan Empire was so vast it spanned the entire world East of the Virdi River. There was learning and culture, and a deep connection to the Gods. There was peace for many, many generations, and all knew nothing but plenitude. When the tides of change finally swept across the land, corruption blossomed and festered in hidden places. The veins of the Empire were too rich with magic and power, and as darkness bloomed, something that should have never happened, occurred. Where the gloaming stifles all light, the wispy edges of Pandemonium caressed our world. The planes crossed, and linked. Thousands of these pathways opened instantly all across the Old Empire at once, and the legions of Pandemonium descended upon towns, garrisons, and homes alike in an instant. There was no war front, there was no army or strike force. The enemy was everywhere, stepping from the shadows as if they'd always been there."

Osirys stared at the diminishing magic. It shimmered curiously, almost innocently. Fernip continued, "Like a torrent, darkness swept across the land, ripping the empire apart at the seams and sewing death and chaos across the realm. Tears and blood mixed on that day. The Emperor was slain, and the immense empire of Eophaetha, largest in all of our known time, fell in one day."

She paused, thinking. "History tells us that evil often follows an Empire's collapse, to lick the syrup of power from the split veins of justice and righteousness, lured by the rotten stench of corruption."

Troodie raised an eyebrow. "You sound an awful lot like my good old Leventus," She said, shaking her head slowly. "Always goin' on about corruption and justice."

"Be that as it may," Pasea sighed. "We need to get Vi out of here, and the platform that granted us passage down has been destroyed. This place is saturated with corruption. Though magic has preserved her life, her wounds will not mend properly here. The foulness of this place will cause her hurts to fester. Not to mention-"

Pasea glanced at her Vipers, three fewer than the number that entered the chamber, the others somewhere in Pandemonium.

The perverse aura that Osirys had felt since descending into Shimmermere had diminished, but not vanished.

What was left of Syndal's field kit had been collected and organized, and she stood, hefting her now substantially smaller pack. She looked exhausted and drained. "We must go."

The Vamanari huddled together, weapons drawn, as they approached the rift. Naivarra stood tall, sword in hand, staring the magical portal down like a hated foe. Troodie pulled a muffin from her pack, breaking off a hunk and handing it absentmindedly to Osirys. "C'mon honey, let's get this party started eh?" She swung her axe up onto her shoulder and trudged forward, the clomping of her heavy boots hauntingly vanishing with her form as she crossed the boundary of the rift, which sizzled quietly, slowly diminishing in size. Naivarra gritted her teeth and bowed her head, squeezing her eyes shut and stepping forward close behind. The Violet Vipers followed quickly, weapons drawn, moving in low, combat ready positions. All except Pasea crossing the threshold, leaving the chamber empty except for the Harbinger and the leader of the Vipers.

Pasea paused just shy of the threshold, turning back toward Osirys.

Osirys stared over Pasea's three foot high shoulder. "Do we even know if there's a way back from Pandemonium?"

"We do not know what we will find, but we have little choice but to find out." She turned and gripped her blade, disappearing from sight.

Osirys trembled, now alone once more in the deep of Shimmermere. She couldn't describe it, but she was horrified; she feared whatever lay beyond that magical curtain. She sucked in air and hesitated. She felt paralyzed, and began to curse herself underneath her breath. She groaned and squeezed her eyes shut, and forced her feet to move. She took several steps, then stumbled. Her sense of balance swam- it was the same feeling as walking down stairs, expecting a final step where there was only flat ground. She felt disoriented, but only briefly. She opened her eyes and turned around.

She saw the room she just left, but it felt fundamentally different, the stone was dull and gray rather than the deep umber of the ones she left. The rock bore deep cracks, and thick, thorny vines sprouted sparsely from the crevasses. She spun, expecting the room to be empty, but her companions were all there, waiting for her to appear out of thin air. It was surreal, she could have extended a hand and touched several of her companions, but it was as if they didn't exist until she crossed over into Pandemonium.

Osirys shuddered, a wave of nausea flooding her senses. She rocked on her heels, putting a hand on the wall to steady herself. It wasn't enough, and she dropped to one knee, reeling. Her stomach rebelled within her, trying to push itself up her throat.

"What is it that you sense, Syn?" Pasea asked, her muscles tensed and body positioned for fighting at any moment.

Syndal shook her head, frowning. "I don't know. Perhaps it is this 'Pandemonium' that sickens us."

"Then we should hope that our presence goes unnoticed until we are rid of this place. Let us employ stealth." Pasea moved to support Olaavi and lift her to her feet, but Troodie stopped her with a hand on her shoulder.

"Don'tcha worry 'bout your friend here, I'll carry her along." Troodie said. Her eyes were soft, and full of concern.

Pasea stalled in thought for a few moments, then slowly nodded.

"Besides, if'n you're gonna try an' go about all quiet like, I'm thinkin' you should keep yourself light. Duarfs are as sneaky as they come, don'tchaknow!"

Naivarra and the Vamanari exchanged looks, as Troodie mimed sneaking gestures and light footfalls, her belongings shifting heavily on her back.

Pasea stepped away shaking her head, while Naivarra chuckled. She looked down the tunnel and seemed to be straining her hearing. "Mirabyll," She said, with a heavy sigh.

"Reckless," Syndal followed, examining the passageway suspiciously.

Wavu called from a few steps down the tunnel. "Pasea," She began.

Pasea turned, looking into the gloaming. She paced for a few moments before speaking, "We will make for the lake. I have faith in Flem and Vim. You all should too."

Syndal frowned. "As you say." She responded flatly.

An uneasy silence enveloped the chamber, the atmosphere felt heavy and oppressive. Osirys moved toward the passageway leading out of the chamber. "Shall we, then?"

Naivarra put her hand on Osirys' shoulder before stepping into the tunnel.

"Stay close, girl."

Osirys smiled. Somehow, Naivarra's touch reassured her, even in the darkest of places.

Chapter Fourteen

Naivarra stepped through the underground tunnel passageway cautiously, weapon drawn. Pasea followed closely, spear shouldered and halfblade drawn and at the ready as she picked their way through the narrow corridor. Syndal and Osirys moved quietly behind. Syndal held a small glass globe into which she channeled an Auric incant, causing it to glow dimly in the gloomy, dark passage, illuminating the way for Naivarra and the others. The remaining Violet Vipers trailed, keeping a close perimeter on Troodie, who carefully carried Olaavi. The feeble light of Syndal's orb was insufficient for Osirys to see anything clearly, but it was better than the absolute blackness that she had endured not long ago. What she could see was indistinct, grayed, and bled of color. There were deep lines in the bedrock of the floor, cracks that felt like they could go to the center of the world. The walls were covered in deep rifts as well, and the same thorny vines that wedged themselves into the crevasses in the cavern where they arrived in Pandemonium clung to survival here as well.

They exited the small passageway that led to what was the underground river, but in Pandemonium, there was no river. It was a dried riverbed. Tumbled, jagged rocks sat exposed. Instead of water, a thick bramble of dark thorny vines knit between the stones, the fleshy stalks of the vegetation were bulbous and bloated looking, as if they had drunk the river completely.

Naivarra had torches with her, but they were soaked from the plunge into the waters of Shimmermere and were now useless. Syndal fed the small dim light steadily, but it was very obvious she was exhausted from her exertion trying to mend Olaavi's wounds.

Osirys had offered to help and Syndal attempted to teach her the illumination technique, but she was once again numb to magic, and wasn't able to reproduce any results. She walked in silence alongside Syndal, ashamed once more of her impotence. Syndal offered no complaint or judgment as usual, and bore the light with a grim look of determination. Though Pasea had offered more rest to the Vamanari healer, she had refused. The feeling of corruption ran thick, and Syndal was adamant that they make all haste to leave the abyss, while her magic held. Osirys felt it too. She couldn't explain it in words, but there was an oppression in the tunnels that grew as they made their way closer and closer to the underground lake. It felt as if the weight of the innumerable tons of rock between her and whatever lay far above were placed directly on her psyche, compressing her thoughts and emotions into hot, dense embers. Her nerves felt exposed to the cold, damp air. She jumped at every uneven footfall from one of her companions, and strained her eyes into the darkness at each muffled sound that bounced off of the cavern walls. Worst were the waves of nausea that rolled over and through her unpredictably, as if they walked through clouds of an undetectable odor that repulsed her and sent her stomach tumbling.

She winced as her insides reeled, rounding a bend in the riverbed. Syndal had paused, and the group stopped moving, turning to look at the two of them. Osirys leaned toward Syndal and whispered, "What is this? Do you know?"

Syndal shook her head slowly. "Aurics are sensitive to the natural magics of this world, for good or for ill. Once attuned to it's workings, an Auric can sense the presence or impact of other Aurics, like fingerprints in the earth left by their magic."

Osirys nodded slowly. "Is that how you found me, in that room?"

The edge of Syndal's mouth curled slightly in what could have been a smirk or smile, "Indeed."

"But you haven't answered my question," Osyris replied.

"Haven't I?" Answered Syndal, "This, corruption, is a fingerprint of magic."

"Of the Pharandi?"

Syndal winced. "No, I don't think so."

"The risen, then?"

Syndal deeply exhaled. "No."

"How can you tell?" Osyris asked.

"It saturates the land, the water, the air. This magic is old. It has been here a long, long time. Perhaps since before the *incursion*."

Silence cloaked the dried riverside, punctuated by the dim trickle of dark water. Osirys felt a shiver run down her spine. She stumbled, and yelped. She couldn't be sure, but it felt like something grabbed her midsection and tugged, ever so gently. Her companions stopped, turning to look at her. She shrugged.

"I thought something touched me." She said, meekly.

Pasea frowned at the noise.

"What could possibly corrupt the roots of the world?" Wavu asked, timidly, moving in to listen to the conversation.

Syndal rested a hand on the young Viper's shoulder. "In Pandemonium, any number of evils. Let us hope we do not find out. This realm holds secrets that none have lived to tell. Let's away before we become unfortunate enough to gain that knowledge." She began walking again.

Syndal was anything but reassuring. Her cryptic responses were vexing to Osirys, and terrifying. She felt a seed of fear sprout within her. It wasn't just a feeling any more. Every time she felt a pulse of toxicity well up and wane within her, she was reminded that it came from *something* lurking in the blackness beyond.

The tunnel opened up as they rounded the bend in the river, revealing the shore of the vast underground lake of Shimmermere, mirrored nearly perfectly in the dim of Pandemonium - the lake was black glass in a lightless cavity in the bowels of the world. Syndal's feeble light could not reach the height or the breadth of the underground lake, but it's stillness was palpable. Beyond the ripples of where the water drained into the tunnel, there was no motion.

Syndal knelt and quietly chanted. Beads of sweat formed on her brow and dripped down her face and nose. Her light grew in intensity, though it taxed her dearly. It became a vibrant beacon, but only served to reveal more of the true size of the lake. The expanse was vast, and featureless. Against the backdrop of obsidian, the water reflected a perfect inverted double of the expansive cavern. The remains of what could have been an ancient structure lurked in the shadows near the edge of the side of the lake they were on several hundred yards further along the shore, a long decayed rope dropping limp into the water from a series of what appeared to be stone pylons.

"Buildings here?" Wavu asked, turning towards Pasea.

"In Pandemonium, this world mirrors the one we know. Where there are structures there, they are made here as well. None know how this occurs, whether there are shadows of ourselves in this realm that follow our actions, or something equally strange. It is a mystery." Pasea replied.

"Look!" Wavu exclaimed, pointing down the shore of the lake. Two small figures moved along the shoreline towards them.

"It's Vim and Flem!"

Pasea's relief was audible as she sighed. The two Musefolk moved with speed along the coast of the underground lake towards them. As they arrived, Flembe and Pasea embraced briefly.

"We tried to find Mira," Flembe said, frowning. "The few tracks we could find end at the shore over there, where we found these." She removed a pair of short blades and two halves of a broken Vaman Spear.

"No," Syndal whispered. "Damnit, Mirabyll."

The Vipers exchanged looks. "We cannot afford to take a long time in the effort, but the effort must be made. Wavu, Fernip, head round the lake and see if you can find any more trace of Mirabyll. We can't just abandon her to the darkness of this place."

The two Vipers nodded eagerly and moved off immediately, disappearing within moments into the gloom.

Pasea paced for several minutes. She seemed to be fighting a battle internally. Syndal sat nearby, hunched over a piece of vellum. She dipped a quill into a small inkwell that balanced in between a pair of fist-sized stones and scratched away noisily, her face scrunched as she focused. She glanced up from time to time, as if she were making sure none of the others were spying on her authorship.

Osirys found a spot to sit as well. She slumped against a smooth patch of stone bordering the shore of the dark lake. She jumped when she felt Naivarra's hand on her knee.

"Peace, girl, it's a friend."

Osirys bowed her head. "Why?"

Naivarra regarded the smaller woman. "Kind of a broad question," She responded.

"Why are you here?" Osirys asked.

Naivarra looked offended.

"I mean, I can never thank you enough for pulling me from the river and for all you've done since. Why do you do it, though? What were you doing before this that was so bad that you'd literally rather be in hell with me?"

Naivarra thought for a moment, picking some dirt from under her fingernails, considering avoiding the question. "I was a soldier."

Osirys let Naivarra take her time.

Naivarra hesitated again. Osirys almost changed the subject, thinking that was as much as she was going to get, but to her surprise, Naivarra continued.

"I was a squad commander for Lord Naros, third in line for regent of Aefemar, one of the core cities. We were campaigning along the Eastern border, land disputes with Eshilar, another of the core cities. I was a year off from becoming an officer, actually."

"What happened?" Osirys asked.

"We met an Eshilari contingent just East of Mathoras' Crossing, we were technically in their territory, looking to grab some acres of farmland and claim a small township. We were lined up on the field, just as day was breaking. We easily outnumbered our enemy. Their defense of the township was barely a formal one, truth be told. Given the chance, the soldiers would likely have let us walk in and occupy to avoid the fight. Just before the horns, one of my scouts reported a caravan was sighted on the southern road. It looked to be a slaver wagon full of merchandise."

"Vamanari," Osirys whispered under her breath.

Naivarra nodded, and continued. "Slavery is still very much illegal in the core cities, you know. More and more the nobles and lords are turning blind eyes to that dark world, and there is plenty of cause to believe that some of the more powerful members of the court are actually funding the whole thing. Anyway, I approached Lord Naros with the intelligence. As part of the King's army, it was supposed to be our duty to enforce its laws, which would very much have included dismantling the caravan and at the very least arresting the slavers. I was told my orders were to remain ready for combat against Eshilar, despite our manpower advantage."

Naivarra stretched her legs and slapped her knees lightly.

"The caravan wound up driving right through the battlefield, smiling and waving as they passed. Both sides, Eshilari and Aefemar waited until they had moved on to begin fighting for a 'noble cause'."

Naivarra shook her head, and there was a long pause. "So I deserted."

Osirys continued listening.

Naivarra breathed a heavy sigh. "I had planned to go to Geagana and find mercenary work. The Outland cities aren't as regulated by the Empirate, it's too remote. Considering my rank, it was possible that they would come looking for me, though. If that happened, I thought I might find my way to Eophaetha, join a treasure hunter's guild."

"Truth be told, I had fallen out of love with fighting. Or at least I thought I had anyway. The adrenaline, the rush, all of it. It had become almost sickening to me. Turns out, it wasn't fighting that I fell out of love with. It was that I didn't love what I was fighting for. I learned that the day we met. Despite all the bloodshed, it was the first time I felt alive in years."

Naivarra glanced at Osirys, leaning into her for a heavy nudge.

"I guess you could say that you saved me in a way."

Osirys and Naivarra sat in silence for several minutes. Troodie was occupied looking after Olaavi while Pasea paced impatiently. The other Musefolk had taken up defensive positions nearby. Without light, the stillness of Pandemonium Shimmermere was frightening. It felt like there was a static charge in the atmosphere. All the while, Osirys wrestled with an impalpable sickness that hung in the air like a poisonous vapor.

"Yeah," Osirys finally said. "I still hate this place."

Naivarra smirked in the dark. "Me too, girl. Me too."

Fernip and Wavu returned without pomp or fanfare some time later. It was obvious by the low voices and bowed heads that they had found no trace of Mirabyll. Pasea boiled internally, fists clenched. She held herself in control, but just barely. It was the kind of anger that had no direction, no objective, but still Osirys could see she blamed herself. Osirys knew what that felt like.

"The good news, is that it seems that all hope is not lost. Look, yonder," Wavu pointed into the darkness.

Osirys followed her gesture out into the center of the lake. Ever so dimly, Osirys could see something that resembled the lift that had brought them into the depths not long ago. It was far away, but she could just make it out. Thick ropes extended upwards into the blackness above. She hadn't dared let herself feel hope since she awoke in the dark tunnels. Judging by the distance that they had walked, Osirys must have been out for quite some time before regaining consciousness on the riverside alone. She wondered how long her companions had looked for her, and how long she had laid helplessly in the depths, and what aberrations she may have encountered without even knowing it.

"How are we going to get there?" Osyris asked meekly.

"The same way we got here," Naivarra said in a gruff tone, affixing her sword into its scabbard on her back and removing her pack. She began to unclasp her armor and roll up the fabric on the legs of her trousers, "Except this time, I'm not going to be wearing armor the whole way."

The vipers removed their cloaks too, and began rolling and stowing them. Osyris looked out over the vast lake, the island could have been a hundred yards or a half a mile away, there were no features to help judge the distance. "We're going to swim?"

"Unless you can fly," Naivarra chuckled, sarcastically.

"Now wouldn't that be somethin'," Troodie giggled. "After all I've seen today, I wouldn't even be surprised."

Naivarra rolled her eyes, but couldn't help but smile at the stout woman.

"I mostly just float," Troodie continued. "Us Duarfs are very, very buoyant, don'tchaknow. We tend to avoid the water anyway, though."

"Even with that weapon of yours?" Wavu laughed.

"Armor and all!" Troodie said, beginning to wade in along the shoreline, sending ripples across the still surface of the lake.

Despite Troodie's antics, Osirys gnawed her lip. Her eyes were fixed on the black depths of Shimmermere. Her companions had begun to follow Troodie into the inky water, but she couldn't move. She tried to block it out, but she envisioned herself exhausted and disoriented, fighting to keep afloat. Unable to find land and totally spent in the darkness, she saw herself slipping below the calm surface without as much as a ripple, never to be seen again.

"Come on, girl." Naivarra urged, sensing her reluctance and snapping her out of her own anxieties. "It's either swim or stay down here." She trudged ahead and sloshed her way into the lake. Osirys felt something brush against her leg as Naivarra passed. She jumped, but quickly realized it was a small cloth sack, presumably left by the strong fighter. Puzzled, she picked it up, turning to Naivarra to alert her that she had dropped it, but Naivarra was already looking over her shoulder with her familiar sly smirk.

"It's for your shiny boots," She called out over her shoulder.

Syndal remained behind as well, panting and hunched, sweat streaming down her face.

"Will you be alright?" Osirys asked.

Syndal's face snapped back to its usual dour visage of determination, as if Osirys saw something she wasn't meant to. In that moment, Osirys realized that exhaustion and the intense perversion of the lake weren't exclusively what afflicted the small Auric. She was in intense pain. Osirys looked out and saw Troodie, floating like a small raft, with the even smaller body of Olaavi atop her belly to keep her from the water, still peacefully asleep.

Osirys snapped her head back to Syndal, who met her eyes. Syndal's large reflective orbs were wet and she was quivering; she could see Olaavi's suffering written clearly in Syndal's eyes, even in the gloom. Syndal nodded slowly, but said nothing, moving toward the lake with beleaguered purpose. She held the illuminating orb aloft in one hand as her small form was quickly enveloped by the dark waters.

Osirys felt herself weaken. The small spit of land seemed so tiny and remote. The vast unknowable depths waited threateningly between her, now alone on the shore and the tiny lump of rock. Air hissed from between her teeth as she clenched her jaw. Naivarra was right. It was either swim, or stay.

THE WATER WAS *COLD*. It was as frigid as it was black, like obsidian ice that sent shockwaves up Osirys' legs as her toes curled and recoiled from the lake.

Swim, or Stay. She repeated to herself. She had removed her boots and stowed them in Naivarra's cloth bag. She thought about those boots - the boots that were given to her by the kind cleric Morvrel in Pearlwater Bend, whose previous owner had lost his young life in darkness. She remembered his words, which now felt like mockery: *'Perhaps his boots will guide you on a lighter path.'*

She shook her head and forced herself to move. She followed the dim, bouncing orb that slowly but steadily crept away from the shore. The slope was gentle for the first few yards, but then it dropped off steeply, and within a few moments, Osirys was up to her waist in the frigid water. A few more, and the floor of the lake dropped away completely, leaving her treading water. She breathed heavily and began to swim, her eyes locked on the one point of light in the immense dusk of the underworld of Pandemonium.

The water sapped her strength, drawing heat from her body. She focused on breathing and moving. The small spit of land did not seem to draw closer as the minutes drew on. She labored and her clothing dragged on her. The small orb of light bobbed ahead of her, ever so slowly. Osirys wanted to cry for Syndal, swimming while holding the light aloft, and bearing the agony of her wounded kin. She focused on that light. Minutes crawled by. Osirys' breath came in ragged gasps. Her arms ached and her muscles screamed, the cold of the water tore at her, freezing her joints and cramping her sinew. '*Swim, or Stay,*' she repeated to herself, sputtering.

She thought the land might have been getting perceptibly closer, until the light up ahead, Syndal's small orb, began to sputter and falter. It started as a slight dimness, but soon it was clear that the small Violet Viper was failing, her light sometimes dipped below the surface of the water, and sometimes its light flickered and then extinguished altogether, plunging her into complete darkness. Her breathing quickened and she began to panic. Suddenly, the depths below her became that much more threatening, and the darkness pressed in upon her like the weight of the land above. Osirys could hear the sound of splashing somewhere ahead, but the sound bounced off of the high ceiling and walls from every direction, making it seemingly come from all directions at once. She was instantly disoriented, unable to discern which direction was correct. She spun in the water, trying to orient herself to the sounds of her companions, but it was useless. She treaded water, exhaustion growing with each passing moment.

She envisioned her arms and legs fighting to their last, until they could not keep her above the water, until she slowly slipped under the black frigid lake, never to be seen again in the lightlessness of Pandemonium. She tried to cry for help, gasping and taking on water, sending her chest into spasms and her nearly frozen limbs to falter. Her head dipped below the surface of the water and she began to sink.

Her clothes were too heavy. Her chest burned for air, her arms and legs wouldn't listen to her, now that they had stopped they refused to start again. She gave some feeble kicks, bringing her face to the surface for a gasping cough and a gulp of air before she dipped back down. She was drowning. She opened her eyes, expecting to see a blackness below her, a never-ending nothingness that would swallow her whole and keep her entombed for all time. What she saw was so, so much more terrifying. A massive, deep red eye glowed far below her, staring upward. The redness of the outside of the eye brightened to a fiery orange that surrounded a yellow slash of a pupil, which eagerly twitched back and forth. She screamed under the water, the last bits of air in her body bubbling out and back towards the surface. Her fear ignited her limbs once more, and she thrashed, surging upward.

She broke the surface of the water and gasped. Nausea rolled through her from below. She felt at once empowered by the adrenaline coursing through her veins, and sickened by the overwhelming torrent of corruption, rising from below her. That was why Syndal's light went out. It was all Osirys could do to endure the perversion of nature that pulsed from the depths below. She cried for help and began kicking franticly. She had no way to know which way she was headed. All she knew was that she had to get out of the water as fast as possible.

"Below! Below us!" She hollered into the emptiness around her. She didn't know if her companions could hear her. She didn't know if they were alive. For all she knew, the monster below her could have engulfed them in all manners of unnatural appendage and dragged them to the depths.

A ripple of light rolled through the rocks of the cavern above, moving down the walls into the opaque waters. It was the light of Mylt, gray and corrupted, thick veins of ore pulsed almost biologically, the light being drawn into the depths. The waves came in slow pulses that began to speed up, increasing slowly in frequency.

"Osirys!" She heard from somewhere behind her. It was Naivarra's voice. She spun, but the echoing chamber confused her again mere moments after the brief instant of clarity. She took her best guess and pumped her legs and arms, surging forward.

"This way!" Naivarra's voice called out again. It was faint, and somewhere to her left. She corrected her course and heaved air. She dared not look down. Her exhaustion was thrown from her as her fear took over, the cold was no less painful but it no longer hindered her.

"That's it! Keep going!" Naivarra's voice was audibly closer. She kicked for her life. The pulsing of the Mylt in the walls had quickened to the point where one wave had already begun before the last had disappeared into the darkness of the water below. The flashes built to a crescendo and then extinguished, plunging the lake back into full darkness. Moments later, she felt and heard a dull boom from below and the water began to boil around her; she felt vibrations around and through her form. An impossibly low tone filled her body, so much that she didn't hear it as much as she felt it. The walls trembled with the call from below, and the glassy still water erupted in standing waves that moved only as the pitch of the tone slowly rose and fell. The sound punished Osirys' insides, the intensity of the vibrations stunning her and pummeling her from all directions, dozens of times per second. Her nausea leapt up within her. She tried to cover her ears, which had no effect on the intensity of the sound, but the water eagerly dragged her down as soon as she stopped pushing herself up and forward. She squeezed her eyes closed and forced herself to move again, despite the acoustic fusillade. She broke the surface of the water once again. If anyone called for her, she could not hear it. All she could experience was the cold of the water and the sonic assault from the submerged terror below.

She pumped her legs and forced down the bile in her throat. She fought for breath, water mixing with air in every heave. Her lungs shuddered as she coughed and her diaphragm leapt into spasms. Still she fought on, impossibly as she struggled in the dark. She thrashed and pushed, the uneven surface of the water washing over her face and head as she battled aimlessly. Her hand struck something soft and she shrieked when it closed around her forearm, attempting to yank free.

"Gotcha." It was Pasea's voice that cut through the droning din. The small Vamanari's strength caught Osirys by surprise. One arm wrapped under her arm and clamped near her collarbone. Pasea swam on her side, keeping Osirys' upper body locked in place on top of hers, supporting her head and shoulders above the water. Her small legs kicked vigorously - Pasea's strength and endurance amazed Osirys.

Osirys kicked weakly to help propel them forward. She gazed back behind, into the darkness, anticipating horrors that she knew were there but could not see. It wasn't very long until Osirys felt her feet bump against rock. It startled her at first, knowing what stirred below. The eerie tone had subsided as Osirys dragged herself up onto the rocky spit of land, still breathing heavily, but it was replaced by a new sound. The sound had created standing waves which disturbed the entire underground lake, the surface now tossed and clashed noisily.

Osirys began to shiver again, her soaked billowy tunic clung to her form restrictively. She heard her companions clamoring about her. She called out for Syndal, "Syn, Syn are you alright?"

She didn't immediately get a response. "Syndal!" She shrieked.

"Peace, Harbinger." Syndal was nearby. Her voice was weak, almost groggy sounding.

Naivarra stumbled around somewhere close by. "Damn this infernal darkness!"

"Here!" Troodie called. "A lever!"

Osirys heard the sound of straining, and the mechanical motion of gears thrust into reluctant motion. Miraculously, the ropes began to roll through their pulleys.

Silence fell over the rocky crop. Suddenly, a deep vibration like the sound of an immense drum rumbled from below, and from above them, another pulse of light flickered in the ceiling and walls. The veins of Mylt in the rock of the cavern shone, running like a wave down the walls from the top of the cavern down into the water, draining toward the deep core of the lake.

"Pasea-" Naivarra began, stern voiced. Osirys stared out into the blackness surrounding them. A pulse of Mylt-light rolled into the lake below the surface. It was interrupted by thick black tendrils that crept upwards from the deep.

Another pulse of light rolled down the cavern wall. A hundred yards from the shore of the small island, a hooked and lethal looking appendage broke the surface of the water silently, reaching its way up from the pit of the lake. Even in the dusky light, Osirys could see thousands of fang like hooks on the underside of the fleshy mass - and *eyes*. Tiny, glowing orange dots lined the center of the appendage, and they dilated and moved independently, twisting about in their fleshy pockets soundlessly. Osirys wanted to scream, but it was frozen in her chest, her lungs trembled helplessly.

"Vipers, attend!" Pasea called, calmly. Osirys caught the flash of steel as Pasea's blade was suddenly in her hand.

Naivarra growled and pulled her sword from its scabbard. The clattering of the gears and pulleys on the ropes echoed through the cavern.

Tense moments passed, more and more tendrils appeared from all directions around the small island, hundreds of tiny orange eyes affixed upon them. Out of nowhere, Pasea whirled and her blade descended, connecting wetly with something near her feet. Instantly, the ground reeled as a detonation rolled upwards from below, and a concussive bulge broke in the center of the water, sending a large wave rolling outward, toward the island. The other Musefolk, Troodie, and Naivarra looked downward as one. Osirys followed their lead, and yelped. Small, wet, fleshy tendrils crept from the waterside towards them. Blades flashed, and Osirys scrambled backwards.

The wall of water sped towards the island, eight or more feet high and growing as it approached. Illuminated only by the flashes of light from the activated Mylt within the walls of the chamber, Osirys only caught freeze-frames of the approaching lake-tsunami as it barreled towards them. It only took moments before they were overcome. The water crashed over the island in a torrent, blasting across the rocks with tons of force. Osirys wrapped her arms around one of the pulleys and buried her head in her arms to endure the onslaught. The water smashed into her, throwing her body backwards. Her arms screamed, her left shoulder took the brunt of the force of the impact, pulling her arm out of its socket and wrenching her from side to side. She howled in agony but held steadfast. It passed as swiftly as it came, rolling over the island and continuing its destruction on through the lake. Osirys sucked in air and screamed again. She opened her eyes. Several of the Vipers had been blasted off the island and were swimming as fast as they could to try to get back to solid land. She heard a yell from behind her. She twisted her head to look and a stinging sharp pain shot through her. Syndal had been washed away by the wave, and now yelled – she was firmly entwined in an oily black, thick appendage that lifted her from the water.

Osirys called out and Naivarra ran, sword lashing out at a dozen or more smaller feeler appendages as they attempted to block her passage. Osirys watched as the hooks of the large appendage that grabbed Syndal dug into the flesh of her body and legs. She screamed and struggled, but she could not wrench free. Naivarra slashed her way into the threatening lakeshore, up to her chest in the black water. Several appendages wrapped around her arms and legs. She tore away from each one that assaulted her, severing it with her blade. She fought her way to the thick thorned arm and bellowed, sweeping her immense sword through the air, its edge singing loudly as it bit deeply into the flesh of the appendage, releasing a spray of inky viscera that showered Naivarra. She pulled her blade free and spun on her heel, even impeded as she was in the water, pivoting the blade and landing an equally devastating cut to the other side of the tentacle, cutting through it clean to her first attack, severing it completely. A shrill noise emanated from the appendage as it toppled, dropping Syndal unceremoniously from her height into the water below, still wrapped by the vicious arm.

Osirys watched Naivarra plunge into the black water after the Vaman Auric, and then screamed as she felt a line of stinging hooks against her left calf and thigh. Her scream was stifled as the hooks bit deeply into her flesh and hauled on her, pulling her backwards, away from the pulleys and across the sharp rocks. The force was unimaginable, and Osirys felt as if she were a minnow caught in the net of a fisherman. She managed a quick breath before the black water overtook her and she was dragged deep into the ice cold abyss.

ONCE THE SHOCK OF the event had passed, she found herself speeding downward. She fought the help-lessness that surged within her - From somewhere deep in her mind she recognized the blackness within as keenly as the blackness that surrounded her in the frigid depths. She felt the familiar sting in her core, the paralyzing fear of having lost all control, a strangely comforting cocoon of loss of agency, where she was no longer the one responsible for her fate. In some ways, she felt like she was back on the stone slab, under the domination of the Pharandi, but there was a very, very important difference. Where that domination was absolute and complete - as if she were a mere observer to her corporeal form, she now could act, she had the ability to strive against the power that controlled her. Her fate was still by some measure, hers. She clutched ahold of that mote of self preservation and fed that ember, nurturing it into a flame for survival. She grabbed ahold of the appendage that rent her flesh and wrenched on it, digging her nails into it and ripping and tearing at it, to no effect. She didn't think about the amount of air in her lungs, she didn't think about the cold, or the mounting pressure of the depths compressing her body and her skull. Realizing that she wasn't making any progress, she changed tactics.

She remembered the Auric Blade tucked into her belt. A moment of hope was immediately followed by a moment of fear - she prayed that it still remained, and wasn't shaken free in the moments leading up to her current crisis. Her hands went to her belly, and found its sturdy hilt. She gripped it in both hands and pulled it free. The pressure of the water kept building. Her ears rang and even though her eyes were squeezed shut, she saw stars bursting in the corners of her vision like fireworks. She was running out of time.

She snapped her midsection downward and plunged the tip of the dagger deep into the flesh of the hooked limb - She felt a hot rush of fluid push by her hands. This was a matter of life and death. She twisted and wrenched the blade, removing it and stabbing again repeatedly. Four, five, six impaling blows, but still its grip did not relent. She was desperate. She grabbed ahold of the hooks that still held fast to her and pulled herself downward along its length and wrapped a portion of the appendage in her legs so she could keep a solid hold. In a tangled knot she descended. She opened her eyes. The maw of the fiend burst into view, its glowing eye was massive before her. She couldn't afford to be stunned now. She gritted her teeth and set to work. She plunged the blade into the arm and began sawing like she was slicing a watermelon, working around the center. She felt the cords of the muscles of the limb break and snap as she worked. Black fluid streamed from its wound thickly like ink. She didn't stop. She felt its grip soften and she doubled down, biting and thrashing as she rent its flesh with the blade. With an audible rip, the limb came free, though the hooks remained embedded deep in her leg. She stopped descending. She looked at the creature, immense and organic, its thorned form spreading out in all directions. She realized the spiked vegetation in the tunnel were not vines - they were the limbs of this monster, extending through the depths of this otherworldly version of Shimmermere.

There was a portion of her that was amazed and intrigued, and wished to linger, but her body would not allow it. She kicked through her agony and shot upwards, her buoyancy propelling her into the blackness above. She had no idea how far down she was or how long it would take to get to the surface. Her lungs screamed in agony, the exertion of freeing herself from the beast had spent most of her muscular reserves, and she fought against the automatic urge to inhale. Her vision darkened even further, bright spots danced along her field of view. She had come this far. Naivarra's words echoed in her mind: *"Swim or stay."*

She forced her body to go beyond its limits, her legs kicking when they had no strength, her arms clawing the water when they had no endurance, her heart pumping when it had no oxygen. Fear and survival was all she knew. She couldn't spare a thought to revel in her victory against the monster, she didn't think about the thousands of other grasping clawed limbs that searched the waters for escaped prey. She saw flashes of light that could have been induced by lack of air, or the Mylt in the rocks, but a concussion ripped through the medium of water around her, blasting the air from her lungs and tumbling her, surging upward. She immediately lost consciousness.

"Now, this is familiar." Naivarra's voice floated as if in a bubble from another reality. "Come on, girl, breathe."

Osirys felt compressions on her chest, but couldn't force her diaphragm to work. She pushed against it, trying to throw herself into a spasm, a cough, anything. She felt air fill her lungs, but it wasn't her own. Her consciousness flickered, and different parts of her body ignited sporadically with sensation. She wanted to try, but she was spent, broken. She hadn't the strength or the willpower to fight any more. She wanted rest.

"Come on, girl. Don't do this now." It was so far away, drifting across a sea to register in the muddy neurons that still struggled for life. She felt lips on hers again, and felt her chest rise and fall. She felt her ribs crack from a forceful impact, but there was no pain. She felt herself drifting away.

And then there was a presence. It was warm, it was bright. It filled her veins and her mind. She felt a willpower that wasn't hers push against her heart, her chest, her lungs. It squeezed the chambers of her core, pushed blood through her veins, expanded her chest, and forced air mixed with water through her lungs. She felt something familiar and alien. Without knowing how, she knew it was Syndal. She felt Auric magic run through her body, forcing it to function. It was both miraculous and terrifying. It was at the same time saving her life and betraying every cell of her being.

She rebelled instinctively, and her consciousness leapt aflame. A spasm rolled through her core and she coughed, spewing water out her mouth and nose. Immediately, the invasion vanished as swiftly as it came.

"Syndal, what have you done?" Pasea's voice echoed. She fought her way towards consciousness

"In absence of Viqua, Auric's blood may substitute…" Syndal's faint reply barely registered, *"I did what I had to."*

Osirys coughed as hard as she could. She feared what she knew. In those moments, their minds and consciousnesses linked. Syndal had gone too far. Osirys leapt from her stunned stupor, rolling and howling, "No! Syn!"

Her vision rolled and she couldn't focus. She clawed her numb and unresponsive hands towards the small Auric. She realized she was on a platform, slowly ascending, but it was of no consequence. All she wanted to focus on was Syndal.

The small Auric sat slumped against a support rope, Pemme's Auric blade plunged deep into her chest, covered in blood. Her arms and legs were rent, flesh hanging in strips from where the massive limb had grabbed and gored her earlier. She was pale and quivering. Blood trickled from the corner of her mouth, and her hands were slick with her own life.

Osirys sputtered, still expelling water from her lungs. She could barely think, but she had to try. She grabbed the hilt of the Auric blade and squeezed her eyes shut; tears streamed from her face. She called out, searching for the rhythm of the world around her, she reached blindly for the power of the Mylt that ran through the walls. She groped in the darkness of the unseen world around her for the door to Auric power. She had no idea what she could possibly do, but she had performed a miracle before, she could do it again. She floundered, in half consciousness, between a surreal world bordering on eternal death and the calamity of willingness to sacrifice everything for another. She called out, it may have been internally, it may have been a mumbled yell, but there was no response. She tried to recall the moment when she and Naivarra stood atop the cliffs near Pearlwater Bend, but it was too murky, her mind wouldn't obey her will. She squeezed the handle of the blade, begging for any response.

"Pemme, if you're in there, please," she whispered. *"I can't do this on my own,"* Osirys gasped for breath; her vision swam, and her muscles quavered. She was still sputtering and coughing, her lungs half full of water.

"Please!" Osirys cried out, her voice hoarse. She tried to pull more air into her chest, but her ribs screamed in pain.

She opened her eyes, losing hope. Syndal's eyes were open, gazing deeply at her.

"Harbinger - Osirys, peace." Syndal whispered. "I was beyond help before I chose this path. I do not regret..." She trailed off, closing her eyes and swallowing hard.

"You will find your way. I believe you are here for a reason. We will all need you before the end." Syndal opened her eyes and forced a smile.

For the first time, Osirys saw her soft face as young and inexperienced. Osirys cradled Syndal's head.

"Syn, I need you. There's so much you need to teach me," She whispered.

"You will find your way," Syndal said, clutching Osirys hands. The blood seeping from her wounds had slowed to a trickle. She turned her head, suddenly aware of how little time she had left.

"Pae," She sputtered.

Pasea knelt by Syndal's side, severe look on her face. "I'm…"

Syndal's words faded, and the darkness of Pandemonium washed over the platform, the slow clacking of the ropes and pulleys rhythmically reminding the group that the world still existed.

It felt like eternity on the lift. Despair gripped Osirys. She failed. She had no idea how long she sat, holding Syndal's body. She couldn't even think about the horrors she had endured. If she had been different, if she had been better, she could have saved the small warrior. She knew she could have. She had the opportunity, but she didn't come through when it was most needed. She sat in silence. Pasea sat nearby, knees to her chest. Osirys couldn't look her in the eyes.

It could have been minutes or hours that they all sat in silence. The dim glow of Mylt illuminated the platform ever so slightly, colorless as it all was. Even Troodie remained quiet. Osirys looked to Naivarra, who knelt, head bowed, sword across her lap. The creaking of the platform changed and slowed, eventually coming to a stop. Pasea stirred first.

"We cannot linger," She said softly. "Naivarra, Troodie," She moved close to Osirys, holding out her hand. "We cannot linger."

Osirys nodded, wiping away spittle and snot from her face on her sleeve.

"There will be time for mourning once we have found our way out of this horrible place. Syndal's sacrifices will have been for naught if we all perish in this dark, miserable hole."

Pasea met Osirys' eyes as she helped her stand. There was a sadness in her large orbs that Osirys could feel. Her words may have seemed callous, but it was very clear that Syndal's death wounded her as deeply as any blade could. She was right, though. They were still in Pandemonium, and more than just the ancient creature of Shimmermere lurked in the shadows. Other aberrant monstrosities could be in any shallow crevasse, waiting to ambush the exhausted and wounded fighters.

For the first time since regaining consciousness, Osirys looked at the other Vamanari. They were stern, but frayed. They hid their emotions behind visages of practiced discipline, but they were haggard, beyond exhausted, with a myriad of hurts. Troodie held Olaavi, who no longer rested peacefully, but was rigid with pain, and vaguely awake. Syndal's incantation had ended in the deep, and she no longer bore the wounded warrior's pain. Osirys wished she could step in and do what Syndal couldn't, but she now stood, impotent, wounded, and useless in the dark of Pandemonium.

She tried to take a step and faltered. The nerves in her leg were aflame. She yelped and grabbed ahold of Naivarra's shoulder, leaning heavily. The warrior was caught unawares, but quickly stabilized, grabbing ahold of Osirys and steadying her. Osirys looked down, for the first time taking in the damage that had been done to her leg by the ancient monster of the deep. Her knees buckled and she nearly toppled. Her leg was swollen and bulging; deep gouges rent through her trousers, and her pale flesh was exposed in several places, deep wounds dotted her thigh and calf, and her pant leg was soaked in blood. What was even worse, however, was the fetid ooze that seeped from the wounds, some measure of venom had pocketed itself under her skin in spots, and the wounds had responded, already beginning to fester.

Naivarra looked down as well and gasped. "Pae," she started. "She needs the healing of your people – we haven't the skill here."

Pasea's frustration was palpable. "Don't you think I *know* that?" She growled. "Even if we find a way to escape Pandemonium, which isn't a certainty, we're still two weeks travel by horse from Eidrdyhn."

"Is that so?" Came a deep voice from the darkness.

The Vamanari reacted as one, instantly in low positions, weapons leveled at the dark tunnel before them.

Pasea held both half blades and stood in front of Naivarra and Osirys, her large eyes smoldering with a flame that desired violence, longed for vengeance for her fallen brethren.

"Come closer, and taste Vaman steel," She threatened in a low tone. Naivarra limped forward as well, wielding her oversized blade in her off hand. Her sword arm hung limply, bound in a makeshift splint.

A dim light grew in the darkness ahead, a glowing orb appearing a dozen or more yards into the tunnel beyond. An old man shuffled into view, thick patterned robes wrapped about him.

"An odd place to find weary travelers in need, I would think," He mused, looking around at the darkness.

"I assure you, I mean no harm to you and your companions, young Va'amirin."

Pasea kept her guard, but softened instantly. "You know the old tongue. Whom do you serve?"

"I am Embraer, of the Silver Cord."

"A Planeswalker, here?" Fernip asked, eyeing the man suspiciously.

"Our order felt something that has not been felt in many an age; naturally, we are here to investigate, and what do I find, but the strangest of parties stranded in the strangest of places-" He moved closer. His eyes were soft and buried in wrinkles, his hands clean. His face was round and his hair was long, it was dark with gray streaks, pulled back behind his ears, which were large and ovular. From his lobes dangled two prisms, and around his neck he wore an amulet on a thick lace.

Pasea hesitated, and then lowered her weapons. "We encountered one of the Pharandi in the depths of Shimmermere. We gave chase, but were waylaid by an ancient aberration of Pandemonium in the deep."

Embraer's eyes narrowed slightly and his lips pursed at the mention of the shrouded wraith. "Ancient enemies – a riddle – are you certain of what you saw?"

Pasea stepped forward, closing the gap between her and the odd man. "We are certain. We followed it here through a rift it created to escape. We can tell you more, but now we must make haste. As you see, we have wounded and fallen among us, and this shrouded demesne is not safe."

He studied Pasea's face for some time, and then moved past her, toward Olaavi and Osirys. He stopped short of Osirys, looking her up and down. He reached out and took a gentle hold of the end of the silvery belt gifted to her by the Muses. He met her eyes after studying it for several moments.

"Riddles, indeed." He turned quickly and began walking away.

"Come, a crossing is near."

Naivarra helped Osirys as much as she was able, while bearing her own wounds. Osirys hobbled along at the quickest pace she could muster, but she felt the throbbing of her left leg intensify with every passing minute. She felt the heat of venom coursing through her, sending spasms of agony up her side and into her spine. Several of the other Musefolk had inflamed wounds as well, but they bore them with poise. Each step became more and more difficult, and as the venom spread, she began to feel sickness within her rise. She began to tremble with fever, and the swelling started spreading to her midsection, moving upwards.

"Planeswalker–" Naivarra called. "We do not have much time."

Osirys shook violently, but kept moving.

Embraer turned and frowned. "You know what we would be risking,"

"And you know what she is." Pasea replied.

Embraer hesitated.

"She will not make it. It must be done."

Osirys could take no more; her eyes rolled back in her head and she dropped to the ground, locked in seizure.

Chapter Fifteen

OSIRYS AWOKE TO THE acrid smell of incense and ointment. She was no longer in the dark. Instead, rays of sunlight filtered through sheer material that formed a canopy above her. She swayed gently, in a woven hammock suspended in an open structure. It was as if she were awaking from a surreal nightmare. She looked about her. Nearby, Naivarra leaned against a stone pillar. She was dressed differently. She was clean, and her hair shone in the evening light. She wore a loose fitting top, cinched across her waist with a beaded cord belt. Her trousers buttoned down, and were tied off at mid-calf. Her right arm was bound in a linen sling, and her eyes were closed. Osirys lingered on her for a while. She was used to seeing the warrior, but here was a woman. She was pretty, even. The material of her shirt was thin, and Osirys could see hints of her toned arms and stomach through the fabric.

"Where are we?" She asked, her voice was shaky, as if she hadn't used it in a long time.

Naivarra turned her head casually, and Osirys was surprised to see her smile.

"Eidrdyhn, home of the Vaman Queen," She responded.

Smoke of incense curled around Osirys in her hammock. She was on a terrace, in a villa that overlooked the city of the Vamanari. The terrace faced North, and the setting sun in the West cast long linear shadows across the valley below. The buildings were low and domed for the most part. The geometry of the Vaman architecture leaned heavily on circular design. There were circular gardens, with arcs and curves built into the structures and landscapes that gave the layout of the city a feeling of continuity, or of multiple ripples on a still pond. The arcs collided and complimented each other, and the small stone walls that lined the streets neatly tied the pieces together. It was serene and beautiful. Osirys took in the sight, absorbing it into the core of her being. Beyond the city proper, there were dozens of wide fields that stretched to the West and East. There were hazy mountains that sat low on the horizon, the bulk of their form half obscured in the dusk of night, only their peaks captured the last rays of day. Nothing looked familiar, even the foliage and grasses were different from the plains that surrounded Tork's Redoubt and Pearlwater Bend. The golden expanse of tall grasses were nowhere to be seen, replaced by verdant green fields, dotted with sparse, large, broad limbed trees that bumped and rolled over small, rippling hills. From the height of the terrace, Osirys could just barely make out the glimmering of meandering rivers in the distance that seemed to surround the city.

"How far are we from Pearlwater Bend?" Osirys asked.

"Two weeks brisk ride in fair weather," Naivarra replied.

Osirys fell quiet. Two weeks? How long had she been unconscious?

Naivarra continued, "The city sits in the floodplain of the Myrn and Dynnin rivers. Both originate from the Virdi further North - near The Virdi Fall - and flow South for a time, before uniting and finding their path through the land together. This is the first time I've ever been in this city. I've only heard stories from some of the other soldiers who had traveled through here, it's nothing like Aefemar. Aefemar is big, dirty, loud. This place is..." Naivarra trailed off, struggling to find the word she was looking for.

"Peaceful," Osirys interjected, finishing Naivarra's sentence.

Naivarra nodded, turning to look at Osirys, "Aye, that word. That's a word I don't get to use often."

Naivarra sighed, stretching her arms over her head. She walked over to Osirys and squeezed her shoulder gently.

"Saving you once was free, you're going to start owing me." Naivarra's smirk betrayed her jest.

"I think you like it." Osirys responded.

"There almost wasn't anything left of you to save. You cut it close this time, girl."

Osirys didn't respond. She wasn't sure that what had happened was real.

"How did we get here?" She asked.

"That old gout used some… trick of his, and poof, we were out of Pandemonium and outside the city here."

"Gout?"

"Clown, what have you." Naivarra waved dismissively.

"You really don't like magic, do you?" Osirys propped herself up on one elbow.

"Is it that obvious?" Naivarra asked sarcastically, stretching her legs.

Osirys thought about what she had experienced. "I think I can understand why."

Naivarra squinted at Osirys. Her eyes twinkled in the fading sunlight. She raised an eyebrow and didn't respond.

"When the Pharandi got me. It used its magic to take over… everything. I would have stopped breathing if it wanted me to. It was like I wasn't me."

Naivarra studied her intently. She continued:

"I tried my hardest to resist it, but I couldn't. I walked right over and laid on that slab. I had no free will. It was the worst thing I've ever felt."

Naivarra nodded, turning away.

"Even when Syn…" She trailed off, "Even when Syndal saved me, it felt like I was being invaded, like my body wasn't mine any more. I can't explain it."

Naivarra didn't turn back to look at her. "I know what you're trying to say." She got up and stepped out into the fading sun.

"Glad you're back with us," She said over her shoulder. "I'll go let the others know you're awake."

She stepped away, her tunic catching the breeze as she descended several stairs, her hair tossing back behind her.

Osirys couldn't help the feeling that she had touched a nerve in the warrior. She sighed and looked herself over. Her leg was bandaged from hip to ankle, nine dark patches where her wounds were treated with oils and ointments spiraled down her thigh to her calf. She tested herself, sucking in air to prepare for any pain.

She wiggled her toes and breathed in some measure of relief. Her leg wasn't useless. She tried to bend her knee, but the wrappings were tight, leaving little room for flexion. She gingerly touched the dark spots, pressing gently. Dull, repressed throbbing rolled through her at the touch. She breathed out through tightened lips. The swelling had gone down some, but her foot still looked puffy and round.

She ran her fingers through her hair. It was clean. She inspected the rest of her. The blood and grime had been scrubbed from her skin. She wore a tunic similar to the one Naivarra wore, without the beaded cord around her midsection. She wrapped her arms around her protectively, she realized that the thin material left the curves and features of her womanliness entirely visible. Her face flushed with embarrassment. She panicked slightly, looking around for her silver belt and Pemme's Auric blade. She relaxed, seeing them nearby, the belt coiled on a nearby table and the dagger resting alongside it. The clothing that Naivarra had given her was there too. The trousers appeared to have been patched and mended, and both articles were cleaned and folded neatly. Her boots sat at the foot of the table. Those too had been cleaned and polished.

She leaned back into the supple pillows that cradled her in the hammock. She survived. She felt a measure of worth in that. She wouldn't have gotten far without Naivarra, Pasea and the others, though. Especially Syndal. Next to their skill and prowess, she was a mewling kitten. She still felt small and terrified. Now Syndal was gone. She shuddered and felt tears well up in her eyes.

She was shaken from her emotions, hearing footsteps approaching. She quickly wiped her eyes.

"Ah, welcome, it is good that you're awake."

The voice was kind, and had an accent. It belonged to a regal looking Vaman woman, wearing a dress unlike Osirys had ever seen before. It was quite plain looking, but the cut was unique, holding tight to the woman's form but accentuating her shoulders and collar bones. It gave her the appearance of height where she had none naturally, standing next to another of her kin of the same dimension, one would swear the former was a head taller. Her hair was braided and coiled down the center of her head delicately, with fine bone pins holding the style in place. Her eyes were large and gemlike, as was normal for her kind, but deep violet, strikingly so.

"I would like to personally welcome you to my city. I am Lavis, Queen of Eidrdyhn and ruler of my kind."

Queen Lavis had a sweet demeanor, but simultaneously, her posture and regard for her surroundings were intense, and frankly intimidating. She commanded respect just by walking into a room. Her skin was stone-gray and speckled with muted colors. She reminded Osirys very much of the Muses, just smaller in stature.

"I suppose I should be thanking you for my survival."

"As have your ilk for millennia, ironically." Her words were careful, but not unkind.

"Ah," Osirys breathed.

"Ah." Lavis said, stepping up on a small stool and taking a seat on the edge of a nearby table. It caught Osirys off guard. Here was a queen, clearly a careful ruler, sitting casually on the edge of whatever furniture she landed upon.

Queen Lavis took a moment and looked at Osirys, as if she were measuring her. The Musefolk had a way of regarding a person that was unsettling. They seemed to be able to dig deeper than the surface, expose feelings that were private; uncover motives and emotions just by their penetrating gaze. Osirys shifted uncomfortably after several moments.

"Pasea and the others tell me that you're a Harbinger."

Osirys bowed her head, nodding slowly.

"Are you, then?" She asked.

"I don't know. I remember almost nothing from before waking up on the edge of the river not long ago. Only what I'm told were the Muses, whoever they are."

"What did they tell you?" The queen asked.

"They said they didn't foresee me." Osirys responded after a lengthy pause.

Osirys remembered their words, as if they were seared into her memory, but she didn't say any more.

"We must trust the River.

It shall weigh her worth.

If she truly serves Pandemonium–

The River will not protect her."

Queen Lavis regarded her in silence for several moments. Suddenly, she slapped her knees, and moved in closer to Osirys.

"You know of the Virdi River, yes?" She asked.

Osirys nodded her head.

"Have you ever heard how it came to be?"

"No, I don't think I have," Osirys replied.

Queen Lavis smiled, "Then, I suppose you'll just have to hear it."

She cleared her throat, then began.

"Long ago, before the Old Empire was born, the entire land was desert. No rain fell from the skies, and no rivers crawled through the mountains or over the plains. There was a girl who lived in a village far to the north, near the cliffs to the Realm of Spirits. Her village survived, because water would drip down

the face of the cliffs, and the village had many hundreds of little buckets to catch the drops. One day while carrying the precious water back to the village, the little girl asked: 'Why do we not go to the top of the cliffs? The water must be coming from there.'

'We do not belong in the Realm of Spirits, daughter', was the reply, and that was that.

Many years later, the water stopped dripping. Without water, the people of the village would surely die. 'Why do we not climb the cliffs?' she asked.

'We do not belong in the Realm of Spirits, daughter', was the reply, and that would have been that, but for another voice, another musical voice that seemed to drift down from the cliffs, calling her.

'Climb the cliffs, and you shall be judged as worthy of the water.'

Determined to save her village, the girl announced she was going to climb to the Realm of Spirits and convince them to let the water drip again so that her village might live. Her father pleaded: 'Please, daughter, you mustn't go. We do not belong in the Realm of Spirits.'

He begged, and she would have listened, but when he cried, no tears came, for there was no water left within him. So she turned and began to climb, and never looked down. She climbed and climbed until there was no ground to see below her even if she looked down, and still she climbed. Finally, exhausted and spent, the girl saw Eight figures standing on the edge of the top of the cliff, not far above her.

'Just a bit more, young one' The Muses urged. With the last of her strength, she jumped and grabbed the top of the cliff, and the rock gave way, releasing the water. As she stood on the top of the cliff, the trickle of water became a stream, and the stream gave way more and more, until a roaring torrent of water surged over the edge to the land far below.

'You have saved your village, young one, you are a true hero' the Muses said to the girl, 'but you cannot go back. We could not let your body enter, because this is the Realm of Spirits.'

For the first time the girl looked down and saw that she was no more than a wispy spirit. Her body had fallen with the rock."

Osirys absorbed the Queen's words thoughtfully. She listened to the tale and studied the small ruler with interest in the telling. When she was finished, Queen Lavis let the two of them sit in silence for a while. She seemed lost in thought also, as if exploring the fable again for herself for the first time. After several minutes, she asked,

"What does it mean to you?"

Osirys wasn't sure how to respond, it almost felt like the Queen was probing her, gauging her responses as some kind of litmus test. She hesitated in her response.

"I guess I'm wondering why the Muses would ask the girl to climb the cliffs knowing it would kill her?"

Queen Lavis held an emotionless expression, her countenance betrayed no hint of satisfaction or displeasure at her response.

"Indeed," She responded. "That is a conundrum,"

The queen toyed with one of the laces on her dress, lost in thought for a moment, before finishing.

"How can anyone ask that of another, to give up their life? I struggle with that still. Would it be that all endeavor could be realized without that ultimate price - Ruling a people would leave me much more sleep at night. Would I make the same choice? How could my people know or trust that I would do the same for them? Proving that I would, after all, would be the end of my reign, and that trust would be bought at the expense of never being able to make use of it."

Queen Lavis lowered her eyes slowly, looking down and crossing her hands in her lap.

"The real question I always have, is would she still have climbed and saved her people if she had known it would kill her?"

Osirys considered the thought. Her mind drifted to Syndal, who knew that her action to save another sealed her fate.

"If she was anything like Syndal, I think she would have." Osirys replied quietly.

Queen Lavis fell silent, but wore a thin, sad smile.

"I think you're probably right." Lavis concluded.

They sat together for a moment before Osirys asked, "What happened to the other Harbingers? The ones before me, I mean. Pasea mentioned that there have been others."

The Queen sat pensively for a moment, considering her answer.

"There have been many over the ages, but the records that have survived are inconsistent. Most agree that the last Harbinger to visit our lands fell in the battle of Tork, sacrificing themselves to provide an opportunity for the grand coalition of Uteriel's forces to strike at the Lich, Or'Qan the Immortal."

Osirys nodded, recalling Pasea's words atop Tork's Redoubt what seemed like ages ago.

"Since then, there have been no Harbingers. Since we, the Vamanari, felt that we had failed in our duties as guardians and our ancestors rescinded our ancient purpose."

Queen Lavis paused, her eyes lingering on Osirys intently.

"None rightly know what became of the Harbinger that opened the way across the Virdi during the *Incursion,* however. Some records say they helped build the first settlements on these shores, others say that they were utterly spent in the massive effort to breach the magic of the river. Still others can't even agree that a Harbinger was involved at all, though our people's histories seem to confirm the presence of at least one such individual. It was a long, long time ago, and very few histories remain from the Eophaethan Empire, only what can be recovered from the ruins."

Osirys thought on the Queen's words.

"Pasea told me that it's a sore subject for all of you. I'm sorry that I'm here. I don't mean to cause trouble."

"I admit your appearance does lay a burden at my feet that I never thought would be mine to bear. Like the girl in the story, a choice is before me that I must make without knowing full well the consequences."

Osirys felt an inexplicable guilt swell within her. She shifted in her hammock, suddenly very uncomfortable.

"Do not shoulder the weight of your arrival, if indeed a Harbinger you are-"

The gaze of the small queen bored into Osirys like a drill. There was a measure of doubt, or of skepticism, that leeched into her words, if ever so slightly. Osirys could not assuage those concerns, in fact she shared them.

"I have much to consider. We will speak again soon. Do not fret, you are safe here, and no harm will come to you or your companions while in my city."

Queen Lavis lowered herself from the table suddenly, breaking the awkward silence that had begun to build between them. She straightened her dress, and moved over to take Osirys' hand in hers. Though the Queen's hands were so much smaller, Osirys still felt like she was the child.

"I am grateful that Olaavi is alive. Regardless of all else, for that alone we are in your debt."

"I tried to save Syndal," Osirys blurted out, her eyes suddenly welling with tears. "I tried, I swear,"

Queen Lavis stiffened, and regarded Osirys wistfully. "I'm sure you did all you could. Syndal, Pemme, Mirabyll, and all of my Vipers knew the risks they undertook in service to their Queen and their people. Though I mourn deeply for those lost, we must all hold to our knowledge that they performed their duties admirably and with honor until their last breath."

The Queen held a stoic visage, but Osirys could see unspeakable pain beneath her demeanor. She released Osirys' hand and turned, descending the stair gracefully. She paused, and turned back, her eyes wet but face as composed as ever:

"The Planeswalker - Embraer, of the Silver Cord - has remained since your arrival. It is highly unlike his kind to linger without purpose. I suspect he has questions. If you would like more rest I will make sure that you aren't disturbed until you say otherwise."

Osirys wiped her eyes with her sleeve. "It's okay, I don't mind. I wanted to thank him for saving me, too."

Queen Lavis nodded and continued down the stairs, leaving Osirys in silence to contemplate her words.

THE SUN SAT NESTLED against the hills in the distance. Her hammock swung gently, though flags flapped steadily from their moorings overhead, the structure where she rested was sheltered from nearly all of the wind. Queen Lavis had called it a city, but nothing about Eidrdyhn spoke to Osirys of urban life. Small dirt roads wound between domiciles and squat domed shops. Along the prominent streets, ornate stonework and masonry decorated corners. The streets were populated but not busy by any means, they were too narrow to permit more than a single decently sized wagon to travel through at once. From her vantage, Osirys could not see much detail, but it seemed that most of the Musefolk traveled on foot, carrying woven baskets with goods and supplies for their homes and businesses. As peaceful as it was, Osirys could feel pensiveness, perhaps even fear in the air. Eidrdyhn was a city under siege, not with machines of war, but its people were a hunted race.

Osirys remembered the caravan, wagons full of these strange folk in link and chain. Their homes destroyed and their populace taken by force. Osirys made a mental note to ask the Queen about the plight of her people when they next met. She had so many questions- and yet she felt like she was expected to have answers, like her mere presence required explanation.

The stars had begun to reveal themselves along the darker edges of the horizon. Osirys smiled. In the darkness of Shimmermere there were no stars. Under the open sky, she felt so far removed from that deep place, as if it were a bad dream that existed far, far away. Her dark bandages reminded her that it was very, very real. The stars twinkled anyway, as they did still when she was underground, just not where she could see them. Their persistence comforted her, and frightened her at the same time. Her world could be crashing down about her, but the stars would twinkle on, oblivious and unmoved.

She became suddenly aware that she was not alone. She wasn't sure how he arrived- she didn't hear or see his approach up the stair, but Embraer was suddenly present, seated in the nearby chair, gazing out over the township and surroundings with her. She had to stifle a yelp of surprise, but her sudden start made him jump as well, as if she were the one that were startling.

"Goodness me!" He said in a huff.

"How did you-" Osirys started.

"I do apologize, I was lost in the beauty of it too." He said, answering and not answering her question all at once. "Where I come from, we do not get these sensible views."

"Sensible?" Osirys asked.

"Hm, yes." Embraer responded, matter of factly.

"Where is it that you come from that isn't as sensible?"

"Ah," Embraer answered, catching on. "My order resides between this realm and all others. I'm sure you have heard others refer to us as 'Planeswalkers', and while that's true, it's somewhat of a simplification."

Osirys did not follow anything that he was saying, and it was clearly shown on her face. He turned to look at her, and frowned.

"Suffice to say it is both near and far, but looks nothing like where we are now."

"If you say so. I think you're crazy." Osirys responded. He moved to talk but Osirys continued. "Crazy or not though, I feel like I owe you a thank you for saving me - us, I mean."

He shut his mouth, and nodded. "Yes, I suppose." He said quietly. He returned his gaze to their surroundings, and fell silent for a few moments, before he rose to his feet, slowly walking to the table with her belongings and effects. She watched him move with more than a little curiosity and a healthy dose of suspicion. She didn't know where to begin with her questions. He quietly looked over her things, and then reached out, running his finger along the silver belt that the Muses had given her along the shores of the Aetheral Lake.

"What are they like?" He asked, suddenly.

"Who?" Osirys replied, cautiously.

"The Muses." He responded, unshaken. "They are both so fascinating and frustrating."

"Seems like you know exactly what they're like," Osirys answered coyly.

Embraer turned and for the first time showed some expression. His eyes twinkled with some joy at her comment.

"Ah!" He chuckled. "I can see why she likes you."

Osirys looked at him, confused. Before she could ask what he meant, he kept talking, changing the subject.

"Consider it humor, or, consider it a warning that the Muses saw fit to provide you with such a clear message to our order, it's likely both. Their involvement with our realm in the past has been on the edge of coincidence – never before have they so boldly interjected, it's as if they don't trust us to see their metaphorical fingerprints all over you."

"So I am a Harbinger, then?" Osirys asked.

"Harbinger of what?" Embraer asked, cryptically.

Osirys didn't know how to tell him that wasn't what she was asking:

"No, I mean, the others, they refer to me as a Harbinger, there have been others like me?"

"It seems you know exactly whether you are or aren't," Embraer echoed, smiling ever so subtly.

Osirys rolled her eyes. "You are as vexing as the Muses too, you know. I don't exactly have a good idea about what's going on here."

"I apologize. It is difficult to explain so much in words." Embraer seemed sincere. His eyes softened and he returned to the chair, her silver belt held gently in his hands. For the first time, she noticed that he wore one that was similar, if not nearly identical.

"I am part of an order called the Silver Cord." He raised her belt ever so slightly, and his bushy eyebrows to match.

"We are cartographers, of sorts. As you are no doubt aware, there are other realms that exist in near parallel to the one you see and feel around you."

"Pandemonium," Osirys said, under her breath.

"That one, and others," Embraer said.

"There are others?" Osirys asked.

"Why yes, many, many more. Some are small and featureless, others are as vibrant and complex as the world you see here. Some are uninhabited, inhospitable, and wholly unnatural. Others are actually quite beautiful."

Osirys had trouble wrapping her head around the concept. "How many are there?"

"If we knew the answer to that question, young miss, there would be no reason for our order to exist." He fidgeted with her belt.

"The Queen says your order is secret, and that you generally do not stay in one place for very long. Why is that?" Osirys asked, narrowing her eyes.

"It may come as a surprise to you that there is more than good and well wishes in the world. There are those that seek power and control, in this realm and others, that greatly desire to reach beyond the veils that have been forced upon them."

Osirys nodded, thoughtfully. Embraer continued, "We have learned much, and that knowledge is, in a word, more valuable than any amount of gold or riches depending on your perspective. Early on, we sought to work with the Kings and Queens of this world to ensure that realms like Pandemonium would never be able to repeat the atrocities of the *Incursion*, but we soon learned our lesson. We became hunted, lobbied, and pursued for political interest everywhere we went. We exist outside of these ephemeral constructs of society. We do not exist for the good of one nation or another. We seek only to understand, and to use that understanding as a means to avoid calamity like we have experienced before. So, as a result, we went into hiding, and only show ourselves when something significant happens that requires our attention. Like you. So yes, the Queen spoke truly."

"So I *am*-" Osirys repeated.

"I should think there would be no doubt in that. This gift that the Muses bestowed upon you will provide evidence enough for the Queen and her court should they require it." He rolled the braided silver between his fingers. "Look here," He lifted out of the chair again and ambled over to Osirys' hammock. She propped herself up eagerly, her spirit lifted by promise of some form of legitimacy.

She took the cord in her hands and examined it, but did not see anything significant. She looked at Embraer, questioningly.

"The clasp," He said. "It is in inscribed with the old Vaman sigil of the first house to serve the Harbingers, before the *Incursion*."

Osirys examined the clasp. It was in the shape of a crest or shield, with a symbol in the middle. The shape was of an X where the tips had been swirled, as if where the lines crossed had been grabbed and pulled counter clockwise a quarter turn.

"What does it mean?"

Embraer thought for a moment.

"The sigil is not used any more today. It used to be a symbol of their people - of their purpose. It was discarded after Or'Qan the Immortal was destroyed, after they disavowed their heritage as the guardians of your kind."

He paused, considering his words,

"Queen Lavis will recognize this."

His face reflected that he considered his answer sufficient, and he moved on.

"The real important question, as is usually the case, is *why*. Why are you here, and why now?"

Osirys hoped that it was a rhetorical question. There was an awkward silence. She started trying to formulate some kind of response, but before she could say anything, Embraer rose to his feet suddenly.

"Embraer, what if you're wrong? What if this is something different entirely?" Osirys bowed her head. "There hasn't been another Harbinger in so long. And..."

She trailed off. Embraer studied her, his jaw set.

"There's something else. I don't remember it clearly, maybe that's why I haven't said anything."

"Said what?" Embraer asked, his eyes narrowed and focused.

"Before the Muses, there was something else. A darkness. I think it was alive. I don't really know how to describe it. That thing in Pandemonium, that monster deep in the lake of Shimmermere. It brought back feelings that I've felt before. Something else chose me, from wherever I belong, wherever I came from. It picked *me* for *something.*" Shame washed over her.

"What do you remember?" Embraer asked, leaning in, his face close to hers.

"Eyes, in the darkness. Six of them." She whispered. "They wanted everything I had, and that wouldn't have been enough."

Embraer remained silent, waiting for her to continue.

"I… I didn't fight it. It was like I *wanted* it to hurt me. I, just don't understand."

Embraer hummed, his face betraying no hint of understanding, but still Osirys had the feeling he knew exactly what she was talking about.

"The other Planeswalkers will be interested to hear of these events!" He said, his voice suddenly louder. "I have been too long. Yes, I must return."

Osirys still had so many questions, still felt so lost. The few tidbits of information she had learned in such a short time whet her curiosity, and ignited her insecurity.

"Embraer," Osirys pleaded. "Pemme, Syndal, Mirabyll, others have died. What if I'm not what they think I am?"

Embraer turned back to face her, his eyes kind, smiling. "I stayed because I wanted to meet you, and I'm very, very glad I did. Farewell for now, Harbinger."

He turned and descended the steps, leaving Osirys alone with her questions and doubts.

Curse that cryptic man! Osirys was sure that he knew more than he let on. She felt so ill equipped for her situation. She wanted answers to questions she didn't know how to ask. Embraer was right, though. It mattered very little how she got to where she was. She had no choice but to trust her life and liberties to people she barely knew, had only known for a few days, and who seemed to idolize her as some sort of symbolic legend, as if she were more important than everyone else. The more she considered it, the more insane it seemed to her. She had heard of people who became completely self absorbed in fictional narrative, so much so that they couldn't distinguish reality from fantasy. She knew she wasn't important. She felt it deep within her that she was sub-ordinary, even base. If anything, she was extraordinary only in the means that she was uniquely mundane in comparison to everyone around her. Alone on the terrace, Osirys battled with herself, feeling entirely alienated from her surroundings. She drifted into an uneasy, dreamless sleep.

Chapter Sixteen

THE FOLLOWING DAYS WERE peaceful. Despite that, Osirys thought of Syndal often. She woke up in her hammock nightly in cold sweats, visions of the small Auric propped against the rope of the lift in the darkness, lifeless. Each dream was the same - Osirys would be alone on the platform with Syndal, suspended above Shimmermere, but instead of dark water, the lake was Syndal's lifeblood, running fluidly from the gaping self-inflicted wound in her chest and cascading over the edges of the elevator. Osirys could never move or act; and she kept calling out into the void for Syndal to wake, for her eyes to open, and for her face to resume her customary dour expression, alive with nearly emotionless purpose. Then Osirys would look down and see that Pemme's Auric blade would be buried in her own chest, pushed all the way to the hilt, the cold metal burning with sickly light - and then Osirys would wake up. All of her visitors had assured her that it was no fault of hers that Syndal was gone, but inside, Osirys couldn't help but feel differently.

Osirys sat near the railing of the promenade, the soft light of morning had come and gone. She watched as the sun touched the tops of the buildings and worked its way swiftly down until the town was awake with warmth and light. The Vaman physician and his aides had already performed their tasks and moved on, her dressings were refreshed with the new day. Now she sat, holding and studying Pemme's Auric blade. The blood of both the abomination of the deep and her friend was thoroughly cleaned away from the metal, not a trace of either lingered in the many angles and hollow corners of the blade. She leaned forward, resting her elbows on her knees, and holding the dagger upright, the rounded hilt between her palms. She rolled it between her hands slowly, watching as the light caught the different faces of the blade, causing it to shine and twinkle in the late morning light. She looked at and simultaneously past the blade. The town below was out of focus, matching the quiet, muddled sounds of life far away.

She smiled when she heard heavy footsteps making their way up the stair. She recognized Troodie's foot-falls long before she saw the stout woman. Her smile grew as she inhaled, catching a whiff of sweet, warm, yeasty fresh baked bread, with a heavy overtone of cinnamon. Troodie's face popped around the corner of the stair, her hair was bundled neatly, and her eyes were as bright as the morning.

"Halloo! I see ya' there, are ya' hungry?" Troodie chirped.

Osirys nodded eagerly, standing and moving one of the other chairs on the terrace near the railing. Troodie held a plate covered in a supple linen towel ahead of her; a thin wisp of steam catching the breeze as she climbed the last couple of stairs. She wore a Vaman style tunic as well, but hers was a bit thicker in fabric, and the buttons were larger, brick colored, and embroidered with little yellow pies. Troodie put the plate down on a nearby table and wrapped Osirys in a hug. Osirys was caught off guard. Still, she felt her insecurities and doubts melt like hot wax. Simultaneously, Osirys felt warm and sad at the same time. She had needed a hug so bad. She felt like hugs were a luxury she knew long ago, but she felt like it must have been so long since she felt that touch of comfort. It was as if her body rebelled against kind touch, like it had been soured or poisoned for her in the life she couldn't remember. What kind of life did she lead, where a hug caused her to stiffen so?

Troodie didn't let go until Osirys relaxed. "There." She huffed. "Everyone could use a big ol' hug every now and again, don'tcha think?" Troodie said, settling into the seat Osirys had pulled over for her. Osirys stood for a moment more.

"Well I thought'cha said you were hungry, don't wait for 'em to get cold now, they're best hot!" Troodie said playfully. She grabbed the linen cloth and pulled it aside, revealing knotted pastry covered in a cinnamon sauce.

"Oh my gosh-" Osirys gasped.

Troodie beamed, her eyes were wide and Osirys noticed their deep emerald color for the first time. "Go'on'en!"

They enjoyed breakfast together on the Promenade, thin clouds building along the hills. After Osirys had given up on her third roll, Troodie sat back, hands folded across her lap.

"How's yer leg healin'?" Troodie asked.

Osirys shrugged. She looked at her clean bandages. "I'll be okay," she responded.

"Good, the Queen has given you the best of the best, don'tchaknow. That physician fellow Olthi knows his stuff." Troodie continued.

Osirys nodded. Not only was Master Olthi good at his craft, but he was kind. His hands were practiced and careful, and his mind equally sharp. Osirys glanced at Troodie.

"How do you know so much about baking and medicine, Troodie? Kind of a strange combination, don't you think?" Osirys asked.

"Oh, ya'know, I'm a lady'a many talents!" Troodie giggled. "The truth is baking is in my blood, but I was never meant to be a baker like the rest of my clan. Yippee, the Divines had other plans for me!"

"What do you mean?" Osirys pressed.

Troodie sighed. "Well, Nan always knew I had the sight, from the first I could say 'hot buns'."

"The sight?"

"That's right. Among my kind, rarely there are some of us born with the ability to see health, don'tchaknow!"

"See health? That's amazing, what does it look like?" It seemed like Osirys was more and more amazed by the little plump woman every time they spoke.

"Well, it's kinda like a glow, but inside here." Troodie tapped Osirys' chest. "The stronger the glow, the stronger the spirit. Anyhoo, Nan knew I had it early. She loves to tell stories of me when I was knee-high to a grasshopper, I always knew which of our egg hens was sick. She said I were blessed by the Divines, and called me 'Pride of Van-Hootan'." Troodie smiled while she spoke, but Osirys heard sadness behind her words.

"What happened?" Osirys followed.

"Oh, nothin' that wasn't s'posed to, dear." Troodie replied. "If you have the sight, you join the Order of Leven, and first thing you learn when you join the Order is medicine to help the sick. That's just what goes!"

Osirys lowered her eyes. "You miss your family, don't you."

"Yip." Troodie nodded. "They say the Order is like a family, and don't get me wrong, it is in many ways; but – there's somethin' to be said for home and bein' where you feel."

"So why don't you go back?" Osirys asked.

"Oh I would dear, but I can't. I'm not allowed. Not until I receive my blessin'. Only then can I return, to be inducted into the Order as a full Leventus. If-" Troodie caught herself, "I mean, *when* that happens, I can finally go home."

Osirys thought for a moment. Once again, she felt like she should have known what Troodie was talking about, like it was common knowledge, but she wasn't privy to it. Troodie read her face, and smiled, continuing without Osirys having to ask.

"No way to know what my blessin' might be, course. That's for the Divines to know and for me to learn once I've earned it - if I earn it."

"I'm sure you will," Osirys said, looking out over Eidrdyhn.

Troodie smiled wistfully. "Only one in fifty aspirants ever receive their gift. It's been over a hundred years now for me, don'tchaknow?"

Osirys gasped. "A - hundred?"

Troodie looked at Osirys, smiling sadly. "Yip. This year will be the tenth Makemoot since I've been away."

"What's a 'Makemoot?'" Osirys giggled, despite the somber context. the word was funny to her for some reason.

"In our tongue it's called '*Yiselhaf*,' Troodie explained. "Once every ten years, it's a fair of sorts, but it's very important for us. Our people are organized by houses, each house is devoted to a single craft. My house are bakers, if that weren't obvious." Troodie covered the remaining rolls with the towel, standing up. "Want to get some air while we talk? Give that there leg a little stretch?"

Osirys nodded. A walk did sound nice. The stair that descended to the village commons below was difficult for her to use, but thankfully the stairs were shallow due to the smaller stride of the Musefolk to begin with, so it was only inconvenient for Osirys to navigate down to the lower level. The stair itself curved and hugged the outcropping that the Queen's estate was built upon. Troodie helped her slightly, but she mostly made her own way. Troodie began talking again once they had reached the street of the square below the Queen's estate.

"Anyhoo, each house is made up of many clans, called Stones. Those stones are ranked, and the elder of the first Stone of each house has the honor of presiding on the High Council. Second Stone of each house has a lot of influence in trade, and the lower you go, the less power you have."

They had made their way into the open market. Osirys eyes feasted on all the strange goods that sat piled in baskets and in carts. There were all manners of raw foods, woven goods, and wares. Troodie periodically paused to browse foodstuffs and spices as she spoke.

"Troodie, you still haven't explained Makemoot," Osirys said.

Troodie chuckled. "I'm sorry dearie I get carried away. Right. Makemoot. Once every ten years, our people hold a year long festival where each Stone of each House endeavors to create one singular submission of their best craftsmanship to the High council to be ranked against the other Stones of their House. We spend six months abroad gathering the best materials, and then six months practicing and working toward a perfect example of our best work. Then on the night of the winter solstice, there's a big feast and the Stones are rewritten. That way our people are always represented by the best of our best. Rarely, clans can even jump two or three Stones for particularly legendary Moots."

Osirys was fascinated. "What Stone is your Clan?"

"Fifth, now." Troodie sighed. "We were third when I left."

"Oh," Osirys said. "I'm sorry. What happened?"

Troodie shrugged. "We got beat, and that's just what goes."

They had stopped at a small cart filled with different brightly colored syrups. Troodie pawed through them skillfully.

"Ooo!" Troodie squeaked, with sudden excitement.

"What is it?" Osirys asked, swooping in over Troodie's shoulder to see what the fuss was about. Troodie clutched a vial of thick amber liquid.

"Is this what I think it is?" She called out to the small vendor. An aged Vaman woman shuffled over and took the vial from Troodie, examining it closely.

"Vespenbee Nectar, yes," The small merchant replied, smiling. "You have keen eyes."

"May I smell it?" Troodie asked. Osirys watched on, blindly amused.

The trader pulled the stopper from the small vial, passing it under Troodie's nose, allowing her to take a deep sniff. Troodie hummed, smiling.

"What is it?" Osirys asked, unable to contain her curiosity.

"Honey. Very, very special honey, from very, very special bees. Come, smell it," The Vaman woman said, holding the vial close to Osirys nose. The peddler and Troodie exchanged knowing looks, grinning.

Osirys drew air, unsure of what to expect. The odors of the Vespenbee honey filled her nose and lungs, and instantly she felt a warmth spread through her core out to her extremities, giving her a tingling feeling that felt like being wrapped up in strong arms, but from inside. Osirys knees quivered, and her loins suddenly ached.

"Oh. Oh my-" Osirys clapped her hand over her mouth to prevent a more involuntary noise from escaping her lips. She felt her face flush bright red.

She shot a look at Troodie, whose cheeks were rosy like apples.

"Teehee!" Troodie giggled. "Now imagine what it tastes like!"

The Musefolk carefully replaced the stopper to the vial, sporting a coy and mischievous smile.

Troodie grabbed Osirys by the hands. "It's still before Middenhaf, which means my clan is still gathering materials for this year's Makemoot. Could you imagine an enormous table of old crustaceans - First Stone of every house - trying a bite of pie with this honey drizzled on the top?" Troodie bubbled with laughter. "The lot of them wouldn't have felt their nethers twitch in such a way for a hundred years or more!"

Osirys couldn't help but laugh through her embarrassment.

"So, shall I wrap it for you?" The merchant asked.

Troodie's face suddenly dropped, the joy running from her eyes and cheeks. "Ah, I wish I could but, ah, I don't think I'll be gettin' back there in time."

The Vaman woman's smile faded, as she noticed the stamped medallion of the Leven Order that hung around Troodie's neck. "Ah, I'm sorry, dear." She carefully replaced the phial of honey, and resumed tending to her other goods.

Troodie turned to leave, but Osirys grabbed her hand. "Get it, Troods," She urged. "I believe you'll get back with plenty of time to spare."

Troodie met Osirys' gaze, her deep emerald eyes welling with sadness and hope. "You think so?" She asked.

"I do," Osirys said.

Troodie wrung her hands. "Ah miss? I ah, I think I've had a change a'heart, I think I will take that there Honey."

Osirys smiled as the old peddler wrapped the phial in a leather pouch, tying it off with bits of chartreuse and pink string. "That'll be one-thousand four-hundred marks, dear."

Troodie nearly fumbled her purse. "Ooo!" She stammered. "Would'ja take nine-hundred an' a muffin?"

The merchant rolled her eyes, crossing her arms across her chest. "What flavor muffin?"

"Garnetberry an' roasted wealdnut?" Troodie asked, squinting hopefully.

The peddler frowned, deep in thought. After a few moments, she finally spoke. "Fine, but only because I feel bad for you."

Troodie lit up. "Oh, thank you!" She handed over her entire purse of coins, and produced an immense muffin from her pack, wrapped in a checkered linen. The vendor's large eyes went wide. The muffin was nearly the size of her head.

"You can keep the cloth!" Troodie said, gingerly placing the pouch of honey amongst her belongings. The Vaman woman would have replied but her mouth was full of muffin.

Troodie and Osirys continued walking through the market, slowly making their way back toward the Queen's estate. The guard, cloaked in violet and clad in shining armor nodded as they passed. They climbed the stair slowly. Osirys leg had begun to ache. Several dark spots had appeared on her wound dressings, and though it was warm, Osirys fell a slight chill run through her as the breeze ruffled her tunic. The morning had waned into afternoon, and Olthi, her physician, sat, with thick spectacles on, in one of the chairs by the railing of the promenade, reading a leather bound book. He glanced up as Osirys and Troodie crested the stair.

"My apologies, Master Olthi," Troodie said, shame tinting the edges of her words. "We got carried away a bit in the market."

The old physician smiled from behind his book, his glasses sliding nearly off the tip of his nose.

"Exercise is good," He said, matter-of-factly. "But it does look like you may have overdone it a bit today. Come, let me have a look."

Osirys nodded, and turned to Troodie. She was several heads taller than the stout woman, and she leaned in so that their noses were mere inches apart.

"We'll make sure you get back to your family before midsummer," Osirys said, "I promise."

Troodie smiled, but didn't reply. She turned to leave the terrace, pausing to look out over Eidrdyhn. "Thank you, Osirys," She said, before descending the stair.

Olthi gestured for Osirys to sit. "Come, we must change these dressings. I recommend some rest after we're finished."

Chapter Seventeen

T HE FOLLOWING DAY, OSIRYS was restless. The very air about her felt uneasy. Master Olthi barely spoke that morning, and after her wounds were carefully wrapped, he bowed deeply, which seemed strange to Osirys, before leaving.

She stood, leaning over the railing of the terrace. She wore a gown similar to the traditional wear of the Vamanari highborn women, but sized appropriately for her stature. The dress consisted of a long linen wrap that hugged her ribs and crossed over her chest and cinched in the back. It was brightly colored and patterned at the shoulder and across her middle, but the strips that covered her chest were muted in pastel blues and greens. She also wore a dress skirt that was long, nearly to the ankle, and very form fitting, but loose enough to hide the bulky bandages that wrapped her still healing leg. Her hair was wrapped in a traditional Vaman *Torayn,* a slim piece of fabric that was woven through tight braids, and pinned with ornate metal decorations. Rather than the traditional hide wrap that would serve as a belt for the skirt, she instead wore the Muse's Silver linked cord, to which a scabbard had been fastened for Pemme's Auric blade. The servants to the queen had dropped off the garments that morning, having just retrieved it from the queen's personal tailor. Though she had protested, it was fruitless - it's not as if anyone else in the palace would fit into it anyhow, and it was already made. After the queen's servants had helped her into the dressings, they held up a mirror. Osirys' dark eyes stood out against the overall colorful brightness of her garments. The Musefolk were predominantly light-eyed, with many hues of amber and yellows being common. The queen's servants spent several more minutes preening her and showering her with compliments for her hair and features, and she did have to admit, she felt beautiful.

Perhaps that was the source of some of her conflict. She stood on the terrace of the palace of the queen, young and beautiful externally, but inside she felt wretched and confused. She felt that she were even more of an imposter than she was before. Here, dressed as if she were of noble birth, entitled to the finest of clothing, free meals, and the doting attention of attendants and physicians, waiting for her liaisons to come calling. She was not noble, she was full of shame. Her arrival had caused the deaths of some of the finest of the queen's warriors, she felt like she deserved to be in a dark cell of a dungeon, feeding once daily on moldy bread, if at all. It felt backwards. Why should she be celebrated and treated as royalty when all she had caused was pain and death? All under the pretense that she was someone *important*.

She heard the light footsteps of someone ascending the stair. Who now? It shouldn't be the physicians, they had come and gone, and it was not time for her dressing to be swapped for another several hours at least. The attendants had left with a measure of finality that morning, indicating they wouldn't return until the evening time, and it was yet early afternoon, with the sun still high in the sky.

A sturdy looking Vaman clad in rich, brightly armored and violet garb similar in design of the sort Osirys wore, stepped lightly up the final few stairs. Instead of a *Torayn,* however, she wore a thick hood that covered much of her face and features. Osirys knew it was Pasea just by the way she moved; her stride was measured and deliberate. She wore an ornamental spear on her back, and two short blades were secured in gemmed scabbards, gleaming in the afternoon light.

She stopped at the top of the stair, and brought down her hood. Osirys met Pasea's gaze. The warrior was even more stone stoic than usual. Osirys could not discern the slightest emotion from her flat affect, so much so that it was almost disturbing.

Pasea bowed deeply, sweeping one arm low.

"The Queen would be honored if you would join her. If it please you, I will serve as your guard and escort."

Osirys stood, dumbfounded for several seconds. Pasea remained bowed, waiting.

"Uh, yeah, alright." She managed to choke out after several moments. Pasea straightened promptly and stepped to the side, in practiced military stride.

"I was beginning to wonder where you all had gotten to," Osirys said, trying to initiate conversation. Pasea did not reply. They descended the stairs in silence after that, Pasea matched Osirys slow stride, still favoring her uninjured leg.

Just before the bottom of the stairs, Pasea paused. Osirys turned, puzzled.

"Har-" The regal warrior began, but quickly corrected herself. "Osirys," She said, looking around as if she were breaking some kind of rule just by speaking to her. "You should know, your arrival here has caused quite a division within our people. While you likely have not seen or observed any disruption, I assure you, there are just as many Vamanari here that would deny your existence as would cheer your coming. There are even some that see you as a demon, and would have you thrown into the Virdi from whence you came."

Osirys took a step backward, looking around.

"I must remain neutral, as ordered by our Queen, until the trial has concluded."

Osirys gasped. A *trial*? Without another word, Pasea turned and began walking again. Osirys had no choice but to follow closely. They worked their way through the residential area of the queen's estate, and exited the promenade through a garden that she hadn't passed through before. It was full of cropped violet bushes and pools full of colorful fish. Shortly, they had emerged from the royal estate and were on a main road that led through the village proper. Osirys began to notice that many of the locals paused their tasks to watch them pass. Shuttered windows would open and small heads with large round eyes would peer from the domiciles and shops. Conversations would awkwardly diminish as they neared. She had figured previously that the behavior of the locals was more or less due to the fact that she was nearly twice their size - out of curiosity, or just because she was an outsider. Now, however, she sensed the unease in the air that surrounded her. The Musefolk were *afraid* of her, of what she represented. She wanted to call out to them, assure them that she meant them all no harm - that she wanted to help. But how could she hope they would believe her? She thought of the old Vaman woman from the caravan, a casualty of her carelessness. She thought of Syndal and her sacrifice, who died in the dark of Shimmermere, to keep her alive.

Osirys felt tears push their way upwards, but she forced them back down. She noticed that a small crowd had begun to follow them as they moved through town. They turned, and Osirys saw the gates to a large wrought amphitheater that she had seen from her chamber on the terrace. They moved through the large gates, at which there were a great number of Vamanari clad in violet wrappings. They stood at attention as Pasea and Osirys passed, and descended the many shallow steps to the basin of the Amphiteater. Pasea motioned for Osirys to have a seat in one of the front benches. Osirys complied, and Pasea took a position closely nearby. For some time, she was alone with the Vaman warrior in the immense amphitheater. She felt tiny. Soon, Musefolk began flowing through the main gate that she had passed through and also several other smaller gates around the edge of the amphitheater. By the hundreds they entered and began filling the seats.

Osirys began to bead with sweat. Why wasn't she warned? It seemed as though the entire city of Eidrdyhn was pouring through the gates. She scanned the crowd. Naivarra's tall frame should be easy to spot amongst the small statured Vamanari.

She didn't see Naivarra or Troodie amongst the crowd. Perhaps they didn't know, or weren't invited. It had been several minutes, and now just a thin stream of stone-colored faces filled in the top rows of the amphitheater; it was a full house. Osirys eyes widened and they instantly welled with tears as she saw Naivarra's comparatively hulking frame under the archway, stepping to the side and lingering in the back, crossing her arms. Osirys forced her gaze forward. Her breathing was hurried, and she felt herself beginning to flush with anxiety.

She heard the gates close, and then heard the rhythmic footfalls of the Vamanari guards as they moved down the amphitheater, taking places between Osirys and a series of ornate podiums, arranged in a semicircle around a central platform. The crowd began to quiet down, and several regal figures stepped from behind a large banner emblazoned with the Queen's sigil. They fanned and took places at all but one of the podiums. Pasea stepped forward, nodding to Osirys.

As Osirys stood, Pasea called out, her voice filling the Amphitheater, "Before the council and citizens of Eidrdyhn, I present Osirys, outlander, and visitor to our lands." Pasea led her to the central platform, set ominously below the podiums surrounding her. Pasea motioned to where Osirys should stand, and then stepped aside. Pasea held her spear in her hand, its shaft planted firmly between her feet against the stone floor, the lethal tip pointed skyward.

Another Musefolk in ornate purple garb that Osirys did not recognize stepped forward, in front of the central, singularly empty podium that remained.

"The council presents Queen Lavis, leader of the free Vamanari people, defender of our lands, and principal of wisdoms."

The queen stepped from behind the banner, taking her place behind the central podium. Osirys noted that the warrior in purple was not watching her, but rather stared at Pasea intently. Pasea did not return the gesture, instead choosing to stare straight ahead and past the entire council. Queen Lavis did not immediately speak. Instead, she surveyed the amphitheater, regarding the thousands of her subjects. Meeting their eyes. Speaking to them without words or expressions, much like their kind were wont to do from time to time. She searched the other warriors beneath the podiums for familiar faces. There were none. Were they intentionally excluded? Were they in some kind of trouble? Her head was flooded with questions, so much so that she almost jumped when Queen Lavis spoke. Though the Queen's voice was not raised, it was loud, amplified by the layout of the geometry of the amphitheater. She spoke in slow, measured words.

"It is said that Vamanari are exceptional at two things: the first being our devotion to duty and the second being our affinity for rumors. Many of you have heard that a *Harbinger* has appeared on the shores of the Virdi River many leagues south, near Tork's Redoubt, outside the township of Pearlwater Bend. Many of you have heard that she is a savior to our people, sent by the Muses to end persecution of our kin at the hands of the cruel races of man. Others have heard that she is a herald of more treacherous evils. Furthermore it has reached my ears that horrors from beyond our realm have been sighted, corresponding uncannily with her arrival. Tonight we convene to dispel rumor. We Vamanari have not been stewards of any Harbinger since the fall of the Dread Lich Or'Qan, some eight-hundred years ago, and in that time, no harbingers have appeared before us, for good or ill."

For the first time, the Queen's eyes fell upon Osirys. They held none of the kindly demeanor that Osirys felt the last time they met. The Queen's face was cold, stern, and commanding. Her stature was rigid, impassive, and imposing. She seemed immense, even while her physical stature was much the same as her fellows. Osirys shrank from her gaze instinctively.

"Speak, outlander Osirys. Tell us what you know of these events, and put our minds and spirits at ease."

Osirys froze. The amphitheater fell to complete silence. She wanted to run. She glanced at Pasea, who stood resolute, and unflinching. She opened and closed her mouth several times, but no words came out.

"Well? Are you a Harbinger or no?" One of the voices from a podium to the side called out. Osirys whipped her head towards the voice.

"I… I don't know." She squeaked out, barely louder than a whisper.

"She doesn't know!" The Vaman noble echoed, tossing his hands.

A hushed murmur ran through the crowd. Queen Lavis held her hand up, and the amphitheater returned to eerie silence.

"Tell us what you do know, Osirys."

"I met them – The Muses." She said, her voice quavering but gaining traction. She inhaled sharply, focusing. "They spoke to me, their words were like a song, but there was no tune or melody."

"And what did they say?" Another noble, this time from the right flank.

"They asked me questions that I could not answer, and told me to trust the River."

"Cryptic! That's not any answer!" Called a third. "What did they ask of you, girl?"

"They asked where I was from and how I got there."

"And? Where exactly are you from? How did you get here?"

Queen Lavis chewed her lip, ever so slightly.

"I told you, I don't know."

The amphitheater fell into uneasy silence.

Queen Lavis spoke hesitantly, "So, you cannot tell us anything about your origin or your purpose?"

Osirys shook her head.

"The girl is clearly a servant of Shadow!" Called the first noble that spoke earlier. Hushed whispers ran through the amphitheater. "She appears with no explanation, claiming to be a Harbinger, the first in nigh a thousand years, claiming to have met the Muses. Death follows her, and no good can come of-"

"Silence!" Queen Lavis roared. "You have as much evidence to your claim as she, Allawer, Alawayn-son. You speak not wisdom." She turned back to Osirys.

"Please, continue, Osirys. Tell us about what happened after your encounter. What else can you tell us about them? Can you describe where you were? What you saw?"

"I was in a forest, full of snow. But it wasn't like any forest I've ever seen. The trees were made of crystals, and it wasn't cold, even though the snow was deep. They spoke to me, and then led me to the shore of a lake, it felt so large, but I had no way of knowing how big it was. I remember floating in the lake, and there was a waterfall. I remember falling."

The Musefolk hung on every word. Osirys felt thousands of large reflective eyes on her.

"And then I woke up on the shore of the river."

"And who did you encounter upon awakening?" Queen Lavis urged her on.

"A warrior named Naivarra helped me, but we were captured."

"Captured? By whom?"

"Slavers, or cultists, I think. There were many of your people chained in a caravan of wagons. I was chained with them."

"Clearly you escaped. How did you accomplish that?"

"The caravan stopped because..." Osiris hesitated. "Because I caused them to."

"And how did you make them stop?"

"I didn't mean to. I thought I was dreaming, and I couldn't stop laughing. They stopped to punish me."

"Yet you bear no scars of the whips? We have seen what these slavers do to punish their prisoners, if they even survive."

"One of your kind intervened to save me." Osirys felt tears begin to run down her face. "She died."

"A selfless act, no doubt," the queen said, solemnly. "But how then, did you escape? Surely, they didn't just let you go?"

Osirys shook her head. "Your Violet Vipers arrived at just that moment, charging from the bluffs of Tork's Redoubt, as I later learned it was called. They fought and killed many of the slavers, allowing us to escape."

"And did those warriors pursue the remaining slavers?" Asked the noble directly to the left of the queen.

Osirys thought about her answer. She knew she had to tell the truth.

"No."

"Why not?"

"They decided to bring me here instead."

"Why would they do that? Why would they betray direct orders to their queen and kin to bring you, a hapless outsider, to a land where you aren't welcome?"

Osirys looked at Queen Lavis, hoping she would intervene, but she remained silent, her mouth drawn to a white line across her face.

"Speak!" The noble ordered.

"They believed I'm what you call a Harbinger."

"Did you tell them you were?"

Tears fell from Osirys eyes. She shook her head.

"Yes or no, outlander."

"No."

"Did you suggest in any way that you are what they claimed you to be?"

"I don't know."

"You don't know?"

"I told them about the Muses, maybe. It was probably my fault. Please don't blame them!" Osirys cried out.

The noble did not relent, his voice was loud now, he knew the answers to the questions he was asking already, his interrogation was obviously more of a formality.

"Did any of the company dissent? Did any speak up to continue with their mission?"

Osirys nodded slowly.

"And they were overruled?"

Osirys continued nodding.

"Yes or no, outlander."

"Yes."

"By whom?"

The amphitheater could have been completely empty, such was the overwhelming silence.

"By *whom?*" The noble repeated.

Osirys glanced at Pasea, who remained steadfast and resolute as the stone beneath her feet.

"Pasea, I'm sorry." Osirys whispered. The warrior didn't respond, or so much as flinch.

"I will not ask again, outlander. Who gave the order to return to Eidrdyhn?"

"Pasea," Osirys said, her eyes falling to her feet. "It was Pasea's decision."

T HE AMPHITHEATER ERUPTED IN clamor. Several of the council members began shouting and slamming their hands on their podiums. The guard that announced the queen stepped forward immediately with two others and strode towards the center platform, spears in hand. Pasea put up no resistance as her weapons were taken from her and she was hauled away. Osirys called out to her, but Pasea didn't turn or utter a single word in reply. Osirys fell to her knees, muttering.

"I'm sorry. I didn't know what to say. I'm sorry."

Osirys looked up at the Queen. Her face betrayed no emotion.

"Please, help her," Osirys begged. "She saved my life, she was only doing what she thought was right."

The queen stared past Osirys, or through her, and did nothing.

Osirys turned to look for Naivarra, but the the spot where she had been standing was now empty, the woman was nowhere in sight.

After several moments, Queen Lavis raised her hand. Where before, her gesture was one of complete command, Osirys felt like she was weaker now, shaken deeply. Externally, there was nearly no difference in her expression or posture, but Osirys could tell that something had shifted. Still, the crowd quieted. The tribunal returned to their places. Some of the council members wore scowls, and were red in the face, while others looked smug. Queen Lavis spoke.

"The council wishes to know what you encountered on your way to Eidrdyhn, from Pearlwater Bend, outlander."

Two new guards had taken positions on either side of Osirys. They helped her back to her feet, roughly, but respectfully.

Osirys shuddered and fought against a tide of emotion that washed over her. Guilt and shame ran like the Virdi through her veins, a torrent of self-disgust roiled across her nerve endings. What had she done? She opened and shut her mouth repeatedly. What more harm would come from answering their questions? She closed her mouth and bowed her head.

"Outlander," the councilman who had just finished interrogating her said, loud and commandingly.

"*Enough.*" Said Queen Lavis. Osirys glanced at the Queen, whose stature now seemed much more her actual size. Queen Lavis stared at the Vaman noble to her left, her eyes full of violence and vitriol. He met her stare and held it for a moment, before quieting his gaze and backing away from the podium slightly, arms crossed.

The queen turned back to Osirys and met her eyes. Osirys saw there a similar softness that she remembered back on the terrace.

"Osirys," the queen repeated. "Please, if you would continue."

Osirys wiped her eyes, and thought hard about her words.

"While in town, we heard rumors that the dead had been seen walking the countryside. While traveling on the road here, we discovered that the rumors were true. We were ambushed by the Risen on the road. They seemed to be coming from the old mine of Shimmermere."

"The Risen? On this side of the Virdi? She lies!" Called a councilman from the far side of the amphitheater. The crowd erupted once again in surprise and alarm.

Osirys began to shake her head. "I'm telling the truth!" She screamed, the uproar died to silence instantly.

"Were the undead the only thing you encountered in Shimmermere?" The queen continued.

Osirys shook her head, squeezing her eyes shut. "No, there was a wraith. Pasea and the others called it a Pharandi. It wore a tattered shroud and an expressionless mask, beneath there was no body, just crackling purple energy, like lightning."

The council shared glances of genuine worry for the first time since the trial began.

"Did the warriors defeat this foe?" Asked an older councilman, one who hadn't spoken yet.

"No, it escaped with a man." Osirys replied.

"Escaped where?" He asked.

"Into Pandemonium." Osirys answered.

A gasp of shock and awe ran through the crowd.

"Are you sure?" The old Vaman followed, holding up his hand to quiet the noise. His tone was urgent, but not unkind. "Are you sure it was Pandemonium?"

"Unless you know of any other places where a giant monster that has hundreds of hooked, venomous tentacles lurks in complete darkness below the ground, then that's where I got these wounds."

Osirys lifted the dress to reveal her bandages, and she grabbed the dressings and tore them free, her swollen and purple leg exposed. The sweet smell of ointments and sick flesh filled her nostrils.

"So it is true, then." The old Vaman councilman turned and looked to his right, then his left. "We cannot ignore these events, they are beyond coincidence. The arrival of this outlander, surviving the wrath of the Virdi, with tales of the Muses that match our records, and encountering the Risen and Pharandi on this side of the river, not to mention a rift crossing to Pandemonium; something that has never happened since the *Incursion*. We must assist this woman - this Harbinger."

"Wyan, you've always been one for superstition." Replied a younger councilwoman from the other side of the stage. "Even if this outlander *were* a Harbinger, our people are no longer responsible for their fate. We disavowed that purpose long ago."

Another councilman spoke up. "And beyond that, we have more urgent matters for our people, namely enslavement and genocide of our kin. Are we to trust blindly in an ancient purpose long abandoned, and allow the persecution of our peoples to continue unchecked? We cannot afford to become distracted. We must act on what we know to be true, and that is saving as many Vaman lives as possible from torment and death!"

Cheers rose from the amphitheater.

Osirys removed the silver belt from her waist, scabbard and auric blade with it. She stepped forward toward the queen. The guards stepped to block her advance, but the Queen waved them off.

"Embraer said that you would understand this," She said softly, placing the belt on the podium in front of Queen Lavis, emblem side up.

Queen Lavis looked down at it, and she closed her eyes.

"What does it mean?" Osirys asked.

"It's the sigil of our forebears," The queen said, firmly. She opened her eyes and pointed at the back of the amphitheater, to a similar symbol carved into the keystone of the archway that served as the entrance.

"It was chosen as a symbol of duty, honor, and purpose. Our people still claim to hold these virtues as sacred, even to this day." The queen shot her eyes at the other council members, many of whom averted their gaze. She returned to look at Osirys. Osirys met her eyes. The queen's visage was a mix of controlled anger, resolve, and temperance. Osirys almost felt as if the queen was asking for Osirys to trust her, without any telling expression. After several more moments, the queen nodded, and motioned for Osirys to return to her place.

"What the council says is true, however." Queen Lavis began. "Our people's need is dire, and cannot be overlooked. We need every warrior at our disposal to fight against those that would burn our villages, and take our people from their homes against their will, to be sold into servitude."

Osirys eyes fell to the ground. She had no idea what would become of her.

"Our ancestors renounced our ancient purpose, and I must trust in their wisdom. This outlander, Harbinger though she may be, is not the ward of the Vamanari, and shall not be afforded the protections her predecessors were entitled, at the cost of the flesh and blood of our people. I have spoken."

Osirys remained silent, head bowed. She didn't know why she felt abandoned in that moment, it wasn't as if any of these strange folk owed her anything whatsoever, but still she felt even more alone, more alienated than ever before.

After a chorus of approving murmurs and nodding heads subsided, the queen continued, "Bring the Queensguard forth for sentencing."

Pasea began walking down the stairs of the Amphitheater, guarded in front and behind by her former comrades. Her violet raiment was replaced with drab clothing. She wore no weapons, and no armor. She stood tall and proud regardless, walking with her chin held high. Many in the crowd hissed at her as she passed. She was led to the platform to stand next to Osirys. Pasea did not meet her eyes, instead she stared at the Queen, perhaps in defiance.

Queen Lavis breathed deeply, and spoke, her voice shaking ever so slightly.

"Captain of the Queensguard, you are accused of defying the will of your Queen and your people. How do you respond to these accusations?"

Pasea held the queen's eyes as she responded. "I honored our sacred duty, honor, and purpose to guide this Harbinger. I did what I felt was right in my heart, and bade my company to follow in my lead, the responsibility of their actions is mine, and mine alone."

"Your vows to duty, honor, and purpose were broken the day you chose to abandon your given orders-" The councilman to the left of the Queen interjected.

Queen Lavis held up her hand to silence him. "*Enough, councilman Sjyhn,*" She quivered with rage, but did not act any further.

"You admit to acting in defiance of your orders, knowing full well the laws of our people?" Queen Lavis asked, her voice shaking.

"I did, and would do so again," Pasea replied.

"Then it is so, before the council and the people of Eidrdyhn, I strip you, Pasea, of your title among our people. You are hereby exiled from our lands, and may claim no kinship to our folk. You are no longer family of the free Vamanari, have no clan, and are afforded no protections to our kind, for all time. You will be escorted from our city at dawn, never to return, under penalty of death."

The Queen gripped her podium as she spoke, her knuckles white. The amphitheater was silent. The queen looked to her left, and her eyes shone with defiance, before looking back to Pasea.

"As it is so that you are no longer Vaman, you are not subject to my decree of neutrality towards this Harbinger. You are free to do what you feel is right, in her regard, and no Vaman law binds you to refrain from performing our ancient purpose therein."

Osirys snapped her head to look at Pasea, then to the queen, then back to the exiled warrior.

Pasea bowed her head, her face full of barely perceptible confusion. "I will do my best, my Queen."

Without another word, Pasea turned and began walking up the stairs of the Amphitheater, past the audience of stunned onlookers.

"How dare you! You can't-" Began Sjyhn.

Queen Lavis shot back, "Those exiled are no longer protected nor bound by our laws. You, nor I, councilman, have power over her actions now."

The satisfaction in her voice was palpable.

Queen Lavis ignored the uproar from the other council members around her and addressed Osirys, "The courtesy of our people will extend until your wounds are sufficiently healed, to the satisfaction of my physicians. Once you are well, you and your companions will be escorted to our borders. You will remain welcome here, as you have committed no crimes nor broken our customs, but I must ask you to look elsewhere for your purpose here. We cannot and will not assist you any further than common courtesy allows. Any Vaman who willingly puts themselves in harm's way on the account of the Harbinger will be subject to the same fate as the Captain."

One of the guards on the outside of the platform surrounding the podiums lowered their hood, placing their weapons on the ground, and removing their cloak. Osirys recognized her as Olaavi.

"Vi, no!" Cried Pasea from atop the stairs. The guards took hold of her shoulders and forced her to keep walking, even as she struggled.

Olaavi stepped forward, removing her vestments, revealing thick bandages around her midsection and kneeling next to Osirys. "I would have died in Shimmermere were it not for this outlander. In repayment of this life debt, I subject myself to exile in service to this Harbinger," She said loudly, rising and bowing her head.

Osirys was stunned. She wanted to shout in protest. She couldn't take any more shame.

"So be it," Replied the queen. "Are there any others?"

Another of the Musefolk stepped forward, lowering their hood. It was a male, of waning youth. He moved to face Osirys, looking up at her. His eyes were a deep amber, and thin wrinkles lined the corners of his mouth. He spoke softly, only barely loud enough for Osirys to hear him. "If Syndal believed in giving her life for yours, then I will trust her judgment." He turned and addressed the queen and council, "I too renounce my kinship and service to my queen."

Queen Lavis winced.

"Then it is done. This tribunal is concluded." The queen turned and raced from the Amphitheater, followed closely by guards. The rest of the council stood, regarding each other, stunned.

Osirys was ushered up the stairs, and soon she was on the terrace once again, utterly and completely alone with her thoughts. As the sun dipped towards the horizon, and the fading light of day left her feeling cold and empty, she felt crushed by the gravity of what had just occurred. She collapsed on the hammock and cried until she was overcome by uneasy dreams.

Chapter Eighteen

*S*HE CLOSED THE SMALL, *square hard-covered book for the last time before he would get home from work. It wasn't thick, only twenty or so pages, but each page was lined with that fancy gold leaf edging, and the contents of each page were more of a risk than Osirys had ever taken in her life. One of her friends had given her the idea for his birthday present. She hemmed and hawed for weeks, but after meeting the photographer and seeing her work, she managed to convince herself. She had gotten out of work early and gone to the studio. She didn't own much lingerie, and what she did have wasn't anything particularly special, but the photographer, Lorrie, had plenty of props to augment the photo shoot. She felt awkward at first, but Lorrie was fantastic. She never felt more beautiful or sexy in her life. She realized about halfway through that she was actually really enjoying herself, which was a complete surprise.*

For days after, she was nervous. She saw a few of the pictures on the small camera screen that Lorrie had showed her with excitement before she left that day, but as time went by, her confidence waned. She was spindly, waifish, and odd. She didn't have the curves of the runway models or the practiced poise of someone who spent time in front of a camera for a living. She almost felt juvenile, and worried that the photos would be more of an embarrassment than anything. Finally she got the call that the book was ready for her to pick up. She remembered walking back into the studio with her heart in her throat. Her concern must have been written plain as day across her face because Lorrie gave her a big smile and immediately told her that the pictures came out fantastic. They went through them together. Osirys definitely was not conventionally alluring in her eyes, but it was way better than she anticipated. The photographer managed to capture a playfulness, even an impishness that made Osirys feel attractive and desirable. Lorrie kept on saying how jealous she was of Osirys' body, and how beautiful she was, especially for someone who had never done it before. She kept saying how she was a 'natural'.

She wrapped the book in a thin silk red ribbon and tied it into a bow. She took a deep breath. She heard the car pull into the driveway. She had to admit, she was excited to give him his birthday present this year. It had been a rough one for him. She smiled, despite how nervous she was.

The door opened. He saw Osirys standing just past the entryway, hands behind her back. He gave her a quick smile as he hung up his jacket and cap on the hooks by the door.

"Hey babe, happy birthday," Osirys said, a playful smile on her face.

"Hey, thanks." He said in return.

"I got you something," Osirys teased, swaying her hips back and forth. Her hair was up and she was wearing one of the few sets of matching underwear she owned under her tracksuit. She thought those pictures came out the best. She thought maybe he'd like to see them in person after seeing them on the photo paper. They were maroon with lace and little bows, two of which adorned the straps where they connected with the body of the bra, and two sat on the front of her hip bones.

"Oh, yeah?" He asked, a grin spreading across his face. It was nice to see him smile. It seemed to happen less and less these days.

"Yeah, do you want it now?" Osirys asked.

"Sure, why not." He said.

She bit her lip and revealed her present from behind her back. The bow shimmered in the light. She was so excited, her heart pattered in her chest.

He cocked his head.

"What's that?"

"It's just for you, not your friends, or coworkers. You understand?" She said authoritatively. "You have to promise." Her fear of just such a thing almost talked her out of it on several occasions.

He approached, taking the book from her and undoing the bow. The outside of the book betrayed no hint of the contents, it was matte black with a leather-like finish. The only adornment on the cover was small letters embossed with gold that said "For your eyes only".

He squinted, looking at her curiously as he opened the book to the first pages. He flipped through slowly. Osirys stood in the entryway waiting for his reaction. He reached the section with the maroon set. Lorrie had given her black feathered angel wings to wear with them. She felt they gave her shape curvature and body. She bit her lip. She couldn't read his expression, his face was turned down to the pages.

"Who took these?" He asked. He lifted his eyes. Her excitement drained from her instantly.

His face was red. No, this couldn't be happening. She fell back on one heel, stammering.

"Who. Took. These. Pictures?" He repeated, stepping toward her aggressively.

"What do you mean?" She answered, tears rushing to the corners of her eyes.

"You let someone else see you like this? Nobody else gets to see you like this, you hear me? NOBODY." He had closed the book and raised it over his head threateningly. She swore he was about to hit her with it, but he threw it into the kitchen instead. It crashed into one of the lower cabinets and lay splayed open, two of the pages bent.

"No, I swear, it wasn't like that." She said, hands in front of herself defensively. She backed away.

"No? Someone had to take the fucking pictures didn't they, you stupid little whore - You couldn't have taken them yourself, could you?"

"No, I didn't take them, it was a professional. I swear. It was a professional photographer. I had them taken just for you. Please, stop. Please-"

"Who was he, huh? Did you know him in high school, and now he does this 'part time' for fun?"

He had grabbed her wrists and squeezed them. His grip was strong. Her wrists and arms hurt. They would definitely be bruised.

"He?" Osirys choked out. "No, it was a woman; it was a girl who took the pictures. I swear. I swear I'm not lying," She sobbed. His grip loosened instantly. She fell back onto the floor, holding her wrist.

He stood above her, wind blown from his sails.

"Oh," He said. He stalked past her, picking the damaged book up from the floor. He looked back to Osirys, who continued to cry. She had scooted away and propped herself against the wall near the kitchen island.

"Whatever." He gruffly tried to unbend the pages, but the creases were deep. He flipped through the rest of the book quickly.

"You don't have the body for this kinda stuff anyway."

He closed it and put it on the kitchen island.

"Get off the floor. It wasn't that bad." He said over his shoulder as he walked away to the back rooms.

Osirys wiped her eyes and stood up. She picked up the little square black book, moved to the other side of the island, and dropped it unceremoniously in the garbage pail.

Osirys was startled when she awoke to find Embraer on the terrace, facing away, out over the sleepy city, which until the previous day had seemed so welcoming and friendly. She felt overcome with nausea, as was common since she had arrived in the Vaman city. Perhaps it was how she slept in the hammock, swaying back and forth through the night, or perhaps it had something to do with the ointments and medicines that she had been taking for her wounds. Most days she could fight the rebellion of her guts, but some she succumbed, retching in her chamber pot. Today she mustered mastery of her insides, more for Embraer's sake than hers.

The sun was just breaking the rise of the Eastern horizon, the wisps of moisture from the distant Virdi River rising high into the sky, building large, streaking clouds that drifted slowly. The light of the sun lit the water droplets on fire, imbuing the river mist with vibrant oranges and reds. Osirys loved the sunrises from the terrace. She would wake up every morning as the sky was set aflame and watch the colors crawl across the heavens as the sun rose, before the doctors would arrive to check her dressings. This morning was no different, except the strange Planeswalker had arrived without announcement. He seemed quite content to watch the morning unfold as well and paid her no attention, but instinctively, Osirys clutched her bedding around her, feeling somewhat intruded upon.

Without turning to regard her, he spoke softly. "I'm sorry to wake you. I didn't intend on arriving so closely. I gather that yesterday did not go as you expected."

Osirys replied, despite her obvious confusion. "No, it didn't." She instantly felt the pang of guilt as she recalled Pasea's eyes, locked with the Queen, as she was stripped of her armor and weapons, in front of all assembled.

"Why did the Queen allow that to happen? She could have just–"

Embraer half-turned, without looking at Osirys. He held one hand out, gesturing at the city below.

"It was quite clever of her, actually." He said, bemused. "This settlement, Eidrdyhn, was carved from the notion that the Vamanari were freed, by their own decree."

Osirys had heard this tale before. She began to protest. "Just because I showed up, Pasea and the others deserve exile?"

"Deserve has nothing to do with it, Harbinger." Embraer's words cut the air, but his tone was not angry. "Think of it this way. The Queen believes in you, but she knows she cannot command her people back into service to your cause, to whatever end that may be."

Her small physician Olthi peeked his head around the corner wall of the terrace.

"I'm sorry, lass, is this a bad time?"

Osirys sighed, with exasperation. "No, please, come in."

He nodded, and then quickly moved to the basins and began filling them with water, which began to steam and bubble with heat. His attitude toward her was much more rigid this morning. Previously, he was friendly; jovial, in fact, but today he kept his eyes distant, and focused on his work. It could have been due to the fact that Embraer was present, but Osirys could not help but feel there was an invisible tension that lingered in the air, thick as blood. The physician's aides worked silently as well, their focus absolute.

Osirys turned back to Embraer. Her face was flushed, and she felt anger rising within her. "If the Queen believes in me, then what sense did any of yesterday make? I don't understand."

Embraer looked at her for the first time. The Muse-folk that worked around her paused in their tracks. The aides looked to the physician, who nervously nodded for them to continue.

Nobody answered her question. Embraer looked at her, thoughtfully. "I know you wish there were easy answers, but rarely do we see the simple design behind the complexity of what's shown to us."

Osirys felt like she was about to scream. Embraer continued. "Master Olthi, our young Harbinger is nearly well enough to travel, yes?"

The Vaman physician nodded his head. "Yes, she should be nearly fully recovered. I would stay clear of trouble for as long as possible, as my professional recommendation."

Embraer smiled at the small physician. "Wonderful. I will escort the Harbinger once she is of cleared health. I will be nearby, if you don't mind."

"Of course, sire." Master Olthi responded. The Muse-folk worked quickly, unwrapping her leg, which was still streaked with purple. Master Olthi checked the wound sites, gently palpating them. They were sore to the touch. Osirys winced several times, but kept quiet. She noted that the old bandages appeared to not be nearly as stained and soiled as they had been for the previous days. He shuffled away with her old bandages, disappearing from the terrace.

The aides steeped fragrant herbs in the hot water of the basins, and soaked warm cloths as the steam billowed about the terrace, to be swept away on the warm morning breeze.

The eldest of the aides approached her and began gently cleaning her thigh, dabbing the warm cloth on her skin with a practiced, measured hand. Her name was Baia. She had been so kind to Osirys every day. She casually glanced down at the chamber pot that sat empty.

"Feeling alright this morning?" She asked, smiling.

"Not really, no." Osirys admitted. Her guts still twisted inside of her, but she forced herself to ignore it. "I think this hammock doesn't agree with me very much."

Baia paused her rhythmic dabbing and gentle scrubbing. "Is that so?"

The other aides exchanged looks, but said nothing.

Osirys furrowed her brow. "Either that or some of the medicine I've been taking-"

One of the younger aides giggled.

"What, what is it?" Osirys asked, annoyed.

Baia glanced around. Master Olthi was still exchanging the soiled dressings for clean ones.

"Young Harbinger, you must know, do you not?"

Osirys stared at her, confused and dumbfounded. "Know what?"

The aides looked at each other, unsure of how to proceed. Baia leaned forward and whispered, "My dear, you're pregnant."

Osirys was stunned. She knew. Of course she knew. How could she have not known? It was like the words cut open a part of her she had lost. Osirys stared at the basins, billowing with steam. The aides remained motionless, their large eyes fixed upon her, waiting for some kind of response.

"Yes, of course." Osirys whispered, lowering her eyes. "Of course, that would explain it."

Baia smiled, and the aides continued to dab at her leg. Baia paused, then asked, "How far along are you?"

"I..." Osirys began, stammering. "I don't know."

"Goodness me," Baia said, her hand covering her mouth. "You didn't know, did you?"

Osirys didn't know how to respond. She looked at Baia, unable to answer properly. "Somehow it's been hidden from me."

Osirys pulled at the memory of the hot smoke in the darkness, before the Muses. She could almost feel the urges, the tip of the inky blackness piercing her belly.

"My apologies," Baia said, wringing the cloth into a small basin and shuffling away, tears in her eyes. "I did not mean to lay more burden upon you."

"No, Baia, please," Osirys said. "You did nothing wrong. Thank you for, telling me."

Baia turned, her face betraying emotion that was rare for the Vamanari. "Master Olthi told me that the records on Harbingers said that their memories were oftentimes broken, incomplete."

Osirys lowered her eyes as Baia continued. "I must admit, there was a part of me that wasn't convinced, until now."

Osirys was overwhelmed with emotion. Her hands had moved without her being aware, and they now touched her abdomen tenderly. Baia returned, lightly grabbing her hand and squeezing it.

"I can't imagine how it must be for you - to be blind to so much that you once saw clearly." Baia collected her things and motioned for the aides, who scurried from the terrace. Before disappearing, she glanced back at Osirys, eyes wet. "Good luck, harbinger."

Osirys nodded, but couldn't think of a reply. There were no words that could begin to describe her confusion, her rage, or her shame. Master Olthi returned shortly, and seemed content to work in silence. His face was somber, his wrinkles slightly more deep than days previous. Before, they had shared conversations, and had become friends. Today, the doctor was as stiff as his physicians tools. Osirys didn't mind. She was glad for it, truths be told. She felt like she would have been incapable of conversation had he attempted it. He worked quickly, applying healthy amounts of ointment and wrapping her leg in fresh dressings, leaving her knee free to move and bend slightly so that she could walk. When he was finished, he moved to the low table which had a small pile of supplies laid out. He began carefully rifling through one of the satchels, one which she hadn't seen before.

Osirys forced her lips to move. "Is everything okay, Master Olthi?"

He paused, as if listening, before he spoke. "Young Harbinger," He began, turning to face her. His eyes were soft, and where Vamanari eyes were somewhat large by nature, his seemed somewhat smaller by comparison, the skin of his cheeks and brows piled up around his orbs, his eyebrows clinging like immense caterpillars to the ridges of his face.

He made no move to hurry his speech, and began to walk back towards her, holding something in his hands. He held them out, taking her hands in his and leaving a small, thick glass vial in her palms. It contained what appeared to be a small amount of water.

Osirys looked at him, puzzled.

"It's Viqua Vitae." He explained, his eyes fixed on the vial, before looking back to her, and, upon seeing her perplexed face, he wrung his hands and smiled. "Some may recognize it as 'Magic of the Muses'. It's an extremely potent supplement for Auric magics," He explained.

"I think I saw Syndal use something like this while we were in Shimmermere," Osirys said, "She used it while she was trying to heal Olaavi, she just called it Viqua, though."

"Ah," Olthi sighed, holding a single, sausage like finger up, his excitement for his craft showing through his muted demeanor for the first time that day.

"All Viqua is not made equally, my girl!" He whispered. "Typically Viqua is drawn from deep underground, from places like Shimmermere, before it was… Corrupted. Those waters are sourced from the Virdi River, its fingers run deep into the rocks and heart of the world, through and under mountains, and the magic of the river feeds the land, which drinks it in and refines it. In the process, its potency is, enhanced."

"So this is water taken directly from the river?" Osirys followed.

"Not quite," Olthi corrected, he paced ever so slightly, struggling to find the words he wanted. "The power of the Virdi's water is in its violence. It has no ability to create, only to rend."

Osirys didn't understand, visibly. Olthi continued, more plainly. "Water drawn from the Virdi seems to have no influence on an Augury, even when performed by a powerful Auric. It cannot be commanded. It is the violence of the river that prevents it. Viqua has been tempered by the land, the chaos of the river left behind, and so its power is in the vitality of the land it serves."

"So what makes Viqua different?" Osirys asked.

"It is simply the potency. Viqua drawn from a deeper, more filtered source is more potent than Viqua that is more shallow, more chaotic." Olthi explained.

"And what of Viqua Vitae?"

"Ah, that is a different matter entirely. Viqua Vitae has never felt either the violence of the river, nor the refinement of the land."

"Never felt the river?"

"No, my girl." Olthi briefly took the phial back and held it so that the light from the morning sun hit into the watery medium. Light erupted from the vial into bright colors, filling the room. If it were possible to be inside a rainbow, Osirys imagined it would have been something similar. Olthi smiled in wonderment as he handed it back to Osirys, his face lit by a thousand thousand colors.

"It is collected as misty droplets directly from the Aetheral Falls, the source of the Virdi River itself, as the water crashes from the home of the Muses, where no mortals may tread, some of it becomes mist. Most of that mist never makes it close enough to the ground to be collected, and is instead whisked away as clouds. But through careful and meticulous methods, minuscule droplets can be harvested, and eventually, may fill a vial such as this."

Osirys looked around the terrace in bewilderment. "I'm guessing this is how you know it's the real deal, huh?" She asked, smiling for the first time since before the tribunal.

Olthi chuckled. "The way you speak brings me joy. Yes, my dear, indeed. It is the 'real deal', as you say, and its worth is nigh incalculable. A single drop of Viqua Vitae is more potent than several vials of even the most potent Viqua. Its magic is rich in ways that most Aurics have never even dreamed of." Olthi's face suddenly became very serious, "And that is why I must be so secretive. After the events of yesterday, even my showing this to you-"

Osirys clapped her hands over the vial, stifling its light. She held it out at arms reach towards him, alarmed. "No, please. Don't."

He stepped forward, closing her hands around it tenderly. "In the past, the lives and futures of all depended upon scared, confused, and utterly lost outlanders just like you. It is a burden none should bear. Furthermore, it was our duty, the purpose of the Vamanari as a people, to give and provide and protect. Even with the might of our admittedly small race, it was never easy. But you..." He trailed off, his eyes turning sad. "You will not have that luxury."

Osirys trembled with shame. Why were so many people willing to sacrifice so much for her?

Olthi straightened his stance, forcing his curved spine to match the arrow-like determination in his eyes. "If I could do more to help you, I would, even at the cost of my home or my life. If you need refuge, I will answer, even if my kin will not."

He produced a small cushioned cloth bag and helped Osirys slip the phial of Viqua Vitae snugly inside. He tied the bag neatly and placed it among her belongings, inconspicuously.

"Many have lived long lives and never lived so fully as the few days I have spent with you, Harbinger."

He offered his hand to help her from the hammock, which she took, putting only a little weight on her leg to test it before relying on it completely. The pain had lessened substantially, just an aching soreness remained.

"The Planeswalker is waiting for you. It is time." Olthi said, sadness lingering on the edges of his face.

"Can I trust him?" Osirys asked, looking deep into the old physician's eyes.

"Though his mannerisms are strange, his intentions are honest. Members of the Silver Cord have always acted in the best interest of the world, even if their methods are unknowable."

Osirys nodded, gathering her belongings, and placing the Viqua Vitae deep within the folds of several sets of clothing that had been tailored for her by the Vaman artisans. Master Olthi smiled, and walked beside her in silence as they descended the terrace.

Her thoughts returned to the life growing within her. How could she have forgotten? No, it didn't feel like she forgot. It was different. It was as if the memory was present the entire time, but absent to her awareness. It was deeply troubling. What else had been hidden from her? She tried to remember anything from before, but once again was met with just vague emotions, even less substantial than she recalled. Clearly, there was a before. The Musefolk, as familiar as they had become, still shocked her, as if somewhere inside she felt like they could not exist. The world around her felt incomplete, and yet she couldn't place exactly what was missing.

They reached the bottom of the long curved stair. Embraer sat on a bench near the gate, reading a thick leather bound tome, though he carried no bags and Osirys was certain she did not see it with him before. Without turning to make eye contact, he rose, stretching, and turned to regard her. She turned and held Master Olthi's hands in her own, though his head did not reach past her hip.

He bowed deeply anyway, and then without another word, turned, and returned the way they had come, back up toward the terrace. Even though it had only been a matter of days since her arrival in Eidrdyhn, she had to admit to herself that it felt like someplace she might have been able to call a home.

Embraer watched Osirys with measured, kind eyes. She took a deep breath and walked through the gate. He stood with his hands, and the tome, behind his back. It was the first time she had ever really looked at him without other distractions. It may have been the architecture that was proportionally smaller, catered to the smaller race of Musefolk, but he looked immense, imposing in a way that wasn't offensive. Almost like a monolithic ward. He stood a full head taller than her, but only when he stood straight. She realized that most of her interactions with him previously, he was hunched over a railing or leaning heavily, but now he stood before her, looking down at her as she left the terrace estate.

"Come," He said, lifting his hands so that his palms faced upward. His skin was rough, weathered. It was surprising to Osirys for some reason. He presented himself as a scholar, someone who spent his life in study, but his features betrayed that assumption.

T HEY PASSED UNDER AN archway that connected two intricate stone towers. Osirys noticed a small crowd gathered on the other side of the arch. The crowd parted as they approached. Osirys noticed the colors of the Queens-guard before she saw Queen Lavis, who was speaking to Pasea. Osirys felt confusion and rage swell within her.

As they approached, Embraer spoke, "As I was saying on the terrace, the Queen was quite clever. For generations, the Vamanari as a people have sought to forge their own identity, a new calling. Given their current predicament, it would have caused riots if Lavis had undone eight-hundred years of their society by swearing allegiance to an outlander. She had no choice but to remain neutral to your cause, politically speaking. But, she believes in you. She believes in you so much that she gave you the very best her people had to offer. By her actions, none can judge the choices of Pasea and the others as politically driven. The Queen has suffered much to give you this advantage, and given up more than you realize. Do not be so hasty to condemn her decisions."

Pasea's head was bowed. She wore a bland color tunic with a gray woolen cloak. It shook Osirys to not see her in the familiar violet cloth raiment that she had become accustomed to. It seemed wrong, and ill fitting, though it was tailored perfectly. She wore no weapons, and by all accounts she looked as any common traveler, with a small rucksack and plain leather shoes. The Queen, by comparison, was dressed in dark robes that were accented with silver laces. She wore a headpiece emblazoned with the sigil that matched Osirys' belt. Osirys felt that there was intentionality there. The two Vaman women stood close, facing each other. The queen lifted Pasea's chin with her delicate fingers so that their eyes met. Though the Queen seemed so much larger, they were nearly the same physical height. They held each others' gaze for several seconds, then the Queen stepped back, turning.

Only then did Osirys notice Naivarra and Troodie nearby, as well as the other two Vaman warriors, Olaavi and the older man, whose name she did not even know, dressed in similar drab fashion, stripped of their customary colors. They did not carry the customary heritage spears, but they retained their short blades, in scabbards fit with crossed leathers on their backs. They certainly had seen Osirys, and were watching her intently. It made her feel slightly uncomfortable. The queen regarded Osirys, and though her face was sad and her cheeks bore the streaks of tears, she smiled.

"Harbinger," She said, "Osirys."

Osirys wanted to yell, to tell her it wasn't too late to change her mind. She could pardon Pasea and accept the others back into their positions. Osirys could leave and deny that she had ever met the Queen or her entourage. She saw plainly the truth in Embraer's words, written in the faces before her. Queen Lavis had told her on the terrace that a difficult choice was before her, one that she never would have imagined would be hers to make. She saw raw anguish in the Queen's eyes and face, but her poise was resolute. She stepped close to Osirys, lowering her eyes for the first time. She seemed to have aged many years overnight.

"I can see in your eyes you do not understand, that you place blame on yourself needlessly, and see my decisions as foolish. I know it's hard for you to trust in my honesty when I tell you that I believe Syndal was right about you."

Osirys face twisted. "What do you mean, right about me?"

Queen Lavis nodded in the direction of the older Va-man warrior. "It is not my place to share such personal things, I'm sure it will be made clear to you in time. Just know that before the end, she believed in you so very strongly, as do I." She motioned for Osirys to join her companions.

Osirys did as she was bade. Naivarra moved close and placed a comforting hand on her shoulder.

Queen Lavis regarded the group, forcing a stoic visage, and speaking loudly enough for the gathered crowd.

"The decree given by my own voice prohibits me from giving you more, Harbinger, and were it not for the wisdom of that stronger Queen, I would falter in my steps today."

She stepped forward and spoke softly, so that only the company could hear.

"I cannot offer you any aid now but this: Intelligence has reached my ears that a fearsome wraith, a man of ill-fated appearance, and one of our kin were spotted near the town of Pearlwater Bend recently."

Pasea's eyes widened. "Mira," she whispered heavily.

Queen Lavis nodded. "The rumor is they crossed the Virdi several days ago, though I must warn you. My heart tells me that a snare has been laid to entice you into foolish pursuit."

Pasea's face flushed with purpose. "Thank you, my Queen."

Queen Lavis placed her hands on Pasea's shoulders. "I am your Queen no longer, child. Now you must go."

The muscles in Pasea's face strained against her forced stoic expression. She nodded and turned, and began walking swiftly down the road, Olaavi and the other small warrior close behind.

They walked together and left the city of Eidrdyhn, passing through the town limits to a multitude of Vaman eyes following them, some filled with suspicion, fear, or anger, some filled with sorrow or shame. Osirys tried not to pay them any mind, but it was difficult.

They had left Eidrdyhn far behind by the time they made camp. Osirys sat near a fire that Troodie had made, rubbing her healing leg. It ached from the day's march, but she did not complain or slow, for Pasea's sake. The small warrior barely spoke at all through the day, only responding to direct questions or to make observations about their progress.

Troodie was busy preparing a soup, her pack was bulging to the seams with vegetables, breads and cheeses. She even unwrapped a slab of dried meat. Osirys realized for the first time that day how hungry she was. Troodie had given her a muffin several hours into the march, but her stomach groaned as the air became aromatic, the steam of a rich stew permeating their campsite.

"Careful Trood," Naivarra remarked, "Mirelings will smell that stew a dozen miles off."

Troodie smiled. "I dare 'em to try and get a spoonful," she chuckled. She produced hand carved wooden bowls from somewhere deep in her pack, along with delicate spoons with a sigil branded into the handle.

Osirys accepted a hearty portion from Troodie. "Go on, lass. Eat up. There's plenty enough."

Osirys knew she had to share the information she had learned that morning on the terrace with the company. They deserved to know. She spooned the stew around to let it cool; chunks of potato, seasoned meat, and leafy fronded vegetables mixed around in a salty brined gravy while she spooned words around her head.

The other Vamanari took portions as well, the older warrior took a seat next to Osirys. They ate together in silence. He seemed to purposely eat more slowly, so that Osirys would finish first. He took her bowl and returned it to Troodie, who was on her second helping. He said some words, and Osirys saw Troodie beam with delight, her cheeks pushing up into her lower eyelids. He returned and sat next to Osirys once more. He seemed to be working up the courage to say something of his own.

"I know how it must seem, for me to be here given the circumstances." He finally said.

The others fell silent. He glanced around and huffed, not pleased at suddenly becoming the center of attention. Undeterred, he continued.

"You may call me Thyndal. Syndal was my daughter."

Osirys hand went directly to her mouth and she couldn't help tears from building at the corners of her eyes.

"I…" She stammered.

"Please," He responded, his eyes firm. "It is not your sorrow that Syndal believed in." He handed her a small folded note, wrapped in string. "This was in her belongings that were returned from the darkness. You should know what she thought of you."

Osirys gritted her teeth, and unfolded the small letter. It was nearly impossible to read in the dim firelight, and the script was tiny, written by the precise hand of the small, rigid Auric. Her eyes scanned the lines, looking for some kind of answer to unasked questions.

'Appa,

I write this letter from the darkest place I have ever known, in the presence of none other than a true Harbinger, brought into our midst by some calamitous fortune. Whether it be for good or ill, she is among us. I say this knowing full well your understanding of my skepticism of our heritage. We had taken our freedom bought with the blood of countless generations from our ancient purpose. Here, now, though, I can understand the choices our ancestors made. This outlander - there is something about her that I cannot describe in words. She is luminous in ways that cannot be seen, but only felt. The Muses, damn their nature, have given us purpose. She can see, Appa. She can see and feel the rhythm of the world. She will surpass all that have come before. You do not need my words, though. You will meet her soon and see for yourself the truth of the matter. This is not the reason I write to you now.

Do you remember when I was young, when I learned that many with our gift are given sight of their own end? I asked you what it felt like, and you told me you didn't know yet, that you hoped to never know. You told me that if you ever did learn, you would share it with me, to ease my curiosity. It seems instead it is my fate to ease yours. It feels familiar, like the last chorus of a well known song. I am afraid, I think, but my purpose is plain. I find myself hoping, after having witnessed a miracle wrought by her hands, that the Harbinger Osirys is able to divert my destiny as well. I pray to the Divines that I may gleefully tear these pages and cast them into the darkness, forever lost to the secrets of Pandemonium. My heart tells me otherwise, though, and I must accept what I know to be true. You will read this letter, and you must know that I am at peace, my place in this story cemented by the necessity of my actions. It will fall to you, Appa, to give her the knowledge she will need. You must, as it is my final request of you, as your daughter. She must learn the ways of the Auric. Our people will shun you, and you will forsake all kinship to our Queen and kin. Know that I would have done what I ask of you willingly, even gladly, if I could have. My last thoughts will be of you, and the love and faith you bestowed upon me. I could not have wished for a better Father.

-Syn

P.S. She will have tried to preserve me. I have seen her heart. She will not view my passing as anything but weakness and failure."

Osirys cried freely. She folded the letter and handed it back to Thyndal. He tucked it neatly into his tunic. His eyes focused on Osirys.

"You see now why I am here."

"No, I don't." Osirys replied, shaking her head. "I know why you think you're here, but I'm not any of those things."

The camp was silent. "If I were, none of this would have happened."

Embraer put down a slice of goat cheese, and leaned on one elbow. "Fate is a curious thing," He said.

"We all wish to believe in the power of some kind of free-will and agency, that we are the authors of our stories, yet we find comfort in the concept that things were meant to happen this way or that." He wiped his mouth.

"In my many years of study, I've found it is a little of both. Our stories are penned by the events that swirl around us, and we are blind to all the possibilities that blow in and about our lives. We are powerless to all but what we choose to do about the path that is before our feet. It is in the decisions that we make that give us power. You, nor I have the foresight to know whether those who have suffered were destined to do so."

Osirys wanted to protest. In her core she felt that she had to believe that fate was a culpable villain. There couldn't be an alternative. Her shame cowed her, and gave her a measure of freedom at the same time. She wished she could believe it fully, but she knew on some level that Embraer spoke the truth. That somewhere along her path, her choices were not made for her, and more accurately, making the decision not to act or change a situation was a decision in and of itself. Relinquishing that agency to observe the outcome was as much a choice as deciding to act, with the notable exception that she had no defense against outcomes that might impact those around her. She forced herself to absorb the words, rather than rebel against them. She rallied around Embraer's words, and gathered her courage.

"There's something you all need to know." She said softly, barely audible above the dim crackling of the fire, which had died down to soft coals.

Osirys looked each one of her companions in the eyes as they waited for her to finish her thought.

"I'm pregnant."

Chapter Nineteen

T HE ROAD TO PEARLWATER Bend was made all the
longer from Osirys' perspective; the awkwardness
that her companions displayed towards her as they de-
parted Eidrdyhn was palpable. Naivarra barely spoke to
her, and averted her eyes whenever she tried to strike up
a conversation. The Vamanari were even more reserved
than what she had gotten used to as their custom. Pasea
seemed completely detached, as if she were on military
assignment. Olaavi was slightly warmer to Osirys, but
still remained distant, on alert, at Pasea's urging. Thyndal
spoke with her daily, mostly about Aurancy. He had taken
it upon himself to begin teaching Osirys the basics of
Auric magic. He explained that Auric attunement was
usually hereditary, and he had been a junior Auric in the
Queensguard when Syndal was born. Aside from their
structured conversations, however, he remained mostly
silent. Osirys could see that he still struggled with the loss
of his daughter. He approached her instruction as a duty
and as an extension of his purpose, but had little room for
much else. Embraer had remained frustrating and aloof.

Speaking to him was an exercise in patience, and Osirys found that she tended to avoid lengthy conversations with the man out of respect for her general mood and temperament. In fact, the only one that seemed to behave more or less normal was Troodie, who, at hearing Osirys announcement, gushed and giggled for the better part of the next three days, asking if there was anything she could do for Osirys every time they so much as paused for a drink.

Aside from being slightly overbearing, Troodie had no shortage of words on the topic of building a family. Osirys had learned that Troodie's people were a long lived race, and that children were often few and far between, and highly celebrated. She was shocked to learn that pregnancies for the Duarfs lasted typically three to five years, and she did admit that listening to Troodie's stories of her clan's experience with her younger siblings did take her mind off of much of her current predicaments. As they traveled, though, Troodie too became less conversational, and during mealtimes, spoke often of her mentor and Leventus. Osirys could tell that Troodie mourned deeply, in her own way. She didn't quite understand what the connection between Troodie and her mentor consisted of, or what he was necessarily mentoring her for, but she did understand that feeling of loss, and let her express it in her own capacity.

They had began their journey Eastward, crossing the Dynnin river before the road had turned Southward. The small mountains on the horizon that Osirys had observed on the veranda terrace revealed their true mammoth size. Known as the Eidynmar range, they rose along the horizon steadily for two days, slowly dominating the skyline, leaving no room for any other remarkable features. The ground sloped gently upward for miles, rippling hills slowly growing in size as they approached the mountains proper, their escarpments piercing the clouds and extending far beyond. Thyndal explained that the Eidynmar peaks were still growing a measurable amount each year. The Virdi River pushed the mountains skyward, the force of the water buckled the bedrock and forced the land away. They held to the road which wound through the Eidemiryl pass, known colloquially as Syrpent's Gap. Stark cliffs rose a thousand feet on each side, leaving a meager quarter mile of rugged, rocky terrain that was mostly flat between them. Osirys had gawked at the landscape, the beauty of which astounded her at every turn. The striation in the rocks were colorful, their lines sharp and angular.

The road turned broadly Southward for several days following the pass of Eidemiryl, and they entered a sparsely wooded grassland that began to look more identifiable to Pearlwater Bend's climate. The grasses were of stockier, hardier variety, built to withstand their relative proximity to the river. The woods became thicker, and Osirys recognized that they had entered the Forrenweald from the Northern side. The forest was much less threatening from this direction, the trees increased in density so slowly that Osirys hardly noticed when the thick, reedy grasses stopped growing completely amidst the dusky undergrowth.

The exiles were vigilant in the forest, stopping frequently. Naivarra seemed alert, but healthily reserved. Facing the Risen had apparently tempered her eagerness for combat against the aberrant undead somewhat. The two nights that they spent under the treetops of the Forrenweald felt interminably longer than the rest of the trip. Perhaps it was the anxiety of facing more of the Risen, perhaps it was the reality of the situation sinking in for many of the companionship, their exile brought into relief by the close atmosphere of the trees. It was so much easier to feel alone in the forest, even surrounded by others. Osirys certainly felt it.

They emerged from the dense wood before sunrise on the familiar road. Though they were still several hours from the outskirts, the small town of Pearlwater Bend huddled among the rocky crags that limned the Virdi, the dull glow of the town before daybreak lifted Osirys' spirits. Pearlwater Bend itself remained much as it was mere weeks ago, though to Osirys it felt like an entire lifetime had elapsed. So much had occurred in such a short time, it was as if she was returning to a place she hadn't seen since childhood. As they traveled, she looked at the buildings differently, and the people that moved about their business. She viewed their curiosity and their superstitious ways less skeptically, after what she had witnessed. She had seen firsthand the horrors of Pandemonium, and if any of the tales were to be believed, any amount of evils that remained in the Old Empire following the *incursion* would be entirely terrifying to behold. As they entered town, they made for the *Lost Lantern.* Osirys, however, tugged on Naivarra's sleeve as they walked through the town in the late morning sun.

"I will meet you all there, there's someone I'd like to visit."

"Do you want company?" Naivarra asked.

"No, I'll be fine. I just wanted to stop by the chapel, say hello to Morvrel, the man who healed me when we were last here," She looked at her boots, that were now dusty and showed light signs of wear. "And thank him for the boots."

Naivarra nodded, and looked to Troodie. "I'm sure Troodie would also like to pay the old cleric a visit as well."

Troodie scrunched up her face. "I s'pose yer truly." She fidgeted with her fingers. "I sorta up and outed on him before, not much the way of a farewell. But, if'n my Leventus had his say, he'd tell me that 'Some wrongs can't be mended. This isn't one of them," Troodie shrugged. "Maybe I'll bring him some muffins. He loves muffins."

Pasea studied Osirys. "Be careful, Harbinger. News of your appearance will have been on the tongues of many townsfolk by now. We have no way of knowing who our allies are - nor our enemies - at this time."

Pasea looked so much smaller without her vestments and regalia. Osirys nodded, placing her hand on the pommel of Pemme's Auric blade, which was tucked securely in her belt.

"I won't lose it again, Pae, I promise."

Pasea held her gaze for several moments, then nodded, turning to Troodie. She seemed like she intended on imparting words of caution to the round Duarfen woman as well, but she was met with a somewhat crushed muffin held out on Troodie's flat palm. "Don't worry yerself, Pae," Troodie assured her. "I'll make sure nobody gets any bad ideas."

Pasea hesitantly took the muffin, sighing, but nodding. "I know you will."

The Musefolk, Embraer, and Naivarra continued through the town towards the inn, leaving Troodie and Osirys at the base of the dirt path that led up to the Chapel of the Divines. Osirys looked down at Troodie, and then started walking, the smaller woman falling into step behind her.

The heavy door announced their arrival, groaning loudly. The chapel looked the same as it had, even though Osirys had somehow felt that it would have looked or felt different. The inside smelled of incense and ointments.

"Hello?" Osirys called. She ran her fingers along the woodwork in the entryway, taking note of the detail in the craftsmanship.

Morvrel appeared shortly, and smiled as he recognized the travelers. He approached them, palms up.

"Ahh! *Pathyk,* and what's more, my favorite baker!" He took Osirys' hands in his and looked into her eyes. "This is wonderful to see you once again." His heavy accent felt reassuring, somehow. "There is much to say. Come. Miss VanHootan, I have need of you as well, your arrival is fortune." He turned and moved to the back rooms, where she had first been healed. As they entered, her nostrils were accosted with the smell of wounds and the thick, pungent aroma of healing ointments and salves. Nearly all of the beds were occupied.

"What happened?" Osirys gasped.

"Evil." Morvrel said softly, over his shoulder. "The rotting dead appeared. Many were hurt." Troodie chirped in alarm from behind.

"My goodness!"

"Yes, it is hard to see. Some healing soup would ease much suffering."

Troodie nodded and scuttled into the adjacent hall.

Morvrel began tending one of the wounded, pulling up an extra stool for Osirys, patting it. She sat down. He took her hands in his again, looking once more into her eyes.

"I know how you must feel." He said, turning to the sleeping man, who was wrapped in the middle with thick bandages. "You may know it was mere days since you were here last, but you feel it has been much longer."

Osirys nodded. "That's exactly how I feel."

"I had that same feeling, after crossing the River." He tugged a bandage free, revealing a long, savage rend in the man's side, stitched, but inflamed. "We were gone for no more than five nights. It may had been five months."

He patted the wound with a light, sweet smelling oil. "I can see in your eyes. You have felt the Shadow."

Osirys looked at her hands folded in her lap. "We found Risen in Shimmermere as well."

Morvrel nodded. "Terrifying, no?" He pressed lightly on the man's side, and he groaned, his breathing labored.

"Not as terrifying as what we found in *Pandemonium*." Morvrel paused. "So it is true, then."

"What is true?" Osirys asked.

Morvrel held a cloth to the man's side and turned to Osirys, his eyes very serious. "You are not safe, *Pathyk*."
Osirys bit her lip. "Why?"

"The Divines have ways of connecting all things," He began. "The slavers, your Vaman friends, their people. You."

"I don't understand," Osirys pleaded. She began to tremble. "All I want is for all of this to stop. I'm not-"

Morvrel grabbed her hand and placed it on the compress, "Press firm, but do not hurt him." He said, cutting her off. He pulled over a small table littered with vials of liquid, and began mixing a new ointment. "I do not turn away those in need. I healed men not long after you left. Slavers. They spoke fearfully. They serve a cult. It seeks to stop the Vamanari."

"Stop them from doing what?" Osirys asked, leaning in.

"*Helping you.*" He whispered. "There is much fear of your arrival. Dark words, blasphemous prophecy from the black mouths of heretics against the Divines."

Morvrel's eyes softened. "I wish I had better news, young *Pathyk*. But that is not why you have come. You will follow the demon to the old kingdom, yes?"

Osirys nodded. "One of my friends was taken."

"Ah, the Vaman fighter. Yes. She was seen. I fear for her, and do not believe the rumors."

"What rumors?"

"There is belief that the musefolk are allied with shadow." He said, looking around the room carefully.

"Never!" Osirys hissed. She trembled with anger. "The Vamanari have fought at every turn against the Pharandi, Syndal *died* fighting-"

"I believe you," Morvrel reassured her. "But there are many that do not." He sighed heavily. "It is unfortunate that fear is often held above reason."

"What are they saying exactly?" Osirys asked, measuring her words to control her emotions.

A deep voice answered from the entrance to the chapel, causing both Morvrel and Osirys to jump to their feet:

"Herald of woe - from the River expelled - tossed from the
bowels of violence.

She bringeth the will of that which resides nearby but hidden
in silence.

Dead shall again walk as never before, pathways long shut will
reveal -
Servants of the most hated Shadow be freed from the bonds of
a most ancient seal.
Old, loyal allies will bend to the call, unable to resist pall or
odium -
Such is the fate of those poor bewitched, to the Harbinger of
Pandemonium."

"Who has entered this chapel?" Morvrel spoke loudly, moving towards the entrance. "There shall be no violence here, cultist. Take your haunting rhymes with you!"

A large dark hooded shape stepped through the frame of the door. She shrunk behind Morvrel, grabbing ahold of his tunic in fear. From the other side of the room, Troodie charged, weapon in hand, snarling.

"Peace, Chaplain." The deep voice spoke. The man let down his hood. His eyes were dark, but they unnerved her. Instead of round pupils, his eyes bore vertical slits. They shone in the flickering light of the chapel. "I do not seek violence. I merely wish to see."

Morvrel stood in front of Osirys. He had no weapons of any kind, but neither, it appeared, did the prophet.

"You best see yerself on out then," Troodie warned. "Otherwise, violence is gunna' seek you."

The man in the dark robes smiled, looking beyond Morvrel and Osirys to Troodie. "I mean no harm to your exalted Harbinger." he turned and moved slowly towards Osirys. "I too only wish to deliver a warning."

Troodie hissed, "She doesn't need any more of your *Nakh di ouru.*"

"We shall see," the man replied. "The tongue of your people is rough in your mouth, little warrior. It must be hard to be separated from your clan for so long."

Troodie growled, tightening her grip, the leather wrappings on her weapon creaking with eagerness.

The dark prophet turned his attention back to Osirys, taking a step backward and revealing his empty hands from within his deep robes. He bowed, slowly bringing his eyes to meet Osirys.

"Who are you?" Osirys asked.

"You may call me Sheol," He replied nonchalantly. "Though I doubt that name has meaning to you."

"Why are you here?" She pressed.

"Ah, a slightly more useful question," He studied her with vicious intensity. "I got word not long ago from a little bird of mine," He threatened, smiling. "Of a girl with a silver belt, found on the shore of the Virdi River, with strange attire and no recollection of where she came from."

Osirys quavered from behind the tall chaplain.

"Naturally, I had to come see for myself, and here you stand, every bit what my Master foretold you would be."

The man brought his hand to his chin, resting his elbow in the other.

"And who is your master?" Osirys hissed.

"You've met," The dark prophet said, turning slightly askew to the side and speaking over his shoulder.

> *"Six eyes set in darkness,*
> *In whose presence no light may shine.*
> *Six tongues, each speak of truth,*
> *To those who will hear their design.*
> *Six hearts beat with malice,*
> *Their hatred for all genuine.*
> *Six hands hold the cosmos,*
> *Abandoned by the great Divine.*
> *Six pillars of onyx,*
> *The throne upon which is enshrined,*
> *The six heads of chaos-*
> *The One Pandemonium Mind"*

"You're a monster," Osirys barked.

He looked at his open palm. "Compared to what you'll become, I'm a mewling calf. But, it is of no consequence. My warning is thus: The river has been restless as of late. The Muses themselves rise against you." He held her sight for several moments, before his mouth curled into a broad toothy smile. "Having seen you now as you are, I believe you will triumph over the challenges to come," he said.

"Yes, you were chosen well. Farewell, luminous one." He backed from the room slowly, humming. Osirys heard the heavy door open and close, and once again there was silence.

Morvrel turned, taking Osirys gently by the shoulders, looking down at her with fear and sadness in his eyes.

"I fear you must go now, *Pathyk,*" He said. "We will be attacked soon."

"How do you know?" Osirys asked, her eyes darting up and down his old face.

"The Divines have given me this feeling. Trust your heart, you will hear them someday."

He looked at Troodie, "The Divines have gifted purpose to you, child of Ijozaan. Whether you harbor belief or not, I believe the good Leventus guided you to where you needed to be, and will guide you still."

Troodie nodded at Morvrel, her eyes wet.

He pressed his lips to Osyris forehead. "As before, *Pathyk.* You will always be welcome. Now, go!"

Troodie rushed past them, grabbing Osirys by the hand. As they pulled open the door, Osirys turned to see Morvrel behind them in the hall. He stood tall, clad in his robes, with a large broadsword in his hands, pulled from its position hung on the walls behind the pulpit. He pulled a shining metal helmet over his head as they closed the door behind them, stepping out into the fading light of the evening.

The small town seemed so peaceful, but Osirys felt Morvrel's words. There were no sound of birds, just the dull reverberating, subtle quaking of the nearby Virdi River just out of town to the East. It was otherwise quiet. Troodie grabbed Osirys by the hand, her heavy axe carried easily in the other.

"Come-'long, lass. We ought'a find our friends quick-like."

They hurried down the path towards town. Osirys drew eyes from nearly every townsfolk. Windows shuttered at their passing, and children scurried from sight.

Clear and ominous, a deep tolling rang out from the bell tower atop the Chapel of the Divines, Osirys stopped and spun, squinting to see Morvrel standing in the peak of the tower, hauling on the bell rope.

"She's here!" One of the townswomen cried out from further down the street. "Just as the prophecy said! The Shadow comes in her wake!"

"C'mon lass, don't'cha listen to any o' that blabberclappin." Troodie pulled on Osirys, but she didn't budge.

"Troodie!" Osirys cried, pointing down the Western road. Descending the hill, the man in the black robes stood atop a rocky outcropping. Around him shambled dozens of small forms. They looked like Vamanari, but they moved strangely. They stalked like feral animals, and they were pale. Their typical stonelike complexion was washed, and eerie. They bore dark streaks on their faces and arms, and their mouths hung open in anguish, pain, or fear; their haunting, unnatural forms lumbered quickly towards the town. Osirys lost her breath when she saw their eyes. It was unmistakable. She saw familiar black, inky pits. These Musefolk were already dead, and had been reanimated as Risen.

"Run!" Hollered Troodie. Her tug on Osirys' arm left no room for resistance this time. Osirys stumbled forward, her eyes locked at the horrors descending upon the sleepy hamlet town like an avalanche.

Morvrel's voice bellowed from the top of the bell tower, "To arms! Defend the village!" though he already seemed so small, his voice so faint.

Troodie and Osirys fled through the town toward the Lost Lantern. Osirys heard shouts and clamorous fighting mixed with screaming rise from seemingly all directions. They rounded a bend in the narrow street, putting the tavern into view. Osirys' heart leapt into her throat. The Lost Lantern was engulfed in flames. The townsfolk scrambled towards and away from the structure that bellowed fire and smoke into the sky. Osirys and Troodie skidded to a stop, mouths hanging open. They exchanged a fearful look, before Troodie launched into motion, much faster than Osirys thought possible for her frame. Osirys stood paralyzed, chaos rising all about her. Townsfolk stared at her, fear gripping their faces. Osirys saw the tips of many pointed fingers aimed at her person, and heard the voices rise above the din, "Harbinger! Harbinger! She brings death and darkness!"

She began to crumble. "Naivarra," She sputtered. "Pae." Troodie barreled through the crowd like a locomotive, throwing townsfolk aside like they were naught more than children, though they stood easily two feet taller.

Osirys' mind raced. She wanted to help but had no idea how. Fear gripped her and she stood idle, hands by her sides, hair hanging about her shoulders, her face swollen with anguish. The shouts and jeers pummeled her like fists. She dropped to her knees. Any of the townsfolk, had they been able to overcome their terror, could have plunged a blade through her core then and there. She wouldn't have even attempted to stop them. A blast shook the air as a window shattered and an eruption of flame spouted from the immolated tavern. Osirys sucked air through her teeth as she sunk, digging her fingernails into the packed earthen road.

Suddenly one of the upper windows of the second floor of the tavern blasted open, in a shower of glass and wooden splinters. A dark robed body careened out into the air over the street, his raiments ablaze, landing heavily on his back. Osirys saw his bald, tattooed head as it bounced off the road from the impact. Like a lioness, she saw Naivarra's shape leap from the gaping and burning hole, blade raised above her head as she fell, roaring. She landed squarely on the robed man, the force of her impact throwing her blade to the side, skittering down the road several feet away. Naivarra didn't move, the fall was a long one from the upper window, even for the sturdy woman.

Osirys scrambled to her feet and started running. The words and stares of the people around her felt like lead on her ankles. She stumbled and skinned her knees on the stony road, but it didn't matter. She needed to move.

The front door of the tavern burst open wide, nearly tearing from its hinge. A tall, bulky figure cloaked in black strode from the door, long dagger glinting in the evening light. He moved towards Naivarra's prone form in the street like a dark storm, his blade raised in one hand. Osirys wouldn't make it. She was too far away. Why hadn't she moved sooner! He loomed over Naivarra, like he was savoring the moment.

The hooded cultist was so focused on his impending victory that he didn't notice Troodie burst through the gathered crowd until it was far too late to avoid her bull rush charge. The Duarfen woman collided with the man with all her force, lifting him from his feet and bowling through him, sending him flying. Without a second thought her axe flashed, and she brought it to bear with an overhead chop, splitting his chest.

Osirys paused, but didn't stop running. She shoved her way through the fray, many moved out of her path preemptively, shouting at her as she passed. Their voices fell upon ears that had focus now. One man stepped in front of her. He was large, and wore a blacksmith's apron, with heavy leather gloves on meaty hands, thick trunk like arms crossed across his chest. She caught a glimpse of Troodie, who glanced at Naivarra's crumpled form in the street, and head bowed charged into the burning structure, axe at the ready. Osirys slammed into the smith, who was unmoved by her momentum. The mountainous man looked down at her.

"You," He spat, his words filled with ire.

"Please!" Osirys pleaded, "I don't care what you think about me, my friend needs help!"

"I could end this madness right now," He growled, pulling his smith's hammer from his rawhide belt.

Osirys fumbled and pulled the Auric blade from its scabbard, holding it shakily in both hands. "I don't want trouble. I just want to get by!"

The smith took a menacing step towards her then halted, throwing his hands up, dropping his hammer to the ground, and falling to his knees. Behind him, Olaavi brandished her twin short blades, their points firmly pressed against his kidneys.

"You simple, mindless fool," the Vaman warrior mumbled. "This Harbinger is here to stop this madness, and I won't have you saying any different."

She slid around him, her blades tracing their way across his body and sliding near his neck. Their eyes met. Olaavi stood at eye level with the man though he had slid from his kneeling position to nearly a full sit.

"Make yourself actually useful and defend your town," She said, gesturing at the sound of battle behind them, to the West.

The smith nodded, swallowing hard at the steel that still lingered near his windpipe. Olaavi looked at Osirys. "Let's away."

Osirys hesitated. "Where's Pae?" She asked fearfully.

"She made for the bridge ahead of us, with Thyn. No doubt these cloaked fiends wish to keep us from crossing."

"There's more than just the cultists." Osirys said, shakily pointing back the way she'd come. Olaavi narrowed her eyes. "The Risen, dozens of them."

"Foulness and evil," Olaavi hissed. "All the more reason for haste."

Osirys nodded and looked at the smith, who still sat, regarding her. "I'm not what they say I am," She said softly, before turning and running towards Naivarra, who still lingered, crumpled on the street.

Osirys skidded and dropped next to Naivarra. She lay on her front, several feet from the cultist who had broken her fall. He was plainly dead, blood pooled from behind his skull, and one of his eyes was open, sightless. Osirys heaved on her ally, rolling her over onto her back. Her face was covered in soot and dirt. Her chest rose and fell, and Osirys breathed a sigh of relief. She took Naivarra's head in her lap and shook her shoulders. She saw that her other arm was twisted in an unnatural direction. She winced, and heard Olaavi calling her name.

"Harbinger! Osirys! Where is Troodie?" Olaavi asked urgently. Osirys wiped away wetness from her cheeks with a dirty hand, and pointed at the conflagration, the door billowing smoke and flame. "She went in, I think she was looking for everyone else."

"Damn that fool," Olaavi growled. "Do not follow me. Get Naivarra up and get to the River!" She turned and pulled her cloak about her face as a mask. "Now, Harbinger!" The small warrior disappeared without hesitation into the blaze.

Osirys shook Naivarra by the shoulders with urgency, but the woman didn't come to.

"Naivarra!" She yelled. "Come on, wake up!" The warrior gave no response. Osirys looked around. The fighting was getting closer. Townsfolk had begun fleeing, rushing past them. There was no time.

Osirys slid the Auric blade back into her belt and tried to lift Naivarra, but it was a fruitless attempt. The woman was just too heavy. She struggled for several moments, to no avail. She screamed at the top of her lungs. Curse her weakness. Curse her frailty. Curse her indecisiveness. Naivarra *needed* her right now, and what could she do? She grabbed her hair and face, trying not to break down. She couldn't afford to fail. She saw the first glimpse of the raging dead, its small form thrashing through the crowd several hundred yards back. The townsfolk had initially rushed the small Risen, given false confidence at its relative size. They threw themselves at the aberration, but it seemed indomitable. She remembered their supernatural strength, burned into her mind from deep in Shimmermere. It's fingers had been transformed, lethal dagger-like claws split leather and flesh, and their inked visages burned with madness. In its wake, tens of torn bodies crawled away, shrieking. The undead Vaman had been female, of middle age. It bore no affable demeanor as she had become accustomed to. It saw Osirys, knelt in the street and hapless, and it howled an unearthly wail before lurching towards her, its eyes fixed and unblinking at her. A chorus of screeching howls of the undead rose above the din in response.

Osirys screamed and stood, grabbing Naivarra by one ankle and hauling on her with all her might, adrenaline surging through her veins. God, Naivarra was *dense*. She dragged the larger woman, foot by foot, away from the burning tavern, which had begun to crumble, sending burning timbers clattering to the road below, showering Osirys and Naivarra in embers and sparks. Osirys felt the hot sting of a coal as it dropped into her tunic, searing a line down her shoulder and back. She wanted to squirm and thrash but held fast to Naivarra's ankle, pulling her down the road, despite the pain. There was no time.

Osirys saw the smith that had waylaid her had regained his feet and was nearby. His eyes darted back and forth between Osirys, struggling to drag her comrade, and the approaching Risen. He shook his head, and ran towards the Harbinger. The Risen was closing too fast. He looked down and saw Naivarra's discarded greatblade which had scattered from her fall. He considered Osirys for a moment.

"Go," He said gruffly, sweeping up the blade in his bear claw-like hands.

He turned and squared against the oncoming revenant, the breadth of his body cutting off her sight of the monster. Osirys didn't waste the opportunity he granted her. She pulled Naivarra out of sight and onto the long stair that led through the rock towards the river, losing sight of the smith just as she saw the flash of Naivarra's sword as he swept it in an arc above his head. She dropped Naivarra's ankle in favor of her arms, to keep her head from banging on the stairs as they descended. Naivarra would have to accept her apology later. With gravity's assistance, they moved down the stairs quicker, Naivarra's legs and feet bouncing at every step.

Osirys stumbled and nearly fell backwards as she tripped over something. She tried to find her footing, and yelped as she looked down. It was the body of a cultist, pierced multiple times, slick blood drenching the stone stair. Osirys slid into the stone wall, grinding her arms and side into the sharp rock, and dropping Naivarra to catch herself. Naivarra slid one or two steps before skidding to a stop. Osirys saw thin lines of blood on her arms, and sucked air between her teeth.

"Damnit," she hissed.

She regained her footing and grabbed Naivarra once more, dragging her down the stairs with as much urgency as she could safely muster.

The roar of the river grew, the rock audibly hummed from the force of the water. The stair passage was thin, and Osirys could not see any of the town, but smoke rose thickly into the sky. The sound of the river had drowned out the sounds of dying and battle, but Osirys knew in her heart that those sounds were there, somewhere within and behind the din of the Virdi.

They emerged from the stair on a wide flat stone. Osirys stopped, eyes wide in amazement. She stood on a flat outcropping of rock. The Virdi was before her, but not as she knew it.

The water was glass for several hundred yards upstream and downstream, calm to the point of unease. Beyond the threshold of serenity, the Virdi crashed and raged against some unseen force. Thick mist rolled across the surface of the water, obscuring a thin wooden bridge that struck out into the body of the River, which extended several miles in width, spanning one shore to the other. Thick wooden pylons supported the wood bridge every dozen strides or so. The wood was aged, but sturdy.

"Harbinger!" Osirys heard above the roar of the River. It was Pasea, with Thyndal close behind her. They rushed to her.

"Are you hurt?" Thyndal asked, taking Osirys scratched and bleeding arm.

Osirys shook her head. "No, not bad. Naivarra needs help. I can't wake her."

Thyndal, without hesitating, pulled a small pouch from his belt, digging his fingers in, producing several small leaves. He smashed them in a fist, grinding them together, and stuffed them up Naivarra's nostrils. Within a moment, the warrior let out a spasm and began coughing, her eyes shooting wide.

"Oh, hells!" She spat, blowing her nose, sending the pungent leaves flying and rolling over, gasping. She tried to get up but winced and grunted. "What happened to my arm?" She moaned.

"I will tend to your hurts, but we must move now." Thyndal urged. Naivarra nodded, and began trying to figure out how to regain her feet.

Pasea nodded and looked back to Osirys. "What of the others?"

Osirys shook her head. "I don't know. Troodie went into the Lost Lantern looking for everyone. Olaavi followed her. They told me to run, so I ran."

Pasea slapped her thigh, frustrated. "At least one of you three has any sense at all. We cannot wait. We must go. Now."

Osirys wanted to protest. Pasea saw her face and cut her off before she even had a chance to speak.

"If their stupidity didn't cost them their lives, they will catch up to us. There's nothing to be gained from foolishness."

Pasea hooked her arms under Naivarra's and pushed her upright. "Come on, let's get moving." Naivarra sucked in air, pain visibly rolling through her.

She shook her head, clearly still disoriented. "My sword…?" She asked, groaning and holding her arm, that was clearly twisted and out of socket.

"Nevermind your sword," Pasea commanded.

Naivarra looked like she meant to reply, but was thrown back to the stone as a small form crashed into her from behind, sending her sprawling on the hard rock. Osirys was thrown aside, she watched as the form of a Vaman Risen, what appeared to have been an adolescent boy - now twisted by undeath - face and body corrupted by dark magic, scrambled towards her after knocking the strong warrior prone. A second undead Musefolk clung to the vertical rock of the stair, moving toward Osirys with purpose. It took less than a second for Pasea and Thyndal to put themselves between the Harbinger and the lethal unliving.

Osirys caught Pasea's eyes. "What is this devilry? What have they done to us?" She hissed. Thyndal's face was wide in awe and horror.

"My kin," he said under his breath, his blades drawn, and in a low traditional Vaman combat pose, which Osirys recognized. In the Queen's employ, he seemed to be trained in the exact manner as the rest of the Vipers. "So, this is the fate of those taken." His sorrow was as deep as Shimmermere. "What cruelty would compel this?"

Pasea growled. She brandished a pair of what Osirys recognized as cultist daggers, taken from the fallen attackers. They weren't quite the size of traditional Vaman short blades in her hands - they still seemed small and inadequate. Even so, Pasea did not complain or seem uncomfortable in their employ. She held one in front of her, in a guarded position, and the other in reverse grip, held higher. Her posture reminded Osirys of a scorpion, ready to strike. The Risen regarded the defenders, though they seemed singularly focused, they were far from mindless. They stalked to flanking positions, drawing Pasea and Thyndal to either side of Osirys. Naivarra rolled to her back once more, groaning.

"I'm getting pretty sick of this," Naivarra said. She pushed herself back up to her feet with her one good arm. "You bastards are persistent, that's for sure."

The Risen leapt into assault at the same time. Pasea spun and dodged the leaping strike, knowing full well the supernatural strength behind the blow. Osirys watched as Thyndal made to block more directly, and was thrown to the side, one of his blades spinning away from his grip. Though older, his balance was superb, and he rolled, launching off his shoulder and landing in a combat stance, one leg out to the side, and his other short blade held before him in both hands.

He exhaled, forcing his diaphragm to work again after the blow. "By the Divines," he whistled through aching breaths. "You learn your lessons fast against these beasts or you don't learn them at all, I suppose."

Even still, it seemed to Osirys that Pasea was having a hard time against the undead that struck out against her in wild abandon. She defended herself impeccably, dodging and weaving her weapons to deflect the flurry of violence, but it was as if she couldn't bring herself to strike back against one that bore resemblance to her kind, twisted and corrupted even as it was.

Thyndal matched Pasea's technique and focused on avoiding the Risen, using their momentum as a tool against their own assault.

Osirys noted that these Risen in particular seemed quicker, and more intelligent. While still driven by a supernatural rage that saw no respite and required no moment to catch breath, they seemed to read their opponents and moved in such a way that was more taxing to defend, rather than the more random, all-out and overwhelming offense of the those that Byzzim Roth had created in the dark of Shimmermere.

Naivarra had fully regained her footing. Weaponless as she was, she gave pause, waiting for a moment to join the fight. Pasea had landed one or two light strikes against her foe, but they went completely unnoticed by the her unliving kin. She was beginning to tire, if ever so slightly. While the Risen's strikes did not connect, she was beginning to lag behind, the pace and intensity of its attacks were ferocious. Unless she did something, she would soon be overwhelmed. Thyndal fared little better. He favored one side, where the Risen first connected with him at the beginning of the fray. His foe seemed to identify the weakness and lashed out at him with increasing ferocity. His breathing was labored, clearly the blow that sent him sprawling had potentially cracked a rib, and every breath caused him to set his jaw. Still, the small warriors held ground.

Osirys gripped the Auric blade. She wanted to act. If only she could see an opening, if only she could sneak her blade in and cause a distraction for a moment, it may be enough to give her allies an opening to finish the fight. Still, she hesitated. She was one clawed swipe away from being rent and torn, life slipping from her once again. She was afraid. She pressed against that fear. Maybe she could use Auric magic to aid her allies? After all, it was on the precipice overlooking the Virdi not far from where she stood now where she first felt the presence of the magic of the world. She didn't understand it much better now than she did then, but she had been taking instruction from Thyndal since their departure from Eidrdyhn. Maybe she could? She held the blade before her, gripping its handle in both hands. She tried to focus on the words of Syndal and her father. She tried to listen and feel for the rhythm of the world around her, tried to identify patterns within the chaos that swirled and danced about her. The Virdi roared and smashed against unseen bonds, her companions fought for survival against tireless and savage foes, each bore a myriad of hurts and fears. Osirys felt the River, it was oppressive and immense, overshadowing all other elements. She tried to push its influence aside, to focus on the cadence and timbre of her allies, if even she could lend them her strength or endurance, it may be enough. It was as if she was standing amidst the torrent of the river itself, it battered her focus, threw her attention this way and that, with each reverberating crack of boulders, it demanded her. It had power and violence that she could not ignore, it consumed her. It was convoluted and chaotic. It threatened to sweep her consciousness away. She began to lose herself in the tumult. She began to feel far away, and panicked.

Osirys realized she had squeezed her eyes shut and had been holding her breath. She gasped, coming back to the present in a jarring snap. She shook her head, disoriented. She brought her focus back to bear just in time to see Thyndal miss a parry, and a clawed fist connect with the pommel of his remaining blade, sending it flying from his hands. Sensing victory, his foe coiled and sprung without hesitation.

It was the moment Naivarra had been waiting for. No sooner had it launched a head-on lunge at Thyndal, than her knee connected with it squarely in its middle. She had launched herself into a martial strike that struck its mark perfectly. Though strong beyond measure from the effects of the magic upon it, Naivarra was still much more massive, and the weight behind her blow sent the Risen flying. It landed heavily on its back and bounced once, sliding over the edge of the stone into the calm water.

As soon as it touched the water, its frame leapt aflame. White-hot, scourging flames coursed across its form, and it shrieked. The noise was unbearable. Osirys covered her ears at it thrashed in the water, its flesh and skin boiling from its frame rapidly. Within moments it ceased animating, and the remnants of its body dropped limply into the water, as if it had never been given power.

"Ha!" Naivarra shouted.

She nodded to Thyndal, who breathed heavily on one knee, clutching his side. She held out her hand and helped him back to his feet, before moving past Osirys towards Pasea, who fought with renewed vigor, despite the horrific noise. Naivarra picked up one of Thyndal's short blades on the way by, testing its weight. It was little more than a large dirk in her offhand. Her dominant arm still hung limply from its socket

"Let's see how you like this," Naivarra rumbled, pushing herself into a lunge directly at the remaining Risen. Pasea rolled to the far side of the small undead, turning it away from the oncoming charge. Naivarra thrust the tip of Thyndal's short blade into its back, lifting it off the ground, thrashing. Pasea stared at it as Naivarra held it several feet off the ground. It tried in vain to grab at Naivarra. It squirmed and gurgled. Pasea dropped her recovered weapons, the cultist daggers clattered to the stone. She stepped close to the Risen, just out of its lethal reach.

"I'm so sorry. I failed you." She said softly. She dropped to her knees, hands clenched in fists as Naivarra turned and walked calmly toward the threshold between the shore and the Virdi. They stood, the Risen suspended above the waters of the river. It had begun to shriek and thrash desperately, as if it knew what was to come. Naivarra unceremoniously dropped the fiend and blade as one into the shallow water. Upon contact with the water it leapt alight, much like its companion. In moments its unbearable screeching had stopped as well, and just bone and cloth remnants bubbled under the surface of the water.

Pasea had pulled herself to her feet. Osirys gasped as she dropped from the flat stone into the River, half expecting her to become engulfed as well, but no such thing happened. She fished in the shallow water, pulling up a pendant from the remains of the boy. Naivarra helped her back onto the flat stone. She studied it intently, hand over her mouth.

"What is it, Pae?" Osirys asked.

"This boy was from Dyrdyndal." Pasea whispered, shoulders slumped, eyes to the sky. She dropped her gaze, shaking her head. "Wavu was right. When we didn't pursue the cultists and destroy them utterly - back at Tork's Redoubt - they continued on to the village to the South, just as she said. They were defenseless. I chose to let this happen to them."

Osirys looked at the charred remains that bubbled softly in the water. She felt the weight of their deaths, and the untold agonies of the other Risen fall on her shoulders like a ton of stones.

"I'm sorry." Osirys said, softly.

Pasea knelt by the water, and let out a scream of shame and anguish. Her fists were knotted and white. Her typical stoic demeanor crumbled and she shouted at the expanse of the Virdi. The tendons in her neck were corded and taught as she howled.

Osirys choked back any more words. She knew Pasea did not blame her. She shut her mouth, angry with herself.

After her outburst subsided, Pasea rose slowly. Naivarra approached and knelt, so that they were eye-to-eye. She placed one hand on Pasea's shoulder and pressed her forehead to the Vaman warrior, but said nothing. Pasea closed her eyes, and tucked the pendant into a pocket in her tunic, pressing on it tightly.

"We all fail sometimes," Naivarra said, too softly for Osirys to hear, but she read Naivarra's lips as she spoke. "Today we didn't."

Pasea opened her eyes, mere inches from Naivarra's. They held each other's sight for several moments, before Pasea pulled away, nodding.

"Mira needs us now." She said, addressing Thyndal and Osirys.

Thyndal nodded, reclaiming the weapons that lay strewn about the rock landing. "It seems the River still holds its potency." He said. "Having heard the rumors of the Pharandi, I had feared the fiends of Pandemonium had found a way to cross, but there must have been another way."

"If the rumors are true, and the wretch Byzzim and the Pharandi that accompanied him have indeed found some way to cross."

"That would be dire news, indeed." Thyndal responded. "But, at least we know that the *Geas* will protect us from the Risen."

Pasea nodded in agreement.

Osirys spoke, confused. "The *Geas*?"

"This is the work of one such as yourself," Pasea said over the noise of the river. "Following the *Incursion,* a Harbinger used their gifts to calm the river, just wide enough for the last peoples of Eophaetha to escape to our familiar shores." Pasea stepped onto the bridge, encouraging Osirys, Thyndal and Naivarra to hurry while talking.

"It is known as the *Geas*, and while we may cross at our leisure, no servant of Pandemonium may set foot beyond the shore. They are set ablaze, and are rendered to naught but dust."

"The Risen," Osirys said, under her breath.

Pasea nodded. "They cannot follow."

Osirys stepped onto the bridge, and looked about her. To the North and South the water was as calm as a winter pond. It reminded her of the Aethereal Lake, in the home of the Muses. She almost felt Mother Mnemosyne in the stillness of the water. The cacophony of the river had not diminished with the violence of the water, however, and she felt the river a mere hundred yards in both directions, boulders cracking against hard stone and the sound of millions of tons of water scouring the land. She looked up and marveled, at the force that kept the Virdi at bay.

"Why is it so shallow?" Osirys asked.

"Well the first people to cross didn't swim the whole way, and there certainly wasn't a bridge for them to use." Pasea called out, "They were, after all, fleeing for their lives."

"Right." Osirys mumbled under her breath.

Naivarra sat against a pylon as Thyndal examined her injured arm and shoulder.

"It's just out of socket," He reassured her. He took her arm gently and carefully aligned it back into a natural position. Her muscles were thick, and Thyndal had to lean into his movements to persuade the limb to return to where it should be.

"Are you ready?" He asked.

Naivarra nodded, "Go on then."

He held her hand firmly and leaned back and away, gently but firmly pulling while simultaneously rotating her arm. Naivarra grunted, but the Vaman was precise with his care. Naivarra's arm clicked into place, and she heaved a sigh, her relief apparent on her face immediately.

"That's not the first time you've had to do that, I wager," Naivarra remarked, rubbing the joint of her shoulder gingerly.

Thyndal chuckled. "No, it is not." He replied.

Above them, the mist swirled, sending prismatic rainbows arcing in all directions. So this was the power of the Harbingers. Osirys faltered. Was this what was expected of her? To subdue the power of nature itself? She couldn't even begin to fathom how to accomplish such a feat. She shrunk, her doubts rising like the waters that surrounded them. She understood now. Anyone who could save an entire people through an act such as the *Geas* was worthy of legend.

But what had she accomplished? She was a clumsy liability. She thought of the smith, who stood for her without her asking. If she had one thousandth of the power of another Harbinger, a *real* Harbinger, like the one in whose legacy she stood, she could have annihilated the entirety of the attacking Risen with a thought. She could have saved Syndal. She could have even destroyed the fiend of Pandemonium, the Pharandi, in Shimmermere. She could not do those things. She was impotent, she was a trifle. She was all that the townsfolk had cast upon her. She brought the town to ruin, whether she intended to or not. Her awe turned to despair, burned away to ash in her mouth.

Chapter Twenty

O SIRYS WAS PULLED FROM her self-absorbed state by shouts from back the way they had come. She turned. Troodie, Embraer, and Olaavi were at the bottom of the stair. They had their backs turned. Osirys could barely see through the mist. They were fighting. Osirys saw Embraer turn them and urge them to break for the bridge. As they fled, she saw several dark Risen in pursuit. The Risen grouped up on the shore of the river, but did not step any further.

The company was reunited. Osirys felt relief sweep across her like clean water. Troodie clapped her arms around Osirys and Naivarra, hugging them close.

"I thought I lost'cha," Troodie mumbled loudly, enough to be heard over the river. Embraer approached more slowly, breathing heavily. Osirys and her companions turned back toward the shore. The Risen chattered and thrashed about, but appeared that they recognized the power of the *Geas,* and would not pursue. They watched each other, uneasily.

"Harbinger," Embraer called out.

Her relief was short lived. His face was severe as he leaned on a pylon. He closed his eyes, and listened intently, before slowly opening them and gazing upstream. He glanced back at Osirys, his eyes filled with concern.

Osirys slowly walked toward him, straining her ears. As she approached, she noticed that Embraer's robes were still perfectly clean, and were not stained with the soot, grime, and blood that the rest of the company wore. It was as if he stepped from an immaculate dressing room, his hair was still neat, giving no indication that he had been fleeing with the rest of them. It was just another peculiarity about the man that Osirys could not place.

It was hard to hear anything above the tumult. She began to tune in to a pattern within the noise. A deep, barely audible rhythmic rumble was followed by a dull quaking boom, slow and deliberate, hidden within the chaos.

She jerked her head to look at Embraer, whose chin rested on his chest.

"What is it?" She asked, too quietly to be heard.

"Embraer, what is it?" She repeated, louder.

He kept his eyes down, but spoke, just loudly enough for her to hear. "A foe I did not expect."

He lifted his eyes and stared into Osirys' orbs, "A *Fury* of the Muses approaches."

She stepped back, remembering what Naivarra had told her weeks ago, standing on the overlook of the river.

"A manifestation of their magicks, made raw and given form." He continued. "It will not tolerate the undead on its shores, and does not discriminate. It will destroy us as readily as it will destroy them."

A familiar deep voice cut through the roar, clear and unfettered, as if amplified.

"Well done, Harbinger!" It called. They all spun and looked back toward the shore. The prophet Sheol stood like an imposing, dark bulwark; his tattooed, bald head shining against the umbral backdrop of the Risen behind him - clustered, and eerily calm.

He held out one robed arm and tossed a cloth bag onto the bridge, which thudded and rolled. Osirys screamed and buried her face in Naivarra's tunic as she saw the helmeted head of Morvrel roll from the sack.

The Dark Prophet stepped onto the bridge. He moved over the grisly trophy like a cloud, paying it no further mind.

"I tried to warn you," He called, lowering his hood. "I told you the river was restless," He gestured at the upstream river. "Do you not hear the Judgment of the Muses? The *Fury of Mnemosyne* comes for you."

"We seek the same thing, you know," He continued. "That wretch of a man that you hunt has taken something very important away from me. He came to us, asking questions that the Aurics wouldn't answer. We took him in, showed him our secrets. I never would have believed the crazy bastard would actually succeed, you know. We sent him on the fools errand in Eophaetha. If he wanted to know the secrets of death, he would have to find one of the Pharandi. When he showed up with one in tow, he could have had any amount of riches he wanted, he needed just ask! Instead, of course, he disappeared with it one night. Even so, it taught us old spells, as you can see, and then some!"

He turned and gestured back toward the Risen, that pressed themselves by the river.

"Come, my pets. By the will of our master, this *Geas* shall not hold you back any longer!" He brandished a dark crystal from deep within his robes, and spiked it downwards, smashing it on the bridge. Black smoke whipped about the air around the Prophet, and Osirys felt more than heard the groaning of the world. To the horror of all, the Risen Musefolk shuddered, and one by one stepped down into the river, the water flowing about them as they began to stagger towards the company.

"You must understand, though, that the Pharandi will be returning across this river with me. It has *so much more* it can teach us." Sheol said as he stalked forward.

"The Pharandi bow to none, no matter how deranged they may be," Embraer said, squaring himself against the Prophet.

"I do not pretend to assert authority over the grand servants," The prophet answered mockingly, "I merely relay what I have been shown in visions."

His robes flared around him in the wind as he walked.

"You are a fool if you believe that you have been shown the whole truth," Embraer hissed. "Your new master shows you only what is required to control your small mind, Sheol Marthyne. I never wished such things for you, apprentice. "

The prophet bared his teeth. "Apprentice," Sheol laughed, "Is that all, now? So be it." He strode forward, suddenly angry. His reptilian eyes flashed, and his face flushed.

"I think you'll find 'apprentice' is insufficient to describe my abilities now, Embraer, Warden of the Silver Enclave. The Pharandi and Pandemonium have seen to that. You guard secrets and knowledge, they give them both freely to those who are deserving. Come, show me your true self once more. I greatly wish to humble you."

Embraer looked over his shoulder at Osirys and her companions, "Go, now. I will hold this demon."

Osirys made no effort to move. The Vaman Risen had lurched into stride, running at them and closing.

"Go!" Embraer urged. His eyes were soft as he spoke directly to Osirys. "I am not helpless."

Olaavi had grabbed her sleeve and had begun to pull her, and quickly they had begun running, disappearing into the heavy mist of the *Geas*. Somewhere behind her as she fled, she heard a tremendous, quaking roar. She glanced back, and through the nearly opaque mist, she saw an immense shadow over the spot where Embraer had stood mere moments before.

T HE MIST OF THE river swallowed her as she fled. Her heartbeat thundered in her chest. The river was miles wide. For what seemed like eternity she ran, her senses bombarded by furious noise and the eerie, confounding wet fog that lashed her and kept her all but blind to anything mere feet from her. She saw a dark shadow on her flank. From behind her, she heard Troodie bellow. She looked back to see the stout woman launch herself from the bridge into the mist, axe raised. The fog swallowed her completely, and she was gone. The roar of the River covered any sound she might have otherwise heard. Naivarra kept pace with her. Olaavi, Pasea, and Thyndal stayed several paces behind. She yelped as the form of one of the small Risen careened at her, with a leaping attack from the mist. Osirys skidded, and Naivarra crashed past her, catching the Risen in the chest with the tip of a dagger she had claimed from a dead cultist, plowing through it as it thrashed furiously. Osirys spun to look behind her. Two more Risen attacked from the sides, pouncing like jaguar from the cover of camouflage, catching Olaavi and Thyndal. They tumbled off the edge of the worn bridge and into the shallow water. Pasea brandished the twin cultist daggers. The other Musefolk struggled to gain their footing, the wet, small rocks challenging their balance and reflexes. Pasea scanned the swirling brume.

"There are four more." Pasea said, turning to Osirys. "Harbinger, fly like your feet have wings."

"Pae," Osirys started.

"Go!" Pasea commanded, her stonelike visage the embodiment of finality. Osirys turned and ran. She ran until her stomach rebelled, her hair stuck in wet matting across her face and nose. She struggled to breathe, but she did not stop. The narrow, old bridge continued on, only ever turning slightly, but never more than several yards in view at a time. A sharp bend could have been mere feet in front of her but she would have never known until it was upon her. She clawed at the hair that sought to strangle her. Her wounded leg screamed with pain. She did not know whether it was tears or the fog that caused droplets to stream down her face. It hardly mattered.

The unearthly roar shook her, nearly knocking her backwards. It was as if the trumpets of the roots of the world rang out around her, combined with the the grinding of continents and the wind of a world ending tempest. Glass eyed, Osirys collided with and clung to a pylon and fearfully looked about. At first, there was nothing. The mist continued to swirl, and she could only hear the tumult of the Virdi beyond the *Geas*. Osirys shuddered. What lurked just beyond her sight? She tried to force her legs back into motion. Before she could command her muscles to move, however, the titanic *Fury* stepped into view, crossing the threshold of the *Geas* before her. It stood as a megalith, the raw power of the Virdi's waters bound by the will of the Muse, Mnemosyne. It towered well over a hundred feet tall, and nearly as broad. It dominated the river, rising above the chaos and moving through it with no difficulty. It was power incarnate; furious magic focused, and made tangible. Though it appeared fluid, it had a definite form. As it moved she could make out a massive torso on four immense limbs, it loomed in almost a gorilla-like stance. Its presence exerted a pressure on the atmosphere, and within its swirling, violent form she could make out three silver eyes that seemed to focus down and upon her. She was enraptured by the behemoth. It stopped shortly after it passed the threshold of the *Geas*. It seemed to be beckoning Osirys. It compelled her to move. Mouth agape, she stepped off the bridge into the water. It was frigid. It lapped and flowed about her ankles and calves, but did not rise above her knees. The riverbed was tumbled stone, packed closely together, almost as steadfast as a road, but her footing was unsteady, the rocks were slippery, as if they were covered in damp moss. Wind ripped around her as she approached, tearing at her tunic, causing it to whip and lash her, her wet hair snapping in the gale. As she approached the elemental titan, she desperately fought against its compulsion, and desired to flee, into the depths of the raging river if she must, to escape. This compulsion, however, was much different than the one she experienced at the mercy of the Pharandi, however. The *Fury* did not force her movement. Her body was still her own, but it *commanded* her. She acted as if her choice was predestined, ordained by a power that she couldn't begin to comprehend. At that moment, the two forms of control felt nearly indistinguishable, but for some reason, the *Fury* felt much less abhorrent to Osirys.

When Osirys looked up, she took in the magnitude of what the *Fury* contained. She felt the rhythm of the river, the hidden pattern of the world. There raw violence, the concentration of which she could not have comprehended on her own, mixed with elemental energy and substance of life. It was searing, cleansing, and terrifying all at the same time. She also felt the ache of many pains, their edges smoothed but never forgotten like the tumbled stones beneath her feet. The *Fury of Mnemosyne* held the remnant recollections of countless cruelties committed over the aeons; it roiled with the furor of atrocities from an entire world's history. She felt the fall of empires within the colossus. She felt the fear and grief of entire populaces that had succumbed to ruthless conquerors. She felt the extermination of armies at the hands of merciless aggressors, the senseless struggles of millions of entrenched defenders expiring in their own filth slowly, succumbing to the basic lack of requirements of life. Her heart was torn asunder feeling the ache of wars fought between brothers, family brought to arms against family, and the weight of baseless hatred of people against people. More than all else, she crumbled under an unstoppable tide of those that hated themselves. Out of the endless myriad of pains, she found her own agony within the swirling elements. Her self-inflicted terrorism shone like a beacon within the *Fury*. It accosted her with hopelessness, and certainty of failure. It felt so familiar, so intimate, and so shameful. Parts of her mind and soul were locked within the titan, motes of her that she knew existed and were real, but could not recall, and could not justify.

Overwhelmed, Osirys screamed, the sound of her voice barely perceptible over the chaos. Her tears mixed with the water of the Virdi. She did not know what good she could hope to accomplish, and before such immense power, she felt molecular.

"*Who was I?*" She howled at the *Fury.* "Who AM I?"

It boiled and its violence strained against its form. She felt all the hatred of the untold millions of endings scored in savagery reaching for her, seeking her destruction – her companionship. She felt it now. The one called *Recollection,* Mnemosyne herself, her will, the raw essence of the Mother of Muses held the *Fury* at bay. All of it.

"*Why did you send me here if I was meant to fail?*" She railed against the elemental. "*Why did you take my memories from me, Mnemosyne?!*"

She threw herself to her knees, the water rushing around her hands and arms. She felt her soul splinter under the oppressive force of the *Fury.* Mnemosyne bore these hurts for all eternity. The ferocity of the *Fury* was borne for all time behind the kind eyes she had seen in the land of the Muses. It was unendurable.

"*How could you let me forget my child…*" She sobbed.

The *Fury* bowed itself, lowering its massive torso close to Osirys. She gazed into its violent depths, and saw her reflection. It was not a reflected image, but rather, a look behind the curtain she had dropped over the old, damaged structures within her. She saw her pain, her fear, her hopelessness, her weakness. She saw herself as she truly was, regret and shame wrapped in a self-contained violence that never revealed itself. It was for that reason she understood Mnemosyne's burden, it was one they both shared in their own way. She saw the theater of her own tragedies; the cast of villains that filled scene after scene, and she was center stage, the largest and most spiteful villain of all.

All three of its silver eyes bored through her being. Its pressure crushed down upon her. She felt like she would be compressed to a diamond, her impurities squeezed from her pores like ichorous venom under the weight of its presence. Osirys bore the agony, it was cathartic, it was liberating. It was all the pain she wished she could inflict upon herself.

> *"You must become,*
> *and yet cannot be*
> *more than you are,"*

Mnemosyne's voice floated from the elemental.

"What does that even mean?" Osirys begged. "Please, give me back what you took from me!"

> *"What cannot be given,*
> *must remain to be*
> *seen from afar,*
> *Your power does not lie*

In the sordid scenes of your past.
The brighter you shine,
The deeper are the shadows you cast.
A paradox, a contradiction
at once and at last,
Fated against fate,
Your power is unfettered, and vast."

The Fury glistened with defiance, its innards bristled with malice, but the surface shimmered with all the measured patience of a mother consoling an infant in tantrum.

Osirys waited for it to *do something*, she hoped and feared that her memories would flood back to her, and she would finally know what it was she needed to feel so ashamed about. She searched the *Fury* for an answer, for any sign it would act, but it remained statuesque, regarding her with emotionless expression.

"What kind of bullshit answer is that?!" Osirys screamed. The *Fury* shifted, as if spurned. "That doesn't help me!"

The *Fury* lurched upward suddenly, the pressure lifting from Osirys in an instant. She surged to her feet, spinning. Anger rose within her, an inner rage mounting to rival that of the river that surrounded them. Vaguely through the mist, she saw the dark shapes of her friends emerge, rushing along the bridge, and in awful condition. They were bloodied and ragged. They skidded to a stop. Naivarra saw Osirys first. Osirys saw her mouth move, saw Naivarra call her name, but could not hear it. Troodie,

Pasea, Olaavi, Thyndal, – All stared at her from the bridge, standing before the *Fury of Mnemosyne,* soaked and wild. She looked beyond them, into the mist, and saw more dark shapes of the dead, swiftly closing. She reached out and shrieked, pointing.

The Vamanari spun, weapons brandished. The Risen descended on her allies like a ravenous swarm.

The Dark Prophet, Sheol Marthyne manifested through the mist behind the legion of hungry dead, arms outstretched, palms up. There was no sign of the Planeswalker.

"Embraer," Osirys mouthed.

The *Fury of Mnemosyne* moved, raising one of its immense limbs into the sky.

Osirys watched in horror. The club-like appendage was thirty feet wide at least.

Sheol's voice cut through the roaring noise like a fel wind. He held his hands aloft, a broad, evil smile on his face.

"Your friends are about to die, Harbinger, unless you *do something!*"

The elemental leviathan raised itself higher up, lifting onto its rear appendages, the second of its front limbs lifting into the sky as well, poised to come down and obliterate everything, Risen, Prophet, and allies alike.

"No!" Osirys called. "Don't!"

The *Fury* ignored her pleas. It was forged for singular purpose. Osirys felt that, now. It would not tolerate the undead, or any that happened to be caught nearby, just as Embraer had said. Its massive weight and force was palpable as its arms began to fall. She felt its anger. It would send the servants of Pandemonium to deliverance at any cost, no matter the collateral. Naivarra had been dropped, pinned under one of the Risen, her eyes fixed on the wrath of the mother of Muses bearing down upon all of them. She turned and met Osirys' eyes as the maw of the undead pressed close to her throat. The warrior strained and was failing to hold the Risen's supernatural strength at bay. Osirys watched as Naivarra's strength began to leave her, realization of the inevitable working its way across her face.

"Do something," The words ricocheted through her soul and ignited her from within. She didn't know when she had reached for Pemme's Auric blade, but she found it in her hands. She stood, the soles of her feet resting on the artery of magic that fed the world. She felt the vitality of the Virdi River, she understood it.

"You will not do this," she whispered, her voice resonating between each of the tiny droplets of mist. She watched as the *Fury* began its crushing descent. Destroying the Risen wouldn't be enough. There was no stopping the violent behemoth's strike now, it couldn't if it had wanted to. She would make it stop.

She found the pathways within her that she felt deep in Shimmermere, and once before on the overlook not so far away. They were plain and unobstructed. The rhythms of the chaos around her were elementary, and she was *angry*.

"I will not allow their deaths," She spoke, her words coming from within and without, as if the entire Virdi River were speaking with her.

From somewhere behind her, she heard Thyndal calling her name, pleading with her.

"Peace, Harbinger – you cannot control it! It will be the ruin of us all!"

She had no choice. She would not sit idle. She would choose. She would *act*.

Osirys erupted into pale luminance, engulfed in white-hot conflagration. Her rage was unleashed. It was as immense, and as violent as the River that surrounded her. It was directed at the Risen, the Dark Prophet, at Mnemosyne, at herself. She had no control, she didn't even try. All that she was, all that she wished had happened and didn't, she threw into the great song of the world, and the River amplified it a thousandfold. She stared at Pemme's Auric blade. It radiated a blinding luminescence, its runes no longer even visible. It burned her hands. The conduit was just too small, it couldn't contain her.

"Osirys! Please!" Pasea shouted. "No!"

She saw the silver eyes of the *Fury*. They shimmered in fear, even as the colossal elemental levied its strike in full swing towards the ruin of her friends. She turned the point downward. She dropped to her knees, driving Pemme's Auric Blade with all her might into the riverbed.

She heard the maniacal cackling of the Dark Prophet Sheol across the cracking of boulder on boulder and millions of tons of water breaking against the mighty magic of Osirys' predecessors. She turned just in time to see him pull aside reality like a sheet, just like the Pharandi had done in Shimmermere, stepping across a rift to another world.

It was of no consequence. She would do anything to save her companions. For once, she would.

A concussive force ripped outward from Osirys in all directions, scouring the earth beneath her feet - clearing the fog in an instant. The pylons of the bridge ripped from their deep anchors, and through the tears, she saw the Risen tossed like leaves in a gale, disappearing into the torrent beyond the protective limits of the *Geas*. Naivarra, Troodie, Pasea, Olaavi and Thyndal were spared her wrath. They huddled in the shallow water as the bridge was torn from existence. The *Fury* that loomed above Osirys took the full force of the eruption, its form instantly pulverized to nothingness. It was pushed up and away in all directions; its impending fatal strike blown away in an instant, reduced to droplets that sparkled in the light. Even the roar of the Virdi was quelled, and for a few brief moments, its ferocity could not match the Harbinger's. It was over in the blink of an eye, and the eerie silence lingered for the span of a heartbeat.

"What have you done?" Pasea said.

Osirys breathed out, the last of her luminance flickering like an exhausted candle. She sat, slumped in the River. The water around her as still as the air.

Within moments, Naivarra was by her side, hauling her to her feet. She teetered, stars dancing through her vision. Then she heard it. The crack. The Virdi surged once more against the magic of the *Geas,* with the force of all of nature behind it. It was as if a fissure opened in a glacier. Osirys looked at her friends. Exiles, just like her. Behind them, the *Geas* shuddered and quaked, the tumult of the river beyond pressing in and bowing the magic, as if it had been imprisoned for millennia and now sought freedom.

"What have you done?" Escaped Pasea's lips once more as a torrent erupted from the *Geas* nearby. Naivarra and Osirys were thrown to their knees by a quake that rolled through the ground. The earth itself groaned and con-torted, buckling and rolling as if it were made of foil.

A large, house sized boulder sailed through the shim-mering *Geas* behind them, smashing through the magical ward and exploding into shards of sharp rock, sending shrapnel in all directions.

It was no use. The *Geas* had mere moments left. The Virdi was miles wide, they hadn't the time to escape. It began soundlessly. Osirys looked back and saw the entirety of the ward give way from both sides, the River unleashed in full ferocity. She knelt with Naivarra in the frigid water. Osirys saw fear for the first time in her friend's eyes.

"I'm sorry," Osirys said, closing her eyes and letting her forehead fall against Naivarra's.

"I have to stop it." Osirys said.

Naivarra grabbed for her, but she shook free, lurching to her feet and taking a step backward, toward the failing *Geas*.

"I have to try."

She brandished the Auric blade once more, holding it before her like it would protect her from the full might of the Virdi. She knew she couldn't stop it. She had used everything she had to save her friends, only for them to be condemned to die by her actions. She felt destroyed. Her wet hair hung on her face as she stared down what was to come, and it came swiftly.

They only had moments left.

"Osirys, I-" Naivarra called, but she was drowned out by the cacophony of crashing water. The deluge rushed in, and they were swallowed. The force of the Virdi River would not be resisted. She was tumbled and crushed and twisted in an instant.

Chapter Twenty-One

"How fitting," Osirys thought to herself. The air was blasted from her lungs from the force of slamming into the riverbed. She started her journey in the tumult of the river, it was pleasantly ironic she should end there. She couldn't discern up from down. She waited for the crush of an immense boulder to end everything.

She felt pressure all around her. She felt her body enclosed, and was dragged through the water. Then something happened she did not expect. She broke the surface of the water, bursting into the sky. Osirys instinctively gasped for breath, and blinked water from her eyes. All around her were silver scales, glistening and wet. She gawked. Her body was in the clutches of an immense dragon, its claws large enough to encircle her body several times over. It shone in the misty sunlight, its wings broad and magnificent - their leather filling with air with every beat. As heavy and immense as the dragon was, it was agile in the sky, deftly maneuvering out of the way of boulders as they were tossed from the Virdi. The dragon banked and turned as they gained height, angling toward the far shore, which was just barely visible along the horizon. The mist of the Virdi concealed the Eophaethan coast, but soon it was forced to reveal the land of the Old Empire.

The jungle extended as far as she could see, and then much farther. There were no roads, no towns, no sign of inhabitants. There was only the immense wilderness that hid the decayed and crumbled remnants of a civilization brought to ruin, wild and lethal.

The dragon glanced down and back, craning its head on its long, silver neck, looking at Osirys. Its eyes were large, and wickedly intelligent. She felt awe, fear, and shame. The dragon's expression was unreadable, but she felt the grip around her loosen ever so slightly. The beast clearly did not intend her any harm. She spun her head. In the other claw, she saw her companions. She was baffled. They soared through the air far above the rampaging Virdi River. Mist and wet wind whipped about her. Her stomach turned and Osirys wanted to escape. She began to struggle, and the claw clenched ever so slightly once more, not enough to cause her discomfort, but enough to immobilize the Harbinger.

Minutes later, they banked north along the Eophaethan shore, and the dragon glided until it found a suitable landing spot. It swooped low, pushing the air with its wings to slow their descent. Osirys was released, the feeling of solid ground beneath her. The dragon flapped its immense wings and came to alight upon the cliff overlooking the

Virdi, sending hurricane-like waves of wind in all directions.

She rolled, sobbing and bewildered. She felt like she didn't deserve to feel the grass beneath her. She felt like she deserved whatever fate would have befallen her at the mercy of the Virdi River.

Instead she sputtered, hair once again full of grit and small sticks, just as she was when Naivarra found her on the shores of the Virdi weeks ago.

She looked for her companions. They were half drowned, but alive. They were deposited on a high bank, several hundred paces from the violence of the river, which thrashed and tossed newly dislodged stones and boulders with impunity. The bank itself rose over a hundred feet above the bed of the Virdi, which had carved itself a canyon that clawed at the foundation of the world. From her vantage, Osirys still could not see the far shore that they had left, just a blanket of mist rose into the sky where it was whipped about and churned into streaking clouds that stretched far overhead, disappearing beyond the tops of the Eophaethan wilderness canopy. The air was oppressively humid, and everything seemed to be damp with watery spray. There was a thin strip of thinly grown grasses and stones before the dense jungle of Eophaetha began, and continued for a thousand miles or more Eastward. The trunks of the trees closest to the river were gnarled, with much evidence of the force of nature that tore at the landscape nearby. A hardy few trunks with skeletal limbs clung to life, sprouting from defensible spots behind boulders or tucked behind natural ledges, where the force of the Virdi was less threatening. The Eophaethan wilderness rose behind them, thick and foreboding. The ruins of the Old Empire were entombed within the tangle of the woods, their dark pasts lost to ages of natural reclamation. Even still, Osirys could feel the faint stomach-turning sickness of Pandemonium that she felt in the depths of Shimmermere. There was no mistake to be made, the threat of that dark place lingered in the open air of the Old Empire like a sweet, foul rot.

Osirys remembered the fields of funerary stones that stretched for miles outside of Pearlwater Bend that marked the final resting places for those fallen in the battle of Tork. This wilderness had felt far, far more death, and no stones were laid to mark their tribute. She looked back at the Virdi, and suddenly wished she could return to the other side, even with the threat of the Risen. Combined with the endless shuddering of the land upon which they sat, the wilds of Eophaetha tied her insides into knots, and she shivered in the wind. She thought of the veranda terrace, fair weather, and friendly nature of the Vamanari in Eidrdyhn. She breathed in, trying to recall the peacefulness of the city. She felt like that brief respite was a dream, the land so far away and remote. There was no comfort here, and there would be none for quite some time, if she was lucky enough to ever feel such things again.

Troodie sat cross legged, her tight braided hair demolished, and her hair knotted and wild. She stared at the form of the dragon that sat, facing away from them, as it regarded the raging Virdi River which had reclaimed the passage made possible by the *Geas*. It's scales glistened wetly. It folded its wings behind it, droplets of water cascading from them in small streams. It shone a dull but lustrous silver, and the droplets of water that clung to the ends of individual scales gave the illusion of tiny diamonds that caught the light of the sun and scattered it, making the fearsome creature erupt in a magical prismatic twinkling as it heaved for air. The dragon was immense, terrifying, and beautiful at the same time, but Osirys did not feel afraid. Rather, she was curious. Something about the dragon seemed familiar. It held itself with aloof precision. Its spine was adorned with a ridge of thick plated scales, and its arms and legs were protected with chitinous natural armor as well. Its tail was long and powerful, and culminated in a thin rudder-like fin.

"Oooo," Troodie sighed. "I didn't see that one comin'."

"Which part?" Naivarra groaned, rolling onto her back.

"Uh, any of it I guess," Troodie said, scratching her head.

Naivarra dragged herself upright, shaking her head.

"C'mon girl," She said, extending her hand.

Osirys took it, and was pulled to her feet once more. Troodie clapped Osirys on the back. "I told ya those ingredients would come together!"

Pasea sat nearby with Olaavi. She looked at Osirys, her expression unreadable. Thyndal had already opened his pack, and had begun to dress the wounds inflicted upon the group by the Risen.

When she looked back, she was shocked. The dragon revealed its true identity. Embraer stood in his more recognizable form, his robes dry and unmuddied. His back was still turned to the rest of the companionship. He didn't speak, but watched the Virdi River rage on, the *Geas* completely gone, along with all traces of its existence.

He turned slowly, his sad eyes coming to rest on Osirys.

"So, that's your secret, then," Osirys said.

"One of many, Harbinger." He responded, walking past Osirys, fatigued weight in his steps like Osirys hadn't seen before. It was as if he actually moved with an age appropriate for his appearance. "One of many."

"What happened? Where were you?" Osirys realized her words were tipped with a venom not intended for the Planeswalker, but she didn't have the self control or patience to prevent it.

He frowned at her. "My old apprentice has grown very powerful."

"It's true then… He wasn't lying?" Osirys asked.

Embraer shook his head.

"He was an apprentice of our order, and I his master, yes." Embraer said, turning around. The words seemed to pain him.

"His master?"

Embraer grimaced. "And… Father, though that failure is far more painful."

"Hooooooo," Troodie cooed.

"Does that mean," Osirys followed.

"That he is of Dragonkind? Yes and no. The power of my race runs thick within him, though Sheol is not pure of blood."

Osirys crossed her arms. "Embraer, please, speak so that I can understand you. I need to know what just happened here."

Embraer studied Osirys.

"Sheol Marthyne was the first apprentice our order had taken in a long generation. His mother was one of Human kind, and I, as you now know, am of Dragonkind. His training was obviously entrusted to me. Though he is only half dragon, he was to become a guardian of the Great Gateway."

"The Infinite Door," Troodie said, softly.

"Indeed. One may walk through it and appear anywhere in reality, as long as you know where it is you're going. It is the sacred purpose of our order, the Silver Cord, to protect and serve the Great Gateway. Due to our… heritage, we are the few that can use it without going mad. It is through these means that we monitor realms like Pandemonium and others. As I was saying, Sheol was to become a Guardian, and serve at the Silver Enclave, where the location of the Great Gateway is hidden.

"When he was to be inducted, he looked upon the Great Gateway. Never before had a half-blood been tested in such a way. It was at this moment that I fear he fell to the thrall of Pandemonium. I believed he was ready, and we had little other choice. Our kind has dwindled to a mere handful over the ages, and we have long been unable to create full-blooded progeny, but that is another tale. Suffice to say, Sheol was our last hope at ensuring a new generation of Guardians, but I was wrong."

"When did this occur?" Osirys asked.

"Mere months before your arrival, as it would happen." Embraer answered. "I have no doubt that you are the Muse's answer to our error."

Osirys wasn't so sure. She recalled the words of the Muses, with their musical voices:

"We did not foresee her,"
"She was beckoned by Shadow,"
Osirys fell silent. Had she been playing into Pandemonium's plan from the beginning?

"What does Pandemonium want with him?" Troodie asked, pulling Osirys out of introspection.

"Many think the *Incursion* that brought about the ruin of the Old Empire of Eophaetha, upon whose soil we now stand, was ends to its own means. Our order believes it was merely a trial; a test for Pandemonium's true ambitions. Since the forging of this world, Pandemonium has sought access to the Great Gateway. If it were to succeed in gaining control of the portal, Pandemonium could invade all realms, this one and others… Including, even, the Harbinger's true home, far away from here."

Osirys' head snapped up. Her true home?

Embraer continued, "The Muses, nor even the Divines would have any means to prevent the invasion, and all of reality would fall to the immortal reign of chaos. Our kind was chosen by the Muses, created and given purpose to safeguard against such a calamity. As such, we are beyond Pandemonium's influence, immune to its persuasions. Sheol's diluted blood however, must have left him open to suggestion. Where he is by all accounts as strong and powerful as any Guardian, indeed, he has now far surpassed me, his mind did not inherit our gift of resilience. Pandemonium has waited untold ages for the moment when it could enthrall one who could access the Silver Enclave, and show it the way to the Great Gateway. Given the chance, it did not hesitate, and its domination was swift. We, of course, had a safeguard in place for just such an eventuality. Hoping for the best and fearing for the worst, Mnemosyne sealed Sheol's knowledge of the Enclave and the Great Gateway beyond the reach of all mortal-kind for all time in the Well of Memories."

Embraer's eyes bore into Osirys. "Your memories are there, too, Harbinger. The ones taken from you, hidden in plain sight but inaccessible nevertheless. The remnants of all recollection make their way to the Well of Memories. Many mortals call such remnants 'Souls'. After they die and pass on, their recollections, their histories, their experiences and emotions are collected, and used by the Muses for the creation of *Ideals*. Mnemosyne forged a guardian from the recollections of violence across history - A being to protect the Well of Memories, and to serve Mnemosyne's will. Not I, nor the others of my order, or Sheol, not even the Dread Lich Or'Qan had the power to overthrow any of the *Furies,* let alone the mightiest of them all, the *Fury of Mnemosyne.* As such Sheol's memories, and the knowledge of the Great Gateway, was secure beyond the machinations of Pandemonium."

Osirys lowered her eyes. What *had* she done?

Embraer looked past Osirys at the raging Virdi. "The loss of the *Geas* was tragic, but I fear the true consequences to be much more dire. Now that the *Fury of Mnemosyne* has been vanquished, the Well of Memories is no longer guarded."

"Well where is it? We'll just guard it ourselves," Osirys said, looking at her companions for support. "I'll be the new guardian." The Virdi river roared nearby, making her voice feel much weaker, and smaller than she wanted it to be.

Thyndal spoke up. "No one knows its location."

Embraer nodded at Thyndal. "Only Mnemosyne may answer that question."

Pasea wrung her hands. Embraer looked at Pasea, and nodded slowly. "Now you see, young warrior. That is why the Pharandi has taken your kin."

Osirys looked at Pasea, confused.

"Our kind were also created by the Muses to oppose Pandemonium and serve as guides for ones such as yourself, Osirys. Legend speaks of a ritual that allows our kind to commune directly with our creators in great times of need, and seek knowledge that only they possess. The Pharandi intends to use Mirabyll to uncover the location of the Well of Memories." Pasea finished her explanation, her face severe. "It will force her, in much the same way it forced you, to betray her people and her purpose."

Osirys stood, head bowed. Pandemonium's words echoed in her mind:

"I will see the light swept from your world, and you will be my tool, luminous one."

"I have chosen my instrument carefully. Always remember, the brighter you shine, the deeper are the shadows cast. We will meet again at the Gateway."

"I didn't know. I just wanted to do something good for once. I just wanted to save everyone."

She turned and began walking away. Pasea stood up and made to follow her, but Embraer put a hand on her shoulder.

"Let her be." He said.

She didn't want to cry. She didn't want them to see her weakness any more. Maybe she was exactly what the people feared. Every action she had taken since arriving had been nothing but service to Pandemonium. Maybe if she was lucky, one of the horrors of the Old Empire would devour her, and they would be rid of her ill-cast destinies. She strode into the Eophaethan wilderness alone.

THE VEGETATION WITHIN WAS thick, nearly impassable. She found the remains of an ancient tree, enormous and decayed. Moss covered its fallen trunk. Even half-buried in soil, the trunk was twice her height in circumference. The thick canopy above already had reclaimed the sliver of sky that the tree had left vacant upon falling. She sat down on one of the massive limbs that may as well have been a tree in its own right. It flexed weakly under her weight, but bore her.

Minutes passed. She lowered the barrier within her, and asked the tears to come, but they didn't. She had none. Somehow it didn't surprise her that even in her best intention, she ruined everything. What was the point of fighting against fate?

She jumped as she felt a strong hand come to rest on her shoulder. She relaxed as she looked back. Naivarra climbed over the limb and sat next to Osirys. She nudged Osirys with her shoulder.

"Thanks," Naivarra said, pulling a strand of hair out of Osirys' face and hooking it behind her ear. "For saving us."

Osirys didn't feel like a savior.

"For saving me, I mean." Naivarra corrected herself.

Osirys nodded. Of course. *Now* the tears wanted to come. She blinked to fight them back and looked at Naivarra. For some reason, she expected to be blamed, or scolded. She had every right to be. It was exclusively her fault, after all.

Naivarra however, met her eyes with kindness. Her auburn hair was also filled with stones and sticks, wet and wild. Her eyes were clear and more blue than gray. She bore several new bandages, but her spirit still burned strong.

"Why is everything I do destined to fail?" Osirys asked, choking back her emotions.

"We can still pull this off," Naivarra said. "Mira is somewhere out there." She tossed her head in the direction of the deepening wilderness. "After seeing what you did to that *Fury,* we can teach that Pharandi a thing or two about destiny, I think."

Osirys laughed in the middle of her first sob, blowing a snot-bubble through her nose.

"I just can't help feeling that I don't belong here, or anywhere."

Naivarra reached for Osirys and pulled her in, holding her in a tight hug.

"The way I see it, there isn't one of us who feels like we belong anywhere."

They were all exiles.

The two sat for a while longer, until Osirys was able to calm herself down enough. She pulled away and stood up, wiping her eyes and nose with her sleeve.

Naivarra stood as well and stretched, adjusting her bandages slightly. "First, though, we're gonna have to find me a new sword." She winked at Osirys. "Saving your pretty little butt is way more difficult without one."

"I thought I saved you this time," Osirys chided, a smile managing to make its way onto her face for the first time in what felt like forever.

"Oh, are we going to keep score now?" Naivarra laughed. The warrior took several steps back towards the edge of the forest, turning back to make sure Osirys still meant to follow. The sun had fallen below the line of the canopy, and golden rays streaked through the massive trunks, giving Naivarra the illusion of being surrounded by a warm, glowing halo of natural light. She held out her hand for Osirys, who climbed back over the limb of the fallen tree. Rather than letting go, though, Naivarra held on. Osirys wanted to pull her hand away, but Naivarra's touch was reassuring, and gave her strength. They began walking together toward the fading sunlight, back towards their companions.

The two made their way back to the shore of the Virdi River and the rest of the exiles in the dark. Osirys felt her heart lift slightly as the warm campfire came into view, and the smell of Troodie's cooking found its way into her nostrils. Naivarra had begun jogging to the camp, turning back halfway and calling to Osirys. Olaavi grabbed what looked like a lumped bread roll and threw it to Naivarra as she approached.

"Must have been important to make you late for dinner," She goaded.

Naivarra made a face and didn't respond, her mouth full of bread. Thyndal was stitching closed a wound on

Pasea's shoulder, but he paused and stood up straight and smiled as Osirys approached. Naivarra rolled a large stone closer to the fire and sat on it, pulling her wet boots and stockings off her feet and resting them near the warmth of the flames to dry. Osirys sat down in the grass and did the same. Her skin of her feet was pruned and the boots that Morvrel had given her were soaked from the waters of the Virdi. Troodie waddled over, a wooden bowl of hot broth and a slab of dried meat and fresh lump-roll in hand, giving it to Osirys.

"Things will look better with a full belly and a few minutes by the fire."

"Thanks, Trood's." Osirys said, receiving the meal and realizing exactly how hungry she was.

"Have as much as you like," Troodie followed as she plunked down nearby, munching on a slice of cured flank, "Don't forget you're eatin' for two now!"

Osirys paused eating, thinking briefly.

"Troodie?"

"Yes'm? Is there somethin' you need?"

"You said you had 'the sight', right? You could see health?"

"That's right!" Troodie responded.

Embraer had returned from the river overlook, seemingly lost in thought, but he perked up, interested in the question.

Osirys placed her bowl of broth on the ground next to her.

"Can you see the health of… my baby?"

Troodie smiled, wiping her mouth and scootching closer.

"After everything, I'm scared… I'm worried that I might have lost it."

Thyndal had stopped what he was doing. Both he and Pasea along with Naivarra and Olaavi watched on in silence, with concern in their eyes.

"We'll take a looksie," Troodie said, "Just like I used to do with the ewes back home!" The only other sound was the campfire as it crackled in the deepening darkness. Troodie smiled wistfully at Osirys, trying in vain to reassure her.

She sat cross-legged in front of the Harbinger. The fire flickered in her deep emerald eyes as she examined Osirys, holding her hands.

"Hmmmmm," Troodie hummed.

"Hmm - what?" Osirys asked, her voice quaking.

"Bright. Bright and healthy." Troodie concluded. "Protected by light. It's warm, almost yellow like the stars."

Mnemosyne's light. Even after what Osirys had done, the Mother of Muses' magic protected her baby.

Osirys thought of the sadness in Mnemosyne's gemlike eyes and the warm yellow glow that surrounded them both on the shores of the Aethereal lake, what seemed like ages ago.

An audible sigh of relief could be heard from around the campfire.

"You're a tough mama, Siry." Troodie squeezed her hands. "We're not gonna let anything happen to you or that little one." Troodie looked around the camp. "Are we?"

Thyndal raised his chin, his own pain on his stonelike face hardened to resolve. All the Vamanari wore their banishment from their homeland on their faces in one way or another, but they were not sad.

Olaavi knelt on one knee, one of her blades across her open palms. "Even if you hadn't saved my life, I'd be here with you." She said.

Pasea joined Olaavi, her expression still unreadable as bare rock. "I will do what my kin could not. By any means."

Naivarra looked on, smiling, though her eyes betrayed a hint of sadness that Osirys couldn't quite place. Perhaps she reflected on her desertion, perhaps it was something more personal. Either way, she could not go back to the life she knew in Aefemar, even if she wanted to.

Even Troodie was an Exile, of sorts. She didn't know if or when her blessing would be granted and she would be inducted fully as a Leventus, and until that time, she was as good as banished from her homeland as well, unable to return, even during her people's most celebrated of traditions.

Embraer had approached, and knelt next to the Vamanari warriors. Of all the companions, he was the only one who could return to his people, but in doing so, it was perhaps a stronger form of exile than any of the others. Though she couldn't picture it, Osirys understood that the Silver Cord to which Embraer belonged had distanced itself beyond the reach of all societies that might seek to abuse it, somewhere in the spaces in-between the material and immaterial planes. His mere presence among them was a risk in and of itself.

"These are strange and difficult times, Harbinger." He bowed his head to his chest, his words coming out slowly, and purposefully.

"Nevertheless, we will find a way." He raised his eyes to the young, lost woman. He wore a thin smile, forced, no doubt, for her sake, but it still warmed Osirys inside and out.

Each and every one of them was adrift in their own way. Osirys felt security in that company. The old physician Olthi in Eidrdyhn had told her that she would not have the luxury of support of Kings and Queens and armies as her predecessors did, and at the time she despaired. Now, though, as she sat around the campfire in the most dangerous of wilds, surrounded by those unwelcome in their own homes, she felt whole for the first time, completed by their collective incompleteness.

Maybe it was her fate to fail, but with the help of her friends, just maybe she could find a way to at least do something surprising.

To be Continued in Book 2:

"The Well of Memories"

GLOSSARY

- Aefemar (ey-fuh-mar): One of the core cities of the Empirate. Known for militaristic tendencies and a flourishing center of arts.

- Auric (awr-ik): An individual that is attuned to the patterns of the world, able to command and manipulate objects by convoking the essence of the object, see *ideal*.

- Byzzim Roth (bizz-eem rah-th): A man bereaved, obsessed with returning his deceased love to the living, by any means possible. (*See Hyara.*)

- Cleric (kler-ik): Member of the Order of the Divines. (*See Divines.*)

- Divines (dih-vahyns): Distant deities that oversee the relationship between material and immaterial planes.

- Dyrdyndal (yer-din-dahl): Vamanari settlement

located near Tork's Redoubt.

- Eidemiryl Pass (eye-deh-meer-uhl): The mountain pass that leads from Pearlwater Bend to Eidrdyhn. (*See Syrpent's Gap.*)

- Eidrdyhn (eye-duhr-din): Capital of the Vamanari and seat of the Vaman Queen.

- Eidynmar Range (eye-din-mar): The range of northernmost peaks of the mountains that run North to South on the Western shore of the Virdi, known for their sheer cliffs and picturesque escarpments, many believe them to be the most beautiful natural formations in existence.

- Embraer (ehm-bray-er): Planeswalker, and member of the secret order of the Silver Cord. Able to move between material planes of existence. (*See Silver Cord.*)

- Empirate (ehm-pur-it): An alliance of the city states of Uteriel, Aefemar, and Eshilar, formed for the mutual defense against the dread lich, Or'Qan. Functions as a diplomatic entity for the purpose of negotiations with the Outland cities.

- Eophaetha (ee-yo-fay-thah): The Old Empire, reduced to ruins after the invasion of Pandemonium, in the event known as the *Incursion. (see Incursion)* Previously a prosperous and sophisticated society that spanned the entire landscape to the East of the Virdi River.

- Eshilar (eh-shih-lar): One of the core cities of the Empirate. Known for the largest Auric Academy, the Auramance, in the alliance.

- Feanar (fay-uh-nahr): Southernmost Outland settlement West of the Virdi River.

- Fernip (fer-nip): Vaman warrior. One of the Violet Vipers.

- Flembe (flem-be): Vaman warrior. One of the Violet Vipers.

- Forrenweald (fah-ren-weeld): Old forest that borders the Virdi River North of Pearlwater Bend. *(See Pearlwater Bend)*

- Fury (fyoor-ee): A physical manifestation of the Muses. *(See Muses.)*

- Geagana (gey-ah-gahn-ah): Capital of the Outland cities that border the Virdi River. Known for the largest library and center of Eophaethan histories, the Avhakamora.

- Geas (gey-us): The magical ward that allowed

safe passage of survivors of the *incursion* from Eophaetha to the lands to the West. Manifested by a Harbinger long ago. (*See Harbinger.*)

- Haltberg (halt-burg): Name of the city settlement that fell during the battle of Tork's Redoubt, rebuilt later as Pearlwater Bend. (*See Pearlwater Bend, Tork's Redoubt.*)

- Harbinger (har-bin-jer): An extraplanar stranger brought to the lands of Virdi through intervention by the Muses or other deific entities in times of great need or strife, usually endowed with enhanced or unique abilities.

- Hyara (yahr-rah): Lover to Byzzim Roth, died young to illness. Returned as a phantom in Shimmermere. (*See Pharandi.*)

- Ideal (eye-deal): Representation entities of worldly objects that exist in the Realm of the Muses. Created by the Muses from the dreams and experiences of those that have passed on, from within the Well of Memories. Any physical object that exists is a manifestation of such an entity.

- Ijozaan (ee-yoh-zahn): Duarfen city state, known for unparalleled craftsmanship. (*See Makemoot, Yiselhaf.*)

- Illumari (ill-oo-mar-ee): The language of the Muses.

- Incursion (in-kur-zhuhn): Event that precipitated the abrupt downfall of the Old Empire, Eophaetha. *(See Eophaetha.)* A ubiquitous invasion of Pandemonium *(See Pandemonium.)* to every corner of Eophaethan society in one moment.

- Ingenshen (ing-en-shin): A small Vamanari settlement.

- Lavis (lah-vee): The queen and current ruler of the Vamanari, located in Eidrdyhn. *(See Eidrdyhn.)*

- Leventus (leh-ven-tuhs): Holy knight of the Duarfen people, leaders of the Order of Leven, a sacred organization of Duarfen individuals blessed by the Divines with foresight.

- Lord Naros (lawrd nah-rohs): A commander of armies for the city state of Aefemar. Former superior officer to Naivarra. *(See Naivarra.)*

- Magisteel (maj-ihst-eel): Common term for Mylt. *(See Mylt.)* A particularly resonant metal that enhances Auric power and may be animated through Auric mastery. *(See Auric.)*

- Makemoot (meyk-moot): Year long festival held

by the Duarfs of Ijozaan once per decade to determine social status and class among prominent clan families, known as Stones. *(See Yiselhaf.)* Each clan is required to submit one example of their finest craftsmanship to determine their place and standing within Ijozaan's society.

- Mathoras' Crossing (mah-thoh-rahs krah-sing): Prominent bridge border crossing between the core cities of Eshilar and Aefemar.

- Middenhaf (mit-ten-hahf): Duarfen word for the summer solstice, marking the halfway point of Makemoot *(See Makemoot, Yiselhaf)* for the Duarfs of Ijozaan.

- Mirabyll (meer-ah-bihl): Vamanari Warrior. Second in command to Pasea of the Violet Vipers.

- Mnemosyne (nem-oh-seen): Demigod, and mother of the Muses, daughter of the Goddess of the Divines Gallamine. Also known as Mother Memory. Arbiter of the Well of Memories.

- Morvrel (moar-vrell): Feanari Cleric of the Church of Divines, located in Pearlwater Bend. *(See Pearlwater Bend.)*

- Mylt (milt): A particularly resonant metal that enhances Auric power and may be animated through Auric mastery. *(See Magisteel.)*

- Naivarra (niv-ahr-ah): Human warrior from the core city of Aefemar.

- Olaavi (oh-lah-vee): Vamanari warrior. One of the Violet Vipers.

- Olthi (ohl-thee): Vamanari cleric of the Divines and Auric, located in Eidrdyhn.

- Or'qan (or-kahn): The dread lich; the undead warlord that waged war against the free peoples of the Westlands long ago. Defeated by the coalition armies led by Villem Uteriel, leading to the creation of the Empirate.

- Osirys (oh-see-reez): A Harbinger. *(See Harbinger.)*

- Pandemonium - Fiend (pan-deh-moh-nee-uhm): Archfiend entity of chaos that dwells within and throughout its self-manifested plane, often indistinguishable from the environment that bears the same name. *(See Pandemonium - Realm)*

- Pandemonium - Realm (pan-deh-moh-nee-uhm): A sister plane and mirror realm manifested by an archfiend of chaos. Features of the material world are mirrored and corrupted. Origin realm of the *incursion.*

- Pasea (pay-shuh): Vamanari Warrior. Leader of the Violet Vipers.

- Pathyk (pah-thayk): Feanari term for wanderer, or pilgrim.

- Pearlwater Bend (purl-wah-ter bend): Smallest of the Empirate settlements, located on the shore of the Virdi River, near the *geas. (See Haltberg, Geas.)*

- Pemme (pem-me): Vamanari warrior, auric, and Violet Viper. Sister to Pasea.

- Pharandi (far-ahn-dee): Phantom legionnaire demons of Pandemonium that destroyed Eophaetha during the *incursion. (See Incursion.)*

- Sheol Marthyne(shay-ohl mar-teen): Leader of a cult in service to Pandemonium.

- Shimmermere (shim-mer-meer): Deep cavern and underground river fed by the waters of the Virdi, rich in Mylt. *(See Mylt, Magisteel.)* A source of great wealth during the age of Or'Qan *(See Or'Qan.)*

- Silver Cord (sil-ver koard): A secret order of Planeswalkers that exists to monitor the material and immaterial realms that border Virdi and other worldly planes.

- Syndal (sin-dahl): Vamanari Warrior and Auric of the Violet Vipers.

- Syrpent's Gap (sur-pehnt's gap): Mountain pass to the East of Eidrdyhn. Rumored to have been the roost of a grand dragon in ages past. *(See Eidemiryl Pass)*

- Thyndal (thin-dahl): Vamanari Warrior and Auric. Father to Syndal *(See Syndal)*.

- Torayn (tohr-in): Cultural hair adornment worn by the Vamanari.

- Tork's Redoubt (tohrks ruh-dowt): Fortress located near the location of the old city of Haltberg. The site of the first major victory for the newly formed Empirate in the war against Or'Qan, the dread lich. *(See Or'Qan.)*

- Troodie Van Hootan (troo-dee van hoot-en): Duarf from Ijozaan, inducted into the Order of Leven but not yet ordained as a full Leventus. *(See Leventus.)*

- Uteriel (yu-tur-ee-el): Capital of the core cities of the Empirate *(See Empirate.)*

- Vamanari (vah-mah-nah-ree): Stone-skinned

race of people created by the Muses as guides and protectors of Harbingers.

- Vespenbee (vess-pen-bee): Rare variety of magically imbued insects that harness the power of the Virdi River in their honey.

- Villem Uteriel (vill-uhm yu-tur-ee-el): Leader of the coalition army that defeated the dread lich Or'Qan *(See Or'Qan)* and formed the foundations of the Empirate.

- Vim (vim) Vamanari warrior of the Violet Vipers.

- Viqua (vik-wah): Water from the Virdi River that has undergone a natural process deep underground. Used as an enhancement of Auric magic to heal wounds.

- Viqua Vitae (vik-wah vahy-tay): Droplets of water from the Realm of the Muses that fell as mist, collected over time. Greatly enhances Auric magic if used by a powerful enough agent.

- Virdi (ver-dee): The great, impassable magical river that splits the land in two. Source of vitality for the land and the root of magic in the world.

- Wavu (wah-voo): Vamanari warrior of the Violet Vipers.

- Yiselhaf (yee-sell-haff): Duarfen word for the winter solstice, and the night of judgement for the year's Makemoot. *(See Makemoot.)* Also may refer to the entirety of the festival.

About the Author

The stories we tell shape the world we live in.

Corbin Kime is devoted to the most noble duties of hus-
bandry and dog-fatherhood. Like Sebastian from "*The
Neverending Story*", he never could keep his 'head out of
the clouds and keep both feet on the ground'. He has
spent the better part of three decades conjuring impossible
worlds and loveable characters as a game master for his
tabletop game group, who had more than a little influence
on the journey within these pages. Like most college
graduates in the 2000's, he earned a degree in early mod-
ern English literature so that he could become a successful
tech engineer in manufacturing instead of following his
dreams writing goofy stories for a living.